Seasons Of Blood

Vampire State book two

Kevin Dickson

Vonsson Press

Contents

For Skye Pyman

I love you more

Chapter One

The New York City of Sara's dreams was a patchwork of the city's various incarnations since her arrival in 1723. Her dream New York was an anachronistic composite that ticked to a ramshackle rhythm favoring the city's hardscrabble dusty bronze early years over its present sleek, antiseptic state. In her dreams, she could feel Mannahatta's black stone spine crumbling under the weight of skyscrapers and expectations.

In this particular dream, Sara was living in one of the many apartments she had occupied several lifetimes over, in the labyrinthine complex on West End Avenue that she shared with her Lock. In this dream apartment, a mid-level three bedroom with big windows, she was moving among short stacks of dusty moving boxes, a modern invention that was completely out of step with the 1920s décor, the muted wallpaper, the Fiestaware drying by the sink. Standing amidst the clutter of boxes, she was searching for something, but as is the wont of dreams, she didn't know precisely what it was.

Moving a box in an explosion of sunlit dust, she disturbed a familiar cat curled on a blanket at the bottom of the box. The cat was feeding very newly born kittens, eyes closed, their paws pressing against their mother. With that rapid focus shift of dreams, Sara noticed several dead kittens, white, gray, stiff, broken, littering the edges of the blanket. In the dream, the cat's name came to her immediately. Iris, named for her blue eyes. Now dead for nearly a century, Iris gazed at her balefully as the surviving kittens suckled.

Distracted from her search, Sara stared into the cat's eyes. Its wishes, in typical cat fashion, were inscrutable. A noise from the hallway startled her, and she glanced up to see the face of a lover she'd taken just after the end of the first world war, soot on one cheek, a panicked expression on his hangdog face. The last time she had lived in this apartment, he had been her boyfriend.

"The kittens," Sara said to him. "Some of them are dead."

The lover, whose name wasn't as readily available as the cat's, shook his head, a tear rolling from his eye, catching some soot on its way to his jawline. He stood in the cluttered hallway, his arms limp at his sides, frown lines at the corners of his mouth. As Sara stared, she noticed his battered shoes weren't touching the floor, but his stance indicated that he was standing on something solid, not floating like a ghost might.

Straightening, Sara stepped toward him, one step, then two, but each time she moved, the distance between them remained the same, the hallway lengthening like a funhouse mirrror. Pausing, she took him in, his brown woolen trousers and once-white linen shirt beneath a plaid vest, black hair combed back and shiny with brilliantine, his dark eyes sunken and forlorn. They stood in silence, Sara flooded by barely-remembered emotions. She knew she had loved him, deeply, and he had cared for her well. But he had never been to this building, this apartment, and the sight of a man in her home was jarring.

"I'm sorry I don't remember your name," she said feebly, horrified when the man began to cry, his fists balling at his sides. "I need to dispose of these dead kittens."

The man floated up further from the floor, and his weeping stopped, his face suddenly dry.

"They're all dead," he said, his voice no longer human, the sound produced by vocal cords as dry and desiccated as a mummy's. His eyes, now bottomless pools of black oil, stared into hers. Horrified, she watched as an oily black tear rolled down his face and landed on the dusty floor.

"No, some of them are still alive," Sara waved a trembling hand in the direction of Iris and her litter.

When she turned her attention back to her lover, she gasped. He was inches from her, floating, the unmistakable stench of death rolling from him in waves.

"Not your feckin' cats, you devil," he said in that same dead voice. "Your witches. Your *sisters*, they're all dead. You killed them."

Jolting herself upright, the sound of her voice echoing back at her, Sara knew two things. She'd screamed herself awake, and this wasn't her bedroom. Her bedroom wasn't this echoey. Inhaling shakily, Sara gazed around the dimly lit, barely furnished room. Her sharp breathing echoed around her like the ghost of her scream, and her mind scrambled to place her.

Iceland. She was in Iceland. Exactly where, she did not know.

Relief flooded her with a comforting security. A single curtained window in the all-white room was edged in a curious blue gray glow. Her suitcase lay on the floor, its top unzipped, flap hanging open. The only furniture in the room was the bed, a side table, and a wooden chair against the far wall.

As she settled back against the cluster of pillows behind her, struggling to get her breathing under control, the too-familiar tug of her addiction clawed at the back of her throat, setting off fresh panic. She needed blood. The hemoglobin pills she'd been taking weren't ever enough to satisfy her curse, not since she'd fed on the body of Laura, her doomed patient, the previous winter.

The memory made her jerk with physical revulsion, but her need for blood spiked at the reminder of that revolting feast. The addiction, once acknowledged, became impossible to ignore, ice at the back of her throat, frost prickling the veins in her wrists and around her heart.

A glass of water on the bedside table caught her eye, and beside it, a small plate with a jumble of heem pills. A wan smile cracked her face and her breathing slowed to manageable as she tipped eight onto her palm, then washed them all down at once. She briefly wondered who'd put them there, so stealthy their presence hadn't woken her. Images of Crina, Silas and Embla came to mind and she swatted them away angrily. She wanted a few minutes to herself before she resumed adulting.

Relaxing back into her pillow fort, she waited for her system to absorb the hemoglobin, drinking the rest of the water to calm her throat for the time being. It tasted of nothing, and she missed the barely noticeable chemical flavor of the water in New York City.

The city where she had left Teddie, the person she cared for most.

Without warning, the dam broke and a jumble of images from the previous days flashed across her mind, vivid and ugly: women she'd protected, loved, all screaming in anger, a broken Teddie, destroyed by her convictions as she voted to sentence Sara to death. The mad dash across three states and the Atlantic with her boyfriend and a new vampire that brought her here. The most recent jagged memory lingered longest: Crina, the woman who made her a vampire, the woman she considered her mother, eyes pleading, after Sara, exhausted and raw, excoriated her for being dishonest with her for centuries, forgiveness far out of reach.

Which brought her to Silas, Sara's boyfriend and savior, who'd failed to tell Sara that he was in fact Crina's son.

At the mere thought of him, she groaned aloud, clenching her fists and scrunching her eyes closed. As much as she understood his motivations, the tidal wave of emotions that swept over her when he and Crina ever so lightly revealed that they were mother and son hit her all wrong, all at once. After a meltdown that frankly could have been worse, she admitted to herself, chuckling briefly, she had demanded to be taken to her room before a combination of jetlag, anger and confusion made her say anything truly damaging. Still, she chuckled again, she'd said enough.

Embla had walked her to her room in silence, Sara barely noticing the hallways that brought them here. As soon as she was alone, the sorrow, delayed for two days, took her out at the knees before she could reach the bed. Falling to the floor, she cried, loudly and wetly, for longer than she had ever cried before, only stopping when hollowness replaced hurt, exhaustion overtaking betrayal.

Her face still wet with tears, she'd hauled herself onto the bed and fallen into a deep jetlagged sleep, the white linen comforter pressing her into the bed as if it were made of lead. With a deep, shaky inhale, Sara banished the twisted knot of thoughts and emotions aside as a single vision filled her mind's eye. Teddie, crying, lost and clinging to the rules of their shared life, despite the cost.

Rather than feeling anger or disappointment, Sara was simply, completely heartbroken, a mother unable to help her daughter. She bitterly regretted ever lying to Teddie, even though Teddie's dedication to the tenets of Lock life didn't leave any room for gray areas, like Sara's accidental feasting on a human, or hanging out with a male vampire.

A sudden need to know the time in New York City gripped her, and she remembered the burner phone that Silas had given her at his home in Connecticut, the day before. Or the day before that. She really didn't know.

As the first wave of heem relief surged through her, she leaned clumsily over the side of her bed, seeing her jeans bundled up on the floor, one leg inside out. Picking them up, she guessed by their weight that her phone was still in the pocket, and in seconds, it was in her palm.

It was 11:57. This was confusing. The date on her phone didn't help her at all. Had she slept for twenty-four hours? No wonder she'd needed to house the heems. There was a red dot over the messages icon, so she clicked it.

> It's Silas. I'm so sorry for making you feel this way. Please let me know if you'd like to talk. If you'd like some space, that's absolutely fine too. I can clear out for a while. Your call.

Nervously, she flipped the phone from one hand to the other and back again. In all of this, it wasn't him that she was angry at. Tears stung her eyes again, and she wiped them away angrily. She needed to pee and had no idea if there was a bathroom in the hallway, or if anyone else was in the house. Locating a bathroom seemed manageable, an acceptable plan for the short term.

Gingerly swinging her feet to the floor, she was surprised to find that it was heated. Standing upright, she wrestled her jeans back to right-side out and dragged them on. Shoes felt like a dumb move when a floor was so warm and inviting, so she padded barefoot to the door. It clicked open, revealing an empty hallway. She paused to listen for sounds of activity, hearing none. The second door that she tried led to a bathroom, thankfully. After peeing, she looked at herself in the mirror. The dark circles under her eyes weren't a surprise but the rest of her face looked sunken and drawn. She pinched color into her cheeks and ran her fingers through her knotty black hair, letting it fall obediently against her neck. She'd never been a vain woman, but nobody needed to see her looking like this. Opening the medicine cabinet, she smiled. It was stocked almost identically to the one in her bathroom in New York.

Crina had prepared for her arrival.

Nice, she thought. Trying to buy me off with La Mer after lying to me my whole life.

After considering and rejecting the thought of a shower, she did a quick concealer and powder job to get her blotchy face under control, happy to find a sense of curiosity rising above the tangled emotions in her heart. After a quick shake of her hair, Sara stepped back out into the hallway, following it past a string of closed doors until it ended at a short staircase that widened into the main living space. As she neared the bottom, she heard Crina's voice.

"Here she is."

Frozen for a moment, Sara considered her options. Her first instinct was to turn and leave, but now that she had slept, that felt childish. Steeling herself, she stepped into the enormous living room. The weird blue gray light permeated the unfamiliar space, making it hard to discern where anybody was. Movement caught her eye in the distance, and she saw Crina rise from the couch, where April Veronica and Embla were also sitting, their thighs touching, their heads down.

When her maker didn't move in her direction, Sara smoothly walked to Crina, reminding her of the ghost in her dream. The image made her shudder.

"Do you feel better after some sleep?" Crina asked, her palms open.

Sara shrugged, unable to trust that her voice would be steady. She saw Silas seated at the far end of the other couch, his eyes on her, his face stricken with concern. At the sight of him, she felt herself thaw a little. He did not move or speak.

"Can I hug you?" Crina asked softly, and Sara nodded. A moment later, she was engulfed in Crina's arms, their heads pressed together. They remained silent, as if both of them were waiting for Sara to cry, but it wasn't sadness that filled Sara. She always felt whole when she was with Crina, and this hadn't changed at a time when so much else had. Eventually, Sara broke the hug.

Squinting, Sara looked out the windows into the electric blue sky. "So, how long was I asleep?"

"About thirteen hours, it's midnight, you arrived this morning," Crina said.

Silently, Sara took in the information.

"Huh," she said eventually. "For a moment there, I thought I'd slept for a full day, and I was quite attached to that concept."

"I wish I could tell you to return to your bed," Crina said. "Unfortunately, we've had some... uh... some news."

A shard of panic ripped Sara's heart.

"Teddie," she asked urgently. "Is she okay?"

"It's not Teddie," Crina said, her voice curiously thin. "It's, well it's Warsaw. The Lock. They took Surrender this evening. They're... well, they're gone."

The news washed over Sara with a nauseating confusion, and she took a step backward, steadying herself on the arm of the couch Silas was sitting in. He sprang to his feet and placed a hand on her shoulder, and she was grateful for the balance it gave her. Moving to her front, Silas carefully guided her back to the couch and pressed her to sit down.

Once Sara was seated, Silas lifted her chin with a curled finger.

"Mom, she needs some blood."

Sara felt the warmth of Silas's callused finger crooked beneath her chin so acutely she could almost feel his pulse. She gazed into his sad orange-brown eyes.

"She's gonna need a few glasses," he called out, his eyes never leaving hers. "You're looking pretty hungry, Sara. Would you like some food?"

Sara shook her head, uncertain that she could stomach anything even though she was definitely starving. "Thanks, Silas, I don't think I could eat right now."

"I know," he said gently. "But you're going to need your strength for the rest of this."

Sara gave him a wan smile and shook her head again. "I think the blood will get me through it," she said. As if on cue, she heard the ding of the warmer oven, and seconds later, Crina was placing a very large glass tumbler of scarlet blood into her hands, and she scrambled to get it to her lips before the virus blacked her out, unable to control the ugly gulps that shook her as she swallowed the whole mug in one draft and fell back against the couch. Silas caught the cup as it slipped from her hands, and as the blackness enclosed her, she distantly heard him tell Crina to warm two more "just like it."

Withdrawn into herself, she felt the blood hit her stomach and instantly, the electric thrum pulsed out along her arteries as if she was being inflated with something better than air, something lighter, cleaner. Feeling the familiar silver glow from within, she groggily opened her eyes a sliver just to make sure she wasn't in fact glowing. Nope. She saw April helping Crina in the kitchen, and Embla staring at her, a concerned look on her broad, elfin face. Closing her eyes again, Sara sank back into the couch and embraced the darkness as long as she could to avoid thinking about Warsaw, but as soon as she thought the word, she sat bolt upright.

"Can you guys tell me what happened to Warsaw?" she asked, her voice thick and congested. April Veronica and Embla exchanged worried glances, and Silas took a seat beside her.

"Sure, I'll start," he said. She turned slightly to face him, noticing the worry lines on his brow. "There was a message from Desdemona a couple hours ago." Sara winced at Desdemona's name.

"Just after seven pm," Embla called from the kitchen.

"Desdemona sent a secure channel message to all Lock mothers at sevenish," Silas continued. "I'll spare you the florid prose, but it was along the lines of 'the brave, selfless women of Warsaw have decided to lead by example and do what's best for the rest of the world.'"

"May we find inspiration in their sacrifice," Crina added from the kitchen.

"That's the florid prose I was trying to avoid," Silas said irritably.

Sara's thoughts turned to the women of Warsaw, and she attempted a quick mental roll call but fell short. Warsaw, like Helsinki, was a very insular Lock, with a very different work structure to New York. Only the working sisters were allowed to leave, and once they had served for a decade, they returned to the compound for a mandatory lockdown that lasted until it was time for them to go back to work, often thirty or forty years. She'd never accepted a transfer from Warsaw into New York, and she knew them as a collection of names at best. Still, they were women, with complex histories and a reputation as scientists, and they were gone.

"Wait," she sat up suddenly. "How did we find out here?"

"Heather," Embla, Silas and April Veronica said in unison.

"She sent us the video too," Embla said, and Crina glared at her.

"There's video?" Sara groaned.

Silas nodded gravely.

"Is it bad?" Sara asked.

Silas shrugged. "It's not violent if that's what you're asking."

April Veronica appeared at her other side, taking her hand.

"It's definitely giving doomsday cult vibes," she said. "White robes, spooky music, and well, Desdemona, being extra. It's just really sad."

Sara lifted her arm and April Veronica snuggled in against her. She wrapped the young woman in a hug.

"Do you want to see the video?" Silas said, giving her a look that told her he didn't think she should say yes.

"Yes," Sara said immediately. "I mean, they've been endorsing ZPG for so long, if anything it's surprising that they finally got around to doing it."

"Alrighty then," Silas said, sounding like a sitcom dad. Without another word he turned and started tapping at an iPad on the coffee table. Embla came from the kitchen with another glass of blood for Sara. She handed it to her and then sat on Sara's other side, pressed against her.

"I know we just met," Embla said. "Please tell me if this is too much."

"This is just right," Sara said, throwing her other arm around the much taller woman until she was distracted by ambient noise coming from the television, and she looked up.

On the screen, she saw Desdemona in a white robe that was so seventies horror movie that under any other circumstances it would have been laughable. Des was sitting on a throne on a small dais, facing the camera. In front of her, Sara saw only the backs of the white robes of the women of the Warsaw Lock. Some appeared to have their heads bowed, others were sitting upright. The only sounds that she could hear were occasional squeaks from ancient chairs, and a lone cough, then Desdemona stood, pushing the hood back from her face. She began to speak in fluent Polish, and English subtitles appeared along the bottom of the screen.

"Sisters of the Warsaw Lock, I welcome you to this, the first Ceremony of Total Surrender. I commend your conscience, and your bravery. I know that you have spent the day in communion with one another, and that now, on the eve of this day, you are ready to begin your next adventure, whatever that will be."

Sara watched with almost clinical detachment as Desdemona turned to a side table and lifted a tray with eighteen small glasses. She carried it to the front row of women, and each woman silently took a glass. Once Desdemona had finished distributing the glasses she returned to the stage, and spoke directly to the camera, her eyes looking directly into Sara's, a shudder coursing down Sara's spine.

"As we say farewell," she said, her voice strong, "please know that you go with my love, my admiration, and my blessing. I will be joining you as soon as I can, when I am the last cursed woman standing, and our selfish threat to humanity is eradicated. You may now drink your sedative."

In a gentle rustling of robes, the women lifted the glasses and uniformly drained them quickly. On the dais, Desdemona smiled benevolently, her arms outstretched, her palms raised like a pieta. Slowly, one by one, the women began to slump sideways, onto one another, or onto the floor. The sound of glasses falling onto carpet preceded louder thumps. Eventually, silence fell again, and Desdemona looked at the camera, and spoke in Spanish.

"It is done. The women of Warsaw have made the ultimate sacrifice. They illuminate the way forward for all of us. They are our inspiration. Let us not make their sacrifice be in vain."

And then the scene faded to black.

On the couch, Sara flashed back to her dream, her dead lover telling her that she'd killed her sisters, and a shudder ran up her spine. She was immensely grateful for the push of young women against her, the warmth they shared with her. She could feel April Veronica's heart pounding against her side.

"She made it all about herself," Sara said. "Why couldn't she let the Lock Mother do it?"

Crina appeared in front of her with a third glass of blood, nodding at the still full glass in Sara's hand.

"Drink up before it cools down," she said, and Sara obeyed, switching her empty for the full one.

"You okay, Sara," Silas said from the coffee table across from her, and she nodded.

"I mean, I guess," Sara said. "I'm probably still a bit numb from New York, thankfully. This is just one more thing to toss onto the dumpster fire."

"I think it's nightmarish," April Veronica said. "I can't downplay it like that."

"I'm not downplaying it, peanut," Sara said, scruffing April's greenish hair. "It's fucking horrendous, but also, this is something that the ZPG Locks have talked about for a while, and it was much less disturbing than the way I had imagined it."

A brief silence fell over the room, broken by a very loud rumble from Sara's stomach. It seemed to be the signal Silas was waiting for, and he leapt to his feet.

"That's it, I'm gonna make us all some dinner."

Sara smiled at him as he moved past her.

"Wait," she said. "Please."

He paused, a vaguely fearful expression on his face.

"I…" Sara paused, glancing at Silas, then Crina. "I need to apologize, I certainly could have handled my arrival better."

"Me too," Crina said, kneeling in front of Sara and moving a strand of her black hair back behind her ear then cupping her cheek in her palm. "I dunno. There's no real etiquette guide for, you know, telling your five-hundred-year-old daughter about your five-hundred-and ten-year-old secret son."

"That's true," Sara laughed then looked Silas in the eye. "What about you? Cat got your tongue?"

Silas didn't smile. If anything, the look of anguish on his face intensified.

"I'm sorry, Sara. I actually planned to head out, give you some space, but then, this Desdemona thing happened and then we uh…"

Silas looked nervously at his mother. Crina took Sara's hand and raised the third glass of blood to her lips.

"My dear, I fear you're going to need this. Heather wants to talk to you now that you're up and she's already on her way to a safe space."

A flutter of excitement ran through Sara, she wanted news of Teddie, and in the midst of her swirling emotions around the demise of the Warsaw Lock, she saw Heather, her rock for so long, as a beacon from home.

"Let's do it," Sara necked the rest of the blood and held the empty glass out to Crina. "As we all know, time, tide and Heather wait for no woman."

Chapter Two

Wriggling out from Sara's embrace, April Veronica and Embla seated themselves on the couch opposite, exchanging brief, warm smiles before settling into silence. At the other end of the couch sat Silas, lost in his phone.

"Sorry, everyone, Heather wants to use a new encryption app, but I still always double-check the VPN," he said, her gaze fixed on her phone screen.

"Set it for Edinburgh," Embla said.

"Der," Silas gave her a smile. "Heather's online"

On the couch, Sara felt a jangle of nerves and realized that the last cup of blood hadn't sent her into a blackout. That meant that her dosage, for want of a better word, was four cups. Before she fed on Laura, she'd been fine on Heems and a ceremonial goblet here and there. Would Crina or Silas comment on her intake, she wondered? A ringing sound from the television jerked her back to reality, and suddenly, the black screen flickered blue, then Heather's face, bigger than she'd ever seen it, filled the screen, pallid, tired lines around her lips and eyes.

"Oh my word, Sara, it's a tonic to see you, it really is."

Blinking herself alert, took the phone from Silas's hand.

"Hey, Heather," she said, her voice steady. "Sorry, I just watched the Warsaw video, I... uh... yeah..."

"What a fuckin' liberty," Heather said angrily. "Can we circle back to that? I don't know how long I have right now. How you doing lass?"

"We just hooked her up with a big mug of the good stuff," Crina said, taking a seat beside Sara and rubbing a hand up and down her thigh. Sara gave her a brief, angry glance, then let it go. Crina always answered for her.

"Where are you, Heather?"

Heather switched the camera's direction on her phone and turned slowly from side to side, giving them a pixelated panorama of Riverside park. Sara knew exactly where she was, on a bench by the dog park for small dogs.

"Any fireflies?" Sara asked, relieved when Heather chuckled as she turned the camera back to herself.

"No, love. Not tonight, it's too windy," Heather said, her face kind, but tired. "Good to see you, all of you. Sara, I know you need to rest, but quite a bit happened after you left."

"You didn't get into any... trouble... did you?"

Heather shook her head. "No, it was exactly like I told you. Nobody pays attention to old Heather. I made sure the furnace got most of the evidence, but not all. I told you those old skeletons would come in handy."

Sara smiled. "I'll never call you a hoarder again."

"I only keep what's useful," Heather quipped. "So, after that, I made it back to mine, but my plan to get shitfaced got sidetracked. Desdemona turned up, so I quickly scrambled all the security codes and locked all the doors. Told all the sisters that we were in a lockdown, told that bitch Desdemona to get a hotel room."

"I'm sorry you had to deal with that, on top of everything else," Sara said.

"Don't worry about me, lass. At least I knew you were alive. Later that night, when people were falling asleep, I went over to visit Teddie... Sara, I've never seen anyone sorrier in my entire life."

Sara's breath caught in her throat like something sharp, choking her for an instant. She swallowed it away. "She's okay? Please just tell me that, Heather, is she okay?"

Heather nodded. "She's been through the wringer, poor lass, but she's fine. I'm sorry, I should have started with that. Everyone is alive and well. You don't have to worry."

It was only then that Sara realized that she was sitting on the edge of her seat, her shoulders knit together behind her, her knees cramped. With a sigh of relief, she fell back into the couch.

"Anyways, I gave her your note, Sara. She was crushed. I took care of her, got her to sleep, then finally cracked open the wine at my place."

Heather paused, looking nervously left and right before continuing.

"In the morning, they discovered you were missing, April Veronica. Then, Rosa and Eleanor forced me to let Desdemona in. And the shit really hit the fan. Sara, that bitch called an all-hands meeting in the big conference room. She insisted on inspecting the furnace, just pulled the whole tray right out!" Heather stopped herself. "Sara, do you want the full story or the bullet points?"

"Tell me everything," Sara said, command returning to her voice.

"The skull was still there, and she kept it. Sara, she bloody kept it. She brought it with her into the conference room and she set it on a table by your throne, which she insisted on sitting in."

Sara winced, imagining what a nightmare that was for Teddie.

"Bitch thinks she's Hamlet." Sara said angrily, making Silas laugh involuntarily.

"It gets worse," Heather said. "So, the first thing she did was declare our votes for Teddie's Lock Mother invalid, because you didn't follow protocols. Teddie said she still wanted to run for the position, but then bloody Rosa raised her hand and said she wanted to be Mother too. So, no surprises here, we took a vote and it was a tie. Imani, me and Yukari voted for Teddie, Liz, Eleanor and Fran voted for Rosa. I said that it was procedure for us to include the scholars, but it was early on a Monday and nobody answered their phone of course."

"Sorry, Heather," Crina said. "We've had our hands full here."

"I know," Heather said with a nod. "Desdemona insisted that as the only Lock Mother in attendance, she could vote. She voted for Rosa."

"Oh come *on*," Sara said, her heart breaking for Teddie, her anger burning at Rosa.

"I know, I know," Heather said. "Then we had a lucky break, at least. Desdemona immediately tried to get us to sign on to agreeing to an end date for the Lock, but she fucked up. Now that Rosa was Lock Mother, Desdemona didn't have a vote, and we tied. So now, Crina, Rosa's scheduling another vote, so you'll need to contact Rosa with your proxy."

Sara shot a panicked glance at her maker, who smiled warmly and nodded. "Heather, I'll head back to America tomorrow."

Sara turned to her in shock. Crina took her hand and smiled. "I was about to tell you, I promise. Anyway, my work here is done and I can be more useful there."

"So what happened next?" Sara ignored Crina, whose style of news delivery was becoming increasingly irritating.

"Well, she announced that she had urgent business elsewhere, and that she'd be taking Eleanor with her. Rosa was pissed but what could she do?" Heather paused, her eyes wide.

"And they flew directly to Warsaw?" Sara felt sickened that Eleanor had most likely been holding the camera for the mass Surrender.

"That arsehole Eleanor was already packed. They both flew on the same plane to Warsaw that afternoon."

Sara shook her head in disgust. Eleanor's departure meant that the weight of supplying blood fell to Liz and Teddie. The thought of additional pressure being dumped on Teddie weighed on her heart painfully.

"Do you think Rosa knew that Des was going to take Eleanor?"

"I think she knew but couldn't hide her anger," Heather said. "I lingered after the meeting, and Rosa and Liz got into an angry whisper argument."

Despite herself, Sara smiled. One of Heather's favorite Lock pastimes was eavesdropping on whisper arguments.

"And we're in a bit of a pickle, I'm afraid," Heather continued. "I spoke to both of the other scholars today."

"I did too," Crina chimed in. "Courtney's against it, Toni's for it."

Sara closed her eyes. Courtney was a grand elder, almost as old as Stefanya. She'd existed as a scholar for centuries and had been part of the New York Lock since 1932. Heather and Crina called her The Ghost. It had been widely speculated that her stint as a Scholar for New York would end in her surrender but so far, she was off doing her thing. Toni had come from Italy via London, and she was a salty, sexy old thing, always entertaining a horde of lovers until it was time to change identities and move. Sara knew nothing about their daily lives.

"Toni's been talking to the Spaniards?" Sara asked irritably. Crina had already spoken to Heather, Sara just wanted to talk to her friend without interruption.

"She's been talking to the Italians," Heather said. "She's a ZPG vote."

"So you're the tie breaker," Sara said. "Just vote from here."

"I'll feel better when I'm in New York," Crina said, turning to Sara. "I know I'm not as close to Teddie as you are, Sara, but I love her and I want to go take care of her. I also want to keep a closer eye on Rosa."

"I'll come with you," Sara said. "It's inhumane to torture Teddie like this."

On the screen Heather shook her head.

"Lassie, right now you're worth way more dead than alive. Desdemona is flexing her muscles because you're not around. If we can keep you secret, we might get to find out what she's up to."

"Then tell Teddie, at least." Sara's voice was steel, the strongest she'd sounded since the chaos in the New York meeting.

"Sara," Heather's tone was calm. "I love you, and I love Teddie, but right now, she's a mess. She's unpredictable. As soon as it's safe, we will tell her."

Surges of anger hummed through Sara's chest and down her arms and legs and she fought against an instinct to just leave this weird house and go home to New York. Sensing her anger, Embla rose and came to kneel in front of Sara.

"I know we just met," she said, her voice low. "You do not know how hard people worked to get you here, and how much work we can do now that you are here."

Gazing into Embla's amber flecked hazel eyes, Sara saw nothing but love, and it melted her anger. Embla took her hands and squeezed them tight.

"I can see that you're not used to being told what to do, and I apologize," Embla said, "but please, if you can trust me, then take a deep breath, and let go, I promise that we will help Teddie, and after that, we will deal with Desdemona. This is a long game and we've been planning it for a while."

"This isn't directed at you, Embla, I appreciate what you just said," Sara paused, looking angrily at Crina and Silas, and then at Heather through the phone screen, "but you guys have too many secrets and I'm tired of looking like an idiot."

In front of her, Embla nodded sagely. "You've never looked like an idiot," she said with a smile. "Sara, meeting you is like meeting my inspiration, at long last. Anyway, let's put a pin in that, we will come back to it, but Heather, anything else before you go?"

"You're right, Embla," Heather said. "I really have to hurry. We are not allowed to leave the compound, and we are all being forced to wear goddamn AirTags like fucking cats."

"And yet, here you are," Crina smiled.

"Well, yes," Heather chuckled. "My poor old AirTag is currently enjoying a nice trip around my apartment on top of my Roomba. Anyway, speaking of AirTags, Liz is in a rental car attempting to track you down, April Veronica."

"She can give my love to North Cackalackie," the young girl crowed, clapping her hands.

"She certainly can," Heather said. "But we have a few more things to get out of the way. Silas, Desdemona wasted no time circulating your photo to all Locks, with a kill-on-sight order, accompanied by some histrionics from Liz about how deceptive and dangerous you are. On top of that, Desdemona has stirred the pot by adding that you're possibly part of a secret all-male order that she has heard rumors of for centuries."

Sara stole a glance at Silas, his face hardened by anger. As if he sensed her gaze, he looked from the television to her, and Sara quickly dropped her eyes before they could meet his.

"Anyways, with facial recognition technology being what it is, it's best for you to hide out for the next little decade or two."

"I was going to come back with my mother," he began.

"NO," Heather said loudly, cutting him off. "I'm sorry, lad, but no. Not now. We need you in one piece."

Sara watched as Silas made an impassioned face at his mother, who shook her head.

"I'm going alone," Crina said. "Heather, have you talked to Stefanya?"

"She's been texting me bibs and bobs," Heather said, her brow furrowing. "Do you know what's going on?"

"Not fully," Crina said. "Stefanya seemed pretty ruffled."

"You guys, I have to get back," Heather said. "Rosa has called a meeting for tonight, and I don't want to get caught in case someone knocks on my door."

"Before you go, Heather," Sara leaned forward. "Is it safe for you to stay there?"

"Safe as houses, boss," Heather said, her voice chipper. "I still have a few things I need to set in motion before I can even think about leaving New York." She paused, staring into her screen. "It makes me so happy to see you all together over there. Sara, I know that you're dealing with Crina's big secret, so take some time to heal, everything is under control here. And Crina, I'll see you tomorrow."

And she was gone.

The TV screen went back to illuminated black and the room fell into an uncomfortable silence and Sara felt four sets of eyes on her.

Taking a deep breath, she raised her head, returning the gaze of each person in turn.

"Are you okay?" April Veronica asked. "It must be so hard to hear all that stuff."

Lost for words, Sara shrugged. "There's not much I can do from here," she said, her voice small. "But first, Stefanya what now?"

Crina stood and raised a cautioning palm at Sara.

"Before you blow your top, my love," Crina spoke and Sara could tell how hard she was working to keep her voice light. "Before we got the Warsaw news, I was planning on having you talk to her tonight. We got a bit sidetracked, clearly, and I also don't want to overload you today."

"But Stefanya, the mythical, impossible to track down elder, just wants a chat and that's normal?"

"She's been in Spain, spying on Madrid," Crina said. "They're up to something."

Embla quickly sat beside Sara.

"You want no secrets, right?"

Sara nodded.

"She made me," Embla said simply. "Stefanya is my maker, and she lives here in Iceland."

Sara blinked uncomprehendingly, trying to grasp the enormity of the machinations that had gone on around here while she slowly flamed out in New York. Feelings of guilt and inadequacy assailed her and she suddenly very much wanted to be alone. She felt Silas's hand rest on her shoulder, then give her a very firm squeeze. It was surprisingly calming.

"I secretly very much want to make dinner for you," he said, giving her another squeeze. "Everything will look a little better after you eat some real food."

Sara glanced directly at each of the people around her, humbled by the looks of concern and care she saw.

"Okay fine it better not be fermented shark."

Chapter Three

Sara had forgotten the brutal toll that jetlag extracted from her, the oily way it insinuated itself into her moods, making her incurably cranky, filling her with a lethargic bitterness that she could do nothing about. Sitting in silence on the couch while four people bustled around her, setting the table and preparing food, she was at least grateful for the awareness that it was the jetlag that was making her bristlier by the minute. She clamped her mouth shut and feigned reverie until Embla called her to the table.

She maintained her silence throughout dinner, a sumptuous, simple farm meal of braised lamb shank, potatoes and chard, resting in a very red pool of au jus. Embla's plate did not contain lamb. April Veronica, seated beside her, clearly sensed her reticence and stepped into the void, peppering Silas, Crina and Embla with questions about whatever crossed her mind: Iceland, music, culture and history. Several times, Sara caught Embla looking at April Veronica with open admiration. Eventually, her mood thawing, Sara forced herself to join in, with simple acknowledgements that cost her more than anyone at the table knew. More than anything, she wanted to be alone, to give herself time to absorb the sudden loss of the women in Poland, and to ease the pain in her heart over what Teddie was going through because of her.

Once dinner was done, Silas and April Veronica cleared the table. Embla opened a cupboard on the far side of the vast room revealing a full bar set up. She poured five pints of Guinness, then returned to the couch area, the drinks on a tray made of a single piece of polished wood. Without a word, she set them on the low table between the two couches, mirroring the seating pattern from earlier, three on one side, two on the other. In silence, Sara walked over to her former seat, lifting the pint glass directly to her lips and draining half of it before sitting back against the couch.

"Embla, you can drink Guinness?"

Smiling, Embla nodded. "Yep, since 2017 it's been vegan."

With a nod, Sara raised her glass to Embla, then drained it.

"Where do you guys keep the heems around here?" she asked, her voice deliberately light to mask the guilt she felt, asking for hemoglobin after drinking several pints of blood.

"Wanna try a synthetic?" Embla appeared at her side, a smile on her face and a brown jar in her hand.

"Sure," Sara took the jar and popped the lid. "Same strength as regular?"

Embla glanced at Crina then back to Sara. "Um, no not exactly, these are much stronger, I brought them down here because your... well your tolerance is high at the minute and..."

Sara felt even guiltier that this person who she barely knew was dancing on eggshells around her.

"How many would you recommend?" Sara kept her voice light.

"I always think of heems like psychedelics," Embla said. "You can always take more, but you can't take less. Let's start you with two." Sara chuckled and shook two pills onto her palm, washing them down with the rest of her Guinness. With a flourish, Embla turned and sashayed back to the bar, returning with a new bottle of Guinness. She refilled Sara's glass, then took her seat on the couch across from her.

In the kitchen, Silas was putting the finishing touches on a charcuterie board. April Veronica finished loading the dishwasher then took her seat beside Embla. Crina returned from the hallway with an arm full of folded blankets, white, patterned with snowflakes in pinks or blues. Carefully, she set them on the couch.

"In case we decide to go sit outside," she said, taking her seat beside Sara. As if on cue, Silas proudly carried his charcuterie platter from the kitchen, setting it among the pint glasses on the table.

"I'd like to break the ice a little," Sara said, raising her glass. "I'm sorry, I know that a lot of effort went into getting me," she paused, looking at April Veronica, "...sorry, us, here, and I am all too aware that my behavior since we got here has been less than gracious. I'd like to take a moment to apologize, to all four of you. And also," she locked eyes with Embla, "thank you, for welcoming us into your home."

"It's our home now," Embla said, her glass raised high. "Skál"

"Skál" echoed the other four.

"I have another question already," April Veronica said. "Is this our house? Is this where we all live?"

"It's one of them," Crina said, her eyes warm. "Iceland is a tricky place. People pay attention, so when we need to go into the city, we prefer to stay in hotels, but we have houses located around the island-"

"Boltholes?" Sara interjected.

"If you will," Crina said, unruffled. "We have many options. If you'd like some space, Sara, please say so. We can set you up anywhere that you like. This is merely our current headquarters."

"It's gorgeous," April Veronica said.

"It is," Sara agreed, then an awkward silence fell. After several moments, Crina stood.

"My friends, I know we are in trying times and right now, we are hurting, some more than others. Even so, I want to tell you that tonight, I am hopeful. I look around this room, and I see not just four people whom I love very much, I see a future for people like us, a future that nobody has dared to envision."

Confused, Sara waited for Crina to begin the benediction that began every Lock meeting. As if reading her mind, Crina shook her head.

"I don't want to throw too much at you, dearest, but it's long been a dream of mine to rethink the whole Lock situation. In my new version of a Lock, we are equals, friends. We utilize the rules of the old ways as discussion points, and we are built to adapt to change."

"But we're still a Lock?" Sara asked, surprised when Crina shrugged.

"If you need it to be, then it is," she said enigmatically. "For me, once I began to leave the concept of the fixed Lock behind, I came to see it as just another boundary. When I made you, we needed our nunneries, mainly for our safety. These days, the benefits of being a pseudo religious order are purely financial. And we have enough money, we have enough real estate, to maintain ourselves indefinitely. So, why cling to the old ways if they don't serve us?"

What Crina was saying made perfect sense to Sara, and that feeling of foolishness surged in her. Such a huge, fundamental change should have at least occurred to her, but she'd never seen the Lock structure as something she could overhaul.

"The laws would still apply, obviously. And I think that Embla's work on vegan alternatives is something we should be working towards. We need to leave the cities, because surveillance is so pervasive and our existence is a greater global threat than anything in history.

We need to become even less visible, but at the same time, we gain freedom."

"Back to the forests," Embla said gleefully, clapping her hands.

Across the coffee table, Sara watched April Veronica's eyes widen alongside the smile that grew below them. A clamor of questions arose in Sara's mind, and she shot them down, aware that they all just made her sound like an old person, and she suddenly cared very much about what Embla thought of her.

"Sara, that's what I mean, this Lock, this group, it would be temporary," Crina said benevolently. "And none of us is the mother, none of us is the scholar. Look at New York. How long has Heather handled the books? How long has Rosa handled the investments? They are positions of power, but because they're hard work, nobody wants to do them. Both of those women are too powerful now. That power should have been divided, shared."

"But I.." Sara sputtered.

"I'm not singling you out, Sara. It's the same at every Lock in the world. Power isn't gender based. People like power, and they'll take it where they can get it. So now, New York has two women, diametrically opposed, holding all the power. That situation will end however it ends, but here, in Iceland, we will all work. We are a small operation. Stefanya and her girls are up in Akureyri. Decentralization works best in smaller countries like this."

In all of the confusion, Sara had completely forgotten that Silas told her there were more women than she'd met.

"And who exactly are Stefanya's *girls*?" Sara asked pointedly.

Crina heaved her shoulders in a sigh.

"Sara we are all on eggshells here, and you really have to choose how you want your information. I don't want to overload you, and that's the only reason I'm going slow."

A flash of rage tore through Sara. She wanted to scream that two nights ago she had faced death and no piece of information would ever be heavier than that. She closed her eyes and counted to ten in Romanian, then slowly opened her eyes.

"Hit me, mama. Overload away."

Crina exhaled, glanced at Silas, then took her hand.

"We currently have Amitra and Fan living with us."

"You're not serious," Sara said, her eyes wide.

Crina nodded slowly. "Once again, there was no way to tell you before we got you here."

"I understand," Sara said, doing her best to sound okay with it when she really wasn't. Fan and Amrita were the warriors who helped Stefanya defeat the cursed men during the Purge. Tiny but lethal, one Indian, one Chinese, they had influenced Lock life more than anyone, and Sara thought often about her time with them. They'd taught her to fight, how to meditate and do yoga, and how to find appreciation in service. Once again, she felt like a child who had assumed too many incorrect things about her parents.

"And they're... okay?" Sara asked.

"I know it's a lot," Embla said, "but they're super normal and weird and goofy. Sometimes they act too young even for me."

"This is amazing," April Veronica laughed, and Sara fought off a wave of anger. It wasn't amazing. It was horrible. Now that she was looking back at her time in New York through a lens of failure, the last thing she felt like doing was facing the scrutiny of the three greatest cursed women of all time.

"What's wrong, Sara?" Silas said, meeting her gaze evenly, concern etching his brow.

"This is the vampire equivalent of dreaming you went to school in your underwear," she said quietly. "You guys, it's okay to acknowledge how very deeply I fucked up New York."

"Well, it might be if that was the case," Crina said, taking Sara's hand again. "It's not. The only thing that got fucked up was you, and looking at you, I'd say that once the glue sets, we won't even be able to see the cracks."

Something melted in Sara's heart as she looked into Crina's eyes, then she felt the sting of tears and one heavy drop escaped, leaving a cold trail down her cheek. She blinked the tears away.

"Uh, is it red?" she asked, and Crina nodded, handing her a napkin. "I'm definitely not fit for public consumption."

"That's another benefit of the synthetics," Embla piped up. "You can take as much as you want and no red tears. You also don't get to be as strong, but that might come in time. Jury is still out."

"Thanks, Embla, I'm sure open to it," Sara said. "But now, back to the elders you have stashed away. Have I passed the test? Can I be told everything?"

"Sara, please don't be a brat," Crina said. "There's not much more to tell. I saw the writing on the wall a long time ago."

"And you didn't try to talk to me about it?"

Crina stood and inhaled deeply, and Sara immediately recognized the broadened set of her shoulders, the arch of her back. She'd offended Crina, and she was about to get it.

"Oh, I tried, honey, I tried. You were a brick wall, and I had to make peace with the fact that you weren't ready for radical change. You and Teddie were experiencing freedom for the first time, running around town, absorbing culture. When Teddie went to Paris, I saw my chance to test out some theories on you, do you remember?"

Wracking her memories of that time, a century before, Sara recalled nothing. She shook her head.

"Can you jog my memory a little?" she said, her tone still defiant.

"We talked," Crina said definitively. "And you listened, and after I presented you with my laundry list of the coming problems for Lock life, you lumped them all into a simple category – that I was a Scholar, too removed from Lock life."

"I'm not psychic," Sara said. "Maybe you should have been a bit more direct."

"We can argue the past forever, but it won't help," Embla said, her voice calm.

"It's truth," Crina said, smiling at Embla, and then Sara. "Also the truth: Telling you was always at the front of my mind, but by the time I arrived at this answer, this Iceland thing, the pace of life picked up in ways I could never have predicted. We went from firelight to electricity, from letters to telephones, from ships to airplanes, and then, in a huge tumble, movies, television, internet and then the complete meltdown that is social media." Crina paused, taking an exasperated breath.

"Each one of these innovations threatened the life we created nearly six hundred years ago. I've been playing a game of four-dimensional chess on a table that changes shape every year or two, for nearly two hundred years. Sara, I don't have any answers, I only have ideas, but I really need to get past one thing with you. I did not tell you I have a son. I can still count the people who know on my two hands."

"Heather knew," Sara said, defiantly.

"Heather helped build this house, Sara, " Crina's tone was firm. "She helped me with finances and paperwork. In time, I came to trust her, and so I confided in her."

Fighting the urge to return to her room, Sara gritted her teeth in silence. Her mind was racing. She cast her mind back to conversations they'd had about Silas, and the fact that Heather knew all along made her anger boil anew.

"Sara, my child, this isn't easy. I did not betray you. I also did not betray myself. Silas was *my* secret. Nobody owes their secrets to anyone else. But this, this life here, I built this for you, and Silas. I dreamed of the day I could bring you together." She paused, giving a frustrated grimace at Silas. "But some people can't do as they're told."

"You're not the boss of me, mom," Silas said jokingly. April tittered briefly until she saw the expression on Sara's face.

"I understand, and I'm struggling with the fact that you all chose such a weird way to entrap me," Sara said. "I need you to realize that no matter what you were trying to do, the end result has hurt the person I love as much as you love Silas, and that's Teddie."

Sara stood, level with Crina.

"You did all this work to save your children, but you didn't give me a chance to save my own."

Silas went to speak, and Crina raised a finger in his direction, silencing him.

"Sara, my love, I need you to know one thing, and I say it without blame. Everything was on track until your levels went off the charts and then Marguerite was killed. Things got messy. And I will fix them."

"Okay," Sara said finally, exhausted by the circuitous nature of the discussion. "Let's move past this. I understand why you lied. I do. And in time, I'm sure it will just become part of our shared history. Are there any other huge secrets that I need to know?"

"Embla, would you mind heating up some blood wine for us," Crina asked, sending Embla back to the bar area without a word.

"Sara, it's worse than we knew," Crina began. "After the murder, I did not return upstate. I went to Paris, then London. I noticed that in each Lock, the two most vocal proponents of Desdemona's agenda were transfers from Madrid."

Sara gasped. "Like Rosa and Marguerite!"

Crina smiled. "Yes. While nobody was paying attention, Desdemona installed sleeper agents in Locks around the world. They've been pushing her agenda and causing friction within the Locks for at least half a century."

Sara's stomach sank.

"I feel sick," she said.

"Of course you do, it's disgusting," Crina said, returning her hand to Sara's thigh. "It's a new discovery, and there's no way you could have foreseen it."

"Nobody plays a long game like an immortal," Embla said from the bar.

"Apparently not," Crina smiled. "Sara, think of the nonsense that has taken up all your time in New York, the fights. What percentage would you attribute to either Rosa or Marguerite?"

Sara shrugged, casting her mind back, shocked at the answer. "It's a lot," she said. "They were always irritating at least one of the sisters."

"Discord, unhappiness, that's what they were tasked with."

"But Crina," said April Veronica hesitantly, "that doesn't explain *me*."

"Marguerite wasn't an obedient person, she never was. Desdemona underestimated just how stubborn Marguerite actually was. April Veronica, I believe that Marguerite was changed by meeting you. In many ways, it's a shame we couldn't save her and have her with us, because ultimately, her heart was pure."

Embla wrapped an arm around April Veronica, her eyes sparkling with tears.

"Desdemona herself killed Marguerite, because Marguerite was about to tell you everything, Sara. She was not murdered because of code violations. Des killed her to shut her up then hid behind that changed rules malarkey."

"This is unprecedented," Sara said, shock on her face. "There has never been a case of a sister murdering another sister outside of formal duel."

"This is fact," Crina said. "In all of our existence, we have never known cold blooded murder. Until now. This is why we needed to act swiftly."

Sara took a deep breath, trying to assess the big picture. She tried to shift her focus away from what had happened to her. Arguing with the past was pointless. Marguerite was dead. Sara's time in New York, for better or worse, was finished. Her main priority was Teddie, and she realized that having Heather caring for her daughter was almost as good as being there herself. The tension in her shoulders abated slightly, and she raised her head.

"So," she asked. "What are you and the other scholars cooking up?"

"Well..." Crina began, only to be interrupted by Embla with four goblets of blood liquor. As she took her goblet, she resumed. "I'd suggest you down this fast. You won't like this next part."

Sara brought the goblet to her lips, inhaling a complex bouquet of iron, rust and earth, with notes of citrus and bay leaf. This was next level.

"Don't sniff it, shoot it," Crina said, nudging her, and Sara obliged, swallowing the whole thing in one gulp.

"Scholars, if that's what you want to call them, are a complicated bunch," Crina began. "A lot of them are watching what is happening and they're content to let it burn itself out."

"What precisely does that mean?"

"Well, one train of thought is to let Desdemona's ZPG cull off a lot of... I don't want to say dead wood."

"They're women," Sara said, her voice firm.

"Yes, that's my opinion too," Crina said warmly. "But we are talking women older than me, well some of them anyway, but their paths have taken them away from Lock life in significant ways. They all really like the idea of a loose, global Lock. So to them, the easiest path is to let Desdemona force the locks into ZPG and then they'll all die out."

"Do we need the other OG bitches to save the world?" April Veronica said, a blood moustache on her elfin face.

"That's the question," Crina said, looking around the room. "Do we save the whole Lock world, or do we just build an ark to weather the flood?"

"Crina, you know how many women have passed through the New York Lock. I have personally known more than half the cursed women currently alive. And now you want me to sit back and let them die?"

"They've changed," Crina said coolly. "Look at Liz and Eleanor in your own Lock. Bright, free thinking women who've been swayed to Desdemona's conservative xenophobia. Fran, that woman's a genius. But she's all of a sudden voting to strip women of their credits, and she's siding with a murderer. People don't stay the same forever, as we are learning. And it's an adjustment that we are overdue in making."

This new information set Sara's head swimming. Blinking twice to clear her vision, she fought to steady her breath. She was overloaded, and she didn't know how to get her synapses to fire the way she needed them to.

"Sara," Silas broke his silence, his voice gentle. "Sara, are you okay?"

A finger to her temple, Sara turned slowly to face him, unprepared for the raw emotion in his eyes. Lying to him wasn't an option.

"I don't think I am," she said, her voice plain and small. "It's not that I don't understand what I'm hearing, I'm literally short-circuiting here."

She broke her eye contact with Silas and turned her face to the wall of glass windows, the sky a rich peacock blue that she wanted to run outside and get lost in. The room fell into silence, and that felt oppressive to Sara. She thought about Crina's new version of a Lock, realizing she was already living inside it and that meant that she didn't have to stay in this room, or be governed by whatever the elders wanted for the future of their kind. As the thought crossed her mind, her heart kicked into gear, and she turned back to face Crina.

"Keeping Cursed women safe and alive has consumed my every waking thought for centuries," she said, relieved that the strength had returned to her voice. "What you're saying, Crina, I literally can't do it. I can't just watch more women die." Her voice got louder. "We just watched a video of a group of our sisters dying like some disgusting seventies cult, and we're sipping blood wine and casually voicing support for more of these massacres?"

Sara could see the emotions twisting behind Crina's eyes as she sought the correct response. It made her happy to see her maker struggle, and she let it play out for as long as it took.

"I am just telling you what the elders are saying," Crina said finally.

"You're an elder," Sara said. "Apparently a very influential one. So here is where I stand, right now. I will only stay here if we are all in agreement that saving everyone, every single cursed sister, regardless of her... politics, is our stated mission."

Once again, Crina fell silent as she formulated her response. The quiet in the room was broken by Silas.

"That has been my position in all of this," he said, his voice low. "I agree to stand beside you in this."

"Me too," said April Veronica.

"I'm a fucking vegan," Embla said. "I'll save any living thing I can.'

"Sara" Crina spoke very slowly. "You're right. It's inconvenient for me, but I admit I've been wrong. No point blaming anyone. My focus was my family, not our entire community. If it means you'll stay, I will agree to begin working on a new strategy."

"That seems sudden," Sara said.

"It's not," Crina said. "Watching that video, for the first time and each time I've watched it again, those women, all dying, all that history, all that knowledge, those hearts, those minds, all of it, gone in a flash. I've been haunted by it and I suppose I was already organically changing my mind."

"So, Iceland is a no kill shelter?" Sara said, looking around the room.

Four goblets raised into the air, and Sara added her own.

"Skál," Embla said.

"Skál," they all echoed back.

"And if we have gotten past the gnarly shit, I have a gift for everyone," April Veronica said, reaching into the pocket of her hoodie and pulling out a familiar bottle of swirling orange oil.

"You smuggled drugs on an international flight?" Silas was aghast.

"Correction," April Veronica said with an impish grin. "This is what happens when you don't tell us where we are going. Also, it's what happens when I forget what's in my backpack because you know, trauma, yelling, fight or flight, mercy dash and whoops, here I am in Iceland with my last bottle of weed elixir."

Embla wrapped April Veronica in a hug.

"Hey," she said into April's green hair. "Who wants to get high and go lay under the Northern Lights?"

Chapter Four

The light flooding Sara's bedroom was golden. The shaft of sunlight piercing the dark through a break in the curtains was somehow softer than the sunlight in New York. A flick at her phone revealed that it was after eleven. She'd slept over nine hours, no interruptions. Blinking the sleep away, she blew a kiss to the bottle of thick orange liquid on her bedside table, the weed syrup from April Veronica.

Then she remembered her behavior the previous evening, cringing at her thorny, churlish response. She'd been such a bitch, sweeping the deaths of the Warsaw women away, focusing on her own hurt instead. Casting her mind back to the disturbingly pristine video of a mass suicide, she was disappointed in herself, she still felt numb, more concerned about Teddie. There was a persistent ache in her gut, an awful feeling of being trapped, overpowered by everyone's refusal to at least tell Teddie that Sara was still alive.

Gazing around the room, she stared at her suitcase on the floor, still unpacked. It felt strangely pleasant to see all of her earthly possessions in such a small container, freeing, not weird. It felt good to leave it there, as if not unpacking was the one defiant thing she was allowed to do. She tried to remember how many pairs of underpants she'd bought at the Target back in New Jersey but couldn't. Then she remembered that she hadn't showered in several days and wondered if that might have anything to do with her sour mood. Leaping from her bed, she saw a slip of paper beneath her door.

Sara I'm heading to New York. I will guard Teddie with my life. I wish we'd had more time to talk and unpack everything that has happened, but things are the way they are. I will be in touch as soon as I get to NYC. I asked the youngsters to drive me to the airport, obviously to give you some privacy with Silas. If that's not to your liking, take one of the cars and explore. He will understand. Love you, so very completely –
C

Crina's new persona as meddling mother was too alien for her to process fully. Flopping back on the bed, she forced herself to see Crina fairly, to accept her unique position, but she balked. As far as Sara could see, Crina was still taking more than she was giving. After spending so many centuries attuned to the needs of those around her, post-suicide Sara was no longer as interested in people pleasing or keeping the peace. All she wanted was to ease Teddie's burden, regardless of the fallout. Snatching up her burner phone from the nightstand, she bounced it in one palm, eyeing it suspiciously. She knew Teddie's cell number by heart, but something deep inside her, something infuriatingly obedient, stopped her from making the call.

Tossing her phone angrily onto the bed, she decided to shower herself back into feeling human. Stepping into the long hallway, Sara paused, the now-familiar silence surrounding her, then continued to the bathroom. The water came out of the showerhead instantly hot, startling her. In her New York apartment, it took minutes for the water to heat up. Keeping the temperature as hot as she could stand it, she stepped under the showerhead, letting the scalding water wash away the tensions of the past couple of days.

As the hot water caressed her skin and needled her scalp, she tried to make a to-do list, quickly realizing that she lacked the basic information necessary for even such a pedestrian task. She needed clothing, food and blood, but she wanted music, books and entertainment, and she knew literally nothing about obtaining any of those things in Iceland.

She'd have to talk to Silas.

As the thought crossed her mind, she listened intently to her pulse. Nothing, no reaction. Unsure if that was good or bad, it was enough to prepare her for the next phase of her day, so she killed the water, dried herself with a thick, absorbent towel from a stack beside the shower, then went back to her room.

Three pairs of undies. That's what remained of the seven pairs she bought in New Jersey. And two bras. She assembled a small, neat pile of laundry, then put on the only pair of jeans she owned, and the shirt she'd worn on the plane, after a quick sniff to ensure that it was still okay.

After pressing her hair as dry as she could manage with the towel, she returned to the bathroom, brushed her hair, considered makeup, decided against makeup.

"Pretty," she said with a smirk. Her stomach grumbled in response, and a double craving, blood and coffee, ran through her like electricity.

Cautiously, she walked along the hallway, then down the three stairs to the empty living room. She opened cupboard after cupboard in the kitchen, finding nothing that resembled anything that would make coffee. The fridge contained a lot of mixers, some spinach and the leftovers from the meal that Silas had made the night before. There was a lone candy bar in the door of the refrigerator, its label read Drammur and there was a photo of chocolate. She tore it open, biting off the end piece, gagging immediately as the acrid tang of licorice filled her mouth. She spat it into the sink angrily.

"Silas!" she called out, her voice echoing back in the huge vaulted room. "Are you here?"

When no answer was forthcoming, she returned to her room to get her phone, firing off a brief text. He answered immediately. He'd be back "in minutes."

Returning to the living room, Sara walked to the curved wall of glass windows, taking in the emerald field that stretched up to the mountain in front of the house, its peak higher than the windows could show. Then she walked the perimeter of the room, a semi-circle. The back wall had closets at either end, then shelving. The first part featured books, records and blu-rays, alongside some ancient VHS tapes. In the center, a large flat television, and below that, a shelf full of bar equipment and bottles. The right half of the room was open kitchen with an island. The couch that she had sat on the night before offered the best view of the windows, which therefore made her feel safest. She sat and waited for Silas.

A noise behind her caused her to jump and spin around. It was Silas coming down the stairs from the hallway.

"Did I scare you?" His face was stricken. "Sara, I'm sorry. I was back in the greenhouse."

"We have a greenhouse?" Sara gave him a half-smile. "Yeah, I guess I'm a little jumpy. Do you know how long it's been since I was alone in a house?"

Silas moved to the kitchen sink and washed his hands. "I'm going to go with either five centuries or never."

"Ding ding ding," Sara said, feeling awkward about standing but if she sat back down, her back would be to him and that would make things worse. "Though to be honest, I don't know which of them is true. I can't remember ever being alone in a house."

"Well, if that's what you want, we can definitely hook you up here," Silas shot her a smile as he dried his hands on a dishcloth.

"I didn't say I liked it," Sara said, hating the defensive tone in her voice even more when she saw Silas flinch. "Silas, we should talk, but first-"

"Sara, I'm so sorry," he said, his hands on the counter.

"I know you are, I really do. What I was going to say, was first, I'm literally dying for coffee and I need to know, is that not a thing in Iceland? I couldn't find a coffee maker or anything."

A wry grin played across Silas's face and he turned slowly, gesturing at a machine on the kitchen counter, so big it would not have fit in her New York kitchen. "Sara, meet our coffee maker. It's not too easy to use, so what would you like?"

"I'd love a dry upside down skinny matcha no foam latte."

"Is that a thing? I'm sorry, I don't know how to make it."

"Nah, I just made it up. I'd love a very strong espresso thing. And I'll need it over ice so I can get it into my system pronto."

With a sharp salute, Silas turned to the gleaming machine, pressing buttons and reaching for a cup as machinery whirred and the aroma of freshly ground coffee beans filled the room.

"Take a seat, I'll bring it over," he called, and Sara plonked herself back into the couch. As the coffee machine buzzed and gurgled, Sara explored her feelings. Most pressingly, she felt untethered, like she was floating, not aimlessly, but not rooted to any reality either. She knew that Silas wanted to talk to her, and she didn't want to muddle her emotions and blame him for a situation that was largely of her own making.

"Sarnia? I have an iced espresso for Sarnia!" Silas was in front of her, on the other side of the coffee table, in one hand a pint glass full of ice and swirling black coffee, and in the other, a second pint glass, this one filled with scarlet blood.

"I'd start with this," Silas said, handing her the blood. She hoped that he didn't notice her hand shaking as she took the glass from him and avoided eye contact until she had downed the whole glass.

"Trade ya," Silas said, taking the empty glass and sliding the fully glass of coffee into her hands.

She took it gratefully, sipping it and immediately banishing a headache she hadn't even realized was forming. As she drank the coffee, she realized that after she drank the blood, she hadn't even swooned.

"Do you mind if I join you?" Silas remained standing.

"Please do," Sara nodded. He sat opposite her, his eyes scanning the room behind her.

"Before we get serious," Sara began, "There's something else that I don't know, and it's unsettling me."

"Shoot."

"I don't have any clothes. I don't have a speaker for my iPod. I don't have any... anything..." Sara paused, shrugging.

A wave of relief passed across Silas's face.

"Oh, okay, that's easy," he said. "Actually Embla and April Veronica are out shopping today. You can text them with any requests, anything at all. I'll warn you. The choices here aren't huge. Most Icelanders fly over to England to do their clothes shopping."

"That's cool," Sara said, draining her coffee. "Is that what we will do?"

"Sure, if you want to. I mean, it's right there. It's easy."

"What about food?"

"If you're up for it, we can go to the Hagkaup supermarket that's not too far from here. They have a lot of everything."

"Actually, that would be nice. We can have an outing."

"After we talk?"

Sara nodded, then answered quietly. "Yes, after we talk."

Silas raised his face to hers, a look of naked openness that tugged at her heart.

"I'll let you begin..." he said quietly.

Sara sighed. "I don't even know where to start. Silas, more has happened in the last two months of my life than has happened in, I don't know, forever. What I need to work on, right now, is what happened between us. Silas, I was falling for you. But I don't know what's real. I don't know if I fell for you because it was illicit, forbidden. Or was I just taking the next step towards burnout? Were you just another bit of self-sabotage? And on top of all that, I don't know your true motives." She paused for a breath, half-hoping he'd jump in and take some of the pressure off, but Silas remained frustratingly silent.

And patient.

"So that's where I'm at. Do you wanna take a stab at any of it?"

"Sure," he replied, way too effortlessly. With a shrug he continued. "I didn't come to see you with any agenda other than to finally begin your extraction from New York. I was supposed to get a sense of how responsive you'd be, and then mom... Crina would step in and see if you'd be open to a new approach."

"She did offer to get me out of New York if I went scholar."

"Yep. That was the original plan. But we underestimated a couple of things. For me, I was thunderstruck by our connection this time. You were different from when we talked in the sixties. You were... I don't really want to say it, it sounds cheesy and it also will sound like I'm telling you how you feel."

"Go ahead, I won't bite."

"Okay, vampire humor, we're doing good," Silas chuckled. "You spoke to me from your heart. We seem to be at the same point in life, and for people like us, that's rare. So something deeper clicked between us. And that's when I went off-script."

"What do you mean?"

"Well, mom and I ... I'm sorry, is it cool with you if I call her mom?"

"She's your mom, why not?" Sara's voice was frostier than she intended, and she looked at the floor rather than meet Silas's gaze.

Silas sighed and continued. "My mother and I had devised a set of hurdles, things I'd bring into the discussion, just for us to see if you were truly burned out on the Lock life. She knew she couldn't ask you directly because you always felt a need to project a strong front to her."

Sara inhaled sharply. She couldn't argue with that one.

"But then I found myself lying to her, mainly to buy myself time with you. I knew that you were burning out, but I told mom I still needed more time to be sure. It wasn't until your blood stink went sky-high that I realized that your situation was more urgent than I'd guessed."

"Did you tell Crina?"

"Not for a long while. I had to warn her before she came into the city, but even then, I only did it because she would have noticed, she would have smelled it on you immediately."

"Was she disappointed?"

"What? No. It happens to everyone. Back to us though, I'd like to be clear. The emotional stuff, it just happened. It was real, and selfishly I let it progress, even though it was a recipe for disaster. Stupidly, I thought I could manage it myself. And, I probably could have, if Desdemona hadn't murdered Marguerite."

"It's still so hard to hear that word in connection to a sister."

"I know. It's awful. But I just want to make that point, while we are here. I went off script. Marguerite went off script. People, apparently, don't like living in a scripted reality. Not when they find love."

After the word was out of his mouth, Silas blushed, and a comfortable silence hung between them. Sara flashed back to him saying it on the plane, a memory that felt like a dream, an important moment that still felt like an illusion. Eventually, Silas resumed speaking.

"Sara, for what it's worth, I love you. I do. That part is real. And now you've seen Iceland, you can see why i needed secrecy. The scene with Liz and San Francisco set us back thirty years. It also showed us how fragile Lock life is, and how difficult it is to introduce new ways of life to people who have lived for centuries under the old rules."

"I got used to you being a cursed man pretty quick."

"Did you think we were both doomed?"

Sara dropped her eyes and nodded. "It was so attractive, to finally have someone to flame out with."

She paused, and Silas went to speak, and she held up a finger. "No. I have something to say. When I was in that-" she paused, and a shiver raced through her. "-that Surrender room, I realized how stupid, how fucking *teenage* I had been. All I wanted at that point was to live, and all I could think of was that I'd robbed myself of something I've never had, which is true love, like equal love. And all I wanted in my last moments was that you got away safely, that they didn't ever find you."

Sara raised her face, unsurprised to see tears streaming down Silas's face.

"I hated lying to you," he said, sobs breaking his voice. "I hated every fucking second of it. In your practice, on our dates. The whole time, I knew that the very facts of it, of all of it, pretty much cursed our success, but for a brief moment, it looked like you would go scholar, and you could live in the lake house, and we would have years before

Iceland even became a thing. Mom would have swept in and delivered that news. And hopefully by then, we'd have become what we're going to become, and we could have weathered it." He stopped suddenly, choking on a sob, his eyes blinking away tears. "I'm sorry, I'm so sorry, I don't know what else to say."

Sara's first response was to comfort him, this broken man crying across a coffee table, in a strange house in a foreign land, but before she knew what was going on, a sob burst from her throat, and she was engulfed in tears, hot and angry. In her chest, her heart split in two, pouring molten lava into her stomach. The pain and the cumulative shock of the past week exploded inside her and nothing else was real except the pain, so intense it bent her double, the hollowness causing her to crumple in on herself.

"I'm not a cryer," she mumbled between sobs.

She felt the pressure of Silas sitting beside her almost as if it was happening to someone else, then the weight of an arm around her shoulders and she leaned in the direction of the warmth, the support of another human body. The contact made the crying worse, and she felt her nose begin to run, and spittle ran over her lips and she struggled to get herself right.

"Sara," Silas whispered into her ear. "It's all going to be alright."

The sound that came from her didn't sound human at all, a long low moan that turned into a "no."

"Nooooooooo, I abandoned Teddie, Silas, I left her to die."

She dissolved onto him, the words silently echoing inside both of their heads.

"I promise you Sara, nothing will happen to her."

"Don't..."

"I mean it."

"You can't... promise..."

"I do, Sara. I give you my word. I'll save Teddie or I'll die trying."

"That's... comforting..." Sara said, a small chuckle finding its way into the sobbing, and she was grateful for it, the way it derailed the flood. "Damn, I'm sorry, I keep on thinking I'm all cried out, and then I'm not."

Silas squeezed her shoulders. "Sara, the amount of stress, just your day to day, was immense. In the past month, I mean, I can't even quantify it. And here we are."

Wriggling around to face him, Sara flashed him a broken smile. Gently, he wiped at her face with his sleeve, leaving watery blood stains on the pale cotton.

"You're gonna have to wash that now," she whispered.

"I don't care, I have other clothes I can change into. Unlike you. Would you like to freshen up and we can head out and get you some things?"

"Actually, if it's okay, I'd like to stay here for a little longer, just like this."

"It's more than okay," Silas wiped her nose and then her chin, then kissed her forehead. "We can stay like this as long as you want."

Chapter Five

Arriving back at the parking garage, Sara felt a glimmer of the familiar comfort of returning home, a fluttering of lightness in her heart. After they parked, Silas hooked the car up to the electrical power supply while Sara threaded her arms through the handles of a multitude of shopping bags in the back of the car.

"Hey, I can help you carry," Silas called.

"I'm afraid you might have to, we kind of went a little crazy."

"No problem," Silas materialized beside her, grabbing up a few bags of shopping. "Actually, we may need to make a couple of trips," he laughed. Sara hauled herself upright, then groaned.

"How are we going to open the doors?"

"Good point," Silas set his bundle of bags on the garage floor, then opened the security door that led to the hallway to the house. "Let's load everything in here and we can get it at our leisure."

As she hauled the bags into the hallway, Sara felt suddenly girlish and ridiculous, she'd lost herself in shopping for clothes and makeup at a string of large retail barns on the outskirts of Reykjavik, even forcing Silas to try on things that clearly made him uncomfortable, mainly pants that made his ass look great. They'd stopped at an organic market and bought all kinds of strange herbs and lots of lamb and extra organic veggies for Embla. She texted the girls that she wanted to make dinner. She didn't know what time it was, and she liked that.

Once all the bags were in the hallway, Silas let the door swing closed and they grabbed an armful each and headed for the front door. As she rounded the glass windows, Sara spied Embla and April Veronica sitting on the floor, controllers in their hands, a video game on the screen.

"I'll say it before you do," Silas said. "This feels weirdly like we've flipped into bizarro world and we are coming home to our kids."

"Get out of my brain, white devil," Sara laughed as she pushed her shoulder against the door, opening it effortlessly.

"You're home," April Veronica called. "If you need any help with your purchases, I'll need a minute, this is the first time I'm beating Embla at Mario Kart and victory shall be mine."

"That's what you think," Embla yelled. On the screen, Sara watched as a cartoon Embla threw a bomb at cartoon April Veronica's car and sailed past her, winning the race.

"Parentfucker," April Veronica yelled, and Embla burst out laughing, a throaty contagious sound that made both Sara and Silas grin as they set their shopping bags on the counter of the kitchen island. The younger women set their game controllers on the floor and stood up, stretched in unison then hurried over to inspect the purchases.

"You guys went everywhere," April Veronica said as she surveyed the various shopping bags.

"This is just the tip of the iceberg. I thought you went shopping too," Sara was confused.

"We *almost* went shopping," Embla said. "After we dropped Crina off at the airport, we went full tourist and spent the day at the Blue Lagoon instead."

Sara gave April Veronica's outfit the once over and saw that she wasn't lying. Her trackpants and sweater both bore the logo of the famous tourist destination.

"Sara, this is literally the most expensive piece of clothing I've ever owned," April Veronica whispered conspiratorially. "I still can't get used to this unlimited wealth thing."

"We got you a present," Embla said, darting to the coffee table and returning with a jar in her hands. She handed it to Sara, who smiled. She couldn't remember the last time a sister gave her a gift that wasn't wine or lingerie.

"Body scrub," she laughed. "Is this a hint? You guys, I showered."

"My skin is so soft," April Veronica presented a forearm, sliding up the sleeve of her sweater. Sara ran a finger along it. "Very nice, but also, you're a baby. Your skin is pretty perfect already."

"Thanks," April Veronica said. "Oh, I hope you don't mind, I went and changed your bedding and I saw your suitcase. Would you like me to unpack for you?"

A curious sensation rolled through Sara, and she paused, her finger still on April Veronica's skin, and it took her a second to identify it. Someone was taking care of her, and she didn't hate it.

"You made my bed?' Her eyes met April Veronica's, and the young woman nodded guilelessly. Sara thought of her suitcase such as it was, a cheap piece of luggage from a big store, its meager contents her entire worldly belongings, and she shook her head.

"I'll take care of the suitcase, but thank you, April Veronica."

As Sara lifted her finger from April Veronica's arm, their eyes met, and April Veronica's widened, boring into Sara's.

"What?"

"You two seem to be on good terms," she said playfully, flicking a glance at Silas.

"We had a talk," Sara said.

"And?" Embla and April Veronica said at once.

"And we good," Sara said before moving to start sorting through the bags on the counter.

"I told you she was enigmatic," April Veronica said to Embla.

"Hey, it's her business," Embla said. "Can I help you unload the food?"

"We're gonna cook for you," Silas said. "Sure, come help with the fridge. We bought half of Hagkaup."

Embla rose and began clearing space in the fridge for the groceries.

"Who wants a cocktail?" Silas said, brandishing a bottle of blood liquor. "I got old school and I gots synthetic."

"All in," laughed Embla.

"Show me the new clothes," April Veronica came around to Sara's side and threw an arm around her shoulders, sending a wave of affection through her. She couldn't remember a time in her life where the pressure was so low, and the camaraderie so high. Every phase of her long life had been a battle. From suspicious villagers and marauding road gangs in Europe to the lawlessness of New Amsterdam, Lock life was non-stop vigilance and subterfuge. This Icelandic model was so peaceful she felt like she was in a movie, a staged reality. She hooked an arm around April Veronica's, and hauled her out to the garage. Several trips later, a fashion parade was in full effect until a sudden image of Teddie flashed into her mind.

"Uh oh," April Veronica said instantly. "What happened in there?"

Sara met her gaze. "Teddie," she said simply. "This doesn't feel right. This whole utopia feels amazing, like this is the most functional night of my life, but then I remember what Teddie must be going through and I feel like the biggest asshole."

"Mom is at the compound now," Silas said, looking at the screen of his phone. "We will be seeing Teddie tonight. Mom will go live from the compound. We will see what she sees." He paused, resting a hand on Sara's shoulder. "You don't have to watch, I know it will be impossible not to, but Rosa is all about the all-hands meeting these days."

"I hear you, but I have to watch," Sara rested a hand atop Silas's. "Now where is this vampire mixology you were talking about?"

After dinner, they moved back to the living area. The image on the big TV screen flickered and vanished several times, then rendered slowly in a boxy low-res that crystallized with tantalizing slowness before revealing a bookshelf, then, moving quickly, a blurry pan around an apartment that Sara recognized immediately as the same one that Crina stayed in for April Veronica's confirmation.

The image dissolved into a pixelated blur and then solidified and Crina's voice crackled into the room.

"Are we good," she asked. "Can you hear and see?"

"So far so good," Embla replied, her fingers darting across the keyboard of the laptop on her thighs. "I'm gonna see if I can stabilize the image. Did you charge both batteries?"

The image on the TV bounced up and down as Crina nodded.

"Mom, you're gonna have to hold your head still or we are all gonna throw up."

"Got it," Crina replied without rancor. "I'll go into frozen elder mode as soon as I get to the roof deck."

"Who have you seen so far?"

"Only Imani and Heather," Crina said. "Sara, I want to warn you. People are upset. It was literally the hardest thing I've ever had to do, not telling Imani that you're alive. I haven't seen Teddie yet, she was sleeping. But that will be even harder. I also know you won't listen, but Sara, you might want to sit this out."

"Silas already tried," Sara said.

"How's everything over there?"

Silence rang out.

"Shit, did I lose you?"

"Everything's fine, mom" Silas said. "There's been talking."

"And shopping," April Veronica said.

"Sara?"

"What? They're not lying. Silas and I had a great day out and about. I have clean clothes and we just made sushi. I know this won't be easy, but I'll be okay."

"This makes me very happy," Crina said. "I'm gonna keep the camera on, but I have to get up to the roof. I'm already late. Do you want to kill the TV for a few minutes? I don't want to make you all carsick?"

"No, I want to see," Sara said. "If I get nauseous, I'll close my eyes."

"Here we go then," Crina said, and instantly the TV image became a swirling blur as she ascended the spiral staircase to her loft room, crossed that room, opened the door to the roof deck and stepped onto the roof. When the image stabilized, it was like a stake through Sara's heart: The sun was setting over the raised garden beds, the water tower, the hedges; things she had built with her own hands, things she'd nurtured with her heart. She felt a tangled mix of homesickness, regret, love and loss. She was suddenly aware of being further away from that building than she'd ever been. When Crina turned in the direction of the roof house, its windows black and foreboding, the pain became almost unbearable. Beside her on the couch, Silas took her hand and squeezed it hard. She squeezed back.

On the TV, Crina pressed a fingertip onto the security pad on the door. It flashed green, Crina turned the handle and it swung open. Disappointingly, Crina kept her head down as she made her way to her throne, now positioned in the rear semi-circle of chairs. They heard muted welcomes, from Yukari and Imani, then nothing but shuffling noises as Crina seated herself, and then, finally she raised her head.

Sara gasped.

At the front of the room, where Sara's throne had stood for over a hundred years, sat Rosa, upon her own throne, walnut inlaid with gold, a relic from a church in Mexico City. Rosa's face was glowing, her makeup heavy and deliberate, black kohl around her almond eyes, mascara thickening her already copious lashes, her hair lightly curled and thick, bouncing as she breathed. Most shocking was her full-lipped red smile, broad and satisfied, as she locked eyes with Crina, in the room, and Sara, via the television.

"Crina, welcome," Rosa said. "I'm glad you decided to join us. In future, a starting time for a meeting is not a suggestion. Please ensure that you're all present and seated before the appointed time."

"This is going to be harder than I thought," Sara whispered, her voice dead.

"Crina?" Rosa's voice was like a schoolteacher's. "Did you hear me?"

On the TV screen, they saw Crina's right hand rise up, its middle finger extended, as a look of consternation crossed Rosa's face. Ignoring it, she stood.

"My name is Rosa, and never have I killed," she said perfunctorily. "I declare this meeting of the New York Lock open. Unfortunately, for the first time in a long time, we will not be starting with the ritual toast since Elizabeth is down in North Carolina searching for April Veronica, and Theodora," she shot a disdainful glance at where Sara assumed Teddie was sitting, "has been unable to work or provide for us. Theodora, I hate to do this to you, but with Elle and Liz out of town, we really do need you to get back to work as soon as possible."

"Give her a fucking break, Rosa," came Heather's voice. "We are good with heems for as long as you need, Ted."

"I'd like to remind you that I'm the Lock Mother now," Rosa's voice was imperious.

"And I'd like to remind you that the operative word in your title is mother," Heather's voice didn't raise a decibel, but the threat in its tone was clear. "It's high time you remembered that."

Crina kept her gaze on Rosa, and Sara delighted in seeing her face fall, then scramble for composure.

"Teddie, of course, take some time, but please remember that we are all relying on you."

"Oh, so she's one of those passive aggressive mothers," Silas said.

"She's even worse than I imagined," whispered Sara, wishing that Crina would pan across to wherever Teddie was sitting.

When Teddie didn't answer, Rosa took her seat.

"I can open the meeting with good news. Liz has followed April Veronica to a women's shelter in North Carolina. She is staking out the building, and given the newcomer's lack of... self-defense training, Liz doesn't anticipate any difficulty in..." Rosa paused, her eyes scanning the room, "...capturing her."

"You're gonna bring her back, right, guv?" Imani's voice was accusatory.

"That is the plan," Rosa said. "Unless she refuses to come quietly, in which case she will be dispatched per Lock guidelines."

Sara glanced across at April Veronica on the couch opposite, her eyes wide, her face pale.

"Rosa, I hate to be pedantic, I really do," Heather's voice crackled into the room. "But which Lock guidelines might you be quoting there?"

Rosa looked briefly flustered, her eyes darting left and right. When she spoke, she kept her eyes lowered. "Fine, it's not Lock guidelines, but pray tell, Heather, what do you propose we do with a runaway Cursed woman who's still dealing with an increased viral load? A woman who has learned none of the survival skills?"

"The number one goal is to return her to us, safely," Heather said. "That should be your primary focus."

"I shall relay your concern to Liz, who volunteered to risk her own life to clean up another one of Sara's messes."

"You shut your fucking mouth," Teddie's voice was hoarse but unmistakable. The image on the screen blurred as Crina whipped her head around, and there was Teddie, standing but crumpled, her face a rictus of grief unlike anything Sara had ever seen. She was leaning on the empty throne in front of her, her face wet with tears, her eyes red. Heather appeared in the frame, wrapping Teddie in a hug from behind. "Sara has been..." she paused, clearly not ready to say 'dead', "...*gone* for four fucking days. This meeting should be a memorial, and here you are, wanting to blame her for the shitty way your life has gone. I won't fucking hear it."

"Theodora," Rosa's voice was steel. "Get yourself together, or leave, now. I am the Lock Mother, and I am going to get this Lock back on track, with or without you."

"Oh, miss me with that bullshit," Teddie wailed. "Just miss me alright? Alright?"

Sara's heart broke in two as she watched Teddie collapse back into Heather's arms, brutal sobs curving her back. Carefully, Heather lowered her back into her throne then stood at her side, a hand on her shoulder.

"Well, now that that's out of the way," Rosa continued, "I will continue. I'm going to rush through things, because apparently we are all still too raw to-"

"Just get on with it," yelled Imani. "No more bullshit. Just tell us whatever you need to and let us get back to grieving."

"Fine," Rosa's tone was snotty. "Firstly, the Madrid Lock has generously undertaken the task of overseeing the dispersal of the holdings from the Warsaw Lock."

"Dispersing them into their own bank accounts, I presume?" Heather's tone matched Rosa's.

"It's not that simple," Rosa said. "You of all people should understand the complicated nature of our real estate and finances. Actually, one thing that might make your life easier is that all of the identities that had been created will be shared with the Locks around the world."

"Yep. That'll make my life so much easier," Heather said. "Desdemona is so benevolent, because with this push to ZPG, who precisely is going to need a bunch of new identities based in Poland?"

"Women will still be cycling through identities, Heather," Rosa said as if she was talking to a child. "Playing stupid doesn't look good on you."

Sara watched Heather, thousands of miles away, swallow her response, hate in her eyes.

"Secondly, in line with other Locks in the world, we are adopting a more cautious way of life. From now on, all sisters spend every night here in the compound."

A minor flurry of chatter erupted, and Rosa silenced it with a palm.

"The new mantra around here is 'responsibility' – we can not go on running around the city like we're on Sex & The City. Additionally, no more outside services. No more beauty parlor, massage, gymnasium or anything at all. Everything happens on site. We will also begin mandatory grocery deliveries. Heather, I want fingerprint locks on every door in this compound, and a daily report of everyone's movements. When Liz returns, she will be the plasma monitor. She will oversee all blood products that are brought into the compound, and she will also be responsible for handling your dosages."

"Hey, Rosa," called Imani. "I just thought of something. I think I need to go to North Carolina."

"I'm sorry, Imani. That's not possible at this time."

"Well, you see, I don't really need your permission, since there's nothing about it in our rules. But it did just occur to me that the vote that we had, the vote to make you Lock Mother, well, it technically wasn't kosher, since April Veronica didn't vote and she's a member of this Lock. And then it dawned on me. You already know that. And maybe you don't want her to come back alive. So, I'm doing this not just for April's sake, but I'm doing it for our own democracy."

A hubbub of voices rose around Crina, and Sara struggled to make out any of the words. When it subsided, Rosa's face was red with anger, and Imani was yelling angrily.

"You'll what, mate? Cut me off? Not in the rules. Kick me out? Again, not in the rules. You sent Liz off without consulting the rest of us. And clearly you've sent her out as a kill squad. That's definitely not in the fuckin' rules. So, I will travel tomorrow morning and you tell that blonde bitch that if anything happens to April, I'll have my Slicer with me."

Rosa's mouth opened and closed wordlessly as she scrambled for a response. Before she could speak, Sara heard Fran's voice.

"We've fucked it all up," the gray-haired woman said, her voice strong. "In five days, we've gone from being the leader of the Lock world, to being a good argument for immediate Surrender."

Crina turned her head until Fran's pale, lined face was in the center of the screen. She was seated away from the group, her throne against the wall.

"The things that I love about this life are entirely absent from this meeting," she continued. "Rosa, you didn't need to do this today. We've lost Sara and April Veronica. The women of Warsaw are dead. No matter how well we knew them, they were us, and we need to grieve. If you keep pushing these changes at such an emotional time, you're going to lose control of this Lock."

"How dare you, Frances?" Rosa snarled, clearly agitated that Fran spoke against her. "I'm already talking to some of the women in Madrid, they'd love a change of scenery."

"You can't bring them in though," Fran continued. "We are dead-locked for votes, and honey, I gotta tell ya, you keep on with this authoritarian shit and you won't be able to count on me. Or my vote. I'm in favor of ZPG, not a return to the dark ages."

"She's right," Heather said. "Any changes to Lock personnel requires a simple majority vote, which you currently do not have."

"And she definitely won't have if we find April Veronica," Imani added, looking up from her phone. "As much as I'd love to stay and watch you get drunk on power, Rosa, there's a 9:45 JetBlue flight out of LaGuardia that I need to make."

"You said tomorrow," Rosa began.

"And now I'm saying tonight," Imani said brusquely. "I've already texted Liz to expect me." Imani stood, turning to face the room. "I need all of you to do some deep thinking. I should not have to travel to another state to protect one of us, from another of our own. But here we are," she paused, gazing about the room. "Here we fucking are. So, Rosa, quit acting like Desdemona. Crina, can you watch Teddie tonight? And Heather, I'll send you my travel details. And if Liz don't welcome me with open arms, or if she's already killed that girl, Rosa, trust me when I say this: I will kill Liz, and then I will challenge you to a duel."

Rosa's gasp echoed around the living room in Iceland, and Sara clapped.

On the TV, Imani brusquely left the roof house, slamming the door behind her.

Crina focused the camera directly on Rosa, as she sat in her throne, her eyes wild with panic, her fingernails tapping nervously on the chair's wooden arms. With Fran at odds, and Liz and Eleanor out in the world, she was outnumbered and she knew it.

"This meeting is finished," she declared suddenly. "Frances, please come with me. I would like to talk to you in private."

As the rumble of female voices started up again, Sara watched as Rosa waited for Fran to get to her, then walked from the room, glancing back over her shoulder at the door as if she expected some sort of attack. She looked scared. Before Sara could gloat, Yukari's face filled the screen, her eyes making contact directly with them all on the tv screen.

"Crina, I'm so sorry," Yukari's quiet voice was breaking. "Are you okay?"

"Definitely not okay, but I don't have time to lose on grieving, not right now." They hugged, the screen becoming a tangle of black hair.

"Can I come and see you later tonight? I want to" Crina's voice dropped. "make sure Teddie is okay."

"She's really not," Yukari whispered. "Also, top secret, I have a large stash of blood that Rosa is not aware of. It's a perk of being a virologist. Come tonight, we can have a drink."

"You're amazing, Yuka," Crina said.

"I'll be waiting for you."

Bowing briefly, Yukari left.

Crina took a deep breath, then made her way to where Teddie sat, hunched over on her throne, Heather stroking her back. As Crina panned the camera past her face, Heather winked, letting them know she was in on the game.

"Teddie, my child," Crina's voice was gentle.

Teddie didn't look up. Her short hair was braided against her scalp, giving Sara another pang. She cherished the nights that she spent doing Teddie's hair.

"I fucked it all up, Crina," she said eventually. "I fucked it so bad, and.. and..." Sobs overtook her. "I can't bring her back, C."

"Teddie, you did what you were taught to do. Sara broke the rules, more than one. Many a sister has been pushed into surrender for less. You're not to blame."

Teddie turned her face up to Crina. "She wasn't just a sister, Crina. She was my mother, she was the best of all of us." Her whole face trembled as a sob rocketed through her body. "I... I pushed it... Crina, I thought I had to."

"Child, that's how we raised you," Crina rested a palm on Teddie's shoulder. "You lost a mother, I lost a daughter. I'd like to stay with you tonight, if that's okay with you. I am not ready to be alone in this place."

"Every inch of this place is her," Teddie said. "I don't want to be *here* anymore."

"I know, I know," Crina said softly.

"Can you take off your glasses?" Teddie asked, her voice plaintive. "I'm sorry, it's weirding me out, I can see myself reflected."

"I'm so sorry, of course I can" Crina's hand headed toward the camera, then some rustling against skin, and then the screen went blue.

Silence fell across the room, until Sara couldn't hold her sobs in anymore. Silas pulled her to him, and she wept, the ache in her heart pulsing through her whole body, her hands, her feet and her eyes. She heard April Veronica and Embla's footsteps moving to the hallway, and Sara pushed herself off Silas's chest.

"No, you two, stay, please. That was heavy for all of us."

Nodding, the young women returned to the couch opposite. Silas pulled a bandana out of his pocket and handed it to Sara, who wiped her face clean.

"What a stupid mess," she said. "April Veronica, I feel so guilty, this is not how your first year is supposed to be."

"Don't worry about me," the young girl said. "It's crazy, just watching how quickly those women, their personalities, have gotten so heightened."

"It's power," Embla said. "You could see it on that woman's face, Rosa. She took this new role for power. Instead, she got responsibili-ty."

"The best thing is that mom is with Teddie now," Silas said. "It's horrible to see her grieving so hard when you're alive, but the Lock is way too fractured for any big moves just yet."

"What do you mean?" Sara sat up, anger in her eyes. "Rosa is thisclose to realizing that the rules actually aren't binding. They don't mean shit for the most part. Our rules are nothing but stop signs. Suggestions for safety. Now that I have some distance, I can see that none of our rules are actually enforceable. What's the penalty for breaking rules? In my experience, it's a lot of yelling. That's it."

"Right," said Embla. "Unless someone has an agenda, and then they can use hysteria, the way they did against you."

Pressing a finger against her temple, Sara remained silent.

"April," Silas spoke quietly. "Would you warm up some blood for us meat-eaters and some synthetic for Embla. It's going to be a long night."

Sara glanced at the wall of glass, out into the deep blue of the evening, and realized she had no idea what time it was.

"Silas," she said, her voice small. "I just want everything to be okay. How can we make everything okay?"

"Well, sure," he said calmly. "I don't want to rush you, but I think the first step, for all of us, is a summit with the elders."

Sara's heart froze. Flaming out in front of Crina was one thing. Admitting to failure in front of the women who led the Purge, the woman who wrote their constitution, no thank you.

"It doesn't have to be tomorrow," Silas said. "We have time, we can go when you feel stronger."

"Sara, if you're nervous, you shouldn't be," Embla leaned forward across from her, the light playing in her brown-green eyes. "Stefanya was running interference in Spain, but she's traveling back tomorrow and she's obsessed with you. I think she'll be more nervous than you are when it comes time to meet. And Fan and Ama are like total vegan pacifists."

Again, Sara marveled at the power of a younger perspective, and the way Embla wasn't mired down by centuries of preconceptions and rules, even when it came to legendary warrior women.

"Well, if that's the case then," Sara chuckled, "let's get the party started."

Embla smiled, then sent a text from her phone. "Let's see what she says. We might get all three, we might get just her. They're like herding cats."

April Veronica returned with a tray containing four goblets, plus a bottle of her weed elixir and four shot glasses.

"I don't know about you guys, but after that, I need a drink."

Looking from one companion to the next, Sara felt something small change in her heart. She felt something close to hope.

Chapter Six

Sara sat up in bed, her ears drowning in silence, the unfocused, repetitive routine of her new life starting to oppress her. In many ways she was already mirroring the dull routine she'd kept in New York, except the Icelandic version went nightmare-freakout-disaster repeat.

Looking at her phone, she saw that it was once again just before eleven. Casting her mind back, she tried to figure out when she'd gone to sleep. Her uncaffeinated mind offered images of a fuzzy game of Jenga with Embla and sitting outside with Silas searching for stars in the deep blue Icelandic night sky. She guessed she'd dragged herself to bed around three, which meant it was time to get up.

Remnants of another nightmare fluttered behind her eyes. In this one, still in the apartment full of moving boxes, Teddie-as-a-child was blaming her because the kittens had died, but they couldn't find Iris, the mother cat. As Sara searched for the cat, the boxes grew higher and higher until she also couldn't see Teddie. Groaning at the dream's obviousness, Sara flopped back into her bed, gazing at the white walls, the white ceiling, her luggage still on the floor, the only change in its appearance the number of clothing items strewn around it. She hadn't even brought the shopping from yesterday into the room.

Today, she would transform the room from temporary to permanent. Put things into the closet. Stash her suitcase. She glanced again at the bare walls, considered hanging art, then decided that she had made enough decisions without coffee.

Rising, she stretched languidly then padded along the hallway, her footfalls the only sound in the house. Still so uneasy in the relentless silence, Sara realized she was more attracted to the concept of solitude than the reality of it. As she stepped down into the great living room, she absently wondered where everyone was, and then wondered if she'd be able to work the coffee machine.

Reaching the counter, she came across a handwritten note from Silas explaining that he'd gone out on some errands but shouldn't be long, and on the flip side of the paper, very painstaking instructions to use the coffee machine, with options for lattes and cappuccinos, and an addendum that there was an americano chilling in the fridge that would be delicious over ice.

Retrieving the Americano and forgoing the ice, Sara decided to venture outside alone, for the first time since she'd arrived. The main door, as usual, was unlocked, a fact that still sent a wary shudder along her spine every time she encountered it, and she stepped through it onto the small cement patio. Gazing from left to right across the green basin that led to the mountainside in front of it, she followed shadows and bumps, looking for the streams that April Veronica had told her about, but nothing broke the endless golden green of grasses in the sweeping meadow.

She came up with a plan. She would walk in a straight line and see where that took her. The grass was stiff beneath her feet, feeling more like straw than lawn, but it protected her soles from any sharp rocks, and the air felt so pure in her lungs that she became lightheaded. After walking for a few minutes, she heard the splashing of a stream, hurrying slightly in its direction and then nearly falling into it, a narrow rivulet hidden in the green, the water crystal clear, and, she stepped her feet into it, freezing cold.

Setting her butt down on the grass, Sara left her feet in the stream and sipped her coffee. Silas made damn fine coffee. Something inside her wanted to fault him, find a reason to be angry with him, but his behavior since arriving in Iceland had been a masterclass, but in what, she wondered? Considerate or manipulative? She didn't know. At no time since arrival had he even intimated that they share a room. He was available, but he never sought Sara out. Age-old conditioning from long-dead men ran through Sara, and she wondered if he was playing games with her, or if he was just really accustomed to waiting for her.

Ask him.

Finishing her coffee and setting the glass beside her, that's what she decided to do.

"It shouldn't be this hard," she said aloud, jumping when a voice replied.

"What shouldn't?"

Turning, she leapt to her feet, landing on the opposite side of the stream. April Veronica and Embla stood less than ten feet from her, a look of horror on their faces.

"We didn't mean to scare you," Embla said.

"We thought you could hear us coming. I'm sorry," April Veronica said.

Both of them stood there, comically upset. April Veronica was still wearing her Blue Lagoon leisurewear, and Embla was wearing an orange fleece jacket over a faded pink woolen dress and green tights. They were both barefoot.

"Hi you two," Sara said, "Come sit by me." She sat, put her feet back in the stream and then patted the grass beside her. April Veronica leapt over the stream and sat on her left. Embla, with her long legs, just stepped across it and sat on her right.

"Do you want to tell us what shouldn't be so hard?" Embla asked. Sara didn't know if it was an Icelandic thing or just an Embla thing, but she really liked her directness.

"Silas," Sara said with a shrug. "I literally don't know what is going on, and what's worse, is I don't know what I want to be going on."

"Ugh boy troubles," Embla said with a soft laugh.

"It's definitely weird," April Veronica added. "I mean, I was with you guys that one night, and all I could see is how much he cared for you. But yeah, I can see that this whole 180 could give you boyfriend whiplash."

Sara laughed. "That's exactly what I have." She paused. "I hate to be this girl, but, uh, has he...?"

"Has he said anything about you?" Embla cut to the chase. "Yes, of course, but if we start running tales here, it will poison our future."

"Ouch," Sara said, rubbing an imaginary bruise on her arm. "But you're right. And that's what I decided just before you guys came along."

"Ah," April Veronica clapped her hands together. "So that's what shouldn't be so hard."

"Good job, Sherlock," Sara took April Veronica's hand in hers. "It also shouldn't be my focus right now. We have so many things to worry about."

"And worrying will solve none of them," Embla said, her eyes scanning the horizon.

"He's literally just waiting for you to ask," April Veronica said. "So, when you're ready, ask."

"I partially asked," Sara said, sounding girlishly defensive. "We sorted out the past. It's the future I need some clarity on."

April Veronica squeezed her upper arm and rested her head on Sara's shoulders. A breeze picked up, frost on its edges. Coupled with the iced coffee, Sara felt it chill her deeply and she began to shiver, taking her feet out of the freezing stream. Without a word, Embla shucked off her fleece jacket and wrapped it around Sara's shoulders.

"There's something we'd like to discuss with you," she said.

"Of course."

"It's Imani," April Veronica said simply, surprising Sara. "I don't think it's fair that she's running off on a wild goose chase to protect me. I feel guilty and I feel responsible."

Sara gazed at her, the fading green in her hair barely noticeable in the bright sunlight, her eyes blazing with compassion.

"What do you think we should do?"

"It's more complicated than that," Embla said, her palms open. "And that's where we really need some guidance. If April Veronica is known to be alive, then she is technically a voting member of the Lock, right?"

Sara nodded.

"So, can they insist that she return?"

Sara pondered it for a minute before she spoke. "That's what I was saying last night. We have rules without penalties, except the formal transgressions that carry a death sentence. Right now, Desdemona is probably the only sister who would enforce it. I'm sure they'll say they want you to come back. When you say no, there's literally nothing they can do about it."

"I see," April Veronica said. "So, for five centuries, Locks functioned solely on good faith?"

Sara nodded.

"But now we are dealing with its opposite," Embla said. "Which is corruption."

Sara's nod became more emphatic. She was slightly jealous of Embla's ability to be succinct.

"So," April Veronica leaned conspiratorially close, "what if I call Imani, via secure line and I set my FTP in like The Ozarks or something, and say that I'm fine, that I left with a huge score of heems and I don't feel safe, but I want her support."

Sara pondered it for a minute in silence, moving chess pieces around in her mind.

"And we would want her to be open with the rest of the Lock?"

"That's why we came to you," Embla said. "That part would need to be strategized."

"Weaponized," April Veronica whispered theatrically, making them all laugh.

"I guess we need to talk to Crina about it, whenever we can," Sara said.

"We don't though," Embla countered. Sara turned to face her. "That's not the way we work here. We have no mother."

Dumbfounded, Sara looked from one to the other, both of them smirking.

"I apologize," Embla said. "I am certain it will be a big adjustment for you, but the three of us can make a decision right here, by this little stream. If we agree to tell Imani that April is alive, then we can make that call."

Sara recognized the forces that were pulling at her, but she didn't know whether they were good or bad.

"What we know," April Veronica met Sara's gaze, "is that, unlike you, I'm more valuable alive, That's a good indicator that we should tell Imani."

"It would destabilize Rosa's hold on the Lock," Embla said. "And we can use April Veronica's fake location as bait if we need to draw anyone away from the Lock."

"It protects Teddie and buys us some time," April said.

"It feels like a huge decision to me," Sara began. "Do you two need my vote?"

"Not really," Embla said. "But we would like your blessing."

Sara sat with the decision for a long moment, weighing up invisible risks against very tangible benefits, before nodding. "Sure. Do it."

April Veronica wrapped Sara in a hug.

"You're good at this," Sara said into her hair. "Marguerite was right to choose you. Maybe she saw the future more clearly than I do."

April Veronica pulled back, tears in her eyes.

"Look," Embla said. "Silas is back."

Shielding her eyes from the sun, Sara looked to the house, which at this distance existed as a long line of black windows, beneath a grassy hill. Sure enough, Silas was walking to the front door, wearing black jeans and a traditional Icelandic patterned sweater, his hair poking out below a black beanie. As he was about to reach the door, Embla whistled sharply, her fingers in her mouth. He turned instantly, and Embla waved him over.

"We are going to go inside now and set up the FTP for the call," Embla said as she stood up. "You can have your chat with Silas and then come inside, if you'd like to listen."

With a quick squeeze around the shoulders, April Veronica stood and took Embla's hand, and the pair walked back toward the house, stopping to hug Silas on the way.

"Want some company?" he called out, and Sara nodded. Arriving at the stream, Silas shucked off his shoes, then sat opposite Sara, on the other bank. "Good morning. You sleep okay?"

Sara nodded. "I did, thanks. And I've arrived at some jobs that need doing, so I feel like less of a slug."

"What jobs might these be?"

"I'm gonna be here a while, right?"

Silas's brows knit briefly, telling her she'd startled him.

"That's up to you entirely," he said, pressing his palms together. "You can stay here, you can go to another property. Probably best if you stay here until you get the lay of the land, but even that's up to you."

"Either way, I'd like to hang something on the walls in my room, put my clothes away, you know, just turn this Airbnb into a home."

Silas laughed softly. "Well, if you need any help."

"I probably do. I'd like to find something to hang on the wall."

"Sure, we can go into Reykjavik later. I was just in town."

"Oh? What took you into town so early on a... what day is it?"

"It's Thursday," Silas said. "I went to the City Library to use the computer. I needed to get ahold of Stefanya to discuss our meeting."

"Uh oh," Sara said. "That sounds ominous."

"Oh, not at all. It's more of a production to get in contact with them than it is to actually talk to them. We just jump through so many FTP and VPN and IP hoops from here that it's way easier from a public internet connection. Anyway, she says hi –"

"Am I supposed to say hi back? Feels oddly insufficient." Sara said quietly.

"Don't think about her as some cartoon character," Silas smiled. "The secret is to engage her intellectually. You'll have no problem with that. Also, she's eccentric and she binges trash TV. The other two are always deeply into something. Right now, they're bolshy students in a college town."

"Literally every Cursed woman presumes that they live in a mud hut in Romania making swords and training every day."

Silas chuckled. "Fan and Amitra, they're like my crazy aunts. They're the longest-living couple on Earth, just two women who've been in love forever, and also they happen to be fierce fighters."

Sara's eyes rolled before she could control herself. Silas paused, giving Sara a quizzical look.

"Wait, am I mansplaining?"

Sara gave a smile and a half-shrug. "I know all that, that's basically the start of the vampire history book, but didn't they have like a huge fight?"

Silas chuckled. "Yeah, they fought then, and they fight now. They're like eternal teenagers. They separated for a long time last century. They're back together now."

"How did you bring them to Iceland?"

"Mom heard they were living in Greenland when we first started coming here, and we went and found them. They're way more engaged in Lock gossip than Stefanya, and they have helped us so much with this... escape hatch. They think the New York Lock is the best version of what they set up with Stef. They want to reunite with you."

"I was around them, when I was just made and learning Cursed life. They were scary, and so exotic. Fan was the first Chinese person I'd ever seen, and she wore trousers, her hair was short. Amitra had an actual ruby in her bhindi, and it just sparkled in the fire light. I just thought they were the most beautiful women I'd ever seen," Sara paused, reverie pulling at her, the memory surprisingly vivid, the aroma of lemon leaves in campfire smoke present in her nostrils. "I gotta tell you, Silas, I'm quite intimidated. What do they want from me?"

"They don't want anything from you," Silas said, shaking his head. "And I'd never speak for them. They knew we were trying to get you out of harm's way, and now they know you're here."

"Oh great."

"No, they're happy about it," Silas said. "They want us there on Saturday. If you're up to it, it's safer to drive, we really do our best to shield them from any chance of being traced. If you're too tired, we can fly for sure, but Iceland, small country, yada yada."

"Driving is fine," Sara said. "All four of us?"

Silas nodded. "Yep. Fun little road trip."

"Did they tell you what they're going to do?"

"To tell Imani?"

Sara nodded, considered asking Silas the question she was dying to ask, about their romantic status. She knew he'd say that they were whatever she wanted them to be, and right now, she wanted him to tell her what they were. She'd grown bored of the early-dating dance, the are we or aren't we, the lack of surety. This thing with Silas was definitely new ground. Perhaps, she reasoned, that was why she was so reluctant to define it.

"Should we get back inside?" Sara kept her gaze fixed on the running water.

Lifting his feet from the running stream, Silas stood and extended a hand which Sara gratefully took, unfolding in one sleek move.

"Wait, I need my coffee cup," she bent and retrieved it, Silas scooped up his boots, and side by side they walked back to the house.

As Sara's eyes adjusted to the darkness of the living room, Silas took her coffee cup over to the sink, returning with a glass of water from the tap which he handed to Sara. April Veronica was bent over a laptop, the tapping of her fingers on the keyboard the only sound in the room until Embla's footsteps sounded in the hallway and she appeared, waving jovially at Sara when she saw her.

"Are we ready?" she asked.

"Where should we locate the VPN in case they manage to track it?" April Veronica looked up from her laptop.

"What's the worst place you can think of, in case they decide to keep up the search?" Embla said with a smirk.

"Fort Lauderdale it is," April Veronica said dramatically. "What? Don't ask. That's what I get for attempting spring break." She fell silent, typing and hitting the enter key several times.

"What happened to The Ozarks?" Sara joked.

"When I realized that I don't even know where that is," April Veronica groaned, "it kind of fell apart as a legitimate cover story."

"A lot of places in America have such strange names," Embla came and sat beside April Veronica.

"Sure," Silas laughed. "Because places in Iceland are so normal and easy to pronounce."

"Okay. We are ready." April positioned a notepad with a handwritten number on it beside the computer, entering the numbers. The dial tone sounded once, then answered. They could hear background noise but nothing else.

"Imani?" April Veronica said.

"Who's speaking?" Sara's heart swelled at the sound of Imani's British twang.

"It's me, April Veronica."

There was a brief pause.

"Oh, the payment didn't go through?" Imani said. "Can you hold one minute? I'll need to get my credit card from the other room." Then they heard muffled sounds of one door opening and closing, followed by another.

"April Veronica, you fucking twat, I'm in fuck knows where with the sorriest slag I know, but tell me, girl, you okay?"

"I'm so sorry, Imani, I really am, but yeah, I'm fine."

"Well that's something," Imani said. "Are you even in North Carolina?"

"Fuck no," April Veronica said, and Imani let out a hearty laugh.

"Course you're not love. Where are you?"

"I don't want to say just yet," April Veronica said with a wince. "For my own safety it's better to just keep it quiet, but I called Crina to see if I could stay with her, and she told me she's back in the City and that you were out looking for me, and I feel terrible so I just wanted to, you know, let you off the hook. You can go back to New York."

"Thank fuck," Imani said with a laugh. "I'm glad you're okay kid. Uh... how are you managing your levels?"

"I didn't leave empty handed," April Veronica said. "I figure I am good for a couple of months, and by then we will know if it's safe for me to come home."

"You're a brave one," Imani said, her voice breaking as she started to cry. "I'm just so happy you're okay."

April Veronica winced and looked up from the keyboard. Embla matched her grimace then drew a finger across her throat.

"Anyway, I'm really sorry you get sent on a wild goose chase, but I'm in no danger," April Veronica said. "I'm fine for you to tell them that I'm alive, especially if that means that Rosa isn't the legal Lock mother."

"Aw shit," Imani said. "I can't wait to spring that on them. Before you go love, do you have a number I can call you on?"

"Not right now," April Veronica said. "But I'll be in touch soon. I promise. And Imani? Thank you. So much."

Terminating the call with a click, April Veronica sat back in the couch, her hands pressed to her face.

"That fucking sucked," she said into her palms, and Embla put her arms around her.

"You gave her good news," Embla said. "She will have some peace."

"I bet she's on the phone to Heather already," Sara said.

"Do we have a road trip in the future?" Embla turned to Silas, who nodded.

"We can leave tomorrow," he said.

"I'll drive," Embla said. "I know the road like the back of my hand."

"Shotgun," April Veronica called out, raising a hand, making Sara smile. This strange new family unit felt altogether too comfortable, too easy. She thought once more about the pain Teddie was in and her body gave an involuntary shudder.

Sensing it, Silas turned to her.

"Everything okay?"

She nodded. "Sorry, I just got to thinking about Teddie."

"I just got a text from mom," he said, holding out his phone. "Teddie has slept in mom's bed the past two nights. She's distraught but at least mom has her eating."

"Is there a plan?" Sara asked hopefully. "Can we tell her soon?"

Silas inhaled so deeply that Sara knew the answer was no before he said it.

"Not yet, but soon," he said. "I know it's hard. It's killing mom to keep this bullshit up while watching her so destroyed, but mom says she's not stable enough for such a big gamble. What if this information makes her feel like she got played and she tells Rosa?"

"It's still cruel," Sara said, suddenly bitter that somehow, she lacked the freedom of April Veronica, who had just made a decision and acted upon it.

Bristling, Sara considered starting an argument. Glancing quickly around the room, she suddenly needed to be alone.

"Okay, cool, thanks," she said, her voice flat as she leaned into the soft comfort of passive aggression. "I'm gonna go tidy my room, since that is something I'm allowed to do. Come get me if anything happens."

Chapter Seven

A soft knock at Sara's door startled her out of the half-slumber that she'd been laying in since she finished setting up her room an hour earlier. The task itself had taken less than twenty minutes, leaving her feeling dissatisfied and slightly churlish.

"Yes?"

"Sara, it's me, Silas. I was wondering if you'd like to go get dinner."

"You can open the door."

Hearing the door open, Sara cracked an eye open to see his earnest face peering through the crack.

"I don't think I'd be very good company," she said.

"I didn't ask you to entertain me," he said with a smile. "The girls have gone off exploring and I'm hungry and I figure you are too."

As if on cue, Sara's stomach rumbled.

"When was your last heem?"

Sara wrinkled up her face. She hadn't taken any for hours, which explained the snag at the back of her throat and her miserable mood.

"Cool. Get yourself dressed and I'll go heat up some sparkling type AB negative. Meet you at the couch in like two minutes."

And he was gone.

Standing, Sara pulled the wardrobe door open, looking at what passed for glamor in her life right now: Two jackets with fur-lined hoods, which Silas depressingly called "summer wear", two pairs of all-weather hiking pants, one khaki, the other navy, and four Icelandic wool sweaters, black, white, dull red and a patterned gray and white one that matched the one Silas was currently wearing. With a sigh she hauled out the navy pants, the black sweater, and after a glimpse at the cloudy sky through the skylight, she added the gray jacket to the pile on the bed, then unceremoniously she dressed herself, her blood thirst, now acknowledged, becoming more urgent.

"You look like a local," Silas said as she entered the living room. He was seated on the couch facing her, two large tumblers of blood on a small metal tray resting on the coffee table. As she drew closer, the scent of the blood reached her nostrils and her vision darkened around the edges.

"Ah come on," she groaned, grabbing for the other couch as her knees weakened.

"Just sit there," Silas said, scooping up one tumbler and bringing it to her hand, which shook so badly that he pulled back, moving the glass to her lips and tilting it. Sara opened her throat and let it spill into her in one long pour, falling back against the couch, then arching her back as the pleasure radiated, her spine made of delicious light.

Absently, she registered the sound of him raising the other glass. Suddenly, she smelled blood close to her nose and then felt the press of the second glass against her lips, downing it instinctively, giving herself over to the blackness in her mind and the warm orange glow pulsing in her veins. She felt the warmth in her body connect with the warmth from his, even through the layers of insulation.

As she returned to her body, her eyes fluttered open into the flood of deep blue evening light, Silas, a backlit silhouette before her, his elbows on his knees.

"I'm sorry, I... uh... I'm really out of my routine."

"Sara, don't be ashamed of drinking enough to meet your needs," Silas began, and she cut him off.

"Yeah, I've been trying to manage but... I'm just gonna say it, sometimes I... I dunno, being irresponsible is attractive."

"Totally fine, but this isn't a Lock, you can have as much blood as you want or need, no judgements. You can carry one of those insulated cups around, just make sure the straw isn't transparent. After a spike like yours, heems just won't cut it, not for a couple of years. We sponsor a bio-research facility and I'm a professor there, they don't question how much blood I take."

"Sign me up," Sara attempted a joke, her voice thick.

"We don't have to go into town," Silas began, and she cut him off.

"No, please, I want to go. I'm starving, and honestly, I think I have a little cabin fever."

Silas laughed. "That's exactly what April Veronica said before they left. Let's head into town."

The drive into the city was breathtaking. Even though the sun shone most of the day, Sara was noticing that each phase of the day had a different hue, in the morning, it was gray. That gave way to a clear blue that aged to a golden light in the late afternoon, then a sunset that never quit would streak the sky with jets of orange and pink for hours, before the peacock blue of near night. The sun was doing its faux setting now, and the bubbly undersides of the clouds were awash in pink and violet.

"It's truly gorgeous here," she said, breaking the silence in the car.

"Just wait til we drive up to see the old girls," Silas said. "You're in for a treat. Once we get, you know, settled, there's so much to explore here. So much."

"I can tell," she said. "Already, I have to bite my tongue from asking to stop at every waterfall."

"Get used to that feeling. And we can stop at them too. No worries. Waterfalls and rainbows, some days that's all you see."

"That sounds so perfect," Sara said, her head falling to the side as she gazed out the passenger window, her eyes scanning fields dotted with chonky horses and herds of very woolly sheep, and beyond that, the ocean. She was filled with an urgent hope that she would someday be able to share this with Teddie, which led her into a solemn reverie that ended with a jolt as Silas pulled into a parking space on a street lined with squat, mismatched houses. Sara hadn't even noticed they'd entered the city.

"Good reverie?" he asked as he gathered up the keys.

"I don't really have good reveries at the moment," Sara said softly, blinking away the cobwebs of worry about her daughter. Silas got out of the car, and came around to her side, opening the door and extending a hand. With a smile, Sara accepted his hand and hauled herself up to standing, taking in the houses and apartment buildings, the scent of wood smoke in the evening air.

Silas turned to walk down the street, and she deliberately kept ahold of his hand, grateful that he didn't mention it as they walked. After several quick turns on short blocks, she saw the harbor, boats bobbing at moorings, and suddenly there were more people walking around.

"Shit, double checking," Silas said, slowing his pace. "You like to eat fish, right?"

Sara nodded. "I sure do."

"Good," Silas smiled, picking up his pace, then stopping suddenly at a restaurant called simply Fish & Chips and opening a door for her. "This place is touristy, but there's one dish I love. Go grab a table and I'll be right there."

Taking in her surrounds, Sara was overwhelmed by a feeling she couldn't pinpoint. It felt like newness. After evolving alongside New

York for so long, it felt strange to be treating Reykjavik like home when she hadn't yet been a tourist in it. In New York, she always took a table toward the rear of a restaurant, and a seat facing the wall. The first room she walked into was crowded, all glass on one side, and not terribly deep. She was relieved to see steps in the rear corner of that room, even happier to see that they led to a smaller, much emptier room. She chose a table beneath a window at the far wall, and sat with her back to the window, feeling like she'd made an uncomfortably grownup decision.

Silas appeared at the top of the stairs, carrying two beers and a number 27 on a metal stand. After setting it all on the table, he vanished again, returning with two large cups of water. As he stood there, organizing the cups on the table and pulling some napkin-wrapped cutlery from his jeans pocket, Sara flashed back to them kissing at his cabin by the lake, a week ago that felt more like a year, and suddenly, she couldn't stop staring at his full lower lip or the way his hips moved as he walked around the table.

You are ridiculous, she scolded herself.

"What?" Silas, now seated, was looking at her, his head cocked.

"Oh, nothing," Sara lied, instantly hating the tell-tale burn of a blush across her cheeks.

Silas lifted one of the beers, raising it in her direction.

"What did we cheers the first time, at that Italian place?"

"Oh, to different paths."

"To different paths, then" Silas waited for her glass to clink against his, then took a long draft.

Sara followed suit, then set her beer on the table, happy in her silence, absorbing her surroundings. Opposite her, Silas alternated sipping his beer with either checking his phone or just gazing around the room. Eventually his beer was finished, so he set his glass on the table, then his phone, face down. His silence began to feel weird to her, and she wondered if he was annoyed, or if he had some more bad news to share. She tried to come up with something to say that didn't feel forced, and was still searching when a lanky, bearded guy appeared with their food. Strangely, he set it on the table, picked up the order number sign and left without saying anything. Sara took in the food on the plate in front of her, a piece of fish, paler than salmon, atop a bed of small potatoes and vibrant spirals of orange and red – beets, carrots – and as soon as the aroma hit her nostrils she was ravenous.

"So what's this?" she asked, grateful for the innocuous question.

"Arctic char," Silas locked eyes with her. "They live in lakes here. Like salmon, but a more delicate flavor."

Breaking off a piece with her fork, Sara brought it to her mouth. The flavor was lighter and cleaner than salmon, and the meat was tender, like sea bass. Her eyes widened and Silas smiled.

"Good huh?" He ate a piece of fish, nodding slowly in agreement and Sara finished her beer. As soon as the empty glass hit the table, Silas rose, wiped his mouth with his napkin and darted back down the steps out of the room, empty beer glasses in his hands.

Biting into a potato, Sara flashed back to something ancient, a sense memory, of boiled potatoes her mother would make. In the blink of an eye, a jumble of fractured memories flooded her mind: Her mother's hand, the log and mud wall of a cabin, and a feeling of security, an awareness of her siblings around her, at least some of them. Fleeting and vague, the memory passed, leaving Sara slightly dazed and absent. Arriving back at the table with fresh beers, Silas startled her back to the present.

"What?" he asked.

Blinking away the cobwebs, Sara gave him a quizzical look.

"You're smiling..." he explained.

Sara's first instinct was to come up with a lie, quickly replaced by the realization that now, she could actually tell the truth.

"So, I ate a potato and had a flashback..." she began.

"Uh oh," Silas smiled. "How far back did it send you?"

"Almost all the way," Sara said, her eyes wide. "Like, I was five or six? Definitely not ten yet. I saw my mother's hand, the wall of that cabin, do you remember? That comfortable, crowded feeling, always the smell of smoke and damp, wool, sweat, straw and earth?" Silas nodded slowly. "I felt that, just for a second."

"That's one hell of a potato," he said and they both laughed.

"At least we know it's organic," she said through her laughter, and Silas cracked up all over again. Eventually the laughter petered out, and they resumed eating in silence, but this time it felt more comfortable and Sara leaned into it, finishing her meal before she spoke again.

"I'm just going to come right out and say it, it's made me feel, I dunno, lost and ancient and alive, and I've been acting like such a weirdo, so..."

Silas shrugged. "Okay."

"That was me apologizing."

"No need," he said, setting his cutlery down. "It sounds like it was a beautiful memory to receive. I haven't had a really ancient memory pop up in such a long time."

"Me either," Sara said, feeling strangely at ease talking like this in a public place, even though the room was deserted apart from them.

"I remember the little hut that I lived in, with the woman mom paid to look after me while she was away, but these days it feels like I'm looking at pictures in a book. I could draw the cabin for you, but in my memory, it's just walls and angles."

"That's what mine was too," Sara nodded. "But that memory, it was so..." she paused, "...so full, so complete, it was literally just what I was seeing and feeling at one tiny moment."

"Well it made you smile."

She nodded. "Yeah, I felt happy in that memory. It also felt fresh and recent, which is what is doing my head in right now. That little girl, that version of me, she was happy, her world was tiny and that was all she wanted. She was warm and there was food, and the memory carried that feeling of complete peace."

"What a great gift," Silas said. "A moment of peace after the week you've had."

She chuckled then took a sip of her beer, trying to cling to the warmth of the memory, happy that it was still there for her.

"It did make me feel better," she said, her voice low. "The things that have happened have all been, I dunno, like huge emotions, and on top of that, they're all complicated and interlinked with all the other huge emotions. That was a nice feeling, you know, simple contentment."

Silas raised his beer. "To simple contentment, probably the most underrated human emotion."

Nodding, Sara raised her glass. "It's weird but I think I need to be my own Lock Mother, like find a way to take my own advice. And that memory is the key."

"I'm not sure I follow," Silas's brows knit, and his deep brown eyes gazed into hers.

"I need to get over myself," Sara said plainly. "Yes, a bunch of shit happened but that's what life is."

"Or..." Silas began.

"Or what?" Sara hated the defensive tone in her voice.

"Or... you can spend as long as you need with your complex emotions instead of brushing past them."

"Gross," Sara screwed up her face. "No thank you."

"I mean, it's up to you, but you just had one of the more brutal couple months of anyone I have ever known, and that's really saying something. I can understand why it's tempting to sweep it all under the carpet and move on, but in my experience, you might just actually be planting some deep landmines that you'll eventually step on."

"I mean, that's quite possible and also, yes, that's been true in my past. This is not my first disaster."

"This time, you have me by your side. And you have mom and April Veronica and Embla and Heather. This new situation isn't you alone fighting the tides. If you don't feel like rowing, just sit back and let someone help you."

"Never been much for rowing," Sara deflected. "You rely on me for rowing, you're going to go around in circles for a while and never get anywhere."

"Mentally withdraws idea for fishing trip," Silas smiled, the blue night sky shining through the window playing off the orange flecks his eyes.

"Silas, I just don't know what we are doing," Sara sounded way more exasperated than she'd intended, but Silas's expression didn't change.

"Can I deflect now? Please? You just did."

"I mean, sure," Sara said. "But that's why I feel awkward. I feel like we dated, then all of the shit hit all of the fans, and here we are, adrift and shit, there's rowing again, and yep, I'm trying to paddle."

Silas reached across the table and took her hand in his.

"It may surprise you, but I'm not pushing for boyfriend status here. What I'd like to be, at least in the short term, is a support network."

"And that is driving me insane," Sara said. "Not your fault. It's just a lot. You're being so kind and patient, but no matter what you say, I am pretty sure that your end game is us as a couple."

"I'm not gonna lie," Silas said. "If things went that way, organically, then of course, it would be wonderful."

"I expected you to deflect."

"The last thing we need right now is more lies from me," Silas said, giving her hand a squeeze. "I'll deflect but I won't lie."

"Fair," Sara said. "Which brings us to here and now, and this whole thing, I just can't shake your expectations."

"I don't have any real expectations from you, Sara."

Sara rolled her eyes and leaned forward.

"Silas, we literally dated four times before we moved countries together and adopted two kids."

Silas erupted in laughter, sitting back against his chair.

"I'm sorry," he gasped between laughs. "I'm so sorry Sara, it's not funny."

A smile played at the edges of Sara's mouth as she watched him wipe the tears from his eyes and struggle to get his laughter under control.

"And you moved us in with your *mother*," Sara said, cracking herself up and sending Silas into fits.

"Oh shit, stop," he pleaded.

"By my estimation," she continued, "in a very short space of time, we've engaged in deception, illicit drug use, a tribunal, a near death experience and human trafficking. I mean, why the fuck not shack up on a remote island near the arctic circle?"

"Human trafficking," Silas managed between laughs. "Sara, stop, you're killing me."

"Oh, but it was fine when you nearly literally killed me one week ago?"

Abruptly, Silas stopped laughing. "Too soon," he gasped. "Way too soon."

The look that came over his face, concern, regret, sadness, instantly made Sara regret her words.

"I'm sorry," she said. "That was supposed to be a joke."

"Sara, if that memory pops up in my head five hundred years from now, it's still going to rip my heart out."

Sara gazed into Silas's earnest eyes, still wet from happy tears, now sad and almost haunted, and this time, the weight of his expectations didn't smother her. He cared deeply and she knew she was lucky that he had come along.

"I get it," she said, feeling her heart tug for his hurt and her own. "I will now attempt to take my foot out of my mouth and get this dinner date back on track."

"It's been perfectly on track for me," Silas said, his hand finding hers again. "I do have something that I've been waiting to say to you."

"Ruh roh," Sara said apprehensively. "Nah, it's not bad, not this time." "Okay, hit me."

"Stop looking at the old ways for guidance," Silas's other hand took Sara's free hand, and he squeezed them tightly. "There is no road map for what I want with you. We are on a different timeline. What we can do is uncharted. We can take centuries to do what other people need to achieve in decades. This is new, Sara. We've established little more than chemistry, and well," Silas paused, his eyes dropping. "On my side at least and I'm not fishing, some admiration. But that's the thing. The fifth date doesn't have to be this week. Or this year. Or this decade. That's what I want to say, now that I can say it. You can harbor as much anger at me as you want for as long as it takes, and I'll have faith that one day that fire will lessen, and you'll see why I couldn't tell you everything all at once."

"Thank you for saying that," Sara began, letting his words resonate within her. "And this is technically that fifth date. I do understand the need for the whole spy tactic. If I was going to be angry, I should be angry at Crina... your mother."

"I'm officially Switzerland between you two," Silas said quietly. "But in the last century, I've really appreciated what a visionary my mother is. She's smart and fearless, and she sees a long game better than anyone I've known, except now, maybe Desdemona."

"Last mention of that bitch before we ruin our date," Sara smiled. "And yeah, it's really crazy. I've known your mom longer than I've known anyone, and for a literal century, I thought she was off navel gazing and preparing for Surrender. Now I find out she's been off masterminding the survival of," Sara paused, habitually gazing around the room for any eavesdroppers, "our kind. It's hard to be angry, because she was being selfless and trying to help me. My resentment is just me being a brat."

"So many tangled emotions. She's preoccupied with her crusade, but I know she'd love to clear the air with you."

"Sure, once she's saved everyone in New York through some miracle, I'll sit her down to talk about my wounded feelings."

"Speaking of which," Silas gave her hands one last squeeze before letting them go. "I got a couple texts from her, she can talk to us in," Silas flipped his phone and tapped the screen, looking at the time. "Twenty-two minutes. Let's wrap up here and get to somewhere private."

After doing the math, Silas decided that they didn't have enough time to make it home before the call, turning the car around and heading into a residential area. After so long in the same surroundings, Sara's eyes tripped from one new sight to the next as the car drove along a wide main road, dipping in and out of roundabouts. While she took in fields and bays and supermarkets and houses, Silas drove in silence, occasionally checking his phone.

Leaving the main road, he turned onto a smaller road that led around another a postcard-perfect bay. In the distance, Sara spied a small church, white with a red roof, on a hill, almost too picturesque to be real.

Following her gaze, Silas spoke.

"That's where we are headed, that church," he said. "There's great service there and hardly any people."

Pulling into the empty parking lot, Sara could see that the doors of the church were indeed locked, and the grounds were empty, as were the fields around them. In the distance a pair of joggers bounced along a paved track, and on the other side of the church, a field of sheep and woolly ponies milled in the dusk, making her smile. Beyond that, the ocean churned and glittered.

"Watch your step," Silas said as he exited the car, and seconds later, as Sara felt her shoe slip across something on the parking lot gravel, she understood.

"It's the geese," Silas said as he came around the car and took her hand. "Don't worry, we're going to be walking on grass, just keep an eye out."

They walked up the gently rolling hill to the church, where Silas ushered her through a small gate to a bench beside a young tree.

"I've taken so many calls here," he said as he took his seat. "Nobody will bother us."

Sitting beside him, Sara looked across the field and the bay at the city in the distance.

"I'm so turned around," she said. "Which way is… home?"

Sliding beside her and putting his head against hers, Silas tilted her face slightly right, raising his hand and pointing. "We are out that way, on the opposite side of the city."

"And where is the airport?"

"Behind us, a long ways."

"Well that clears that up," Sara laughed, leaning against Silas, relieved he didn't move back to his space on the bench.

"Sara, don't feel like you have to stay here," he said, out of nowhere.

"I hate how well you pre-empt me," she said, taking his hand in hers.

"A place is just a place," Sara whispered, not wanting to disturb the peace around them. "And as far as places go, this one is gorgeous. I could definitely spend a few years watching the seasons from the living room of the cave house."

Turning, Silas kissed the top of her head.

"Do you know what Crina... what your mom wants?"

Shaking his head gently, Silas squeezed Sara's hand.

"Just an update, I think."

Pulling his phone from his pocket, Silas lay it face up on the bench beside him. A wind whipped up, a chill around its edges, and Sara pressed against him, inhaling the pure air. She knew she was close to simple contentment in the moment, and she also knew that Crina's call would likely put an end to that feeling, so she pushed all thought from her mind, focusing on what she could sense in the moment, looking for the same contentment as a memory of a long-gone childhood.

She was still calm when Silas's screen lit up minutes later, black background, blinking red phone symbol, no contact info.

Silas lifted the phone and swiped it open, holding the screen face toward them. After a short delay, the screen came to life, showing

Crina, outside on a gray day, her dark hair peeking from beneath a knit cap, an umbrella over her head.

"Look at you two," she said, beaming. "You're at the church!"

"Yeah, we didn't have time to make it home before your call time," Silas said.

"Hi Crina," Sara said, the normalcy of the moment making her feel weird.

"Hey my child," Crina said. "Did you pick the right time to get out of dodge or what?"

Sara's stomach clenched. "What's going on?"

"Oh, no, no, don't panic," Crina said. "What I meant was, just be grateful you're not here. Your peacekeeping skills would be stretched to their limits."

"Or, I could just not get involved in that bullshit."

"That's my approach. It's just strange. Rosa used to be so reasonable, but she's decided that identity politics are the way to get ahead, and she's all or nothing for ZPG as if she invented it. If she had her way, we'd all be getting into an extinction machine tomorrow." Crina laughed, amused by what she said. "But for the most part, everyone is staying in their own apartments. Imani called in with her news, which has obviously ruffled a few feathers. Nobody knows how to handle a satellite newbie with voting rights. Rosa and Desdemona have been talking day and night, but you know what? So have I. We can't even vote until everyone is back in town, but it looks like Teddie will be reinstated as Lock Mother. I've taken the position that it is in April Veronica's safest interests to stay away, given Desdemona's murderous streak. And once that happens, we will block all communications with Des, until we get through this."

"Crina," Sara interrupted. "How is Teddie?"

Crina paused and inhaled deeply.

"I'm not going to sugar coat it," she said. "She's struggling."

"I want to call her."

"It tore my heart out, for sixty years, to watch you get so unhappy in your life," Crina said, her voice warm. "I had your get out of jail free card in my pocket, but you wouldn't take it from me. That's where you are with Teddie. So, I know what you're going through, and that's why I feel it's fair to ask you to be as patient as I was."

"I guess," Sara nodded. "How is she really?"

"One of us, either me or Yukari or Heather, is with her at all times. She sleeps in my bed. She's not eating, she's not doing much of anything. But Heather has the security to the Surrender room as high as it can be, and we are not even sure that she's considered it. If it comes to that, I'll call you immediately and we can tell her together."

Sara continued nodding as a deep, broad pain settled back across her heart.

"Mom, when will Liz and Imani be back in New York?"

"Any minute. Once they're back, we will convene a meeting. Would you guys like to be in on that?"

"Yes, very much," Sara said. "Thank you."

"There is one other matter, which is really why I called."

"Oh?" Sara felt nervous sweat on her neck.

"I talked to Stefanya, she told me you're going to visit."

"Yeah, I was messaging her from the library today."

"I know. But Sara, I want to warn you, these women aren't like normal Cursed women. They are unpredictable, and on the wrong day, I find them especially draining. I wanted to warn you."

Sara shot an alarmed glance at Silas.

"They're my annoying aunties," Silas said. "I love them all, so much, but every time I leave their place, I need to decompress for a week."

"Me too, so that's what I wanted to advise for you Sara. I've learned that the best approach is to stay silent and let them swirl and fuss and then they'll calm down," Crina said, the background behind her suddenly blurring out. "Sorry, someone just came and stood near me."

"Where are you?" Sara asked.

"The North Woods baby," Crina said. "Your favorite place. It was sunny when I set out, but these clouds just came in out of nowhere, hence the twenty-dollar street umbrella." The camera flipped and Sara saw the pond where she liked to sit at night, gray clouds reflecting on a surface broken by little ripples from raindrops and big ripples from a pair of ducks. She was surprised that she didn't have a reaction to seeing it.

"How long do you think you're going to be out there, mom?"

The camera flipped back around to Crina's face, her eyes gazing upward in thought.

"It's gonna be a little while, this time," she said. "We need to secure Teddie, and then we can begin the next phase, whatever that is. Sara, I don't want to burden you with too much just yet, you still need to heal, but if you have time, please just think outside the box on what we can do with New York."

"What exactly do you mean?"

"We have so many options," Crina said. "Just open your mind to ideas for the future of New York, the city and the Lock."

"Isn't the goal to bring everyone here?" Sara asked, and Crina shook her head.

"Not entirely," she said. "You and I worked so hard to build what we have here. I know that emotional attachment to buildings is weird, but Sara, we drew the plans for that compound. If we sold it, we'd have to brick up all the back doorways, we'd have to seal off so much of what makes it amazing. I don't want to do that. But a fractured Lock isn't sustainable either."

"We've never been through anything like this," Sara said.

"No, my love, and things are going to get more different before they get familiar again."

"Now I understand why you guys hid out in a cave!"

Silas and Crina laughed.

"You seem to be a bit happier," Crina said.

"I'm settling in," Sara said. "It still feels like I'm crashing someone else's cool Airbnb."

"It's your house, Sara," Crina said. "Make yourself at home."

"We went out to look for things to decorate but..."

"Yes, I know. Iceland isn't a country for shopping," Crina said. "Wait. Silas, did you tell her or not?"

Silas shook his head. "I thought that was why you were calling."

"You guys," Sara waved her hand in front of the camera. "No more secrets or in-jokes or whatever this is."

"I gotta head back," Crina said with a wink. "I took the liberty of boxing up some stuff from your apartment and I sent it your way."

Sara's heart leapt.

"Stuff like what?"

"You had some prints in a tube in your wardrobe?" Crina said, her finger to her cheek. "Oh yeah, I included a few things from your closet. You know. Things you may have kept on the back hanging rail?"

"Oh my god," Sara said, a broad smile on her face.

"That smile makes it all worthwhile, my love," Crina said. "Silas, give her the tracking information, and then give Stefanya a call. Today she's panicking about the menu, when you get there she'll forget to feed you. Gotta dash, love you both so much."

"Love you mom," they both said at once, and she was gone.

"That's weird," Sara said.

"What? That she sent your clothes over?"

"No, it's weird to be dating a person who calls my mother mom too."

"If that's the worst of our challenges, I'll take it," Silas kissed the top of her head again. "Wait, we're dating?"

Sara nodded. "You just bought me dinner and made me laugh. It was a good date and I'd like another. Ergo, dating."

"Good, and now it's time to head home," Silas stood and held out a hand to help Sara up. "It's getting late and the kids don't have a sitter."

Chapter Eight

"**I**s my phone out here?" Sara asked from the top of the stairs into the living room, a fist rubbing sleep out of her eyes.

"Sleeping beauty," called Embla, chopping vegetables at the kitchen island, turned and gave her a smile. "It's about to be ten in the morning. I put your phone over on the coffee table."

Half-awake, Sara clomped down the small staircase, enjoying the heated concrete beneath her feet.

"You feeling any better?" Embla called out. "And can I get you a coffee?"

"Yes and yes," Sara said, collapsing dramatically onto the couch that faced the windows. Outside, pale gray clouds filled the sky while a billowing wind sent a light rain sideways.

"Wait, is it Friday?"

"Indeed it is," Embla said, switching from the counter to the coffee maker. "Would you like an oat milk latte?"

"That sounds fancy and altogether too much trouble for you."

"Not at all, I fancy one myself," Embla turned to give Sara a smile, but stopped halfway into the smile. "Sara, when was your last heem?"

Wrinkling her nose, Sara cast her mind back. "Just before I fell asleep?"

"Doll, you've been out for nearly twelve hours, you have two black eyes."

Abandoning the coffee maker, Embla went to the fridge.

"Can you drink blood cold, or do you need it warmed?"

"Cold makes me nauseous, I'm sorry," Sara said, wondering just how bad she looked.

"Okay then, day drinking it is."

Sara hauled herself up to sitting as Embla appeared beside her with a goblet of blood liquor in one hand, and a Guinness in the other.

"I'd never be so gauche as to make you drink alone," she said with a pert smile, handing the goblet to Sara, and cheering her on her way down to sit beside her.

As soon as the liquid hit Sara's tongue, the thirst in her chest and throat flared up, worsening its raspy clawing, and she was powerless as pure instinct raised the goblet, her throat bobbing as she swallowed it in one draught.

"Would you like another?"

Sara nodded, licking blood from her bottom lip. Silently, Embla set her beer on the coffee table and returned to the kitchen, returning with a fresh goblet for Sara.

"Thank you," Sara smiled. "It doesn't bother you, being around... what would you call us?"

"Carnivores? Is that what you're asking?"

Sara nodded.

"No," Embla said, snuggling against Sara, making her smile. Since her arrival, Embla's open, affectionate nature had stolen her heart. "I knew what I was getting into here. I was a vegan in my old life, so I carried that over. So far it has been sustainable, although I have some new gray hairs that mean I might not be getting the full immortality benefit. I'm a bit of a science experiment, you may have guessed. Since

I was born with male plumbing, this is all new territory, and I'm as scared as anyone that something from that old physiognomy might be triggered by real blood. I don't think that it's as intense for me, when I ingest the synthetic. And that's fine, I don't need a potential addiction. For now, it seems to be working."

"So you never ate meat?"

Embla scoffed. "I'm Icelandic, love. I mainly ate meat til I was nine or ten, but then, as I grew into myself, it was easy to leave it behind."

"Well, if it ever bothers you, please let me know."

"You're too kind," Embla said, finally taking a sip of her beer. "I have one philosophy in life, and it works well for me: You do you, boo."

"I'm sorry?" Sara's mind was still fuzzy from sleep and she wasn't sure Embla hadn't lapsed into Icelandic.

"You do you. You do what's right for you. I do what's right for me. If we both have empathy and integrity, then our world will have harmony."

Sara smiled and rubbed Embla's thigh.

"Thank you for making me feel so welcome."

"Please. I was like a kid waiting for the Yule Lads once I knew you were on the plane."

Sara laughed, then fell into silence, still freaked out that it had taken so much effort to get her here. "What are Yule Lads?"

"Sorry, Icelandic Santas, kinda. Do you feel better for the sleeping?"

Pausing, Sara did a quick body scan, happy to discover that she did feel rested and a lot lighter than she had since... well since before she left New York.

"Yes, I think I do feel better. I'll know more after I get a coffee." Embla went to stand, and Sara grabbed her hand.

"I wasn't hinting. I'd rather have you sitting here with me."

As Embla sat back down she pointed with her chin.

"The others are coming back."

Following her gaze, Sara saw figures materializing out of the gray. Silas and April Veronica, black ponchos whipping in the wind. When they opened the front door, a gust of wind accompanied them in, blasting arctic chill across Sara's face.

"I thought it was summer," she yelled, nestling into Embla's side.

"Sorry," April Veronica pushed the door closed then wrestled the wet poncho over her head. Silas already had his off and stood there patiently waiting for April's. He bundled them up and took them to the sink.

"I'll dry them later," he said, spying the bottle of blood liquor on the counter.

"Are you guys day drinking?

"In my defense, I asked for coffee," Sara laughed, the bloodbuzz strong in her ears.

"Well in my defense, someone looked like a raccoon when she woke up."

"The bruises under your eyes are lightening," April Veronica said, taking a seat on Sara's other side.

"So, I'm gonna make coffees for all of us. April, would you like a cocktail too?"

"I'm good," she called out. "Sara, just wait til you check out all the crazy shit they got going on here. Silas just showed me how to retract the bridge, and I'm learning how to work the geothermal setup. We had to get it all set so we can leave it for a few days."

"Also, everyone," Silas's voice boomed in the domed room. "Let's manage our expectations. There's always a chance that we will get there and they won't show up."

"Has that happened to you?" Sara was surprised.

"More than once," he said without rancor. "I don't mind. It's not a horrible drive, it's just long. But I'm always happy to kill time in Akureyri. Stefanya's last message was promising."

"Wait," Sara exclaimed. "Are Fan and Amitra still lovers?"

"Why don't you ask them?" Silas said with a wry smile as he delivered a steaming hot coffee into her hands.

"Why don't you tell me so I don't have to?" Sara kicked him in the shin.

"What I know," Embla said grandly, a joke playing across her eyes, "is that they've never been spiritually apart. Their entire journey since they met has been shared. They argue and take mental health breaks, but they're basically one unit."

"Shut the front door," April Veronica yelled, pushing herself out of her slouch. "Two women and how many centuries?"

Sara and Silas shrugged in unison, both smiling at April's reaction.

"Five and a half?" Sara said, and Silas nodded.

"And they're monogamous?" April Veronica raised an eyebrow.

"Again," Silas said with faux seriousness, "I suggest you ask them."

"I wouldn't," Embla said. "I really love them, I really do, but they scare me. They're the most formidable women I've ever met. They appear light and flighty, but that is a disguise."

Sara thought back to the stories that Crina had told her of the Purge, when two women fought like warriors, exterminating the cursed men with calculated violence that relied equally on their martial arts skills and the predictable natures of men. They invented the Slicer, and trained women in combat. And as soon as the last man was dead, they vowed never to spill another drop of blood.

"Wait!" It was Sara's turn to sit bolt upright. "Silas. They're cool with you being a cursed man?"

"I've known them my whole life," he said. "But it's only since they came here that I'm in regular contact with them. They've stayed at the lake house." Sara's eyes widened incredulously, and Silas raised a hand.

"I know, but Sara, honestly, there's a million things that I need to tell you, and that one just now felt like…" he trailed off.

"Namedropping?" offered April Veronica.

"Kinda sorta," Silas laughed. "Sara, I would not say I know them well. I would say I know them the way a child knows an aunt. They're kind, they give nice presents sometimes, and I don't ask much about their private lives."

"It just feels like I'm walking into a lion's den, and everyone knows more about the rules than I do, and I'm not being paranoid."

"Nobody said you were," said Embla. "I mean, I'd be nervous too. But I'll tell you this. They're lovely. They're what I want to be when I grow up."

April Veronica reached across Sara and high fived Embla.

"Are you hungry, Sara?" Silas went back to the kitchen. "You must be. I'm gonna make lunch for all of us, then we can prepare for the zoom with New York."

"That's at two, right?" Embla bounced off the couch. "I'll handle lunch. I was getting started on a ratatouille when mama here woke up."

"Any updates from Crina?" Sara asked.

An awkward silence fell, and Sara watched as her three companions all looked from one to the other.

"Yeah," Silas said, taking a step toward her. "She says no spoilers but you're gonna love this."

After a hearty lunch, Sara was cleaning the kitchen, deep in thought, when she suddenly heard Heather's voice.

"It's me this time, pets," Heather's voice echoed from the speakers by the television. The screen was all blurry movement that gave Sara vertigo, forcing her eyes closed. Keeping her eyes on the floor, she made her way to the couches, then looked back at the TV. She saw Heather's apartment, the crocheted rugs atop the couch, the orderly confusion of knick knacks on the mantle. A mix of homesickness and security washed over her.

"You know I can't hear ye, right?"

The camera bobbed around as Heather opened the brick wall door at the rear of her apartment and slipped into the dim hallway behind it. This time Sara forced herself to watch, somehow expecting that in just over a week, things might have changed.

"I so want to go to this building," Embla said enthusiastically from her spot, cross legged on the floor in front of April Veronica. Beside her, Sara sensed Silas turning to look at her but kept her eyes fixed on the screen.

Wait, if this was a meeting, why was Heather going down to the basement?

"Silas, have you heard anything? Why isn't this meeting in the roof house?"

"Radio silence, I'm afraid," he said. "I know as much as you do."

For once, Sara thought, a little bitterly. The night before, she'd lain awake, gazing up at the rich blue night sky, trying to figure out the cause of her general irritability. A breakthrough just before 4am was that she felt under-equipped in terms of what everyone else knew, and she didn't. Embla, a delightful woman, cursed less than twenty years, had had experiences with the elders that nobody else on this planet had had.

And Silas thought of them as his aunties.

She was jealous.

"What?" she had said aloud, in her dark echoey room. "I lived five hundred years and all I got was this lousy t-shirt?"

On the screen, Heather drew near the door to the conference room and a wave of nausea rolled through Sara with sudden force. For a panicked second, Sara thought she might vomit, swallowing back against it, making herself burp suddenly.

"Better out than in," Silas smiled, his attention fixed on the television.

As Heather entered the room, Sara shook her head. The divisions among her old Lock could not have been clearer. The seats never had any formal pattern of placement, but now there was a clear path down the center, with Eleanor, Liz and Fran clustered on the right, Yukari and Imani seated side by side on the left, and further left, Teddie, her chair against the wall, her knees drawn up to her chest, her face heartbreakingly despondent.

As if sensing that was too much for Sara, Heather turned her attention to Rosa, sitting on her throne on the dais, scrolling on her phone, not paying attention to the women in front of her.

"She's absolutely on Pinterest," April Veronica said. Only Embla laughed.

On the screen, Rosa looked up.

"Did anyone remind Crina that we have a meeting today?" she asked imperiously.

"She texted me she'll be a little late." Heather's voice was suddenly loud in the room, and Silas lurched for the remote.

"Of course she is," Rosa said. "Well, I don't have all day, so we are starting now. We're still low on blood for obvious reasons," she paused, shooting a death stare at Teddie. "So I hope you're all heemed up. We have some very unusual business to deal with."

Rosa stood, revealing a floor length black crepe dress, buttoned bodice and pleated skirt. Sara remembered taking her shopping to buy it, from a designer on the lower east side in the early nineties.

"I am nominee Rosa, never have I killed. I declare this meeting of the sisters of the New York Lock to be in session. I know there's been a lot of gossip, so I'm just going to start with the facts as we know them. Somehow, our missing sister April Veronica has managed to communicate with Imani."

"Somehow?" Imani hissed. "She used a fucking cell phone Rosa."

"From a blocked number, leaving you with no way of contacting her."

"I'm not a liar," Imani stood. Sara focused on the floor in front of her, the rapid jerking of Heather's head was making a bad situation worse for her. "I spoke to her. She will return when we can guarantee her safety."

"That's why I sought counsel from Desdemona," Rosa said. "In Europe it would be considered a serious defection, for someone to vanish from the Lock. The dangers inherent in such a situation are clear. The repercussions for all of us are almost unthinkable. She must be located immediately, and she must be dispatched."

Sara winced even before she heard the gasp from April Veronica.

"Rosa," Yukari's voice was barely audible. "There is absolutely nothing in the foundational writings about these circumstances. You say dispatched, but I hear killed and that, in case you've forgotten, is against our creed."

"Al contrario, Yuka. There is a period in which a newly made sister can be deemed to be dangerous, or defective, or posing a threat, and that period is most definitely still in force."

"I repeat," Yukari stood, and her voice hardened, "killing is against our creed."

"Aiy, this is the exact kind of bullshit that got us into this trouble," Rosa said theatrically. "You want to pussyfoot around the problems, pretend that-"

"Murder," Teddie called out, her voice hoarse. "Sorry. *Murders.*"

"Which brings us to the elephant in the room," Imani's voice, normally a throaty rasp, could turn full foghorn when she was angry. "Your role as Mother, voted on in a tie-breaker with Desdemona casting the deciding vote? I asked April Veronica, and she would have voted for Teddie. Which means that since we voted without a member, that vote is invalid. The vote as it stands, unless anyone wants to change their mind, would retain Teddie as Lock Mother. Congrats, Theodora."

A jumble of chatter filled the room, and the screen jerked from Rosa yelling from the stage to Liz screeching "pic or no proof" like an incensed teenager to Teddie, eyes wide in shock. It was an ugliness almost on par with the scene before Sara's surrender. One voice rose above the melee, and Sara instantly recognized it. Crina.

"Come on, Heather, let's get this party started."

The screen pixelated again and then Crina was standing on the stage facing them all.

"As the founding mother of this Lock, I am taking control," Crina said, her voice almost regal. "No votes, no bullshit. Fuck the rules. This shit is over. Does anyone care to disagree?"

Silence fell in the room as Crina stared into Rosa's eyes.

"Nobody? Good. Now, Rosa, get your damn chair off this stage."

With an angry huff, Rosa lifted her chair and carried it to the back of the room. Crina looked at each woman in turn, her expression fierce and focused. Sara hadn't seen her like this for centuries. "Whatever is going on here, this division, this" she looked at Rosa, her face stern. "This ugly, unnecessary brutality, it stops. Now. And if you can't play happy families with every woman in this room, it's time to go. If you're so in favor of Surrender, the door is that way. If you're full of hate and anger, you'll be right at home in Madrid."

A noise from behind Heather caused her to turn. It was Teddie, rising to her feet, tears streaming down her face. When she spoke, her voice was almost inaudible.

"If Rosa takes Surrender, I'd like to push the button."

The camera jerked back to Crina, who extended open palms, stepped down from the dais and walked to Teddie, wrapping her in a long hug. When they separated, Crina wiped the tears from Teddie's face with a knuckle, then kissed her on top of her head.

"It won't come to that, my love," Crina said gently. "Rosa, like Desdemona, wants everybody else to Surrender. And there'll be no killing for you. You're a gold star vampire. You don't want blood on your hands."

"Wait?" Liz yelled. "What the fuck is happening here? The rules are finished?"

Crina shook her head. "Look at yourselves. This is how the men acted. This is what happens when you thirst for power like a man. This is not how a Lock should function."

"If we can get back to the business at hand, Teddie, congratulations."

The camera whipped around to Teddie, curled up in her chair again.

"I can't..." she said quietly. "Not now. Thanks but I can't."

"Heather?"

The camera bounced left and right as Heather shook her head no.

"I have an idea," Crina said. "I think it's a good one. Yukari, would you like to be our new Lock mother??"

"Me?" The shock almost raised Yukari's voice to a normal volume.

"Yes," Crina stepped to her and wrapped an arm around her shoulders. "Hopefully some of your patience and kindness will rub off on these women."

"Okay, I guess," Yukari shrugged. "I'll do it."

Crina lifted Yukari's throne and carried it to the dais.

"Ladies of the New York lock, I present your newest Lock mother, Yukari."

The sound of a single pair of hands clapping filled the room. It was Imani. Heather joined in, then Crina, who glared at the baleful faces of the other side of the room.

"Don't make me come over there," she said, and suddenly, they heard more clapping, slower, less enthusiastic, but clapping nonetheless.

"Sorry about the drama, ladies. I think it was necessary to get us back on track. If any of you have a problem with it, please see me personally. Yukari, is this meeting adjourned?"

"Yes please," Yukari said with a smile and a polite bow. "Yes, please."

"You heard the woman," Crina said, leaving the dais and heading for Teddie. "Show's over, get the fuck out."

A rustling sound filled the room and the screen went black.

"That. Was. Amazing." Embla said, jumping to her feet. "Blood liquor all round?"

Silas turned to Sara. "You okay? That was intense."

Sara smiled. "I haven't seen Crina like that in so long," she said. "And yes, I'm very okay with what just happened."

Silas put an arm around her shoulders and kissed her on the head.

"I got a text during the meeting," he said. "There's a delivery for you that I'd like to go get before I start drinking."

"A delivery?"

"I would presume it's items from your wardrobe, judging by the customs charges for importing an arctic fox fur."

Chapter Nine

Embla pulled the SUV into a parking lot in front of a pair of low rise, boxy buildings, one painted red, the other blue, and killed the engine.

"Welcome to Akureyri," she said with a yawn. April Veronica bounced out of the passenger seat, dancing excitedly on the asphalt.

"You guys, get out, look at this bullshit," she said.

In the backseat, Sara and Silas remained motionless, her hand warm in his. They'd traveled like this, in silence, since the last rest stop a hundred kilometers ago.

"I can't believe how endlessly beautiful this country is," Sara said.

"I'm glad you think so," Embla said, exiting the car.

"We gonna get out?" Silas tilted his head, looking at her through his thick lashes.

"Eventually?" Sara laughed. "I just don't..."

"You don't what?"

She looked down at their hands. "I don't want this to end," she said softly. "I haven't done the whole hand holding thing in a really long time. I forgot how... nice it can be."

Silas gave her a smile then turned his head, looking out his window at April Veronica and Embla, now across the road on the banks of a sparkling river or bay, Sara wasn't sure which. Across the water, green fields extended up the sides of mountains topped with snow.

"Things would have been so different if I'd come here instead of going to America," Sara said wistfully. "I considered a lot of countries, but Iceland just felt too raw, too brutal back then."

"I remember," Silas said. "Mom told me she was thinking about Sweden, Norway. I am the reason all the Nordic countries couldn't work. The towns were too small, it was too obvious to have a stranger hanging around. I'm glad she chose America, in hindsight. I think it was the right choice."

"I agree," Sara said. "It was a great place to be anonymous, I think we would have stuck out here."

"Yeah, people pay attention here," Silas said. "It's a great quality, but it's not good for us."

"After living in America for so long, that's actually terrifying," Sara laughed. "Hey, can we still hold hands outside of the car?"

"In front of the kids?" Silas mugged.

"Stop it," Sara said, snatching her hand from his and unbuckling her seatbelt. "Let's get this over and done with."

Silas put a hand on her shoulder, restraining her gently. "Sara, there's nothing to worry about, we aren't seeing them until tomorrow. Tonight, we will just wander around town, get some dinner. Maybe walk through the botanical gardens, they're gorgeous."

"That's easy for you to say. No matter what anyone says, I'm pretty ashamed of how I flamed out."

"Everyone flames out," Silas squeezed her hand. "They'll offer compassion, not judgment."

April Veronica appeared at Sara's door, tapping on the glass.

"Are you locked in?" she asked, the sun glinting on her hair. The green had washed out, leaving her with gray streaks in her brown curls, and the sunlight turned her eyes into golden brown explosions that reminded Sara of the eyes of a wolf.

Opening her door and stepping out, Sara wrapped the girl in a long hug.

"I was just taking my time," she said into April's hair. "I hate to say anything because I don't want to curse it, but that whole drive, I think I was happy."

Sara felt the arms around her tighten.

"I don't want to curse it, but I think things are about to get good for us."

"Why is everyone so worried about curses right now?" Silas came around the car.

"Must be something in the atmosphere," Embla appeared beside him, making heavy metal horns. In her mirrored aviators, blue jeans and Wet Leg t-shirt, Sara thought Embla was the most rock n roll sister ever, which made her think of the women in Desdemona's Lock and the dreary clothes they were forced to wear.

"No time for a reverie," April Veronica said, reading her mind. "We need to get the stuff out of the car and go check in."

"No need," Embla said. "We own these buildings, and they are presently vacant. I have keys to the rooms."

"Can we please share?" April Veronica turned to Embla, who nodded. "Good, thanks, I still haven't spent a night alone since my conversion." Sara raised an eyebrow, surprised that she'd missed that April Veronica had been sleeping in Embla's room since they got there.

"No need for explanations," Embla said, opening the rear of the SUV and lifting out Sara's suitcase. "Separate rooms for you two?"

Sara glanced at Silas, who was suddenly engrossed in something across the bay.

"How many beds in each room?"

"Two twins, you can push them together or have them apart."

"Silas, is it okay if we share?"

Suddenly Silas was able to hear again, turning to her with a smile spreading across his face.

"I don't know, I like my space."

Sara socked him on the arm, and he stumbled back from the force.

"Ouch, I was joking." Silas rubbed his arm theatrically. "Sure, fine, whatever you want, just don't hit me again."

Sara went over to Silas and threw her arms around him. "I'm sorry, I didn't mean to hit you that hard."

A strange voice joined the fray.

"I never could resist the sound of laughter."

The laughter dried up and Sara whipped around to see Stefanya, once the most feared sister in the world, walking toward them between the two buildings. Blinking a double take, Sara took in the woman who'd taught her to fight, a woman who lived in stiff leather armor and never went anywhere without a chainmail bodysuit that covered the top of her head and her spine.

The Stefanya that was walking to her, arms open in greeting, had glossy red lips, thick black eye makeup, her raven hair cut in a loose shag, and she was dressed in purple and black striped trousers and a neon yellow mohair sweater. She would have been at home anywhere in Red Hook.

"Hey mamma," Embla waved.

"Welcome home," Stefanya said with a warm grin. Her first stop was to kneel in front of a clearly awed April Veronica. The fact that Stefanya took a knee in front of her did nothing to ease the young woman's shock. "April Veronica, welcome to the sisterhood." Stefanya took April Veronica's outstretched hand and kissed it, then rose, turning slowly.

"Sara," she looked her up and down. "You've been here a week and they've already got you in head to toe Icelandic GAP?"

Releasing Silas, Sara stood still, completely disarmed, then decided to lean into whatever Stefanya was serving.

"You know, between imploding, falling in love and being forced into surrender, I didn't have time to pack my haute couture."

Abandoning April Veronica's hand, Stefanya's smile softened into a look of concern, and she stood, moved in front of Sara.

"Too soon, you're right. Those bitches really put you through the wringer, huh? My love, I've been dreaming of this day for so long. I'm sorry, I use humor when I'm nervous."

Sara's mind was racing. Should she hug Stefanya? Should she kneel?

"And here I thought I was the one who'd fall into reverie at the sight of you," Stefanya clicked her fingers in front of Sara's face. "Snap out of it and give an old woman some sugar!"

With that, Stefanya took Sara's face in her hands and pulled it to her, kissing both cheeks.

"You scared the fucking life out of me, Sara," she whispered into Sara's ear.

"I'm sorry," Sara mumbled.

"Don't be, not one bit," Stefanya separated herself. "Now, let's empty the car and we can figure out dinner."

"Where are Ama and Fan?" Silas asked.

"Get a load of this one," Stefanya laughed. "He's been too busy in America to ever visit me, and as soon as he gets here, he wants the others."

Silas groaned like a schoolboy. "Stef, I saw you five weeks ago."

"You didn't even have time for dinner," Stefanya turned to Sara. "All he could talk about was you."

"And we really should get our stuff up into the rooms," Silas interrupted, winking at Sara. "I'd like to show Sara the botanical gardens before they close."

"And I'd like to show you a cup of our new synthetic, young man, so dump your crap and come up to the house. The gardens can wait."

After showing them to their rooms in a whirl of off-the-wall chatter, Stefanya bid them farewell suddenly, saying she'd left something "on the stove." Finally alone in a rustic townhouse set up, Silas busied himself with putting things in the fridge while Sara explored.

"These beds are tiny," Sara laid herself onto one of the beds in the room, her feet still on the floor.

"Welcome to Iceland," Silas said, sliding Sara's suitcase into a small wardrobe. "We can push them together, but it doesn't really add much room for each person."

Sara pondered that fact for an instant, then bounced away from it.

"You came here that week after our first date? And then you came back to New York early!"

Silas nodded, sitting on the bed beside you. "I came to ask for guidance."

"Did you get it?"

He shrugged. "Kinda? You'll understand more whenever we see Ama and Fan. They were all confident that you would survive."

"Are they out of touch? Do they know how violent Desdemona's movement has gotten?"

"Oh they know everything," Silas said. "Don't for one second fall for this whole hippy vibe. They hear all the Lock drama. They just don't intervene."

"So they would have let me die?"

Silas shook his head. "No, they were certain that you wouldn't."

"Why did you let me go back to New York, after the lake house?"

Silas came and sat beside her.

"We all misjudged how that would go, and Heather and I argued about whether you needed to actually go into the Surrender room," he said. "Heather thought it was better to go through with it all, in case someone came to check up."

"Fucking Heather," Sara said, again wondering why her old friend hadn't just set her down and said, we need to get you out of here.

"I'm happy to spend the next decade apologizing," Silas said patting Sara on the leg.

"No need," Sara sat up, looking out the window of the small room, over the parking lot and road, across the bay to the hills so green they reminded her of absinthe through candlelight. "It feels symbolic now, like I literally ended that phase of my life and now I'm starting another one."

"Except for Teddie."

"We will get her, I see that now."

"Good," Silas kissed her on top of her head again, disappointment surprising Sara. "Shall we go up to the main house now or do you need time?"

"I'm as ready as I'll ever be," Sara said, leaning forward and kissing Silas on the lips, lingering for a few seconds. Noting the surprise on his face, Sara leapt from the bed and headed for the door. "Wait, are we driving or walking?"

"Walking," Silas said, not moving from the bed. "Go knock on the girls' door and see if they want to walk up with us."

Sara noticed the spring in her step as she walked down the hallway. She was still smiling when Embla opened the door.

"We headed up?"

Sara nodded, then noticed that Embla had changed out of her driving clothes and was now dressed in a sleek pink jumpsuit, its zipper low enough to show a lot of cleavage.

"Shoot," Sara panicked. "I didn't pack anything nice, I just brought the stuff I bought at 66 Degrees North." Her mind flew to the immense shipping box that Crina had sent her. She'd barely opened it last night, a single peek at the contents threatened to send her into a vortex of reverie and regret.

"I took the liberty of packing your Care Bears onesie," April Veronica appeared beside Embla in a matching jumpsuit in a neon green, a bundle of peacock blue fake fur in her outstretched hand. "I thought it would be a fun way to defuse the situation."

"Be right back," Sara took the onesie and returned her room, where Silas was at least standing up, dancing strangely from one foot to the other.

"Apparently dressing like a vintage cartoon animal will help what's about to happen," she said querulously. "Do you have any adult babywear?"

Silas shook his head no.

"Then what the hell is that weird dance?' Sara said, hating the sound of mild paranoia in her voice.

"Sara, I had a boner," Silas said. "That's it. We can just go up dressed like this. Don't worry."

"Embla says I should wear my onesie."

"It's not a terrible idea," Silas agreed.

Minutes later, two jumpsuits and an adult onesie accompanied a lone man up a narrow road that curved up the mountain behind the guesthouses. Embla held open the first gate, a faded, sprung wooden fence that opened with a smoothness that belied its ancient appearance. After the gravel road went from asphalt to river stones, another gate appeared, this one a no-nonsense metal and wire affair which Silas opened by pressing a fob on his keyring. As they waited for it to open, Sara noticed thin wires stretching horizontally between the twisted low shrubs, an almost invisible security fence. As she walked through the gate, she felt her anxiety spike and she realized that subconsciously at least, she was still expecting something bad to happen.

The road climbed gently as it swung back into a tight valley and the group continued in silence, each lost in reverie, until in the distance, Sara saw a building on the crest of the next rise. A typical Icelandic home, two story, high steep red roof, no visible windows on the side they were approaching from, a pair of battered Subarus parked in front of it.

"Is there a front door?" Sara broke the silence.

"Yeah, you just can't see it, it's in the wall right there." Embla said, pointing. Sara couldn't make it out, but as they got closer, the faint outline of a door appeared in the wall, seconds before the door opened, revealing Stefanya, now clad in a sparkling, bobbing dress that looked like a constellation, or frog's eggs.

"What the hell is she wearing?" Sara asked.

"I heard that," Stefanya called out. "I thought you liked fashion. This is brand new Ninomiya."

"And this is vintage Walgreens," Sara replied, curtsying in her blue onesie.

"I'm dead with envy," Stefanya replied. "I can't join you, those rocks will ruin my heels."

They completed the rest of the walk quickly, each one hugging Stefanya as she ushered them into a living room so vast it made April Veronica gasp. The façade revealed nothing of the house behind it.

They stepped into a long curving room, white walls, all glass windows on one side, overlooking rocky outcrops and a higher viewpoint of the bay that was outside the guest houses. The floor was polished concrete, the only furniture a long sleek custom couch in cloud gray, facing the windows, and a thick shag rug the same color on the floor.

"Come into my humble abode," Stefanya said appearing beside them. "Please, make yourselves at home while I pop into the kitchen."

Vanishing through a door at the other end of the room, Stefanya let the door swing closed behind her, its latch echoing off the walls and floor.

"What is it with you guys?" April Veronica turned to Silas. "Do you share an architect? What do you call this? Postmodern Vampire Eco minimalism?"

Silas laughed. "Yeah, that's what they're calling it on Zillow."

"I bet the hipsters are dying for it," April Veronica said.

"Not literally, at least," Embla said, and they all laughed at her clumsy joke.

Shifting her weight from one foot to the other nervously, Sara wondered if they should sit. Or stand. Some sit some stand? She didn't know. The Stefanya she'd known was fair but exacting, and Crina used to be fond of saying that the Purge had changed her, shortened her fuse. Sara was still intimidated by her.

"So standing is what's comfortable?" Stefanya swept back into the room, her otherworldly dress bouncing sensually around her hips. In one hand, she held a glass pitcher filled with blood so scarlet that Sara knew immediately she had aerated it, like wine. Her other hand supported a silver platter, atop which sat three metal mugs, and two tall glasses of a liquid so black it looked like oil.

Without warning, April Veronica plopped down onto the couch, her eyes on Stefanya. Sara briefly wondered how this delightful young woman remained so resilient considering the tumultuous, violent events since her conversion.

"She hasn't said a word and she's already in reverie," Stefanya appeared in front of Sara, startling her. "Take a mug."

"I'm sorry," Sara cast her eyes down as she took a mug from the tray, and Stefanya poured it to the rim with the cherry red blood. The scent hit Sara immediately, and the rich, layered bouquet made her salivate, and she fought to keep her hands from rushing it to her mouth.

Stefanya poured drinks for Silas and April Veronica, then handed one of the glasses to Embla, took one for herself, then set the tray on the floor.

"Skál," Stefanya raised her glass, and everyone followed suit. The blood that hit Sara's palate was exquisite in flavor, with complex notes of something floral atop the usual notes of iron and rust, and as she sipped, Sara waited expectantly for the heady rush of the virus receiving new fuel, but it did not come.

Realizing that she'd closed her eyes out of habit, she opened them slowly to see Silas staring at her curiously.

"What?" she said.

"Well, what did you think of that?"

"Delicious, but something's strange," she said, licking her top lip clean.

"For fuck's sake, sit," Stefanya said, carefully arranging the skirt of her dress and sitting beside April Veronica. Embla took the spot on the other side of April. Silas remained standing, waving his hand at the couch, waiting for Sara to sit beside Stefanya. She'd been hoping for a buffer, but reluctantly took the seat.

"It makes me happy to have you here," Stefanya said, her gaze moving to each of them. "April Veronica, I'm hoping that we can offer you some stability, for your time in our world has been fraught with so much loss and anger. And Sara, you've been a pillar, an absolute rock. I hope we can give you a respite from the work you've done for so long."

"Thank you," Sara said, feeling more unsettled by the second.

"I remember you as a lot chattier," Stefanya said.

So many responses rushed at Sara she felt herself overload, her eyelids fluttering, an attendant blush rising across her throat.

"I'm-" she began to apologize.

"No more sorry," Stefanya said softly, reaching across Embla and stroking Sara's thigh. "Take your time. Accelerating after a long period of a slow life is going to take a minute."

Sara nodded. "Yes, that, plus also I didn't think we were seeing you until tomorrow, so I hadn't gotten around to recalibrating. Silas said we were going to walk around a garden. That was what I was set up for."

"Totally understand," Stefanya waved a dismissive hand. "And if you'd like to go for a walk, we can, or if you'd like to do it alone, that's also fine."

Sara shook her head. "No, I want to see you, I've wanted to see you, I've thought about you so many times, I wanted to talk to you, but Crina always said you'd gone very silent."

Stefanya roared with laughter. "She wishes! I'm just such a terrible liar, they couldn't trust me not to tell you," she said between laughs, turning to Embla. "Can you imagine? Me? Silent?"

"I mean," Embla made an exaggerated face, "there have been so many times I wish you would be silent…" Stefanya fell back on the couch in hysterics. Embla turned to Sara. "Seriously, this old witch is a total chatterbox. She talks in her sleep." Stefanya nodded, wiping tears from her eyes with the back of a hand.

"It me!"

The confusion swirling inside Sara became too much, and she reached for Silas's hand, relieved when his warm hand wrapped around hers, squeezing it, anchoring her.

"Did you learn anything on your trip to Spain?" she blurted.

Stefanya shook her head. "Yes, I followed some sisters out to a facility in the forest outside the city. It seems to be some sort of halfway house on a grand scale," she said. "It's owned by the Madrid Lock and it's the one place that sisters are allowed to go, and they take care of a lot of young women who live there. The townspeople all gossiped about the young women, clearly battling addictions, but they are kept away from them. The women never go into the village."

"I can't believe Desdemona does anything altruistically," Embla said.

"Right," Stefanya said, looking at Embla with pride. "But there's nothing to forbid her from doing what she's doing. I will return to Spain once we get Teddie out of New York, grab a few elders, see what we can find out."

"Thank you," Sara's voice was soft, her conscience eased by the woman's words.

"De nada," Stefanya smiled. "It's time for me to come out of retirement anyway."

"Stef," Embla interrupted. "Where are Ama and Fan? I thought they'd be here too."

"Oh, of course, they were going to be here, but some band is rplaying at the university tonight, and typical of them, that's where they have to be."

"Which band?" Embla sat upright. "Not Dauðyflin?"

Stefanya nodded. "Yep, that's it."

"Fuck, why didn't they tell me?" It was the first time Sara had seen Embla get angry, her eyes darkened, her brow knit.

"I'm telling you now," Stefanya said. "You can go if you like."

Embla turned to April Veronica. "Wanna?" April Veronica shot a glance at Stefanya, who nodded. "Yep, you too. Go, get out. Have a great time."

Embla leapt to her feet like a kid who just got out of detention, then hauled April Veronica up. They were halfway to the door when she stopped.

"Silas? Car keys?"

"On the dresser in our room, it's not locked," he called out, and they were gone.

"That worked perfectly," Stefanya said, grabbing the tray from the floor. After taking the glasses from both of them, she returned to the kitchen.

"This is weird," Sara whispered when the door clicked shut. Silas leaned his head against hers and kissed her cheek. "Just roll with it," he replied, and they sat in silence, both gazing out of the windows at clouds scudding across the mountain tops, across the bay.

After several minutes, the sound of the door clicking brought them back to the moment, and Sara looked left, smiling when Stefanya bounced into the room in denim cutoffs and a Dauðyflin t-shirt, holding a dark green bottle aloft.

"You guys," she enthused as she settled by them on the couch. "This is the best batch of blood liquor that I've made in fucking eons." Confusion turned to amusement for Sara as she watched the elder pop the cork, sending it hurtling into the ceiling where it left a small spray of dark blood before bouncing to the floor.

"Do you want me to get glasses? Silas asked. Shaking her head, Stefanya raised the bottle to her lips, her throat bobbing as she swallowed. When she was finished, she smacked her wet, red lips together, passing the bottle to Sara.

"Tonight, we drink like the warriors we are," she smiled. "Straight from the bottle."

Following suit, Sara tilted the bottle to her lips, her mouth instantly filled with a more familiar, but complex flavor. As she swallowed, she felt the telltale rapture cloud her vision with a renewed intensity, handing the bottle to Silas as she fell back against the firm couch. In her mouth, she tasted something reminiscent of the way whisky used to taste when she was young, a memory floating above the swoon that was taking its sweet time returning her consciousness.

"Good, huh?" Stefanya asked. Sara opened her eyes to see the woman taking a second, longer swig. When she was done, she offered the bottle to Sara, who declined, waving a hand.

"Embla is such a narc," Stefanya said. "I'm so glad she took the bait, now we can get on with having the night I wanted to have with the two of you."

"I don't understand," Sara said.

"It's such a drag," Stefanya said. "I'll spill the tea. That stuff I gave you? It's lab grown. We made it. And it works. But it's still blood, technically, chemically, so Embla is still deciding if it works with her belief system, so when she's around, I try to be a supportive parent, and drink the godawful synthetic that she came up with. I mean, it works, but it's like eating the pizza box instead of eating the pizza."

"This is so Absolutely Fabulous," Sara said. "You're the naughty indulgent mom."

"I am, and I love it," Stefanya said. "I wanted to have some time with you, outside of the way it's going to be with Ama and Fan."

"Oh?"

"They're like Embla," Stefanya said. "They're militant vegans now."

Sara raised her eyebrows.

"I know, I'm surrounded," Stefanya said with a groan. "I just think, after what you've been through, it would be nicer to offer you a more... traditional welcome."

"Thanks," Sara said. "I guess it has been a rough couple of months."

"Bitch please," Stefanya rolled her eyes. "It's been a rough century for you. You do realize every other Lock has cycled through Mothers every five minutes."

"Of course I knew," Sara said.

"Well, did you know that's why everyone wanted to go to New York? Because it was known that they wouldn't get forced to be Lock Mother, everyone knew you'd never quit."

Her shoulders slumping, Sara let out a frustrated sigh.

"That's the worst part of this whole thing, honestly," she said. "I feel dumb. Or at least, I've been made to feel that way."

Stefanya fanned a hand in the air. "Nope. Not dumb. Not for a second. You know that each Lock is different? Each Lock is an experiment, an unplanned, organic, social experiment. And your selflessness, your sacrifice, created the closest that any Lock has come to a semblance of something fair, sustainable and worthwhile. But all Locks crumble eventually."

"What do you mean?" Sara pressed herself upright, her eyes fixed on Stefanya like a hawk's.

"Girl, I wrote those rules five hundred years ago, to get us out of the situation we were in at that time," the elder said, leaning forward confidentially. "They seemed to work, and I stopped paying attention. I'm sure you remember, when things kind of changed, or started to, like I dunno, eighteen hundredish? Things got disorderly, people began to want strange things, a selfishness came up that was new. It was tied to progress, it was tied to class, to sex and rejection and fear and religion." Sara nodded.

"I feel like it was later in the States," she said.

"Yeah, for sure," Stefanya agreed. "Started later, accelerated faster."

"And now the States is like a truck hurtling down a steep hill without brakes," Silas said.

"Most of the world is in that truck too," Stefanya said. "You, dear child, have been so preoccupied with the States for so long."

"There's still so much good there."

"Spoken like a junkie licking a spoon," Stefanya said with a throaty laugh. "Look, it's not a race, and to be honest, I don't care too much about the world at large, I don't need to. The damage is being done, there's nothing I can do to stop it. I'm not going to spend my days stomping out bushfires with my bare feet.

The bloodbuzz was wearing off and Sara couldn't help but stare at a woman she only knew as a fierce enforcer of the rules that she wrote, now reinvented as an eccentric aunt.

"So here's where we are," Stefanya said, tipping the bottle to her lips again. "Desdemona used my rules to emulate the Catholic church, which was unexpected and unfortunately is turning into the ruling solution. Her doctrines are not even vaguely connected to my original goals. Even you, Sara, you saw my rules as the box you lived in, not the materials to build a better life."

"It was honestly probably the way you delivered them," Sara said, her voice strong. "I was there, remember, when you and Crina, Fan, Amrita, us youngsters, the numbers were agreed, the rules were accepted without any discussion of their evolution or change. And now you're faulting me for not knowing I could have changed them?"

"I'm not blaming, not at all," Stefanya put a hand over Sara's. "Who has time for innovation while they're raising a rotating crew of underlings? If there's blame to be cast, it rests upon me, and upon Crina, but hindsight is always perfect. But this is why I wanted to get you two alone, before you meet with the others tomorrow. You will not like what you hear, and I wanted you to be prepared."

"Hit me," Sara said. "No, wait, hand me that bottle, give me a minute and then hit me."

With a smile, Stefanya handed the bottle over. Sara drank deeply from it, deliberately drinking more than she normally would, losing herself in the trance of intoxication. As her vision cleared, she opened her eyes to see Stefanya grinning eagerly.

"You good?"

Sara nodded.

"Okay, well here goes. The new Lock must be free from the attachments or burdens of the past."

"You've already lost me," Sara said.

"This is just a sketch to prepare you for tomorrow. In New York, you were crushed by the weight of your responsibility to history. Now, imagine a century of leadership where you lived on a day to day basis."

"Nope, can't do it."

"Of course you can't, dear, but that's what I'm asking you to see. The fruitless human habit of living in the past and worrying about the future. It's not why we are here, as people, and I certainly don't think that's why we, as Cursed people, are here."

"Why are we here?"

"To love," Stefanya said. "To love animals and people and the planet, to love experience and to love nurturing. We don't need to pretend to be nuns, we don't need so much money, we are now able to live fully outside of society, and we can keep our minds sharp by embracing technology."

"That's all very nice," Sara said. "And I would adopt all of that in a heartbeat, but what about places? What about my New York?"

"Go back in a century," Stefanya said. "That's my point. Take your-self out of the human schedule. I wrote a plan that looked backwards, not forwards, and I did not consider the difficulty of living such a long time. I forced the daily routine of the regular human life on to women who could live on the timetable of the earth."

Blinking, Sara digested the information.

"That's why we are not planning to intervene in Desdemona's ill-advised crusade. I know you're going to try to sway me with pas-sionate talk about the women of your Lock, the amazing fortress you constructed in that city, but it will not work."

"It doesn't have to work, for you," Sara said, her voice deliberately light. "But I get to decide what works for me."

"Yes, exactly," Stefanya clapped her hands. "You're already here. You get it. Every morning, my only decision is whether I will live to see the end of that day. If, at the end of the day, I decide to kill myself, then, that would be it. But every day, I fall asleep thinking, 'I'll die tomorrow'"

"Those days are a human timeline," Sara said, and Stefanya nod-ded.

"Yes, but those days, for us, they're microseconds. Forgive me for saying this, but your flameout last week, the readiness of your willing-ness to go to Surrender, that was the weight of centuries of frustration and exhaustion getting to you."

Fucking Heather, Sara thought, as she realized that somehow, the elders had seen her dramatic tribunal.

"But you said the point of it all was love?" Sara said, trying to regain control of the narrative. Stefanya nodded. "I love Teddie. But I can't rush in there and save her."

Stefanya nodded. "We know how important she is to you, and that's literally why Crina is there now, she knew it was the only way you could find some peace here."

The news hit Sara like a truck, the enormity of Crina's love for her, something that she had assumed the years had tempered, reduced. Now she saw Crina's absence from her life for what it was, a brave attempt to save them all.

"I feel sick," she said.

"It's a lot," Silas said, and she knew he understood immediately.

"I just wanted you to be prepared, because once you get Fan and Ama on a rant, you'll need your defenses up. Basically, they're of the opinion that the existing Lock network around the world needs to convert to a new model."

"Which nobody will go for," Sara said.

"Right. So, if we let Desdemona's vicious nature take its course, we stand to inherit a lot of real estate, and substantially less neo-conservative brainwashed sisters who are terrified of their own shadows and who refuse to live life. These sisters have already opted out of living a life of love. They're slaves to fear and nostalgia. They see Surrender as a release, not an ending."

"But these are women, not, I don't know, ants on your picnic."

"And these women have known truly special lives," Stefanya said emphatically. "Some more special than others. I risked my life time and time over to create this world. I oversaw our expansion, into the old world and then the new. But then it was time to sit back and observe. Sara, I believe in time you'll see things from my vantage point."

Sara shrugged. "I wonder," she said. "It's not too revolutionary, It's just too, I dunno, clinical, it's too black and white."

"It's both clinical and black and white, but it's built on heart and shades of gray," Stefanya said. "And it's also a work in progress. If you can think of a way to undo Desdemona's fear and insecurity and her ravenous appetite for control, and the way she's convinced people to think, then I'm all ears."

"She said something interesting at the last meeting," Sara said.

"Oh, you mean the thing about finding out what she's really up to?"

Sara nodded, blindsided once again by the fact that everyone was watching Lock meetings in New York and who knows where else.

"Yes, that. She has a plan.'"

Stefanya nodded. "There is travel in the future, for some of us. We need to talk to people we can trust at other Locks. I will travel to London in the coming weeks, then Paris, Milan. Fan and Ama will attempt to contact old friends in the ZPG Locks, Helsinki, Edinburgh."

"We should come with you," Silas said. "Sara and I could-"

"Nope," Stefanya said, holding the bottle out to him. "Every Lock knows what you look like. They think you're a hunter, that you're onto us, and the general consensus seems to be capture and kill, even though I'm pretty certain that the majority of sisters have gone soft. I think Desdemona is the only one with a murderer's soul. Either way, you're grounded."

"Fucking Liz," Silas said. "Why was I so stupid?"

"We've all been stupid," Stefanya said. "That's what life is: Being stupid and then cleaning up the mess."

"It doesn't mean killing."

Stefanya began to stand, steadying herself with one hand on the arm of the couch.

"I'm going to get us another bottle, because we need to continue this discussion. But Sara, please remember who and what I am. I have killed to save our kind before, and I'll do it again."

As she walked to the kitchen her phone pinged in the pocket of her shorts, and Stefanya paused, retrieving an iPhone in a bejeweled case. As she glanced at the screen, her expression darkened.

"You guys, it's Yfke, in Bucharest," she paused, glancing at Sara. "Do you talk to Yfke?"

"Only when I have a spare two hours," Sara giggled, tipsy from all the blood liquor. "I love her, she's hilarious, but she's just not capable of a short phone call."

"I've been dodging her all week. She's strategizing our moves."

"Does she know about Iceland?" Sara asked, and Stefanya shook her head vigorously.

"Hell no she doesn't. Nobody does. She thinks that we are in Scotland or Ireland."

"I don't know her, but I love hearing about her life," Silas said with a smile.

"Such as?"

"Wasn't it her, Stefanya, that told her Lock she was Scholar like in Norway or somewhere but she was really in Ibiza partying for a decade with the gays?"

Stefanya snort-laughed and nodded. "That's her."

Stefanya's phone rang again.

"She's being persistent," Stefanya raised a finger. "Don't go anywhere, I'll say I have company and can't talk."

Stefanya answered her phone. Sara could hear panic in the female voice on the other end of the line, and consternation washed across Stefanya's face.

"No, I've been away from my phone, I'm sorry. I'll look now. When did it happen?"

Sara glanced at Silas, who shrugged and widened his eyes. The voice on the line chattered rapidly, and Sara watched a bloody teardrop fall from Stefanya's eye, a trail of eyeliner following it down her cheek.

"Yes, yes, my love," she said, her voice low. "I will do that now, and I will call you back right after. Okay, bye, I love you."

Slowly, Stefanya lowered the phone to her lap and turned her head to face them.

"Helsinki took Surrender this afternoon," she said, her voice breaking as a flood of tears coursed down her face.

"No," Silas said. "Ah, fuck no."

Sara looked from one to the other, watching Stefanya's hands clasp and unclasp in her lap as she wept. Her mind racing, she forced herself to remain silent to give Stefanya the space to process this information. A torrent of questions raced through her mind; a rapid roll call of the women she knew in Helsinki, three had been part of New York. Was Desdemona there?

"Wait," she blurted. "Did they post the video?"

Desdemona nodded, three short slow nods, the universal confirmation of bad news.

"We should watch it," she said with a sigh. "If you're not up to it, it's okay to leave."

"No, we will stay with you,' Sara said emphatically, even though she wasn't sure she had the bandwidth to watch.

Sobbing, Stefanya rose and pressed a button on the wall. The windows darkened, and a glass panel descended from a slit in the ceiling. Stefanya turned it on with a remote, the glass turning into a screen.

"It's smart glass," Silas said, noting her confusion.

Sara nodded, not understanding that either. The three of them moved to the couch facing the television as Stefanya signed into her Signal, which was now displayed on the hanging screen. As soon as she signed in, they all saw a screed of new messages, and Stef scrolled down until she came to a message from Desdemona entitled A Proud Day For Helsinki.

"Before you open it," Sara said, "if it's okay with you, can we just go to the video? I don't want to read Des's propaganda before we watch."

"My sentiments exactly," Stefanya said, flicking away the words and clicking on the video attachment.

On the television, once again the camera was on a stand at the back of their meeting room, delightful folk art carved into wooden beams, flowers and vines stenciled on the walls. Two rows of women, once again wearing white nun robes, sat, their backs to the camera. On the dais were two thrones. Desdemona, in black robes and full makeup, her hair immaculately curled, smiled with false benevolence. Beside her sat Helmi, Helsinki's Lock mother for half a century. Her blond hair was braided with blue ribbons that framed her elfin face. She stood slowly, spreading her arms to the women seated before her.

Speaking in Finnish, she addressed her Lock, speaking slowly, her voice cracking several times. After several minutes, she bowed deeply and returned to her seat. Standing, Desdemona bent and kissed her forehead, then turned to the camera, clapping her hands at someone offscreen. A young Latina entered the frame, carrying a silver tray of small, elegant goblets. She moved through the rows of sisters, each one taking a goblet as she passed, until finally she returned to the dais, and Helmi took the final one.

Remaining seated, Helmi raised her goblet high, and the women in front of her responded in kind.

"Maailman turvallisuuden vuoksi teemme tämän," Helmi said, her voice strong, regal. "Valaistuneille sisarilleni rakastan teitä kaikkia ja kiitän teitä tästä elämästä, jonka loimme yhdessä."

"Do you speak Finnish?" Sara asked Stefanya, who shook her head without taking her eyes off the screen.

Without another word, Helmi brought the goblet to her lips and finished it in one draft. Delicately, she set the silver mug on the floor beside her, then she sat back and closed her eyes, a drop of blood trickling from the corner of her mouth. In front of her, the women of her Lock followed suit, one by one their heads falling backward as the opioids in their final cup of blood took effect.

When the last woman had gone unconscious, Desdemona stood, gazing beatifically around the room.

"What a fake fucking bitch," Stefanya said through clenched teeth. She began to say something else but a violent sob erupted from her chest and she fell back against the couch, her eyes pressed shut. Sara watched as Desdemona signaled to the camera, and the screen went blank. With a sinking realization, she figured that Eleanor was probably with her, operating the camera.

Silas wrapped an arm around Stefanya and she collapsed against him, her back heaving as she sobbed. Sara took her hands, caressing them with her thumbs, and they sat, waiting for Stefanya to regain her composure. Silas's eyes met Sara's, and he mouthed "are you okay?" Sara shrugged and nodded.

"You guys," Stefanya lifted herself from Silas's chest, his shirt now smudged with kohl. "I.." she took a deep breath. "I need to make a bunch of calls, there are so many messages to answer and I...is it okay if I kick you out? I really need to be alone. Those women... they were the most peaceful Lock in the world, they weren't radicalized, they weren't anything. I have to talk to Yfke, she's going to get a group zoom happening with a bunch of elders and I want to be on it."

"Can I be on it?" Sara asked.

"A) they think you're dead and B) honey, you're in a Care Bears onesie," Stefanya said with a short chuckle. "Thanks but no. I'll tell you everything tomorrow."

Standing, Sara extended a hand to Silas.

"Walk me home?"

Chapter Ten

A light rain pattered the ground, sounding like small cymbals as they made their way down the hill to the guesthouse. Slipping on a patch of wet grass, Sara grabbed onto Silas's arm for support, then let her hand slide down until she was holding his hand.

"I'm glad you were there for that," she said simply.

"Me too," he said quietly. "I won't ask if you're okay, I don't think okay is a goal right now."

"Considering the week I've already had, I think I *am* okay though," Sara said, causing Silas to slow his pace, and then stop.

"I might need your help then," his voice was a whisper. "My mother worshiped Helmi, I loved hearing about her, the work she was doing."

Sara nodded in agreement, then turned to face Silas, taking his other hand.

"It is deeply sad, like sad in the soul sad," she said, her eyes gazing into his. "But it's done. We have forever to grieve and to remember those women. Right now, we need to derail Desdemona, before that happens again."

"You're talking about Edinburgh?"

Sara nodded, releasing one of his hands and beginning to walk along the path again.

"Yeah, they're the last officially ZPG Lock-

"What about Madrid?" Silas interrupted.

"Please," Sara groaned. "Desdemona is never going to destroy her seat of power. But Edinburgh, they only went ZPG recently. I just don't want to lose them."

"We should call Heather when we get to the room," Silas said, surprised when Sara shook her head.

"I'll text her," she said. Suddenly, she didn't want anything more than to be alone with Silas.

They walked in silence for several minutes, raindrops splashing small explosions of cold on her cheeks and the tip of her nose.

"Don't you feel like we could just walk away from all of this?" Silas said, squeezing her hand.

"Probably a bit too soon for me yet, I'm afraid," she replied, returning the hand squeeze. "But I do want to live. Especially after what we just witnessed. Life is just so... I dunno, we make out that it's this huge thing but basically it's just yours til a switch flips and then it's gone. I really, deeply, want to feel like I've lived as much as I could.."

"I hear you," Silas said. "I'm ready for that life too. I hope you have room in your boat for the two of us."

"There's room for you, April Veronica, Embla and Teddie," Sara said. "Wouldn't that be something?"

"Let's go get Teddie," Silas said. "There, it's as simple as that."

Sara raised her face to find his eyes staring into hers, his expression kind.

"You are basically Vampire's Most Wanted, you can't go anywhere, they'll kill you."

"You forget," Silas said gently, "I survived the fucking Purge. I'm not afraid of a bunch of soft, unfocused assassins. As much as they're annoying, Fan and Ama have trained me as hard as they trained themselves. I can disarm them most of the time in training."

"It's the rest of the time I'm worried about," Sara said.

"The question right now is, would Teddie embrace this life?"

Sara pondered the question in silence. If she brought Teddie to Iceland, it would be like breaking the polar bear out of the Central Park zoo and setting it free in the Arctic. She didn't even know if Teddie had a survival instinct, she'd never needed to develop one. She tried to remember the last time Teddie got a black belt in martial arts and hoped that her answer of sometime in the seventies was incorrect.

"In time, I think she would see it as a positive thing," Sara said cautiously, her heart racing at how badly she needed that statement to be true. "The one thing is, she's never had to share me before."

"Yay, the elephant in the room," Silas smiled at her. "So, tell me this: Are you happy to keep on hanging around with me?."

"Hanging around huh?" Sara smiled. "Is that what the kids are calling it?" She considered his question, the answer surprisingly clear and rapid. She nodded. "Yes, and I'll be honest here, it wasn't until today, at Stefanya's, I felt like I had an ally."

"Sara," Silas took both her hands. "I'm so on your side I *am* your side." He raised her hands, kissing them, then holding them against his face. "This, this between us, is something I can fight for, and I can see it going on for a long time. So, in this weird choose your own adventure, we are now a we."

"Does that make today some sort of anniversary?"

Silas nodded. "If you want it to be, but I think it's healthier if we only celebrate it every ten years."

"Sure, whatever," Sara said, the pounding of her heart in her chest making her aware of how badly she wanted this all of a sudden. "But that's a huge gamble for you. We can't just all of a sudden tell everyone that, you know, hey, I'm alive and I'm dating a cursed male."

"Exactly, our relationship cannot exist within the current Lock structure."

"So, you're in favor of the end of Locks?"

"That's quite a conclusion to draw," Silas slowed his pace. "Sara, one of us has never lived within the Lock structure, so I don't feel its pressure the way you might. And to me, being part of a Lock was always such an impossible dream. I'd love to be in a Lock. But I also want to live a life. We live a long time but we aren't immortal. We can keep on kicking against the darkness, but we never escape the ultimate question, what is life? What happens after life?"

Sara paused, enjoying the biting rain on her face, her eyes burning into Silas's.

"That took a turn," she said with a laugh.

"Tell me there's a day that you don't ask yourself that question. We've lived half a millennium, no amount of philosophy or science has gotten us one micrometer closer to an answer. I think that's the burden that is causing the system to crack."

"Der," Sara said. "That's been obvious for centuries."

"But in our most secretive hearts, all of us hope for an answer, or at least, an inkling."

"You think the answer is love, huh?"

Instead of answering, Silas resumed walking, leading her by the hand.

"Sure," he said finally, and she felt his gaze upon her but she kept her attention on the slippery path ahead of them and the increasingly sodden Care Bears onesie.

"So I finally understand Icelandic fashion," she said in obvious deflection. "This ridiculous outfit is now so soaked I could drown in it."

Silas stopped walking.

"Take it off," he said. Raising her eyes to his, her heart began to race. He gave her a wolf's grin and nodded with his chin. Without a word, she drew down the zipper, then flicked her head backwards, knocking the waterlogged hood from her head, its weight dragging the onesie from her shoulders. She straightened her arms so that gravity could continue to undress her. Slowly the onesie sank down her body, each newly exposed part of her body needled with exhilaratingly brisk raindrops. When finally it surrounded her ankles like a ball of blue moss, she stepped from it, wearing only her last pair of Target panties. She felt the rain hit her hard nipples and a deep sigh of pleasure radiated out from her chest and the only thing she wanted in the world was his lips on hers, his hands on her back. She reached her hand out to him.

"Let's keep walking," he said, stepping forward and brushing his lips across hers, sending white lightning through her body.

"What?"

"Trust me," Silas said, turning back to the path. Horny confusion clouded Sara's mind.

"Aren't you going to ditch your clothes?" she asked.

"Don't need to," he said. "I'm dry as a bone."

Great, Sara thought to herself. The guy with the endless erections is suddenly playing hard to get. She bent to pick up her onesie, then decided to get it tomorrow. Standing upright, she dashed ahead of him, then walked the rest of the way back to the guesthouse.

"You know what you're doing to me," he called out. Sara ignored him until they reached the shelter of the guesthouse. Stepping into the dimly lit entryway, Sara waited for him, unsure if the girls would have returned yet.

When Silas caught up to her, he pulled her against him, and she did not give him the option of a gentle kiss, pressing her face hungrily against his, her tongue prizing his teeth apart and connecting with his, sparks filling her head. As they kissed, she lifted her legs, wrapping them around his waist, and he carried her along the hallway, step by step the kiss increasing in urgent intensity. A million miles away, Sara heard the click of the opening door and they passed into the blue semi-darkness of their room, and Sara felt herself being lowered onto the bed, the kiss not breaking for a second.

Silas laid atop her, his hands grabbing her ass, then roaming up and down her spine, his rough fingertips tracing tactile paths that stayed illuminated after his fingers moved on. Desperate to feel his skin, she unbuttoned his shirt and slid a palm against the hair on his chest, her fingers toying with his nipple until he groaned into her mouth and her hand moved down to the button on his pants.

To her disappointment, one of his hands moved from her back and grabbed her wrist.

"Come on," she growled, breaking the kiss.

"Not yet," he said, his voice hoarse. "I have something I wanna try."

"Me too," Sara said, wrapping her legs around his waist, feeling him hard against her.

"You're not making this easy," he chuckled, twisting suddenly and freeing himself from her legs.

Cupping her cheek in his hand, Silas kissed her lips briefly, a concerned look passing across his face. "We need to get some fuel into you first, your eyes are getting dark."

A flare of frustration almost made Sara snap at him, and she bit it down. Standing slowly, Silas shucked off his wet shirt, then bent to untie his shoes. After he shucked his shoes and kicked them into the corner, he turned to her.

"May I also unshoe you?"

Sara nodded, and he quickly slipped her shoes and wet socks from her feet. When he was done he turned to the small kitchen.

"Ahem," Sara coughed.

"Yes, m'lady?"

"The pants," Sara whispered. "Lose the pants."

With a nod and a cheeky salute, Silas unbuttoned his pants, and in one movement, shoved them and his underwear to his ankles. Stepping out of them, he gave her an impish grin, then went to the small fridge and withdrew a metal flask and switched on an electric kettle.

Hungrily, she watched every move. The way his weight shifted from one round buttock to the other as he walked, the glimpse of dark hair between his legs when he bent over, the way the muscles in his back moved when he stood back up.

"This better, m'lady," he called out as he fussed around the small kitchen, setting out glasses and tidying up while he waited for the kettle. Gently, he poured the boiling water into a bowl, then emptied blood into a coffee cup that he then sat in the boiling water. As he was putting the flask back into the fridge, Sara fixated on his ass, thinking of nothing but the scent of him and the gorgeous curves.

"You're the sexiest blood barista I've ever seen," she said, and Silas froze mid-bend before standing and turning to face her, a wide grin on his face, his eyes twinkling, his erection bouncing playfully.

"Thank you ma'am. Your half-caff upside down mocha matcha red drink will be up on the bar in just a minute."

"I'm gonna give you the best Yelp," Sara said.

"I've never been more disappointed to hear the word yelp in my whole life," Silas walked slowly towards her, raising her chin with a crooked finger, then kissing her, languidly, his full lips gentle against hers. She inhaled his scent, and her mind went blank except for him.

The kiss rolled on, the barest flick of his tongue between her lips sparking a groan deep in her throat.

As they kissed, Silas's free hand found Sara's and he threaded his fingers between hers, then clasped down, pulling her against him. Pushing back, Sara rose to her feet, lifting Silas, never breaking the kiss. She walked him to where the blood was warming on the counter, and wordlessly, he reached over and lifted it from the boiling water, breaking the kiss to whisper, "go back to the bed."

Turning, she faced the bed, and carefully, the coffee cup of blood held above his face, she lowered him on to the bed. He shifted the mug to one hand, and with the other, he grabbed the waist of her panties, yanking them off as if they were made of paper. Smiling wickedly, she knelt on the bed, straddling him, her eyes locked on his. She took the mug of blood from him with one hand and took a swig while her other hand reached down and guided him inside her.

Dropping her weight on him, she held the cup over his mouth as the blackness hit her mind and a scarlet throb pulsed out from her groin. He parted his lips, and she poured a thin stream of neon red blood neatly between them. With each swallow, he pushed against her. When the cup was half empty, she brought it to her own lips, holding the blood on her tongue, feeling the wave of rapture in her chest melting into the warmth lower down. Swallowing, she tipped the mug to her lips, drinking the rest down as Silas began to move rhythmically below her.

With an angry fist, she grabbed the back of his neck and hauled him up to her, mashing her mouth against his, their bloody tongues slipping against each other as the swooning blackness crowded out sight and thought, and they gave themselves over to the rush of darkness and she felt him inside her like a column of light.

Sara kept her eyes closed as consciousness returned, Silas's hands had moved to her hips, his thumbs against her hipbones, his fingers digging into her ass as he tilted her forward and she ground herself down onto him. In unison, they moved as one until Sara heard the telltale hitch in Silas's breathing that told her he was getting close.

"Wait right there," she said breathlessly, lifting herself off the bed and retrieving the flask with the blood from the fridge before mounting him again. This time, she didn't care that the blood was cold. She twisted the top from the flask and looked down at Silas's face, his chin smeared with blood.

"Open up, buttercup," she said, pouring it into his mouth until his eyes widened and a small trickle escaped and ran down his cheek onto the white bedding. "One more for mama," she laughed, returning the flask to his mouth. As his eyes glazed over, she brought the bottle back to her own lips, chugging down two large drafts in a hurry, she wanted to join him when he went under.

She barely had time to screw the lid back on before the wave of ecstasy hit her, and she heard the flask fall to the floor and roll away. She felt his hands up over her stomach, brushing across her breasts like sheet lightning, pleasure everywhere at once as the darkness consumed her and she felt an explosion begin around him inside her, but then it blossomed out and up along her spine, out to her fingers and toes and as he began to wrestle and thrash beneath her, the wave joined with the intoxication from the blood and her head filled with wave after wave of pleasure, blasting out from her hips, rolling up her spine like an ocean wave that smashed up into the dome of her skull as she felt his hands now on her shoulders, bringing them together in a kiss that went forever.

Afterwards, their breath in unison, Sara laid beside him, their skin touching from toes to lips, sweat tinged red dotting their brows and cheeks. Time passed slowly as they exchanged kisses, their eyes staring into each other, occasional fingertips tracing a line on the other's body.

"Back there, on the walk," Silas said.

"Yes?"

"When you asked if I thought love was the meaning of life."

Smiling, Sara kissed him deeply.

"Yeah, what of it?"

"Were you trying to corner me into saying something cheesy?"

Silas looked suddenly vulnerable and Sara's heart ached.

"I aspire to being that manipulative," Sara said lightly. "Sorry, I'm just blunt."

"I mean," Silas stepped into the room and then turned to face her. "What if a lifetime, a long one, devoted to love, is, if not an answer, but a reason?"

"I don't hate it," Sara said, staring into his deep brown eyes. "The relationships we've been allowed to have, four years maximum, they're, not enough for our soul. I figured that out a very long time ago."

"I'm talking big love, like huge fuck off whirlwind love," Silas said. "Sure, there's parental love, that's clearly hard to break. There's love of a deity, which is kind of an easier love to maintain, but just as hard to break. I've always wished I could live with love as my focus."

"That's what Ama used to say when she taught me to meditate."

"Yeah, me too. But it never felt like it was possible."

"Oh no?" Sara nudged him in the ribs. "That wasn't your goal with me?"

"Honestly, let's go with thirty per cent of my goal. I wasn't just some sad sack roaming around pining for a vampire girlfriend."

"When was your last girlfriend?"

"When was your last boyfriend?"

"Touché," Sara laughed. "I honestly don't know." Her mind ran back through time. She had never availed herself of an offsite apartment for a serious relationship. "Like a casual boyfriend who I kinda liked? Probably sixty years. I was more of a hot and heavy month or two person."

"Yeah, me too. And it's been.." Silas paused, thinking, "around forty years."

Sara watched as his eyes clouded over in remembrance.

"She was special, huh?" she said, her voice warm.

"He," Silas said with a smile. "It was a he."

After a brief feeling of surprise, Sara felt stupid for not seeing Silas the same way she saw her sisters, all of whom cycled through periods of bisexuality. Why should Silas be any different?

"Wait, did that get weird?"

She shook her head. "Not weird," she said plainly. "Not at all. I just haven't gotten accustomed to the male vampire thing. I haven't filled in your blanks, and that made me realize just how much I still want to know about you."

"I'll tell you everything you want to know," he said, his voice low. "Sorry, I haven't thought about him in a while."

"No problem, was he hard to break up with after four years? Wait, did that rule even apply to you?"

Nodding, Silas gave her a half smile. "I've chosen to live by all the rules. He... uh yeah, he would have been hard to break up with, but he, well he died."

"Oh, I'm so sorry," Sara wished she hadn't pried. Being playfully curious was always risky with sisters, and now, it was doubly so with a man she was in love with. "We don't have to talk about it now, I feel kinda shitty for prying."

"Nah, don't feel bad. The memory trap is always lurking just below the surface. You know this just as well as I do. Sara, that's the thing that excites me most... well," he looked her up and down. "What excites me the *second* most is that we can talk, like nobody has ever talked before."

"Be warned, I'll probably always have one foot in my mouth."

"And that's beautiful," he said, kissing the tip of her nose.

"I love you Silas," she said, the feeling bursting out of her mouth before she knew she'd formulated the thought. "And this is really, embarrassingly overdue, but thank you. Thank you for everything, and I'm sorry I was such a stubborn mule."

"I've always wanted a mini donkey," he said, and she knew he was deflecting. "You know, with a bonnet and a little basket."

"Dork," she said, kissing him. "But sure, tell me again why we don't have a bunch of them chonky horses at the house?"

Chapter Eleven

Sara was in her dream apartment again, but this time the light was different, the air suffused with the golden light of a Reykjavik sunset, dust particles floating lazily around the jumbled piles of moving boxes. A fetid smell was caught in her nostrils, and she knew it was the dead kittens. She walked a box she hadn't seen before, it was the size of a wardrobe. Standing on her toes, she pulled open the top flap and peered in. Instead of kittens, she saw a jumble of dead women, the white robes of surrender torn and stained, their faces skeletal, dead. Strangely calm, she closed the box and stepped away.

In the hallway, she saw Silas, his back to her, crouched on his knees in vintage garb, the twill pants and dirty singlet of her former lover. She tried to speak, but a harsh sound of static came from her mouth. The noise startled him.

Dream Sara watched, queasy nausea in her gut, as he unfolded stiffly, his long, thick legs ratcheting mechanically as they straightened, until he was upright, facing away from her. She wanted to warn him about the box of dead women, but her mouth only spoke more static. Slowly, he turned towards her, and she screamed, abrasive static echoing in her ears. His eyes were gone, and viscous, blue-gray fluid congealed as it flowed from the holes in his face. Slowly, he began to drag his feet in her direction, and she turned to flee, the air around her feet thickening, holding her still. Across the room, she saw Iris the mother cat dart onto the top of another large, battered cardboard box, its eyes widening in horror as the box flaps collapsed beneath it, and it vanished into the darkness. Suddenly, Sara was at the edge of the box, her hand thrusting down into the blackness to retrieve the cat, but encountering something else, clothing, a feeling of coldness. Her other hand pulled the top of the box open, and deafening static screaming filled her ears as her eyes took in Silas, naked, dead, knees up against his chest, his arms crooked and painfully broken, a slicer embedded in the back of his neck. In a flash, his face turned to hers and he spoke.

"Sara! Sara, it's okay," She felt arms around her and she fought against the cables constricting her, arms swinging furiously. Her static scream turned to her normal voice, still screaming at unbearable volume and her eyes flew open, Silas's face inches from hers, his arms around her, her fists flailing at his side.

"Ssssshhhhh, Sara," he said quietly, holding her tightly as the dream endorphins drained and consciousness returned. "It's safe, you're safe, it was a nightmare."

She went to speak, then hesitated, certain that only static would come out, swallowing drily, her mind racing, appalled that she'd had her worst nightmare after the first night she spent with Silas since the lake house.

A brief knock sounded at the door then Embla burst into the room.

"It's all good," Silas said without turning. "Our girl had a nightmare."

"Sara?" April Veronica appeared behind Embla, terror in her eyes.

Struggling to speak and still unsure about her vocal cords, Sara forced herself upright as Silas released his grip across her shoulders.

"Can you pass me my water bottle?" he said, and Embla obliged. He brought the glass bottle to Sara's lips and she drank deeply, her throat so parched that it felt like the water was sliding over her esophagus without wetting it.

"Sorry you guys," Sara said finally. "Fuck…"

"Must have been a hell of a dream," Embla said. "We thought someone was getting killed in here."

Silas shot Embla a stern look.

"I've just…" Sara said, embarrassment mixing with the tendrils of the dream. "I've been having these recurring nightmares since I got here, they really mess up my head."

Silas settled comfortably beside her and she pressed against him.

"You were dead in this one," Sara blurted.

"Oh," Silas replied noncommittally. "Sounds gnarly, but hey, I'm alive and we can all go get coffee in a minute."

"I'm pretty shook," Sara said. "These dreams feel like they're building up to something."

"Most likely you are just reacting to the large amount of stress that you are under," Embla said, and Sara smiled at the woman's reliably methodical brain.

"Most likely, yes."

Embla glanced from Sara to Silas, then turned to April Veronica.

"I think you and I will go into town and bring back coffees and such for all of us."

Without waiting for a reply, Embla threw an arm around April Veronica and led her from the room, the door latch echoing as their footsteps moved down the hall.

"Silas, these dreams are just…" Sara shuddered against him. "They're disgusting, and they're a fucking greatest hits of triggering shit."

"You know what else they are?" Silas kissed her cheek. "They're just your subconscious under massive stress. I'm sorry they're so vivid, and

I'm also sorry we didn't anticipate your PTSD more fully. Have you had a bath since you got here?"

Confused by the sudden turn, Sara shook her head.

Another kiss, then Silas bounced off the bed and went into the bathroom. She heard water splashing into the tub and then he reappeared, in the bathroom doorway.

"No pressure at all, but if you'd like me to scrub your back," he extended a hand. Taking his hand, Sara pulled herself upright.

"That sounds nice," she said, kissing his nose. "But I need some alone time first. I'll give you a holler."

Silas chuckled.

"What now?"

"Uh.. while you're doing that I'll pop next door to a spare room and have some alone time too."

Closing the door behind her, Sara tested the bathwater. It was too tepid, so she turned off the cold, then used the toilet. Standing, she caught herself in the mirror. Despite her hair being a tousled wreck, she looked surprisingly good, her skin tone was clear and even, almost too clear. Getting closer to the mirror, she pushed and prodded at her chest and face. She'd never been vain, using mirrors more to make sure she wasn't a disaster than as a tool to apply makeup. She looked ethereally beautiful, like she had a filter on, her lips darker, the skin under her eyes light and smooth. She killed the water to the tub, stepping in one foot at a time, the water almost too hot to bear, crouching gingerly until she was submerged up to her chin, the water to the rim of the tub.

Swirling her hands in the steaming water, her skin delighting in the eddies that rolled against it, the opposite of the icy rain from the night before. Letting her mind wander, she hoped that Teddie was asleep beside Crina in New York, then her thoughts turned to the elders.

Today was going to be weird. The meeting with Stefanya had left her with a sense of hope, if only for Teddie. Then she remembered that she had forgotten to text Heather, and on top of that, she remembered that her phone was still in the pocket of her onesie, saturated and abandoned on the path to Stefanya's house. In New York, a sister losing a cellphone was one of the worst things imaginable. Here, it felt like little more than a minor inconvenience.

Slowly sliding her back down the porcelain, Sara let her head submerge and enjoyed the echoing silence, her mind harkening back to the night she and Marguerite went running in Riverside Park. It felt like a memory from childhood, not something that had happened recently, and it was followed by a pang of grief for Marguerite, a woman whose mysteries had died with her. The need for air forced her back to the surface, and she heard rustling out in the room, and suddenly the idea of Silas scrubbing her back felt very appealing.

"I'm ready for my body scrub," she called out, mortified when Embla replied.

"I'm standing here with a strong americano and some muffins, but sure, if you want."

"I thought you were Silas," Sara called back.

"I knew that," Embla said. "Your coffee and snacks are on the little table."

"Thank you Embla," Sara said. "Sorry I startled you."

"Not at all," Embla said, her foot tapping nervously. "Uh, Sara, when we got back last night, Fan found your onesie by the road, your phone was inside."

Sara winced. Of all the people in the world to find her fucking phone it had to be Fan.

"Uh yep, massive security risk number one at your service," she said.

"She thought it was hilarious," Embla said. "Don't worry about it. They took it up to the house to put it in a bag of rice to dry it out. And Sara?"

"Yes, Embla?"

"I don't blame you for ditching it. I got so sweaty at that show, I had to lose mine also. And I'll tell you one thing, you haven't lived until you've stage dived in a bra and panties."

"Didn't it hurt?"

Embla turned, lifting her shirt to show Sara a scrape all along her ribs.

"You fell?"

"April Veronica tried to catch me," Embla laughed. "Anyway, I will go back and have my coffee with her. She's feeling a little guilty."

After blowing Sara a kiss, Embla left, closing the door behind her.

Wondering where Silas was, Sara quickly ran the bar of soap over her body and face, slid back under for a quick rinse, and got out, drying herself with her new favorite indulgence, a fluffy towel. She took a second towel and wrapped it around her wet hair, stepping back into the room just in time to see Silas return.

"I was gonna scrub your back," he said sheepishly.

"Well yeah, I think I scared the shit out of Embla," Sara laughed. "Where'd you go?"

"I found a bathroom downstairs in the lobby," he smiled. "I gotta keep the magic alive as long as I can. Want to get back into the tub?"

Sara considered it for a minute.

"You know what?" she said eventually. "Yes, I would like to, but right now, I'm freaking out about seeing Fan and Amrita again. And before you tell me I'm being silly, guess who left their phone in the pocket of their onesie, and guess who found said onesie."

"Oh no," Silas said with mock horror. "Not the group of women high on April's weed liqueur? If anything, I should be embarrassed. They've been texting me. They quite accurately pieced our night together, and I fully expect a solid ribbing when we get up there."

Silas walked up to her and planted a string of kisses on her lips before turning to get his coffee.

"I'll need your help on this whole don't worry thing," Sara whispered. "Without worry, I'm nothing."

"Alles klar, herr kommisar," Silas said, opening a brown paper bag and tossing her a muffin. "I think it's gonna rain today, so let's dress accordingly."

"Right, and those bitches will come out in haute couture."

"Who cares? It's Iceland. If you see sun, dress for snow. And if it fines up later, I'd like us to go to the gardens, just the two of us."

Setting her muffin on top of the bag, Sara picked up her iced coffee and took off the lid, inhaling its delicious aroma before drinking half of it in one gulp. She needed caffeine to help banish the dream, which was proving particularly stubborn.

"I was talking to the girls," Silas said, lifting his own coffee. "They had a good night."

"I'm glad," Sara said, looking for somewhere to sit but not wanting to get her bed wet. "April Veronica could use some fun."

Setting his coffee down, Silas moved behind Sara and began to massage her bare shoulders.

"Oof," he said softly. "Feels like someone else could use some fun. Your back feels like steel cables."

"Shit, you're right," Sara said, leaning back. "I haven't stretched or done any yoga since before we went up to your place."

"You're having a rest month," Silas said, kneading her shoulders.

"I need to get back to it," Sara said, finishing her coffee. "What time are we expected up at the house? Actually, shocker, I have no idea what time it really is."

"We can go up whenever," Silas said. "I texted Stef that we were awake, she said they're cooking and getting ready, but there's no set time."

"It's crazy but after so long dealing with those women in New York, I see every open-ended plan as a potential trap."

"Not here," Silas said. "I think the thing that's hardest for you is, everyone here is on your side and nobody needs you to do anything for them."

Breaking from his grasp, Sara turned and put her arms over his shoulders. "If you wanted me to come to Iceland in 1964, that's literally all you had to say," she smiled, kissing him on the lips.

"Doubtful, but okay," he said, beaming, when she pulled back.

"Do you need to shower before we head up?"

He nodded.

"Okay, you do that while I get dressed. And Silas? Leave the door open, I want to watch."

The rain was light, but the whipping wind made it feel much worse as they trekked up the road to the house. Sara was grateful for her all-weather pants and her pink hooded slicker. Silas slipped on a muddy patch, and she grabbed his upper arm, steadying him.

"Good catch," Silas said quietly, "now we're equal." He shot her a sly grin.

To her left, April Veronica was smiling mysteriously.

"Someone's got a secret," Sara said, nudging her.

"Not really, I'm just excited," April Veronica said. "Sara, I had such a fun night, you wait, Fan and Ama, they're just, I don't know what I expected, but literally, if you told me they were my age, or even a little younger, and just, you know, regular, not changed, I'd believe you."

A rush of memories came to the front of Sara's mind. The first time she'd met those women, during the final days of the Purge, their scars still healing. Fan's single-minded training with an early Slicer, Amrita teaching her how to pour molten silver. She'd seen them fight, she'd seen them be tender. She'd never seen them be fun. She decided not to cloud April Veronica's experience.

"So the band was good?" she asked.

"They were so good," April Veronica enthused. "All girls, but not punk, like harsher, angrier, it just hit me like a wall. And Ama was in the pit, getting tossed around. I dropped Embla on her head. Fan was at the back, selling vegan food, I'm like, you know, just kind of blown away."

Blinking away visions of fierce warrior Fan manning a food stand at a university post-punk show, Sara looked along the road ahead. She wanted to ask if either Fan or Amrita had asked about her, but she knew that April Veronica would call her a thirst trap.

"Oh and also," April said, changing the subject. "If you want to, you know, stop the dreams, weed will do it."

"Huh?"

"Take weed at bedtime, you won't dream," April Veronica said.

"I've dreamed after taking it," Sara said.

"Then take more next time, our metabolism processes it really quick. Take it like a sleeping pill."

"Is there any left after last night?" Sara asked with a wink.

"I have a grow room," Embla said. "Everyone in Iceland does."

"I started making some batches of edibles before we left," April Veronica said. "There's already weed butter in the fridge. We can bake cookies when we get home."

"I am very good at making weed brennevin and also weed tequila," Embla chimed in.

Sara thanked them both, then squeezed Silas's hand, walking the rest of the way up to the house in silence, marveling at how stress-free her immediate life was, unless she thought of Teddie, Helsinki, Warsaw, Edinburgh, New York or her imminent meeting with the elders.

That's called denial, she chided herself.

Rounding the final curve, the house materialized in front of them in the rain, and as they drew close, the door opened, revealing Stefanya, barefoot in a black bodysuit, her hair freshly curled.

"Good afternoon," she called. "Come on in."

Pausing briefly in the small mud room, Sara untied her boots and left them there. She was about to unzip her jacket when Fan, shorter than she remembered, her hair in two small pigtails, bounced into the room and threw her arms around her.

"Sara, Sara, Sara," she said, her voice thick with emotion. "What a breath of fresh air to have you here." Sara returned the hug, keeping one eye open on the room, wondering where Amitra was. Seconds later, the petite Indian woman bumped the kitchen door open with her hip, emerging into the living room with a tray of hors d'oeuvres in her hands. Wearing a black bodysuit beneath a hot pink wool tunic, her trademark ruby bindhi and her long black hair trailing behind her, she set the tray on a small table against the rear wall, then turned to Sara, smiling and waving happily.

Unwinding herself from Fan's tight embrace, Sara walked across the room to Ama, who took her hands and gave her a once over.

"They've already got you dressed like a Reykjavik soccer mom?" she said, her accent, once Indian, now wildly British, surprised Sara more than the offhand comment.

"You missed a sexy onesie yesterday," Sara said.

"You were always such a tease," Ama said in a low voice before leaving her to go hug Silas, Embla and April Veronica. Sara felt an easy love in the room, and it took her words away.

As the sound of small talk filled the air, Stefanya reappeared with a tray of glasses containing what appeared to be blood, but on closer inspection was a shade too orange. Once she was done handing them out, she hauled an embroidered meditation cushion into the center of the windows, and sat, facing everyone. Without a word, Fan and Ama followed suit, and the other four took seats on the couch, facing them.

"This feels like a University peer review," April Veronica said.

"Not at all," Fan said. "We discussed it, and we agreed that for us to sit and just look at you, all four of you, together, would be a blessing for our souls."

"No pressure there," Silas joked, and Sara didn't know whether to laugh or cuff him. When the three elders on the floor laughed, she joined in mechanically.

"Sara, I feel that we should start by saying, primarily, that we love you, so much," Fan said, her voice booming in the open room, startling Sara, who'd forgotten that the tiny woman had the loudest voice of anyone she'd ever met. Unsure whether Fan had more to say, Sara leaned forward expectantly.

"That's it," Fan said with a quick grin. "I sense you are stressed, and I wanted to set you at ease."

Sara nodded. "Thank you, Fan. I love you also."

"She never writes, she never calls," Ama joked from the cushion beside Fan, and Fan whacked her on the leg. Sara decided to lean into it.

"Yes, I really should have bored you two to death with the minutiae of my last century in New York," she said with a misleading smile.

"Au contraire," Ama looked Sara dead in the eye. "You kept the lid on that crucible better than anyone in recorded history, at least for our kind. What happened when you took your eye off the prize is not your fault, rather, its savage violence is in direct relation to how effectively you kept it managed."

"I'm not sure I follow," Sara said cagily.

"It will become clear as we speak," Ama said. "You were visionary. Be proud of what you built."

"You built a vampire utopia," Fan said. "We left you alone on purpose, but I assure you, we watched you avidly, we watched all the Locks so closely."

"Without interfering," Ama added.

"Non-invasive zoology," Stefanya said with a small laugh. "Now please, I would like to begin with a toast, simply recognizing the amount of love and potential in this room."

Obediently, all seven raised their glasses, then drained them in a single shot. As hers was partway down, something in the taste triggered mild disgust in Sara, and she guessed that this was another synthetic. She forced herself to swallow it down and wasn't surprised when no intoxication followed.

"What was that?" April Veronica asked, wiping her lip.

"I invented it," Ama said proudly. "It's lab-grown plasma. I've been working very closely with Yukari in your Lock and several other scientist sisters." Sara knew Yukari led a full life in the science community, but she never suspected she was working with the elders. She wanted to ask if Ama had instructed Yukari not to reveal who she was working with. To be fair, Sara had also never asked.

"It tastes weird," Embla said. "This batch." Ama shrugged and nodded.

"Yeah, it's a bit off," she agreed. "I was playing around with protein levels and trying to see if we can use luteins as effectively."

"You're getting there," Silas said, turning to Sara. "Some of these experiments were like drinking boiled sneakers."

Stefanya angrily snapped her fingers in the air, in a circle. "Don't be sassy just because you finally got to bring a girlfriend around."

A crowd of booing rose up, making Sara smile. This was weird but it wasn't terrible, she decided.

"Okay, okay, fiiiine," Stefanya caved. "Bite me."

"Last night was fun," April Veronica tried to change the subject.

"It was amazing," Fan said. "Did you see me stage dive?"

"The stage was barely twenty centimeters," Embla laughed. "I know that's tall for a shrimp like you."

Fan flipped Embla a finger.

"It was high enough to fuck you up, kid."

Sara sat back against the couch, trying to figure out how to approach whatever was happening in this room. She'd expected this trip to be a pilgrimage of sorts, and she'd anticipated guidance from these elders.

They're not that much older than you, she reminded herself.

"So anyway," she began, and the room fell silent. "Hi! I'm Sara, and for the past two weeks, I've been living in a constant state of what the fuck, and it's not fun. So, is there more bad news or can I either relax or enjoy myself or both?"

"Well played, sister," Ama crawled forward and high fived Sara. "We are all nervous. But we have mostly good news to share, we've seen the future of our kind and it is –"

"Decentralized," Fan said from her cushion. "Locks are like lighthouses, and the seas have gotten rougher and rougher, and they're all in danger of getting swept into the sea."

"Yes," Stefanya said. "A Lock is like a tortoise hauling around a huge heavy shell, it's protection, but sure, you roll over on a hot day and you're dead in ten minutes."

Sara pondered their words, unsure of the full picture. It felt like she was watching something very precisely rehearsed.

"Stef told you that we plan to abandon the rules," Fan smiled at Sara. "As enlightened as those words were, once you write something down and say it's law, people subvert it for their own means."

"Which brings us to Desdemona," Ama said, standing slowly, her back pressed against the glass window, on the other side of which, raindrops joined and trickled.

"How do we solve a problem like Desdemona," Fan sang.

"By killing her," Ama said coldly, making April Veronica gasp.

"That won't work," Sara said. "The last thing we need is to canonize the witch."

"We do have something to share with you all, information," Fan said. "And after you hear it, you can tell us if you still want her to live."

Ama glanced at Stefanya, who stood in silence and left the room, returning with a tablet. She clicked it on and flicked at its surface and suddenly, the weird hiss of an audio recording filled the room. Sara looked around for the source of the sound. Sensing her question, Silas tapped her on the arm and pointed to circular speakers embedded in the ceiling.

The crackling continued for a few seconds, then they heard footsteps and a knock, then a door opening, then Desdemona's voice, tinny and flat.

"Marguerite, thank you for agreeing to this visit."

"What choice do I have?" At the sound of Marguerite's throaty rasp, Sara glanced at April Veronica, whose eyes were pressed shut.

"You have every choice."

"As far as you're concerned, my only choice is to do your bidding. This time, I put myself first. Confirming this girl was not a mistake, it was my right. And yet here you are, in my apartment."

Footsteps fell and suddenly the voices got louder, clearer. Sara guessed that Heather had bugged Marguerite's apartment, and the microphone was in the living room of her apartment, where the women were now seated. Where her body had been found. Why had Heather not shared this with her? Again, she felt the ground beneath her lose some of its solidity, and she squeezed Silas's hand.

"Marguerite," Desdemona's tone was condescending. "You have been among the best of my soldiers. And we are close, so close. Why have you thrown it all away on a child?"

"I've done no such thing," Marguerite spat angrily. "I was entitled to convert April Veronica, I have the credits, regardless of the future."

"Que idiota," Desdemona hissed. "I expected more from you, of all people. We had the numbers, once Sara is out of the way. Either you or Rosa would be Lock mother."

"No, it was always going to be Rosa," Marguerite said. "All of us who you sent, all *soldiers* in all of the Locks, we all are promised Lock mother, but that's a lie. You'll give it to Rosa, and I will get nothing. I have been so miserable, so lonely, banished to this shitty island because you want what? To punish Crina for leaving you behind?"

Silence fell for a period, then Desdemona spoke again.

"This child, where is she?"

"She is sleeping," Marguerite said. "You know what the first days are like."

"And you believe she will vote the way you tell her?"

"She trusts me, she will be easily convinced," Marguerite said, and Sara's heart ached.

"I'm sorry," Desdemona said. "That is not a guarantee. Marguerite, what has happened to you?"

"I could ask you the same thing. I look at you and I see hate, and anger, and also, I see a thirst for power. These are things we attribute to men. I'm sorry I agreed to this meeting."

"How dare you speak to me this way."

"I can speak to you however I want," Marguerite's voice was firm. "You haven't been my Lock mother for sixty years! You gave me instructions and shipped me here. I've done what you asked, I've been a miserable bitch, I've ruined every meeting, I've sabotaged everything, and yet, the wheels keep on rolling. And you know what? This next thing, it's not going to work, so finally, I think of me. I brought a woman into the fold who is inspiring and smart, the kind of woman who can help us enter a new era."

"You sound like Sara," Desdemona whispered, her voice dripping in venom.

"You know what? She's always been kind to me, always. Even though I've been fucking up her mierda every step of the way, she takes the time to ask how I'm doing. When was the last time you asked how I was doing?"

"Oh spare me," Desdemona's rage was brewing. "Are you a wounded child? Do you need your mimis? Does Sara care about your feelings? You've become such a pinche Americana, you make me sick, all this self-pity."

"What's done is done, Desdemona." They heard Marguerite stand with a sigh. "Now, please leave, and remember this: I ain't your bitch. Get out of here before I tell Sara everything."

"I will not tolerate betrayal," The implicit threat in Desdemona's voice chilled Sara.

"You are nothing to me," Marguerite spat. "You can leave now. I was stupid to ever let you use me."

"What's the American idiom?" Desdemona asked, her voice flat. "I'm sorry you feel that way?"

"I don't want you to feel anything for me," Marguerite's voice moved back into the hallway, growing tinny.

"Don't worry, I won't."

In Akureyri, thousands of miles away, they listened in horror as one set of footsteps moved slowly away from the living room, while another took two steps, then paused, then charged in a rapid staccato that ended with a groan, a thump and then the sound of something being dragged.

"Stop it," Sara hissed at Ama. "Stop it now." Ama pressed the screen on her tablet and silence fell, only to be broken by a sob from April Veronica.

Sara's mind swirled with the horror of this ghastly radio play. She watched as Embla comforted April Veronica, then looked at the three elders, all of whom were staring back at her.

"Do you know more, beyond what was on that recording?" Sara asked.

"A little" Ama said. "We have compiled a tracking system of movement between the Locks, and there's a lot of suspicious stuff coming out of Madrid. Every couple years, it seemed that a sister got recognized and needed to transfer out."

Sara nodded. It had become a running joke that either men in Madrid were way more attentive than men anywhere else, or these women were deliberately getting recognized as a means to escape Desdemona.

"You're telling me she was destabilizing Locks around the world, with a view to what?"

"All we have right now," Fan looked apologetic, "is that she hates you so much and that's become a hatred for the things that you stand for. She's conservative because you're liberal."

"She needs to be nothing like you," Ama said. "She's set out to destroy our world, because she wants to hurt you."

"She rushed to New York because she wanted to push the button in the Surrender room," Stefanya said. "She wanted to kill you."

"And in the days since your death," Fan said, making quote marks in the air, "she has supervised Surrenders in two Locks, all heavily populated by former Madrid sisters."

"Hate," Ama leaned forward, "is as addictive to women as it is to men."

"I need to go for a walk," April Veronica said, standing and leaving the room without waiting for a response. After they heard her close the door to the driveway, Embla stood and left the room too.

"That was a theatrical way to tell me something I already knew," Sara said to Ama. "That was callous."

"Life is callous," Ama replied. "I would have hoped you'd be more incensed to discover that at least two women you've cared for for over half a century were sleeper agents."

"Crina already told me that part, much more effectively," Sara said angrily. "I'm actually more incensed that one of our kind casually murdered a woman under my watch."

"It's more than one woman, under all our watches," Stefanya said, her voice calm. "We are talking, we are gathering information, but a lot of the elders who chose surrender in the last century may have been led astray by women trained by Desdemona. She's been working on this for as long as you've been Lock Mother."

A wave of black hate towards Desdemona blossomed in Sara's heart.

"So we kill her," she said slowly. "Then what?"

"Precisely," said Fan. "If we kill her now, her work will continue. The women she indoctrinated will continue to believe that they must continue her crusade."

"So, we have to discredit her?"

"No," Ama said. "We have to kill them all. Anyone who transferred out of Madrid."

"Right, of course," Sara said, sarcasm in her voice. "That's at least two women per Lock, five in Edinburgh."

"She's not the only one with a network," Ama said. "Did you train Theodora in combat? Is she effective with a Slicer?"

Sara rolled her eyes. "Yes, I trained her. Two centuries ago. And since then, she's lived as a pacifist. She's never touched a gun. She still cycles in and out of martial arts training, she's a black belt many times over."

"So, she's not good with a Slicer?"

"How, precisely does one get good with a Slicer? It's not like you can go around killing people as practice."

"I did," Fan said. "And I realize those options have... dried up in recent centuries."

"So let me get this straight, because I'm confused," Sara's voice was commanding. "We let Edinburgh take Surrender and then slaughter the remaining women who transferred out of Madrid at any point?"

The elders all shrugged and nodded at once.

"There has to be another way," Sara said. "Each of these women was welcomed into our way of life because they were exceptional, smart, compassionate."

"And now, they've been exploited by Desdemona," Ama said. "As we are learning, gender is no barrier to stupidity."

"That's no reason to kill them," Sara's voice was getting louder.

"We are forced to live in secret," Ama's steely eyes locked on hers. "At this point, that is the one tenet that remains unbreakable. We have to protect our secret."

Sara turned to Silas. "Did you know any of this?"

"No," Stefanya said. "He's been too preoccupied with you."

"I'd like Silas to speak for himself."

"Sara, no, I didn't know what Desdemona was up to, outside of the stuff that we've discussed, you and me." He turned to Ama. "Does my mother know?"

"Heather told her once she returned to New York. Heather also didn't know," Ama said. "We had her install microphones for us a few years back. We get the recordings. We archive them. We didn't listen to this until a few days after Marguerite's death."

"And you didn't think to let us know?" Sara's struggled to derail the anger blooming inside her, grateful that Heather hadn't kept this secret from her at least.

"We didn't have a way to tell you without telling you way too much," Stefanya said simply.

"And we don't intervene," Fan said.

Sara clenched her fists in her lap

"Sara, we respect your commitment to peace," Fan said. "We do not require or expect you to take part in anything we plan to do."

"Take part," Sara was incredulous. "Take part? I stand in opposition to any plan to kill a single person."

"Even Desdemona?" Sara hated it when Amitra used this condescending, wheedling tone, even after not hearing it for centuries.

"I'm committed to get to the end of my life without ever killing."

"We've created a world of soft bitches," Ama said to Stefanya. "I told you she wouldn't be into it."

Stefanya glared at Ama, then stood, her arms wide. She inhaled deeply, about to reply when the sound of the door opening interrupted her, and seconds later, April Veronica appeared, a determined look on her face, wet from tears and rain, followed by Embla a few seconds later.

"I didn't want to come back here," April Veronica began, an open palm splayed in Ama's direction, "But I guess you people are going to be in my life moving forward, and that's what made me come back."

Sara watched as the elders all shared quick, nervous glances.

"I'd like to set some boundaries," April Veronica stepped into the middle of the room. "Let's start with basic fucking respect. What you did just now was you all being extra, just for the sake of it."

Fan and Ama both stared at the floor. Only Stefanya met April Veronica's angry gaze.

"Wow, cool, you got some evidence," April Veronica continued. "Good for you. You don't have to be so bombastic, so careless in how you drop it. I know everyone expects the new girl to be quiet and just like some passive kind of student for y'all's great experience, but seriously, my sensitivity isn't my weakness, not one fucking bit. And if I can't get a guarantee that you will at least follow some sort of basic moral compass, I'm out."

A lone, slow handclap started on the couch down the way and Sara watched as April Veronica looked to its source, Fan.

"No, really, I mean it, kid," Fan said, her loud voice bouncing off the stone walls. "You're right. We totally fucked up. It was basically us as the cat bringing you guys a dead rat in greeting. We were just so excited to…"

"To be able to have a legitimate reason to kill Desdemona," April Veronica said sarcastically. "I get it. You're badasses. You killed a bunch of men. You killed Dracula. Oooohhh wooooh."

"I actually did kill Dracula," Fan said, nonplussed.

"I'll get used to that someday," April Veronica said, "since apparently I can't expect you guys to be mindful of other people. I mean, do the three of you just sit around jerking off about how fierce you used to be? Because that's a drag."

Sara's heart was bursting with pride. She considered jumping in when April Veronica took a breath, but she didn't get the chance.

"I didn't want to come back here at all," April Veronica's voice grew steely. "But if we keep on letting people get away with shit, nothing will change, and," she paused, looking around the room, "you bitches are as out of touch as Desdemona is. You still talk like feuding and ritual slaughter are the appropriate modern responses to a crisis. You're as dangerous as Desdemona, and not even in such different ways. Anyways, I guess I just came back to say that I don't need any training to be like you. I'm smart enough to save my own skin. I wish you well, but, Embla and I are returning to Reykjavik."

On the couch, Sara felt Silas's elbow nudge her gently. She slowly faced him.

"Go or stay?" he mouthed, and Sara felt her heart swell, she'd felt stuck in place, unable to leave, but he must have read her thoughts. By way of response, she took his hand and stood up.

"Well said, April Veronica," she said before turning to the elders. "You guys, she's right. The old ways won't help us, they won't help you, and respectfully, I can see that I'm not going to find the answers that I'm looking for here. Thank you for your... hospitality, I guess, and I wish you well but we're going to head home now."

It wasn't until the door closed behind them and they were almost to the first gate that they heard the loud, muffled argument break out behind them.

Chapter Twelve

Sara followed Silas down the hallway of the Reykjavik house, her hands knotted nervously behind the small of her back, her heart racing. Taking deep breaths to still her pounding heart and feeling stupid the whole time, she kept her footsteps in pace with his. It was only when they reached the stairs down into the living room that she realized she was totally hiding behind him.

"Ladies?" Silas called out into the living room, his voice echoing in the cavernous space. "I don't think they're here," he muttered, turning. "Wait, are you hiding behind me?"

Sheepishly, Sara nodded. In the four days since they'd returned from Akureyri, she'd spent every night in Silas's room, a large bunker room at the end of the other corridor from the living room. The skylight in his room was much larger than hers – "You're the first person I've shared this room with" Silas told her proudly – and three nights ago, they'd lain naked in each other's arms while the northern lights exploded and unfurled above them.

"Not intentionally," Sara mumbled, then scurried behind Silas's back again when she heard the door to the outside open.

"Did you call us?" Embla's voice echoed in the room.

"I did," Silas replied. "We did. You probably can't see her because she's hiding behind me, but we wanted to let you know that we've decided that Sara is going to be sleeping in my room from now on, which makes it our room, not my room."

Behind him, Sara realized she'd been holding her breath, but Silas's nervousness made her splutter laugh, and she stepped out from behind him.

"Well at least I can say I've seen a five-hundred-year-old woman blush," Embla said.

"You guys," April Veronica chimed in. "Why the big announcement? We know. Your rooms are in different wings, it's not like it was a secret. Wait," she paused, "am I missing something? Is there a vampire custom I don't know about? Shit, are you guys registered someplace? Is this a gifting thing?"

Sara stepped down into the living room and walked over to April Veronica, wrapping her in a hug. "I just feel stupid, is all."

April Veronica and Embla exchanged knowing eye rolls, then Embla sat on the couch and patted the cushion next to her. Obediently, Sara sat down and instantly was enveloped in Embla's cold arms.

"How long were you outside?" Sara asked, rubbing her palms along the woman's chilly skin.

"We got to talking," Embla said. "And somehow several hours passed." She elbowed Sara. "I'm sure you're familiar with the concept."

"Lil bit," Silas said, walking over to the open kitchen. "I don't suppose anybody went food shopping? And by anybody, I mean you two because..."

"Yes, it's hard to go shopping when you're either naked or in bed or both," Embla said, making herself laugh.

"And... uh..." April Veronica stammered, "I want to, I mean... uh..."

"What she's trying to say is that statement applies to both of us," Embla said, and Sara leaned against her.

"This makes me so happy," she murmured into Embla's sandy blonde hair.

"Me too, definitely," Embla said.

"Congratulations, you guys," Silas said. "Shall I order a celebratory feast?"

"Sure," April Veronica pushed past him and switched on the warming oven. "You two look like pandas with those black eyes, so let's get that under control first."

Pulling himself up onto the kitchen counter, Silas buried himself in his phone.

"Anybody want anything in particular?"

"Don't worry about me," Embla said. "The vegan delivery options are limited. I have some leftovers."

"Is it okay if I get a steak?" April Veronica's voice was small, and Sara's heart swelled with happiness. To see this extraordinary young woman weather the hell she'd endured since her conversion and emerge in a relationship was almost overwhelming her. She wished Marguerite could have seen this.

"Sure, just make sure you floss before you kiss me," Embla said with a laugh.

"Now who's blushing?" Sara tickled her, and laughter filled the room until it was interrupted by a discordant electronic buzzing that Sara hadn't heard before. Silas tilted his head, listening.

"You expecting anyone, Embla?'

Beside her on the couch, Embla shook her head. "Who would I expect? Almost everyone I know is here." She sat upright. "Oh shit. Almost."

"What?" The hairs on Sara's arms rose.

Silas pushed himself off the counter and walked towards the front door. As he passed Sara, his phone buzzed in his hand and he looked at it.

"You guys," he said, his voice low. "The elders have brought us dinner."

"This is what I was telling you about," Embla said to April Veronica. "They never give a warning, they just turn up."

Sara looked at April Veronica, whose stricken face told her all she needed to know.

"Remember," Sara whispered to her. "Every girl is a slayer."

April Veronica giggled quietly.

"How are we gonna get through this?" she said softly. With a conspiratorial glimpse around the room, Sara took April Veronica's arm and almost lifted her off the couch as she leapt for the kitchen.

"They're probably loaded up with that synthetic crap," she said when they reached the counter, her hands already grabbing for the half-full bottle of blood liquor. "Shots?"

Nodding eagerly, April Veronica took the bottle from Sara, popped the cork and then tipped the bottle to her lips. Sara watched as the girl's throat bobbed with each swallow, grabbing the bottle from April's hand as she swooned against the counter, a thin rivulet of blood trickling from the corner of her mouth. Making sure that Silas and Embla were preoccupied with frenzied tidying, Sara tilted the bottle and sucked on it as if it were a baby bottle, filling her mouth and gulping down mouthful after mouthful, knowing she was overdoing it.

As she began to lose consciousness, she set the bottle carefully on the counter then turned until she felt the support of the counter against her lower back, and she pulled April Veronica to her, waiting for the light to come back into her vision.

She heard Silas's voice, but it sounded like he was talking to her from another room, then the sound of muffled laughter and she forced herself to open her eyes. As her vision cleared, she saw Stefanya in the middle of the living room, pulling a large green canvas cart, its contents covered by a Buddhist prayer shawl. Behind Stef stood Fan and Amrita, and another cart, this one filled with brightly wrapped gifts.

"Sara, April Veronica," Stefanya walked toward them. "We owe you an apology. We were so awful, so rude to you, no wonder you need a drink."

In her arms, she felt April Veronica stir, so Sara helped her upright.

"Hey, you guys," April Veronica's voice was fuzzy. "Did you come to kill me? Is that what this is?"

In an instant, Fan was at April Veronica's side, wrapping her in a hug.

"No, *qīn qīn*, we came to make things right."

Ama appeared beside her.

"You were right, April Veronica," she said, stroking the girl's hair. "We've been alone in that house, plotting this moment for years, and when the moment arrived, we just kind of word vomited all over you. It wasn't until after you left that we realized just how grossly old-fashioned we are."

"Oh," April Veronica said, shock on her face. "Yeah, you were pretty intense. I don't know how this works. Am I supposed to apologize now?"

Fan hugged her. "No, what you said was fucking perfect, sister. I've always said that we should listen to the youngsters, the newly made, because your perspective is fresher than ours."

"She was so upset," Ama said as she shucked off her floor length puffer, revealing a pink and gold sari and bright orange hiking boots. "Apparently I made us sound like angry old witches, right my love?"

"Well you did," Fan said testily.

"Not this again," called Stefanya. "Hey Silas, are you too drunk to help an old lady lay out a picnic?"

Smiling, Silas flipped off Stefanya, then effortlessly pushed the large couches away from each other. Embla retrieved a batik blanket from the cart, shook it open and spread it on the floor.

"You guys have been busy," Sara said to Fan, who shrugged. "We were about to order delivery."

"Can I get you guys anything?" April Veronica pushed herself off the counter, wobbled, then fell back against Sara.

"Probably best if you just come chill out," Embla said, pointing at the couch. Obediently, April Veronica tottered to the couch and unceremoniously plonked herself down on it. Sara gazed around the room, Stefanya and Silas opening brightly colored Tupperware containers and setting them on the picnic blanket, Ama picking up a large, flat wrapped gift and bringing it to her.

"A peace offering," Ama said as she handed the package to Sara, who didn't break eye contact as she tore the paper open to reveal a bolt of lush violet silk, embroidered in golds and yellows and blues.

"Ama this is beautiful, thank you."

"Do you remember?" Ama's eyes twinkled playfully, a smile lifting the corners of her full lips, and Sara nodded as a memory flooded her.

"Tell me!" April Veronica called from the couch.

"The first time I met Sara," Ama said warmly, "I was dressed to impress, I wore my best sari, and do you remember what you said Sara?"

"Yes," Sara said dutifully. "I had never seen such bright, vibrant fabric."

"You said I looked like a dragonfly," Ama said, her hand cupping Sara's cheek. "A beautiful dragonfly. Anyway," she cleared her throat, "I bought this fabric for you, I dunno, Fan, when did I buy this for Sara?"

"I think it was in the 1940s, thereabouts," Fan replied from her seat on the picnic blanket, a pair of chopsticks in her hand. "Can everybody get down here? I'm starving."

Ama took Sara's hand and led her to the center of the living room, and they sat together, across from Stefanya and Fan. Silas sat on Sara's other side, and Embla and April Veronica sat beside Stefanya.

"Before we start," Stefanya said, causing Fan to groan. "Tonight, let's get to know each other, and keep the talk of war and murder to a minimum."

"Or," April Veronica raised her pointer finger, "how about we don't talk about violence or killing at all?"

"It was nice of you to tell us you were coming," Silas said with a smirk.

"Please," Stefanya snorted. "Even with two minutes warning, you guys needed a drink. We didn't want to turn up to a house full of drunk vampires."

Ama rose to her knees and gathered a stack of bamboo plates, then busied herself serving each person. When everyone had a full plate of food in front of them, she smiled.

"Everyone, eat."

For the next little while, they all lost themselves in the food, Indian stews and Chinese dumplings. Embla rose and returned with a tray of glasses and several bottles of Guinness, smiling as she handed everyone a glass of the inky, foamy booze.

"I literally don't know where to start with the talking," Fan said suddenly. "I've been so focused on, you know, what's going on and how we will deal with it, that now that it's forbidden, my tongue is tied."

"You don't always have to talk, you know," Ama said, blowing Fan a kiss. Grumbling, Fan resumed eating. Turning to Sara, Ama continued. "Sara, if you're up to the discussion, I'd really love to ask you something."

Caught off guard, Sara's eyes narrowed cautiously. "Sure, go ahead."

"How did it feel to accept Surrender?"

Instant silence fell around the room and Sara felt everyone's eyes on her. Instead of anger, she fully understood the urgency of Ama's curiosity. She inhaled a long, shaky breath.

"It didn't feel like anything familiar, but it also didn't feel significant, except that I had to accept that there were things I wasn't going to be able to set right," she said quietly. "I wished I could tell Silas some things, I wished that he was okay and that he would escape. And I wished I had more time to talk to Teddie."

"So selfless," Stefanya said.

"But what about you? How did you feel about the end of you?" Ama's eyes burned into Sara's.

Sara chuckled. "You sound like me with my patients, and this is going to disappoint you but I didn't feel much of anything, it just felt unavoidable, inevitable, it felt like I was on a moving object and the destination was out of my control so I just busied myself with writing my letter to Teddie and then it was time to take the pills. I just watched the fire until I drifted off. I'm sorry, that's kind of what happened. I know it's not what you wanted to hear."

"Actually, it's exactly what I wanted to hear," Ama said. "Fan and I talk about it all the time, like if we knew we had just a short time left, what would we do? And you chose to love, to caretake, and that is probably the best response I could have hoped for."

"That's kind of how I've lived my entire life," Silas offered, and everyone turned to him. "At the start of every day, I tell myself this day is all I have."

"That sounds exhausting," Sara said.

"It is, but the results outweigh the effort," he said, taking her hand and smiling.

"I'm terrified of spontaneity," Sara said. "For five hundred years, I've second guessed the consequences of every action. I can't be in the moment."

"My child," Stefanya blew her a kiss. "Spontaneity is the new black. Just throw caution to the wind and live your fucking live, sweetheart."

"It's not that simple," Sara began, and Stefanya raised a palm.

"If everyone just lived their lives and left everyone else alone to live their lives, we'd be in an era of unprecedented peace," she said, dipping a naan bread into a bowl of spicy lentils.

"You do realize that the entire vampire world wants my boyfriend dead, and if they knew I was alive, we could announce our relationship on a wanted poster?"

"All problems are temporary," Fan said. "Nothing stays in focus anymore. Just wait it out, and you'll be forgotten. In a year or two, you guys could walk right past the Madrid Lock unnoticed."

"If it's even standing in a year," Ama said under her breath, and Stefanya cuffed her across the back of her head.

"So, April Veronica," Stefanya waved a piece of naan in the air theatrically. "Have you gotten to play Who's Your Favorite Movie Vampire yet?"

"Nice segue, mamma," Embla said. "Good coverup."

"You're going to give me whiplash," April Veronica said. "I don't believe I've had the pleasure. Are there rules?"

"No," Embla said dourly. "Just ridicule."

"Fine," April Veronica said. "I'll go last."

"I'll start," Stefanya said through a mouthful of naan. "Hang on." After swallowing loudly, she continued. "I have a new one! Bill Paxton in Near Dark. Stupid brutal and super heteronormative, but that goofy grin gets me every time."

"I don't think mine can ever change," Fan said.

"Blah blah blah Salma Hayek in From Dusk Til Dawn," Ama groaned theatrically.

"Bite me," Fan blew her a kiss. "And the answer is Salma Hayek in anything."

"Her name is Salma Hayek Pinault these days," Embla said.

"Fact check on aisle two," April Veronica said, and the pair of them fell about laughing.

"Guess mine?" Ama directed her question at Fan, who slumped theatrically.

"She never played a vampire," Fan said. "Disqualified."

"Bitch, Janina Gavankar was hot on both True Blood and The Vampire Diaries." Ama gathered a handful of rice from a bowl, threatening to throw it at Ama.

"Technically not a vampire," Embla said without looking up.

"Okay, I don't remember their names, but I'll go with those women from Vampyres," Ama said.

"Marianne Morris and Anulka Dziubinska," Embla said. "I looked them up last time we played this."

"That's my girl," Stefanya said, beaming proudly at Embla.

"You're going to hate mine," Sara said, pausing for effect. "Udo Kier in Blood for Dracula. He's just so over the top and those massive blue eyes. Teddie and I got really high and went to see it in 3D and it really stayed with me. Teddie hated it."

Silence hung in the air and Sara immediately regretted mentioning Teddie. Sensing the tension, Embla leapt into the void.

"Teddie was right, that movie is insulting," she said. "Anyway, for me, I really like two vampires. Klaus Kinski in Nosferatu, he's just so creaky and sinister. That's what I want to be when I grow up. But I also love Johnny Alucard in Dracula AD 1974, because he made it all look like so much fun. What about you Silas?"

"He doesn't like this game," Ama said.

"It's not the game I dislike," Silas said patiently. "It's that I don't go see vampire movies."

"Is it okay to not give an answer?" April Veronica asked, hope in her voice.

"Not tonight," Stefanya said. "Come on, Si, give us an answer, any answer."

Silas set his cutlery down on his bamboo plate and looked into Sara's eyes.

"This isn't a vampire movie, but this is the first movie that reflected my life to the point where it made me cry, I literally couldn't move when it ended."

Sara watched as everyone stopped eating and turned their attention to the strange man seated beside her. Without lifting his face, he continued talking, his voice low.

"There's a movie called Orlando, it's about someone who lives forever, they change gender, they reinvent themselves almost organically. It's got Tilda Swinton and it's..." he paused sheepishly, his gaze down. "Anyway, I know it's not right, Embla, but it's all I got."

Sara took his hand and squeezed it, then went to speak but her voice was gone. Swallowing, she tried again.

"Silas, I... I love that movie too, so much."

"Oh hell nah," April Veronica said. "You guys are too much."

Sara threw her arms around Silas and buried her face in his neck, inhaling deeply, drinking in the scent of him, his sweater, his hair, as she felt something inside her give a little, something that still cost her too much to believe in.

Her reverie was shattered by the fake camera noise of phones taking photos and she pulled back slightly, to see everyone else at the indoor picnic taking photos of them.

"No paparazzi," she said with a warm smile.

"You get it, right,?" Fan said. "For us, for our kind, to be able to be open and in love with each other, to be supportive and receptive and just, gosh, this is what we should be doing, right?"

"If you meant to make a toast, you should have told me to get the goblets ready," Embla said, standing and heading to the kitchen.

"I see what you're doing there, Embla," Stefanya called after her. "Trying to take yourself out of the line of fire, hoping that nobody asks you what's going on with the new girl."

"I didn't say my favorite vampires," April Veronica yelled suddenly.

"Nice try," Stefanya purred with a cheeky grin. "Tell us your vampires, and then tell me your intentions with my daughter."

"Whatever," April Veronica grinned. "I'm team Twilight. All of 'em. I want my vampires pale and angsty and I want them to glitter and stutter and stammer and then be like super strong."

Stefanya looked over at Embla and nodded. "Looks like you found your perfect match."

"I don't sparkle," Embla called out as she set seven goblets in the warming oven.

"You do to me, honey," April Veronica said, a beet-red blush sweeping over her cheeks before the words were even out of her mouth.

Sara watched as Fan and Ama tilted their heads until they touched, and their hands sought each other out, then she noticed Stefanya, sitting in silence and sighing absently while she picked at the food on her plate.

"What about you Stef?" Sara blurted. "Got a secret lover stashed away?"

The elder shook her thick black hair with a laugh. "Gimme a break, I just became an empty nester," she glanced at Embla. "I've been so preoccupied with this one, I did the full-on single mom thing, so right now, I'm... adrift. It's not a priority."

"It's also not so easy here in Iceland," Embla said, returning with a tray of drinks. She handed them out carefully, and Sara realized that she'd made both synthetic and real. "Too small of a country, and the people have such strong memories. You had that nice gentleman in Brighton. Is he still around?"

"He likes me too much," Stefanya said quietly. "I don't want to hurt him, so I've been distancing with love."

Embla crouched beside her maker and threw an arm around her, hugging her tight. Stefanya rested her head on Embla's upper arm, then entwined her fingers around her wrist. In any other living room on earth, Sara thought, this would be an average, functional dinner party. For Cursed people, however, this was definitely new ground, and she felt that recurrent surge of optimism in her chest.

"Did I get a present?" Silas said. "Or just Sara?"

Stefanya snatched the goblet from Embla's tray. "Can we at least drink first?"

"That's real blood, mum" Embla said.

"Yes, I know. Silas can have my synthetic for being such a brat. Is it any wonder I drink?"

Each of them leaned forward, and Embla guided them to whichever glass was right for them.

"I'd like to make a toast," Sara said, and everyone nodded.

"My name is Sara, and never have I killed-"

"Not even yourself," Fan burst out, making Ama crack up.

"Too soon," Silas said, a smile playing at the corners of his mouth.

"My name is Sara," she pushed on. "And never have I killed anyone or myself." She paused. "This," she looked each of them in the eye. "This is what I've always dreamed of for Lock life. Just love and laughter and small talk. My toast is, may we be blessed with an eternity of days and nights just like this, surrounded by friends and love."

"I know we aren't talking serious tonight," Ama said, "but yes, this is the alternative to Lock life that we've been trying to make happen. Instead of trying to fit in or pass as regular society, we just retreat and be insular and live."

"Is that what you two did?" April Veronica's eyes were still glazed from her blood drink. "Because, by my estimation, you two are the longest relationship in the history of this planet. What's your secret?"

"That's easy," Fan said, kissing the top of Amrita's head. "You just have to find a heart you can trust. Trusting people is relatively easy, which is why it's usually disastrous. You have to get to know someone's heart, and then, if you can trust that heart, everything else will be easy."

"Yeah," Ama said. "So easy she needed to be away from me for like forty years."

"Once," Fan said. "Once, and you know why."

"I know why, yes, and honey, it felt like eighty years."

"Can I ask?" April Veronica leaned forward.

"You can always ask,' Ama said.

"But it doesn't mean you'll get an answer," Fan finished the sentence.

"It's worth a try," Embla said, wrapping her arms around her girlfriend.

"Why did you separate for approximately forty years?" April Veronica looked expectantly at Ama, who glanced from Fan to Stefanya and back to Fan, who was smiling impishly.

"I wanted to live in Hawaii," Ama said. "It's that simple."

"Nothing is ever that simple," Fan said gently. "The full story is that she wanted to leave this life behind, she wanted to stop being whatever we are, and just go and I dunno, surf and eat pineapples."

"It was just after they started making sunscreen, and I was just so tired of all this training and hiding and living in cold places. I just wanted to be a nudist pacifist beachbum."

"So we had an argument, and she left," Fan said simply.

"Was it worth it?" April Veronica's question clearly took them both by surprise. After a moment of silence, they both shook their heads in unison.

"No," Ama said. "I was impatient and unrealistic and ultimately, our journey as the longest-lasting couple in human history, or more simply put, our love, is my purpose. Without Fan by my side, I kind of just farted around. Of course I got bored in Hawaii after what, Stef?"

"I think it was two or three years," Stefanya said, her eyes squinting.

"And then what?" Sara was gripped.

"Then she was a proud bitch, and I decided to play hard to get," Fan said. "Plus, I was heartbroken that she actually went. I misjudged it, I thought it was just that I wasn't giving her enough of something, love, attention, spiritual growth. Then I was pissed. So by the time I heard she wanted to reunite, I was angry, and I wanted to have something of my own, like she had Hawaii, , an adventure on my own terms. Sunblock gave us freedom. I traveled too. I joined different humanitarian groups as a scientist. I traveled South America, I spent years in the Galapagos, Micronesia, Australia, New Zealand."

"She chose places that were remote, places I'd never suspect."

"It wasn't about you, my dear," Fan said gently. "It sounds so corny, like something a divorcee would embroider on a pillow, but I needed to find myself."

"It sucked for me," Stefanya said, draining her drink and holding the empty glass up to Embla, who immediately took it and went to the kitchen. "I had to stay in one place as their anchor, and also both of you bitches made me promise not to breathe a word of your whereabouts to the other. We were beginning our life here, but I was doing a lot of the groundwork from Bucharest and my little fortress in the Black Forest."

"It was particularly hard to get from Palau to Bucharest," Fan laughed.

"Do you remember we used to package blood liquor in professional looking bottles?"

"That's right," Fan laughed. "And we would declare them as Duty Free booze."

Sara leaned back into Silas's arms, envy burning inside her. While she was caretaking a rotating roster of women in New York, Fan and Ama traveled to countries she had deemed as impossible destinations.

"I've always dreamed of seeing the Galapagos," Sara said. "And Palau, I want to swim in the jellyfish lake."

"Me too," Silas said, kissing the top of her head. "It's like we have a shared bucket list."

Embla returned with Stefanya's drink, taking her seat beside April Veronica.

"Tell them how you got them to reunite," she said, making Stefanya smile, and, Sara noticed, puff up like a pigeon.

"I tricked them," she clucked. "I said that I was considering Surrender."

"On a fucking *postcard*," Ama said dramatically.

"Whatever," Stefanya sniffed.

"Yeah, that sucked, that mission of mercy dash from Burma to Reykjavik," Fan said. "At least you only had to come from Bucharest."

"Burma is Myanmar now," Embla said to April Veronica, who nodded then turned to Ama.

"Was it weird when you saw each other?"

"She burst into tears," Fan crowed.

"Of course I did," Ama said. "I was so ashamed, and I was worried. What if you met someone else? What if you liked being a solo traveler?"

"I did both of those things," Fan said, "and yet, I always felt like half of my heart was somewhere else."

"And here we are," Ama said. "Eternally inseparable from that day forward."

Extricating himself from behind Sara, Silas went to the kitchen and grabbed two bottles, one of blood, one of synthetic and returned, filling glasses on his way.

"I thought we were getting gifts," he said when he returned to his place.

"Oh yeah," Fan and Ama sprung to their feet, pulling a cardboard box from the little cart and walking to April Veronica.

"We respect your pacifist nature," Fan began.

"But," Ama continued, "it's simply too risky to be captured, be assaulted, by anyone. Without training, you'll just trigger your adrenalin, and at full strength, in a year or two, you'll literally tear the attacker apart, and then it's police and jail and we've gone to great lengths to avoid any combination of those two."

"So first, this," Fan held aloft a taser. "Never, and I mean never, go anywhere without this."

"And then, we begin your training. Nonviolent, sure, but it's tae kwon do, martial arts."

"Lots of yoga and stretching," Stefanya added from her spot on the floor.

"You don't like the idea of a Slicer," Ama said. "But you're a likely candidate for an attack from one of Desdemona's bitches, so-"

"I made you some jewelry," Fan continued, raising a leather hinged box that Ama helped open. On a bed of cream satin lay a set of silver rings, each one topped with a razor-sharp blade that twinkled menacingly in the lights from the ceiling.

"They click together," Fan said. "If you put them on in order, left to right, they will interlock into kind of a mini Slicer."

"Won't get right through any vertebrae on a horizontal strike, but they'll work vertically," Ama said, too enthusiastically for April Veronica. "Sorry, I can see that upset you, but in time you'll understand the need for this, and the training that comes with it."

"I can see the need now, I just don't have the stomach for the act. Killing shouldn't be the first answer to a problem."

"I was the same way," said Embla. "Let's look at it as doomsday prepping."

"I am okay with dying on the first day of a zombie apocalypse," April Veronica said quietly. "It's just a little tricky to get my head around suddenly being Viola Davis."

"The queen," Stefanya said. "That's who I want to be when I grow up."

"We can train together," Embla said. "It was against my beliefs at first also. Now I see it as a necessity."

"Will it be fun?" April Veronica said.

"No," Fan said brusquely. "It's not like a montage in a movie. It takes a while. But we have time."

"We got you something else, April Veronica," Fan went to the cart and returned with a very thick, very old book. Effortlessly, she handed it to the young woman, who nearly dropped it due to its weight.

"It's The Anatomy Of Melancholy," Fan said. "Do you guys remember? We were obsessed with this."

Sara's eyes widened and a reverie pulled her in before she could derail it. She was living in Cadiz, with Desdemona and Crina, when they'd gotten word of a book that promised to expose the secrets of the human soul. Eventually, they'd been able to get a merchant to bring them a copy, and for years, they learned English and read and reread it, marveling at the insights that were particularly pertinent to the existential issues they faced. She'd gifted her original copy to Teddie, and it still sat proudly on her bookshelf. She looked at the version in April Veronica's hands, clearly a new edition, and the fact that it was still in print filled her heart with joy.

"You guys, this is fascinating," April Veronica said.

"It's the first self-help book," Embla said. "We can read it together."

Smiling at Embla, April Veronica began to thumb through the pages, pausing to read the introduction. In silence, Sara watched the tendrils of warmth spread around the room, love and humor flowing between these strange humans, like her and yet, kind of not. She wondered if she'd ever truly be able to lose the rigid sense of responsibility she'd carried for eons, then she was distracted by Silas's strong hands, squeezing her forearms reassuringly, and she felt like it might be possible.

"Hey," she said suddenly. "I thought there were gifts for everyone. You said everyone. Does Silas get anything?"

The elders all burst out laughing, and Stefanya rose from her cushion.

"Oh, Sara, we nearly forgot," she said through her laughter. "Of course we got something for our boy."

Turning suddenly, she presented a perfectly giftwrapped rectangular box, and Sara chuckled at the "it's a boy" wrapping paper.

"Don't encourage them," Silas whispered. "They always use that paper." Stefanya tossed the present to him and he caught it deftly. "Do I have to open it now?"

The elders nodded, their eyes sparkling.

With a deep sigh, Silas tore off the paper, revealing a box containing a pair of what looked like dog clippers.

"My boy," Stefanya said, barely able to contain herself. "We know it's been a hot minute since you had anyone, you know, intimately, so we can only imagine what a wreck you've let your bathing suit area become."

"They say that these don't nip at your wrinkly bits," Ama said, as if she was talking to a child.

Sara turned to see a beet-red blush completely consume Silas's cheeks and forehead, his mouth ajar in protest.

"Ahem," Sara said. "Whilst I acknowledge that this gift is primarily for my benefit, without telling tales out of school, I can assure you that my boyfriend is a very well-kempt gentleman."

"It's waterproof," Fan said. "You can tidy yourself up in the shower."

"I'll keep that in mind," Silas said as he set the package on the couch beside him.

"Don't be mad, Si," Stefanya, still laughing, came and put a hand on his shoulder. "You're a five hundred and something year old Romanian man. It's not like you read GQ, and nobody likes a shag carpet down there."

"Seriously, you guys, it's okay to stop," Silas said. "Sara, April Veronica, welcome to my life as the only son of the fucking witches from Hocus Pocus. This is why I hate birthdays, Christmas, any day that involves gift giving."

"We never get to shop for men," Ama giggled. "We get to live out our weird fantasies at your expense."

"Wait, you celebrate birthdays?" Sara was aghast. She didn't know her birthday. She knew Teddie's, of course.

"We chose birthdays a couple hundred years ago," Silas said. "Because someone," he paused, glaring at Stefanya, "heard about another reason for gift giving."

"When is your birthday?" Sara pushed herself upright.

"We all tried to guesstimate based on seasons. My mom remembered that I was born a few weeks before the winter equinox, so I settled on the sixth of December."

"Oh good, well at least I didn't miss it," Sara said. "I was born just before the last frost, probably around the end of March."

"Well I promise to make it up to you next year," Silas said with a laugh, and the room dissolved into smaller conversations, Embla and April Veronica sharing their birth dates, Silas scolding his aunts for humiliating him, Sara peacefully enjoying everything that was happening around her until suddenly, a chorus of various phone alerts rang out at once, silencing everyone.

"This can't be good," Stefanya said, pulling her phone out of her pants pocket. Sara pulled her phone out, unsurprised that she didn't have an alert. The only people that had her number outside of this room were Crina and Heather.

"Oh Sara," Silas said. "Teddie's been made."

Sara's heart froze. To be made meant to be recognized. She turned and Silas held his phone in her direction. She took it, scrolling through a series of posts on Instagram, all in black and white, by a photographer, each one titled Who Is This Ageless Woman? The first post showed Teddie seated in front of a young Jimi Hendrix, her hair a wild afro. In the next she was sitting in the front row of an early Patti Smith show at CBGB, a man's fedora on her head, wearing a sleeveless torn t-shirt with the union jack on it. The third photo was of her sitting piano-side, watching Bill Evans at the Village Vanguard in the late fifties. The last photo was of Teddie, her hair in braids, at the last show at CBGBs, in 2006, again standing in front of Patti Smith, now grey and careworn, while Teddie looked identical to the way she looked in the photo from thirty years earlier.

Sara's stomach froze and she scrolled up and down. In two of the photos, Bill Evans and Patti Smith in the seventies, Sara was in the photos too, but looking away from the camera. In the recent photo, at the closing of CBGB, she stood next to Teddie, her eyes locked on Smith, her hair a messy ponytail.

"Isn't that Heather at the Hendrix show?" April Veronica broke the silence. "The things you guys have seen..."

"This is so bad," Embla said, her fingers dancing across her phone and she followed link after link. "This has gone viral," she continued. "People are saying that the photographer has used photoshop but they're offering to show complete negative proof sheets."

"Fucking hell," Ama said. "Just what the poor girl needs right now."

"You guys, Desdemona is saying that she needs to be locked down in Madrid," Fan said.

"And who do you think set up these photos?" There was panic in Sara's voice. "The chances of one photographer being at all these shows is literally zero."

"Nobody plays a long game like an immortal," Silas said, "but do you really think Desdemona did this?"

"Of course she did," Stefanya said, fury in her voice. "And this, the deliberate publicity of it, crosses a line I never even thought of adding to the rules."

"We have to kill her," Ama said flatly. "I don't care if this isn't technically breaking a rule, we don't know if anyone out there suspects us, we don't know if we have watchers. This has been my literal life-long stress. She's inviting scrutiny when our entire existence has been secret."

Sara looked at Fan and nodded slowly. "You're probably right," she said quietly. "She is doing this because Teddy stood up to her, she knows she'll never be able to control her so she's making her life impossible."

"She's making all of our lives impossible, potentially," Stefanya said, anger fraying her voice. "First she murders, now she tries to pull the rug out from under all of us? You guys, if she has photos of the New York girls, you can bet she has photos of women from all the Locks."

"She's weaponizing social media," Embla said. "Against her own kind."

"Teddie is already at breaking point," Stefanya said. "Desdemona's trying to push her into Surrender. She knows she'll never agree to transfer to Madrid."

"Can we bring her to Iceland?" April Veronica's face looked hopeful, but her words hung in the air. Nobody said anything, and in the silence, Sara looked around the room. When nobody spoke, she stood.

"We need to get her out now," Sara said, her voice strong. "I don't need permission, I need to go."

To her relief, Silas stood and took his place by her side. As her mind began to overload, visualizing countless threats to Teddie, Sara began to feel faint, until she felt Silas wrap his arms around her and pull tight.

"Sara, we will leave tomorrow," he kissed the top of her head. "I'll call Heather now."

Chapter Thirteen

Nervously, Sara wrung her hands together, irrationally certain that she would be arrested as soon as the plane landed at JFK. Arrested for what, exactly, she did not know. She had become unaccustomed to international travel, and customs felt like a bottleneck of problems. As she shifted position in her first-class seat, something she'd done every minute since boarding the plane five hours earlier, she glanced at Silas, asleep beside her. His head was turned her way, his full lips parted slightly, his eyes darting below closed lids, his breathing deep. His palm lay face-up on the bench between them, and she curled her hand inside his, his fingers closing slightly around hers in slumber. His stubble was on the verge of full beard, thick and full, obscuring the even, pale skin of his cheeks.

Turning away, she opened her window cover, instantly blinded by the sunlight reflecting off a rippled sea of clouds. Blinking while her eyes adjusted, she pondered the madness of what she was doing: arriving back in America without so much as the simplest of plans, aside from saving Teddie.

Closing her blind, she straightened herself up, pulled her blanket up to her chin, and tried breathing exercises, but she could feel that the plane was tilting forward, which meant it had begun to descend, and soon she'd be breathing the same dusty air her lungs had loved for centuries.

And then they'd arrest her.

She couldn't shake the ridiculous thought. And testing out this new passport at JFK felt riskier than when she used it at Boston. Glancing at him again, she felt the now-familiar tug at her heart. He'd been so understanding and supportive, he offered to fly into less-restrictive Canada or Mexico and tackle a land border. He'd even suggested flying to the Caribbean and sailing into New York. All of which sounded romantic and lovely, except for the whole Teddie going viral ticking bomb thing.

An early morning call with Heather had made things worse. Teddie had informed the Lock she'd rather take Surrender than transfer out of New York. Quickly, Yukari had dosed Teddie with Xanax in addition to her antidepressants, and Heather locked her in her apartment. Heather assured them both that absolutely nobody was able to get into the Surrender room. After that phone call, Silas insisted that they both leave their phones behind in Iceland to avoid any tracking that they might be unaware of. Silas had a random Icelandic phone in his pocket so they could order a car when they landed. Sara felt cut off at a time when she wanted in-flight Wi-Fi and regular updates on Teddie's safety.

Crina and Heather both tried to talk Sara out of the trip, fully aware that their entreaties were pointless. Heather went about preparing a safe house for them to stay in when they arrived.

"There are ten women in all of New York who'd be surprised to see me," Sara had argued, wanting to stay in a hotel. "It's New York, Sara," Crina scolded her. "The first person you bump into in New York City is always the last person you want to see."

So, as things stood, Sara and Silas were headed to a brownstone on East 90th St, not far from the Lock compound as the crow flies, but due to the vagaries of New York geography, it may as well have been on the moon. Sara couldn't remember the last time she'd been to the Upper East Side, always feeling repelled by its strange, sleepy bourgeoisie, like she'd wandered into a film set or a social experiment for rich old people. It was strangely arduous to cross the city from Upper West to Upper East, and on top of that, nothing exciting ever happened there.

Why the hell am I thinking about the Upper East Side? she wondered angrily, as the grinding of the plane's wheels lowering rumbled her feet. She pushed her window shade up again, happy to see nothing but gray cloud flashing upward and panicked drops of rain skittering over the double glass. Soon, they dropped below the cloud cover, and the expanse of a steamy New York City afternoon opened below her like an endless tapestry of grays and silvers and terracotta, the river flowing like mercury on this overcast day.

Her heart swelled and tears sprang to her eyes, surprising her. She was home.

Placing a hand gently on Silas's thigh was enough to wake him.

"We're landing," she said quietly, and he smiled, blinking away the sleep, plopping one of his large, warm hands over hers and squeezing it.

"You look happy," he said, his voice still fluffy with sleep.

"I guess I was homesick," Sara said.

She leaned over and kissed his soft lips. When she pulled away, he was smiling too.

"I was homesick for that," he said.

An hour later, after breezing through customs with a cold, nervous sweat on her brow, they were in a good old-fashioned yellow cab, creeping slowly through Jamaica, occasional glimpses of the New York cityscape thrilling her. An almost clandestine silence fell over their ride, as if even their taxi driver might be a spy, and Sara fidgeted nervously, wishing she could focus on one thing, anything, and get lost in a reverie to kill time.

Now she understood why Crina always traveled with a video game.

Eventually, they crossed over into the City and began wending their way to what Silas assured her was the "safest of safe houses." After habitually traveling to the West Side for over a century, Sara was surprised when the taxi stopped midway between First and Second in front of an imposing brownstone that was mostly obscured by a thickly verdant tree.

As Silas paid the driver, Sara stepped out of the taxi on the driver's side, jumping when the trunk opened automatically. She heard Silas get out on his side as she lifted the two suitcases out and set them on the street behind the cab. She reached up and grabbed the top of the trunk and pulled it down, revealing a short woman staring straight at her. A scream escaped her lips.

"Well that's a nice greeting," Heather said, mock indignation on her face. With a belch of smoke, the taxi lurched out into the street, and Sara, overwhelmed, remained stock still.

"I'm not going to bloody well hug myself," Heather said, walking to Sara with her arms open. In seconds, Sara was engulfed in her friend's arms, Heather's face pressed against her chest. It had been a long time since they'd hugged, and Sara always forgot that Heather was so much shorter than she was. Sara hugged her back, hard, smiling when she felt several vertebrae pop. To Sara's horror, Heather burst into tears.

"Now now," Heather sobbed, breaking the hug. "Let's get you inside quickly."

Sniffing away the tears, Heather wiped at her eyes with the sleeve of her shirt, turning to face Silas. "C'mere you big lug," she said to Silas, darting over and giving him a similar hug. "Thanks for taking care of our lass."

"Any time, auntie," he said, lifting her off the ground.

"Put me down," Heather said , her voice still thick. "Welcome to my short-term rental."

Turning, she scampered up the sandstone steps and unlocked the door with a set of keys from her purse.

"This counts as a surprise," Sara said to Silas as she lifted one of the suitcases and began to ascend the steps.

"You can blame me for this one," Heather called out from inside the house.

"I'm sorry, I knew you'd be pissed," Silas said, appearing beside her.

"You can carry her over the threshold if you like," came Heather's voice.

"Don't even try it," Sara said, stepping into a long dark hallway that could have been any one of the hundreds of New York City houses she'd been inside over the centuries. Dark wood paneling, threadbare carpet on the hallway runner, a familiar smell of dust, cooking, paint and upholstery. She followed Heather into an expansive living room, freshly painted judging by the smell, two deep blue midcentury couches, a large flat television, and curiously empty bookshelves.

Once Sara got inside the darkened interior, she turned to Heather.

"What's wrong, Heather?"

As Silas closed the door behind him, Heather went to speak and broke down, leaning back against the arm of an overstuffed tartan sofa. Panic flooded through Sara and she flew to Heather.

"Is Teddie alright?" she said, gripping Heather's arm too tightly. Heather yanked her arm away, nodding.

"Yes, love, Teddie is fine, it's..." Tears consumed her.

"Heather! What's wrong?" Sara's concern was turning to angry fear, her mind racing through countless possible tragedies.

"Edinburgh is dead," Heather said between sobs. "I got the message an hour ago. They're gone."

Sara engulfed Heather in a hug, feeling her sobs echo in her chest. Sara met Silas's wide-eyed surprise.

"Can I get you anything?" he asked softly.

"I need a whisky, pet," Heather said, pushing herself out of Sara's embrace. "Sorry, I've soaked yer bloody shirt, Sara. You'd never know it, but I'm bloody happy to see you."

"Seeing you makes me feel like I'm home," Sara said. "I love you very much. Here, sit down."

Sara ushered Heather onto the couch, then sat beside her, sitting so close that their hips were pressed against each other.

"I don't know anything else," Heather volunteered. "There was just this bullshit email from Desdemona saying it happened and the sisters requested privacy so there was no video. Short and sharp. Sara..." Heather's voice cracked. "I've been talking to my friends there ten times a day, they all told me that they were nowhere near making that decision."

"Maybe they had voted to not discuss it outside of the Lock?"

"I hope that's it," Heather said as Silas appeared, handing her a very full tumbler, mostly whisky, a few rocks. Heather's hand shook as she accepted it and brought it to her lips, sipping slowly until her sobs subsided. "Thank you, love."

"I'm so sorry, Heather. And I'm sorry that I put so much work on you when you clearly could have been doing other things."

"Don't be daft," Heather said. "This is me home. You're me mate. This is what I do. Now I just need to keep myself busy and get a good night's sleep and I'll see it all a bit more clearly."

Heather took another sip and then set her glass on the coffee table, smoothing the front of her skirt with her palms.

"So, this place, we own it?" Sara asked, knowing Heather would welcome the distraction.

"Well, not exactly," Heather said. "I own it, I bought it when I first got here, I run it as a short-term rental."

"Everybody needs an escape hatch," Sara quoted Heather's words back at her, and smiling, Heather nodded. Silas appeared beside her.

"Full disclosure, Sara, I've stayed here before," he said. "I hope I don't get in trouble for that." Sara shrugged, relieved that these disclosures were getting less irritating.

"Do you want the grand tour?" Heather sprang from the couch and headed for the kitchen. Sara stopped her.

"Actually, I think we're good," Sara glanced at Silas. "He can show me around later. How long are you allowed to be out of the building? Can we talk?"

"I do need to get back soonish," Heather said absently, continuing into the kitchen.

Silas kicked off his shoes and set himself down beside Sara, resting one hand on her thigh. Sara smiled at him and he kissed the tip of her nose. From the kitchen, Sara heard Heather puttering around, glasses clinking. She rested her head on Silas's chest, finding peace in the beating of his heart.

"Okay, lovebirds," Heather quipped. Sara looked up in time to see Heather walking back into the room with three mason jars of blood, a bottle of pinot noir and three glasses on a tray.

"You really are the hostess with the mostess," Sara said. "I'll give you five stars."

"I don't do this for every tenant," Heather said, setting the tray down and pouring.

"I'll say," Silas joked. "The last time I stayed here, all I got was a bag of stale Cheetos."

"The last time you stayed here, you had hair down to your arse and a beard to match," Heather said, handing Sara a very full glass of wine.

"So," Sara began, gulping down half a jar of blood without waiting for anyone to cheers her. "Are you okay to talk?"

"As long as it's not about Edinburgh," Heather snipped. "I need to keep me denial up til I get home."

Sara took her hand. "How are things on West End?"

"Right to business I see," Heather said, handing Silas his jar and then drinking half of hers in one gulp. "In a word, annoying. If you mean Teddie specifically, she's numb. She can't see a way forward, which explains the Surrender talk. I was thinking we'd get you two together tomorrow."

"Yes, this has been so cruel," Sara said. "She's not untrustworthy, can you bring her here?"

"Not here," Heather said sharply. "This is my secret, and trustworthy or not, I've learned that a secret shared is a secret no longer," she paused, winking at Silas. "She's still too unstable for me to risk all of this on her."

"Oh right, of course, please, I'll just pop over tonight and ring her buzzer then, shall I?"

Heather shrugged. "If you're going to be like that..."

"I'm not going to be like anything," Sara said testily. "But all of a sudden, I'm on the flipside of who makes the rules, and I just am supposed to what? Guess my way into the available options, or are you going to tell me what you've planned?"

"I know you're feeling a bit out of sorts," Heather wiped out the rest of her jar, then poured the glasses of wine and handed one to each of them. "I'll heat you up some more deep red to take the edge off. Sorry, I underestimated. Pardon my manners."

"Where would you like to meet Teddie?" Silas turned to face Sara.

"Well it depends entirely on where I'm allowed to meet her," Sara said, with a bit more snark than she intended. She made a mental effort to dial it down a notch, knowing that Heather's heart was as broken as her own.

"I don't know her," Silas said, ignoring her tone, "but I can't imagine this is going to be a quiet meeting. Let's figure it out."

Closing her eyes, Sara took a deep breath. Adjusting to being told what to do was weird at best, but accepting help was even harder.

Heather returned with two ornate bronze goblets.

"Now now, lassie," she said, handing one to Sara. "None of us have much freedom right now, I know it's rough. There's been a lot to get used to."

"I know that," Sara said. "I'm just not used to everyone around me handling me with kid gloves."

"It's fine," Silas began, and Sara cut him off angrily.

"Stop being so fucking patient," she snapped. "It's not your fucking fault. It's mine. Fuck. There. Now we can all get on with planning meeting my internet-famous suicide-adjacent daughter who thinks I'm dead?"

In silence, Heather met Sara's gaze, then glanced down at the goblet of warm blood in her hands. Sara knew Heather was right, she'd feel better if she drank it, but right now, her agitation was all she had to stop a torrent of guilt.

"Damn, I'm sorry," she said quietly. "I'm way out of line."

"Drink up, lass," Heather reached over and pressed the bottom of the goblet to Sara's lips. "You'll love this," Heather continued as Sara drank. "The Teddie story made the Post today. It'll blow over, these things do, but there's a lot happening, to be sure. I have to get back and sort out a nursing degree for Imani so we can find her work. Yukari is buying blood in bulk, and hopefully we can phase out the nurse nonsense too. Teddie is presently pretty knocked out, and by the look of ye, some Xanax might not be a bad idea. There's some in the cabinet."

Finishing the fresh goblet in one gulp, Sara felt it finally hit the spot and a calmness settled over her. She wondered if Heather suspected just how high her needs remained. As her vision cleared, she heard Heather take a breath, and a hundred years of friendship told her that she was about to speak. Sara slowly raised a single finger.

"Ssshhhhhhh" she said. "Just shhhhhh."

Allowing herself to slump back against Silas, Sara leaned into the stillness, not a thought on her mind. Gradually she became aware of sounds, Silas breathing so close to her, a truck accelerating somewhere distant, and she let her eyes flutter open.

"Sorry I'm such a bitch," she muttered.

"Us old bitches don't switch gears quickly," Heather clucked.

"Don't make excuses for me," Sara pushed herself upright. "I'm being a child. I am alive because of you two. I mean," she paused, looking from Heather to Silas and back again. "Seriously. Why am I even trying here? Just tell me where and when I can see Teddie and I'll take it from there."

"It'll be very early tomorrow. Are you free?" Heather asked enigmatically.

"My whole future is free," Sara said. "Any chance I can get some more…"

"Wine? Sure," Heather bounced off the other couch and vanished into the kitchen.

"You're quiet," Sara said. Silas shrugged and nodded.

"That's still quiet," Sara slugged him on the arm.

"We've been inseparable for three weeks," Silas said, rubbing his arm theatrically. "I don't think Heather wants to hear about that."

"Absolutely zero interest in your sex life," Heather said, reentering the room with a fresh bottle. "Fuck ton of interest in your meeting with the elders."

"Pish," Sara said, knowing it would make Heather smile. "Wait, how long since you've seen them?"

"Oh, lordy, it's been a donkey's age," Heather said, pouring the wine. "I let Crina handle them."

"I'm not sure if handle is the right word," Sara said. "Heather, they're batshit. They're like a weird cross between like Kill Bill and the suffragettes. The night we were supposed to meet, they blew me off because an all-girl hardcore band was playing at the university and they needed to sell vegan food to the students."

"And stage dive," Silas added.

Heather raised an eyebrow. "That tracks," she said. "And I'm not going to lie, it also sounds like a bloody good night out."

"I'm sure it was," Sara said. "But their response to all of this Desdemona bullshit is to let the fire burn out, no matter how many good, decent women die in the process."

"That's what they're saying," Heather said. "But you and I both know that they're all itching for a battle."

"Oh yeah, that too," Sara said, switching to wine. "But wait til I tell you how their meeting with April went."

Heather leaned forward and raised an eyebrow.

"I'll tell you later," Sara shook her head. "Now that we've said her name, has there been any movement on Des?"

Now it was Heather's turn to sigh and roll her eyes.

"She's told Yukari that if Teddie resists coming to Madrid, she will come and get her."

Sara sat bolt upright and Heather placed a hand on her thigh.

"Don't react, love," Heather said. "It's classic Des and you know it. Hot air. We haven't told Teddie, and I'm only telling you because I don't want to get in trouble when you find out later."

"Fair," Sara said. "I'm on the warpath against secrets."

"It's true," Silas nodded. "She's got a good right hook on her."

"And you've got your work cut out for you if you're going to war against secrets with any Cursed woman," Heather said with a sniff. "All of us are ninety per cent secrets."

"Yeah, I'm figuring that out myself," Sara said, waving her hand around the living room. "Secret houses.." she pointed at Silas. "...secret sons. You know. The usual."

"Sara, Sara, Sara," Heather said with a smile. "You're the only one without secrets, as far as I know. When this is all over, ask Teddie about her secrets. The lovers she kept from you. The girlfriend she wanted to make but didn't have credits for. It's human nature to keep important things close to your chest."

Sara closed her eyes, feeling adrift again. This time she refused to let herself get bogged down in self-recrimination.

"I'll bring that up with her after I tell her that I'm not dead," she said flatly. "I'm sure she'll welcome the conversation."

"And with that," Heather stood, draining her wine on the way up and setting the glass on the coffee table, "I'll be off. But be careful and don't leave this house without telling me. Oh, I brought you these."

Reaching into her purse she produced two AirTags, handing one to each of them. "Carry these at all times."

She handed the small discs to Sara and Silas and moved for the door.

"I'll be in touch about tomorrow, sooner than later. Now, I'll leave you two lovebirds to it."

"Heather," Sara got up and went and hugged her old friend. "Thank you so much, again, and sorry I'm such a bitch."

"That's fine, love," Heather giggled. "It's not like it's a new thing."

Chapter Fourteen

After wandering around the various rooms and floors of Heather's annoyingly secret Airbnb, Sara couldn't settle on a room in which she felt safe enough to sleep. All the rooms had one door, and no potential escape hatch. The two front rooms had windows but she didn't feel like leaping into a tree. Tamping down a growing sense of paranoia, she meandered from room to room, surprised by the lack of personality in the décor. She heard Silas pottering about in the kitchen downstairs. Heather had been kind enough to stock the kitchen with anything that they might need, but strangely, no cooking smells had wafted up to her. She wondered what he was doing, too irritable to bother finding out.

Plonking herself down onto a twin bed in a small room on the second floor, Sara was overcome by a rogue wave of disconnection. It felt like she was seeing New York through frosted glass, everything obscured and at a distance. Being on the East Side made it oddly more intense.

Silas appeared in the doorway.

"You're worse than Goldilocks," he said. "I can hear you going from room to room. I'd be sad if this bed is just right, because there's only room for one of us."

"It's not that," Sara said, patting the bed. Silas came and sat beside her, taking her hand. "I don't know this house. I don't feel safe here. And I also don't feel like I'm in New York."

"You really hate the Upper East, huh?"

Shrugging hopelessly, Sara leaned her head on his shoulder. "That might actually be part of it, I don't know this neighborhood, which is ridiculous considering how long I've lived here."

"Not if you consider how deep your ruts were for the past hundred and some years."

"I mean, I've spent more time walking around Bushwick than I've spent walking around this area."

"So what will make you feel comfortable? Do you want to go to a hotel?"

"Do you know a hotel that has a bolthole at the back of every room? Because that's the hotel I need right now."

"We can go to the upstate house." He squeezed her hand.

"I have to be back for Teddie tomorrow."

"Which is probably also stressing you out."

"Not really, I know how that will go. It won't be easy, but it will be a relief."

They sat in silence for a long time, Sara listening to the sounds of the city, finding them not familiar enough. Too few sirens, no trucks, and an alarming absence of raised voices from the street.

"Do you think you can sleep here?"

Sara shook her head.

"What if Desdemona has people here and they followed Heather?"

"I already thought of that," Silas said quietly.

"I'd actually feel safer back in my old apartment," Sara said wistfully. They fell into silence again, and Sara began to think about leaving the building, not knowing if Heather had been followed, if there was a sister from Madrid waiting behind a tree. She knew that Heather would always use a different exit from the compound, but every train of thought resulted in a new unfounded suspicious, and she fell into a reverie, pondering the extent of Desdemona's cold war.

"Do you think we can call any of the elders for advice?"

Silas wrapped an arm around her shoulders.

"Might take a minute," he said quietly, pulling his phone from his pocket. After checking his VPN was on, he sent an encrypted group text, his phone pinging almost immediately with a reply.

"Well you're not going to like this," he said with a chuckle. "Fan says when she's uncertain of her surroundings, she lives on public transport."

Sara groaned. "Why was I expecting something actually doable?"

"Wait, there's more." Silas read in silence, the phone pinging as more replies came in. "Houseboat? No. Police cell? Um no. Oh wait, this might work. How pissed do you think Heather would be if we pulled up some of the stair risers? We can sleep on the top floor, in shifts, with the steps in the room with us. If anyone tries to come up the stairs in the dark, they'll fall through."

"I'd say that's ridiculous, but then you have to consider what those women have survived. Sure, let's vandalize Heather's secret income property. She won't mind."

"Well that's sorted. Shall I order some dinner?"

"Because I can't seem to do anything right, I really, like right now urgently, need to get out of here."

"Not sure I follow..."

"Silas, I can't shake the feeling that Desdemona has assassins waiting on the street, and the worst part of it is, that wretched, stupid bitch is ruining my New York. I think that's what's got me so riled."

"Fair," Silas said. "So how's about we cover up in hoodies and facemasks and go for a walk?"

"Will we bring a Slicer?"

"No," Silas said, causing Sara's head to turn sharply toward him, a look of anger on her face.

"Why are you smiling, Silas?"

"Because I have something better… Fan gave me a pair of tasers so intense they make the victim black out. We have one each."

"Do you have a minute for some quick fight training? I'm afraid all of mine has been blade focused?"

"Sure," Silas tousled her hair. "Do we have to wear clothes?"

Sara kissed him briefly, laughing.

"Yes, or we will never get out of here."

By the time the two hooded figures emerged from the brownstone on East 90th St, darkness had fallen. The taller one moved quickly, darting as fast as he could without arousing suspicion, across the street and back, circling each tree on the block as he headed east, finally stopping at the intersection and giving a thumbs up sign.

Smiling beneath her N95 mask, Sara sprinted up beside him.

"So, where are we going?"

"I thought you were hungry?" Silas's eyes were playful above his mask.

"After all the blood we just drank?" Sara laughed. "I'm good for a little while."

"Excellent," Silas took her hand and led her along the street until they were standing at a pier.

"What the hell is this?" Sara said looking around. "They have ferries up here?"

"My point exactly," Silas said, pointing to a ferry boat puttering into the dock. "Feel like going for a little sail?"

A weird feeling of warmth, completely different to the bloodbuzz, suffused Sara with an amber glow. She realized it was love, seeping deeper into her bones.

"Sure," she said, her voice coming out several octaves higher than usual. Silas didn't seem to notice, and she was grateful. They filed onto the ferry, Silas showing tickets from his phone to the conductor.

"So, you planned this?" Sara asked. "You knew we were going to take a ferry so you bought tickets?"

He shook his head. "Sorry, Dr Holmes. I love taking the ferries around the city, I've been doing it since I got here."

"Oh, they used to terrify me back in the.." she looked around the Ferry at the desultory commuters. "You know. Back in the day."

"I threw up on the Brooklyn Ferry once," Silas said. "The river was so rough."

"Wait, do you even know where this is going?"

Silas shook his head.

"First rule of spy club. Never know your destination."

"And what if our destination doesn't have food?"

"It's New York, there's always food."

Sara smiled and leaned against him.

"Thank you for going the extra mile today. I know I'm not easy."

"You're not as hard as you think," Silas said happily. "I figure that tomorrow night, we'll be sad and drunk, so tonight, let's party."

Sara chuckled. "Do you know how long it is since I've done anything that could remotely pass as partying?"

"Lemme guess," Silas said. "I bet your nineteen seventies were wilder than your nineteen eighties."

"They were, indeed," Sara said. "But not as wild as my eighteen nineties."

"I'd like to hear about it," he smiled. "I love a good party, or at least the idea of going to a place and that space being open to conversation, or hedonism, or both."

"Do you think we'll ever be in a phase like that again?" Sara faced Silas, her hand around his upper arm for stability as the ferry crossed choppy waters.

"I dunno," he said, thinking. "Those parties were also very invasive and strange, I suppose. Excess was acceptable then. The drugs of today are quieter, more insidious. You're not going to go to a party with a pocketful of fentanyl and GMO weed that would put an elephant on its ass."

"You're right, I'm never going to do that." Sara smiled, gazing out the bow windows at the twinkling lights across the river.

"You feel any safer here on the water?"

Sara nodded and rested her face against his chest, staying like this until the ferry docked.

"Welcome to Astoria," Silas said as they prepared to disembark.

"Really? You can get from the Upper East to Astoria in ten minutes?"

Laughing, Silas guided her up the gangplank and out onto the street. Glancing over her shoulder at Manhattan, Sara felt the tension slip from her shoulders. Twisting her head left then right, she smiled when her vertebrae cracked loudly, sending fireworks along her spine.

"Someone needs a massage," Silas said.

"You offering?"

"Always," he said. "Now come on, I just made a reservation and they won't hold it if we are late."

A short walk later and they were seated in an intimate Italian restaurant called Vesta. A kaleidoscope of scents was making Sara salivate. Moments later, a wave of tiredness washed over her, and she pushed herself back in her chair, stifling a yawn.

"You okay?" Silas's eyes were glittering in the candlelight from the table.

"I just got used to Iceland time, so hello again, jetlag," Sara said. "And we still have to get home and rip up a flight of stairs."

"I'll take care of that. What do you feel like eating? Apart from a good rare ribeye?"

Sara quickly pointed at a slew of things on the menu, and Silas placed their order.

"You look very beautiful tonight," Silas said. "Despite everything, it seems that New York agrees with you."

"I knew this racy hoodie and jeans combo would get you," Sara said dismissively. "And yeah, it's good to be back but I don't know if it's the City per se, or if it's unfinished business. No matter how tomorrow goes with Teddie, I'll feel better when it's done."

"And what about after?" Silas leaned forward.

"After I see Teddie?"

Silas shook his head, his curls bouncing. "No, after all of this, this whole cycle of change that you're in. What would you like to do after?"

So many thoughts rushed Sara that she was grateful for the arrival of their bottle of wine, and she took advantage of the time that Silas spent tasting the first pour to ponder it.

She didn't know. The problems in her world were so big, she couldn't see past them. Until Silas asked the question, she hadn't even seen a future beyond tomorrow. She had been so focused on talking to Teddie that she'd seen the reunion through a needle's eye.

Silas held up his wine for her to cheers, smiling as she left him hanging.

"Sorry, did that push you down a rabbit hole?"

Blinking away cobwebs, Sara laughed and clinked her glass against his.

"You really did," she said. "I actually have never gotten as far as seeing anything past this current Teddie and Desdemona tangle. And subconsciously, I think I still believe it will all just go back to the old ways."

"I'd say the chances of that happening are kinda sorta, at best," Silas said quietly.

"Wait," Sara set her wine down as a thought hit her like a shock. "Have you ever met Desdemona?"

Silas nodded. "I wouldn't say met exactly, but I've put myself in her path a couple times, just to see how she presents to the outside world."

"Did... your mom... have you do that?"

"Some of the times, yeah. Some of the times, I did it of my own volition."

"How many times have there been?"

Silas counted in silence for a minute, a mild panic rising inside Sara as the time went on. How many fucking times had he been around Desdemona? With mild disgust, Sara realized she was jealous.

"I'm gonna say eight times," Silas said, taking Sara's hands. "And most of those interactions were a long time ago. Did my mom ever tell you she's considered," he paused, switching to a whisper, "killing Desdemona a number of times?"

Sara sat bolt upright. "Hell no. She has always said that she's equally proud of both of us."

"Weird," Silas said. "And sorry, not to downplay your feelings, but mom has always suspected that she shouldn't have made Desdemona. And for the last fifty or sixty years, she's been certain."

"I literally don't have room for that information at the moment," Sara said, smiling at her new clarity about Crina's delicate parental juggling.

"Understood," Silas didn't let go of her hands. "So, do you think you'll want to stay in New York? Let's try that one again."

"My kneejerk reaction to that is, yes I want to stay here," Sara looked around the dimly lit room, taking in the faces of the New Yorkers around her, all involved in their complex lives, lives that intersected briefly with hers in this room. "I love so much about being here. I know you are thinking Iceland, but just this, what we are doing now, taking a ferry I never knew about to a part of the city I've ignored, it's all new. And I think that's key for me being satisfied in such a long life, the constant discovery of new things in an old framework."

"I can see that, completely."

"You're not hurt?"

Silas shook his head. "Iceland is an escape hatch, a bolthole, I've never stayed there longer than six months. Don't feel like I'm trying to make you settle down there."

"Oh, good," Sara said, watching his face intently for a reaction that didn't come. "I don't know anywhere else, I've literally never thought about moving. I'm way too attached to that building. Silas, it was so fun to plan it, to work with all these unrelated architects, and then when the thing was finished, your mom and I-"

"You knocked down the walls connecting all the back passages?"

"Of course you know that."

"Yeah," Silas said sheepishly. "I guess when mom planned some of it with you, the idea was that she would tell you about me, and I'd be able to live there, in those protected interior rooms."

Whenever Silas revealed these things, Sara felt a sense of completion, an ancient puzzle piece falling into place in her mind. She remembered Crina's insistence on these rooms, and how confused she'd been that the rooms only had one entrance. "It's just a last resort," Crina explained at the time. "Better to be safe than sorry."

Then it occurred to Sara that Silas must have been very hopeful that he'd be allowed to move in, become part of Lock life.

"Silas, did you have your heart set on moving in with us?"

He looked away, his shoulders moving up and down with each breath, before nodding.

"Yeah, but I understood the reasoning," he said, not meeting her eyes. "Mom saw your potential as a Mother, she said she wanted the building to be a place where you could mold all of the sisters who passed through, and that was more valuable than having me live in the shadows inside it."

"I'm so sorry, I really am," Sara reached across the table and hooked a finger around his bristly chin, pulling his face back to hers. "I need to get better at seeing your life outside of the lens of my own. I promise I'll try to get better at it."

"In hindsight, she was right," Silas whispered. "Look at the women who've passed through, Lindsey is running the London Lock on the template that you founded. Imani was desperate to join you. Yukari knew that the only place she could do her virus studies was here, because she knew you'd be open to the truth of science. It almost feels like mom saw all of this shit in advance, New York is now a battlement against the rest of the world."

"Did your mom tell you what she saw?"

"Not completely," Silas said. "Her reveries are one hundred per cent long game. As she's gotten older, she sees everything strategically in a way I still can't comprehend."

"And yet, I nearly died in one of her long games" Sara's voice was bitter, she still couldn't shake the idea that making her go through with Surrender was unnecessarily cruel.

"She's ruthless," Silas said. "She knew you'd survive. She was certain."

"I mean, it *had* been a while since my last deeply scarring life event," Sara sipped her wine, and smiled when a server delivered plates of appetizers, brussels sprouts, fresh bread, butter.

Silas refilled her glass, watching as Sara buttered a slice of bread, then heaped a mix of appetizers onto her plate then ate in silence.

"Is there anything I can do to help you ahead of tomorrow?"

Sara shook her head and continued eating, pushing to see if Silas was always comfortable in silence with her. She hated testing him but sometimes it was easier than engaging. He always seemed to read her cues effortlessly and was now intently making his own plate of food, meticulously buttering a hunk of bread from edge to edge, then sprinkling some salt across the top.

"Holy shit," Sara said. "I totally forgot about salting the butter."

"How? How the hell did you forget? It's the most delicious thing on the planet."

Nodding, Sara took the salt grinder and ground it over the bread she'd just buttered.

"I forgot a lot of stuff, Silas," Sara broke her silence. "I had my day to day, that was enough."

"Sorry, my enthusiasm for salty buttered bread just got the best of me."

Placing her cutlery on the table, Sara fixed her gaze on him.

"Moving forward, I'm gonna need a lot less sorry from you, if that's okay," she said gently. Silas fixed her with a curious stare. "I'm not a baby, I'm not fragile and I know that you had this long, unpredictable life while I was having my long, oh so predictable one. But every time I stumble across some info and it takes me a minute to unpack it, you don't need to apologize."

Silas took a bite of his bread, nodding as he chewed. "Noted."

"Actually, to answer your question, I don't know what's next. I think I'm just fighting for New York out of habit, out of loyalty to a piece of land. Once the battle is over, maybe I won't feel like staying here, I don't know, it's strange to reconsider what territory means and how I'll feel after – what did you call it? A battle?"

"A metaphoric battle at least," Silas said. "I'll be square with you, I don't feel the same things I felt for America, not right now. It's a strange, ugly, visceral place to be at the moment."

"If you let it be," Sara said. "but if you just avoid the chatter, it's pretty much the same place it always was. Think about it, the all-or-nothing political dramas that never end, they just morph into a newer version of the same fight. People are ridiculous now, but they've always been ridiculous. This is the land of hellfire preachers and snake oil salesmen, traveling carnies and get rich quick. That's how it was, and that's exactly how it is."

Silas stood carefully, leaned across the table, cupped the back of Sara's head with his hand and pulled her face to his, kissing her passionately. After the kiss broke, Sara's eyes were crossed and unfocused as Silas returned to his seat.

"Sorry, I had to do that."

"That apology, I'll take," Sara said, her lips still zinging from his whiskers.

"Sara," Silas pressed his hands together in front of his face. "Sara whatever your last name is these days, I love you."

The words bounced around comfortably in Sara's head.

"Thank you," Sara said. "And anything else I say that isn't I love you back will sound trite, so can I just leave it at thank you?"

Silas nodded, and a server appeared with their mains. When he was gone, Sara looked at the table of food, which smelled great, but she wanted none of it.

"I don't know what's wrong with me," she said. "I was starving, but those hunks of bread have filled me up."

"Do you want to get another bottle of wine and just chat? We can take the food to go."

Sara nodded, taking in the strange, earnest man in front of her. She thought of all the sisters who'd come to her for advice after falling in love with another sister. Her advice was always supportive, but wary: "Eternity will feel a lot longer when you spend it with an ex" was her trusty advice. But there was something elusive and wary about Silas that told her that if things soured between them, he could still vanish. Oddly, the thought gave her anxiety, which indicated how heavily she was falling for him, which in turn gave her more anxiety.

"Fine, I love you too," she blurted just as a new server delivered a bottle of wine. Smiling, Silas instructed him to pour the wine without testing it. When the server finally left, Silas was beaming.

"Yes," he nodded. "You may have mentioned that."

"Well?" Sara glared at him. "Are you happy now?"

"Yeah," he said with fake casualness, "feels pretty good right now."

"Don't be smug about it."

"I'm not, what do you want me to do? Dance a jig?"

"Yes, Silas, that's what the kids are saying these days on the Tik Toks. Dance a jig."

To Sara's horror, Silas stood up, and began doing a strange horn-pipe dance around the table.

"Excuse me," he said to the smiling couple at the table nearest them. "She just told me that she loves me, and apparently this is the appropriate response."

The two guys applauded.

"Silas, stop it," Sara said, her eyes wide. "I was joking."

"But it feels so right," he laughed, now dipping and bowing. "You're not going to let me dance by myself?"

"Oh yes, oh yes I am," Sara said, noticing that all the patrons of the restaurant were beginning to stare. "Silas, please sit down."

After turning and bowing to the restaurant at large, Silas stood upright and declared, "She loves me! I'm the luckiest guy on earth." A surprisingly loud round of applause swelled in the small space, and to Sara's horror, Silas extended a hand.

"I'm not dancing," she said through clenched teeth.

"All's I want is a kiss," he said, and a chorus of "kiss him, kiss him" broke out, egged on by the gays at the next table, who were clearly living for her embarrassment. "Fine," Sara took his hand and began to rise. Halfway up, Silas twisted her hand, forcing her to twirl clumsily, knocking her seat back a few inches. When she returned to facing him, he stepped around the table and wrapped her in a hug, kissing her deeply while the restaurant cheered. As the kiss broke off and the cheering died down, they separated and returned to their seats.

"How's that for another deeply scarring life event?" Silas asked cheekily.

"It's up there with near-death," Sara said, slapping his hand. "What's gotten into you?"

"Can't we just be happy?"

On the table, Silas's phone lit up, and his picked it up, nodding as he read something.

"Good news," he said finally. "Sorry, I guess I forgot, but Heather says to tell you that the top floor bedroom has a…" Silas paused, glancing at their neighbors who were deep in conversation. "It's safe. You have nothing to worry about."

"Let's box this food up then," Sara said. "I suddenly need to be in that room with you."

Chapter Fifteen

Alone in a cab speeding down Columbus just after dawn, Sara fought to remain calm. A million scenarios were playing in her mind, her attention skittering from one to the next. She inhaled deeply, trying to banish them and settle into something resembling calm. She stared out the window, a faint smile on her lips. She loved early morning New York, the city always felt cleaner, somehow almost innocent.

After much discussion with Heather, it was decided that Heather would bring Teddie, masked and covered from head to toe, to Sara's barely used Murray Hill love nest, the apartment that they'd hurriedly set up for her literally the day before Marguerite's murder, a lifetime ago. Peering out the taxi window, she caught glimpses of the Empire State before the taxi turned and stopped in front of the building. After paying the driver, Sara stepped out into the cloudy, dim day, the city noises soundtracking the knots in her stomach. She briefly wondered if she was going to throw up.

As Heather had promised, the front door was propped open, and Sara slowly made her way up the stairs to the top floor. She smelled fresh coffee and heard noises from inside the apartment. Was she supposed to knock? Heather hadn't told her what to do. As she reached the landing, the door to the apartment opened a crack, showing Heather's right eye behind glasses, then opened wider.

Heather turned back into the apartment, and Sara guessed that Teddie was seated on the couch.

"Okay then pet," Heather said. "I'll be outside." She turned to Sara. "In you come."

Hugging as they passed, Sara didn't even look back as they separated, stepping out of the entryway and into the apartment, letting the door swing closed behind her, her eyes taking in Teddie, seated on the couch, thinner, more drawn, in an oatmeal workout suit, one of her beloved Diop headwraps around her hair, checking something on her phone.

"Teddie?" Sara's voice cracked, and Teddie raised her eyes, first widening in shock then narrowing in disbelief.

"No," she said, her voice a whisper. "No."

Sara didn't know what to do, frozen to the spot, her eyes riveted to Teddie's.

"No, no no no no hell no," Teddie mumbled, her chin trembling, her phone falling from her hand and bouncing off the couch, landing on the floor.

Sara forced her feet to move, one step forward, then another. Teddie pushed back into the couch, her face an expression of confused terror.

"Ted, it's me. I'm alive. I'm sorry..." and that was all Sara got out before a wrenching sob tore her throat out and she was bent over sobbing, her knees suddenly unreliable and the room spinning. Gripping the back of the loveseat to keep herself upright, Sara forced air into her lungs, gulp after gulp, her eyes finally opening to see Teddie still pressed against the far end of the couch.

"I don't understand," she whispered eventually, her voice barely audible. "Are you real?"

Sara nodded, surprised she was able to stand and then take several steps until Teddie was close enough to touch. Sara reached a handout gingerly and was upset when Teddie recoiled.

"What the actual fuck is happening here?" Teddie's head whipped left and right as if she was looking for an escape hatch.

"I'm alive, Ted," Sara said, slowly regaining control of her breathing, standing upright, her arms open.

"And you're just getting around to telling me now?" Teddie's face twisted into anger and she pulled her knees up against her chest and for a moment Sara wondered if she was going to kick her.

"I got here as fast as I could, my love. I'm so so so sorry."

"Sara, I thought I *killed* you. Do you know what that feels like?"

"I dunno," Sara said, "does it feel worse than being pushed into Surrender? Ted, I need you to breathe and we need to talk."

"Sara, whatever you are, I *need* to get out of here." Teddie's voice was mocking as she lurched forward and snatched up her phone from the floor and called Heather.

"Get me out of here," she said angrily into the phone, then listened. "Fine, five minutes. No more."

Sliding the phone into her hoodie pocket, Teddie turned her face to Sara. "So talk."

"I did it, Teddie. I went in there and I took the pills. It was fucking awful. But Heather switched them out, it was aspirin. I lit the fire, and when I woke up, Heather hustled me out of there."

"Right, this all tracks," Teddie glared at her. "Self-absorbed woman saves herself, destroys everything else."

"Did you hear what I just said? I thought it was the end. I made peace with you pushing me into the Surrender room! I didn't know. And now you're mad because I didn't bounce back and take care of your feelings?"

"Something like that, yeah," Teddie said, her voice lower. "You always have."

"I'm doing that now," Sara took another step, and reached out for Teddie's arm, running the back of her fingers along her forearm. At least Teddie didn't flinch. "At least, I'm trying to."

"Where the hell were you?"

"I went out of town, Teddie, sorry, I was a mess."

"Did April Veronica help you?"

Sara shook her head. "Can I sit by you?"

Encouraged by Teddie's shrug, Sara sat on the couch, one cushion away from Teddie.

"I bumped into her on the street," Sara said. "She was running away. It wasn't planned, she was just there, so I took her with me."

"Where is she now?"

"She's safe," Sara said. "She will come back when she feels safe here."

Blinking away tears, Teddie turned her face to the windows, and Sara knew she was jealous.

"Teddie, you realize that we are at war right? Our entire, tiny community is at war. It's so much worse than you know. April Veronica doesn't want to tell the Lock where she is."

"And you don't trust me?"

"I trust you implicitly," Sara put a hand on Teddie's thigh. "But right now, can we just talk about us?"

"This is you controlling your narrative," Teddie said, her face still gazing away.

"Did you hear what I said?" A note crept into Sara's voice, and Teddie slowly turned to face her. "I'm not being hysterical, Ted. Heavy, heavy shit is going down. The Surrenders are just the tip of the iceberg."

"Can you at least tell me that stuff?"

"I can," Sara said, her voice gentle. "Which would you prefer me to start with?"

"Just talk, since you're the one putting restrictions on my questions."

"Teddie, I made peace with dying, and you know what? All I learned is that at the end, I wanted more time, and I wanted to make peace with you, but since that was out of my reach, I went to my death at peace, because you're my life's greatest work."

"Miss me with that bullshit," Teddie said, her voice throaty, and Sara took her hand.

"I'm not going to argue with you about what passed through my mind as I died, Theodora. It's waaaaay too soon for that. I did it to save you, I did it to save..."

"That guy? Or is that topic off limits too?"

"Fine," Sara took her hand from Teddie's, and stood up. "I was trying to sugar-coat all of this, but here goes, kid. First, tell me, please tell me, since you sentenced me to death, have you had any regret? Any regret at all? Like at any time, did you maybe think, these rules don't really work anymore?"

"I'm not sure why you're attacking me, and I don't understand your question."

"Why? It's pretty straightforward. Your blind obedience turned you into my enemy, Teddie."

On the couch, Teddie scoffed.

"So," Sara walked behind the other couch, "my question is, at any time since that night have you thought that maybe it went too far?"

Blinking away tears, Teddie nodded rapidly.

"Well good," Sara said, her heart aching as she sensed Teddie's tears approaching. "We have somewhere to start."

"You don't understand," Teddie began, then tears consumed her. "Every... every night since, all I can see is your face when you said you wanted Surrender, the look in your eyes." She paused, her head bowed, and Sara saw mascara-stained teardrops land on Teddie's thigh. Unable to resist, Sara went to her, cupping a palm against her cheek.

"You did what was right, at the time," Sara said quietly. "But our world has changed. Do you remember a million years ago, we read One Hundred Years Of Solitude?" Teddie nodded. "It's time to read it again. We've lived by old rules for too long, they need to change."

"But they've never changed, and we've survived so long."

"The world has changed faster than we expected, Ted. People have changed. The basic laws will always apply. No killing, ever. And integrity always. But after that, we need to think of new ways."

"So with all the Locks at war, we come up with new rules. It'll never happen."

"Who says we have to live in Locks? Who says we have to pretend to be nuns, or never contribute any lasting art or poetry or writings?"

"Wait," Teddie sat bolt upright. "Are there other people like us? Have you met people like us who live in other ways?"

"Kinda sorta," Sara said. "I'm not being evasive. I'm being careful, because, Teddie, the enemy is not out there, it's in Madrid. At least, I hope it is."

"Desdemona?"

Sara nodded.

"Teddie, haven't you ever wondered why Madrid has so many transfers out? Every Lock in the world has at least two women, and usually more, who came from Madrid. And the Locks with more than five are all now dead."

Teddie's eyes widened. "You're talking about transfers over how long?"

"Not saying it's a coincidence, but Desdemona started this around the time I became Mother in New York, so over a hundred years."

"That's a hell of a long game, if you're right."

"I'm right," Sara said coldly.

"And you expect me to believe that you didn't know Heather was going to save you?"

"It's the truth," Sara said, staring into Teddie's eyes.

"Do you know how fucking awful that makes me feel?" Teddie curled her legs up to her chest. "And when you woke up?"

"Heather was dragging me to safety. She dumped me on the street, and Silas found me and put me in his car. As we were driving away, April Veronica ran in front of the car, so I called to her and she got in."

"She never went to North Carolina did she?"

Sara shook her head.

"And you won't tell me where she is?"

Another shake. "She doesn't want anyone to know."

"So what do you want from me?"

"I want you to blindly come with me!" Sara slid along the couch until their thighs were touching. "Think back on your entire life, Ted. Can you think of a time I didn't do everything in my own life just for you? So now, I ask you, is it possible that you can trust me on blind faith, knowing that I'd never hurt you? Because I'll tell you one thing, the only thing I cared about saving from this whole mess is you. You're the reason I returned."

"Even after what I did to you?"

"You stuck to the rules, which is how I raised you. It's hard to be resentful when someone does the thing that they're taught to do, especially when it was me who did the teaching."

"So what does this all mean?" Teddie finally swiveled around, crossing her legs and directly facing Sara, the morning sunlight sparkling on her tear-streaked face.

"I honestly don't know," Sara said. "Maybe we will be able to keep New York, maybe we won't. We need to secede from the rest of the Lock organization. We need secrecy, which is why I can't tell you anything until I know you're one hundred per cent on board."

"And if I don't want to come with you?"

With an exaggerated shrug, Sara leaned close to her daughter. "Then this would be the end of the road for us."

Teddie recoiled as if she'd been struck.

"No hard feelings, Ted, but I came back to ask you to come with me. If you don't want to do that, that's entirely fine, but that would leave me with one option, and that would be for me to go on with my life, without you. You'll transfer to a new Lock, hopefully London. You can tell people I'm alive, or not. Sisters will hunt me, but Ted, that doesn't worry me."

"Feels like blackmail," she said quietly. "Do I get time to think about it?"

"Do you need time to think about it?"

"Let me spell it out for you, Sara. You want me to be faithful to you, but you can't tell me a single thing about what that involves. You want me to forget that you ran off with a man who hasn't aged in fifty years, but you won't even confirm that he's like us. You have a twinkle in your eye that tells me that you've learned something new and special, but you can't tell me that either, and you can't even prove that April Veronica is still alive."

"Do you want to call her right now? We can call her."

"No, I don't want to call her," Teddie said sheepishly. "I don't even know why I threw that in there."

"Look, it's pretty simple," Sara said. "The fundamental question is, do you want a future with me, or a future without me? Both are available."

"I will always pick you, mom."

Sara felt the tears start like something breaking at the base of her throat, only realizing at that moment that she'd lost faith that Teddie would choose her. Opening her mouth to speak, the tears got there first, and she collapsed forward, her head on Teddie's knee, the weight of the conversation settling over her heart like a smothering glove. When she felt Teddie's hand slide over her hair, again and again, she felt a wave of love so strong it could crush her.

"Teddie," she said snottily into Teddie's thigh. "The only thing I've been able to think of since all that shit went down is you. They didn't want me to come back to New York."

"Who didn't, mom?"

Sara winced at her own indiscretion, took a deep, rattling breath and stood up.

"Teddie, I was with Fan and Amitra. Stefanya too."

"The fuck?" Teddie's eyes were saucers.

Sara nodded. "Apparently, the near-death of an elder brings all the girls to the yard."

"I haven't even thought about those women in so long," Teddie said. "I guess I just assumed that they'd be somewhere in a cabin with cats, like non-verbal and almost turned to stone."

"Oh, yeah no," Sara said. "Let me put it this way. They're vegan militant feminists in a college town."

"Huh?"

"Anyway, I don't even know if my future is connected to theirs," Sara wiped her eyes. "I honestly don't. All I know is I couldn't face a future without you."

"Now can I ask about your male friend?"

"Think about it, Ted," Sara said. "Think about what you suspect, what you want to ask. Think about how my answers, in the wrong hands, could destroy him. Can I offer you one thing, and see how we go?"

Teddie nodded.

"What if I told you that whoever, whatever he is, he has lived a life that has followed our rules as absolutely, as closely, as you have?"

"A man living by Lock rules?" Teddie shook her head incredulously. "For what? Fifty years?"

As she started to formulate her reply, Sara rapidly took stock of the situation. The whole Lock knew he hadn't aged since the San Francisco fiasco, and the only explanation was that he was cursed. Gazing into Teddie's imploring eyes, she decided to risk a little. It was the least she could do.

"He's older than I am," Sara said, and Teddie gasped. "And never has he killed."

"Not buying that for a second," Teddie said.

"That's your prerogative," Sara said. "I'm not advocating bringing in a load of cursed men. Not at all. We've learned so much about gender since the rules were written, Teddie. We know that physical gender doesn't equal true gender, and that gender identity is separate. It's something for us to consider as we move forward."

"Do you see this guy joining our Lock if we stay in New York?"

Sara shrugged. "You know, I never even asked him that. But, after nearly six hundred years on his own, I am not sure that he's a joiner."

"So where are you saying we will live?"

"I'm not saying, that's the thing. In the past few weeks, I've had to digest a lot of new information, and it's for your own damn good that I'm not just dumping it all on you. But what if I told you Fan has created lab-grown plasma that works for us?"

Teddie crinkled up her nose. "Does it taste better than that weird tofu stuff Yukari invented a while back?"

"Only a little bit," Sara said. "But she'll get there. At that point, we are free from the whole..."

"You're gonna free us from the vampire industrial complex?" Teddie laughed. "No more nursing scrubs? Because sister, you should have opened with that."

"That's the least of it," Sara said, hope in her voice. "I feel like I carried the West End compound on my back like a sack of rocks ever since it was built. And I'm exhausted from it. What if we could travel lightly, moving cities whenever we felt like it or had to."

"Apart from ten years in Paris, I've never lived anywhere but here," Teddie said. "I'm not sure how I feel about this whole world approach."

"Then live here," Sara said. "But you loved Paris, and there's a whole world we have never seen. Will we always live together in the same city? I hope so but I don't know. I love it here too but imagine just bouncing around every ten years.?

"It sounds almost as exhausting as carrying the Compound on your back," Teddie said.

"All of that will work itself out, and it will always work out in your favor," Sara said. "This is the future I'm presenting to you. Less responsibility, more growth."

"I like the sound of that," Teddie said. "But what about the rest of the Lock, we can't just leave Yuka and Imani."

"I don't plan to leave anybody behind," Sara said. "It's just a matter of whether they want to come with us."

"And what the hell do we do about Desdemona?"

"That's where trust comes into it," Sara said, taking Teddie's hand. "That's why I need you to be quiet about me being alive. It's so much safer for her devotees to think I'm dead. But I do know one thing."

"And what's that?"

"I need to confront her sooner than later."

"Holy shit, are you selling tickets?"

"Honey you're on the guest list."

Teddie let out a belly laugh, and Sara felt something shift as a world of weight slipped from her shoulders.

"I'll take two tickets please," Teddie said playfully.

"Two tickets?"

"Yeah, if I'm gonna spend eternity with your boyfriend, I guess we should meet officially."

"You've already met," Sara said playfully.

"I blamed him for your death," Teddie said coldly.

"You can thank him for my life," Sara replied.

"One step at a time," Teddie said.

"Fair," Sara continued. "Do you want to leave New York for a while? Just until your Tik Tok fame subsides?"

Teddie shook her head. "I can stay inside the Compound. It won't be the first time I've vanished for a decade."

Sara winced and closed her eyes, remembering the violent summer of 1919 which drove a terrified Teddie into hiding and then a ten-year sojourn with the Paris Lock.

"I'm sorry this has been so hard for you," Sara said quietly. "All of it."

"Thanks, mom," Teddie said. "I'm sorry too. After you... were gone, I saw the pressure you were under, my eyes were opened to it, and girl, running a Lock sucks."

"For now," Sara said.

"Enigmatic much?" Teddie gazed into Sara's eyes. "And you won't tell me anything else?"

"I'll tell you one thing, my love," Sara took her hand. "There's a war on the horizon, a little one for sure, but a war nevertheless, and the rules, those damn rules you love so much, if they don't bend, they're gonna break. And that would be a disaster."

Teddie exhaled loudly and squeezed Sara's hand.

"I am starting to see that," Teddie said. "I broke a rule, I had to."

Sara barely caught her reaction, raising her head slowly. "Yes?"

"I didn't burn the note you left for me," Teddie said, her eyes wide with emphasis. "I just couldn't do it."

Sara felt tears well in her eyes and she blinked them away.

"That's more of a guideline than a rule."

"Give me my propers," Teddie said. "This is me we're talking about. This is huge."

"I know, Ted, I know."

Sara threw her arms around Teddie, and they both burst into laughter that soon turned into more tears.

Chapter Sixteen

After Teddie disguised herself in a hoodie, face mask and large mirror sunglasses and Heather spirited her away, Sara spent some time on the couch in the apartment that had almost been hers. She looked at the Mapplethorpe photograph of a lily, its beauty and mortality captured in perfect balance on a shifting field of grays.

Like my life, she thought, almost glumly.

Something about the Teddie meeting didn't feel right. She felt uneasy and unfinished, and certain that she'd forgotten to say something important.

Like my life, she thought again.

Misery loves company, as Heather was fond of saying, so she pulled out the ancient flip phone that Heather had left for her in the rental and called Silas.

"How'd it go?"

"I'm still alive," Sara laughed. "Wanna subway to me and we can walk back?"

"In broad daylight?"

"You're only young once. Come to the 33rd Street and Lexington station. Northeast corner."

"You're sure?"

"Silas, nothing has ever happened on Lex."

A short while later, Sara spied him appearing aboveground diagonally opposite her, across the intersection, a bewildered expression on his face. Unable to remember how to text on a flip phone, she bolted down the stairs and over to his exit.

"I said northeast," she said as he wrapped her in a hug.

"You're mistaking me for someone who ever took this line north," he chuckled. "This walk will be my first time heading north on Lexington, maybe ever."

Slipping her hand inside his, Sara led him across 33rd, their linked hands swinging, bounce in her step, the morning sun bouncing off skyscraper windows in fractured slices.

"I like it when you're happy," Silas said.

Several answers flooded Sara at once, and she took a second to unpack them before choosing the least complicated answer.

"You make me happy," she said, then watched as the compliment landed on Silas's face. He kept on looking ahead, but his smile broadened, and his eyes twinkled.

"So what happened with Teddie?"

"Well, first, still not comfortable using her real name in public."

Silas rolled with it. "So how did things go with Nakeah?"

"You're so fucking smooth," Sara laughed. "I guess it went well. I mean, that poor girl has a lot to process but she seemed open to what I said."

"Was she surprised that you're alive?"

"Teddie will always respond like I'm her parent. She was much more interested in how I could do such a thing to her."

"That's also a good sign, right? Your relationship made it through unscathed?"

"I hope so," Sara said. "I think so. What did you do while I was down here?"

"I bought a car," Silas said.

"Of course you did. No really, what did you do?"

"I bought a car. On the internet!," he said proudly, turning his head to make eye contact. "I didn't feel safe not having one, so later today, I'll go pick up…" he switched his voice to game show host, "our NEW CAR."

"Okay Soupy Sales, what are we getting?"

"Is that how long it's been since you watched a game show?"

"I got rid of my television in the eighties," Sara said. "Since then, I've only watched stuff at either Heather's or Teddie's. Oh wait, and Imani. She made me watch Downton Abbey."

"I hope I get to meet her," Silas said. "She always seemed like a really nice person."

"You will, I'm pretty certain."

"Did Teddie want to kill me?"

"Teddie doesn't want to kill ants. I actually think she wants to meet you."

"You mean Nakeah," Silas said. "And we've already met."

"That's what she said. Which car did you buy?"

"Oh, nothing, just an electric Subaru. You can take the boy out of Iceland…"

"That's exciting," Sara said.

"They're great," Silas said. "And when you're done, you just park one in a bad part of town and it vanishes like magic."

"You're so street," Sara teased, and Silas puffed up his chest and did his best pimp walk and Sara laughed so hard she had to stop and lean against a building.

"What was that?"

"That's how he walks at the start of Saturday Night Fever," Silas said dejectedly, making Sara laugh harder.

"Silas that movie is almost fifty," she gasped. "I thought you'd hurt your back."

"Remind me never to take you out dancing," Silas said, his eyes playful. "Come on, I have to pick up the car in a few hours and the way you're walking, we won't be home yet."

While Silas went to get the car, Sara prowled the house on East 90th Street, feeling rootless and confined. Since building the compound, she had never lived below the third floor, finding freedom in open windows, delighting in scents of food and flowers in the summer, and ozone and ice in the winter. On one of her laps of the house, she'd paused, considering opening the bay windows in the living room, but she'd locked eyes with a passing nanny and panicked. At least she'd been able to wait until the nanny moved on before drawing the drapes and plunging the room into suffocating darkness.

A text arrived from Heather.

> How you holding up, pet?

> Cabin fever is setting in. Feel a bit trapped and vulnerable.

Sara's phone rang immediately.

"Don't shoot the messenger," Heather rarely bothered with pleasantries. "But I have an option for you."

"Is it shopping? You know I hate shopping."

"Worse," Heather replied. "I think I can get you in here, tonight. If you'd like to come and see Yukari and Imani."

"What about Sir Hopsalot?" Sara felt excitement flutter in her chest.

"I'm sure that can be arranged."

"I'm in," Sara said. "What time and where?"

"I just need to find out where the other miserable bitches are going to be."

"Has Fran changed her tune?"

"Not as much as I'd hoped, unfortunately," Heather said. "But she's Fran, she's slow to consider and slower to decide. All she sees is the risk we pose to society. That's what's blinded her."

"I can see that," Sara said. "I mean, I've known it. But she's such a gentle soul I think we can reach her."

"Don't get your hopes up," Heather said darkly. "Liz was a much bigger hippy in her day, but now she's all about authoritarianism."

"Heather, how much do you know about what I learned in..." Sara paused, then whispered, "the other place?"

"Well handled, love. I think I know as much as you, I just haven't had the pleasure of seeing the finished product in person. Yet."

"I think that's what Liz needs," Sara said. "Now that I'm looking from the outside in, I'm not as angry as I was with those women. Eleanor too. I feel like their goodness, their freedom, has been poisoned by Rosa and now it's up to us"

"You can't save everybody," Heather said. "A wise woman once told me that."

"I'm not trying to save the world here, Heather, I just don't want to abandon anyone who could still have a great future."

"I give it five minutes."

"What?"

"You heard me lassie," Heather sounded jovial. "Since you left, Liz and Fran have been huddled around Rosa like baby witches around a boss witch. It's gross."

Sara felt a wash of frustration that was quickly replaced by anger. She took a deep breath and pushed it aside.

"What's the game plan, Heath? Am I rejoining the Lock? Am I worth more alive or dead?"

"Good question," Heather said slowly, clearly thinking. "And you know what? That's a question for Yukari tonight. She's Lock mother."

"Her decision is only binding if I return to the Lock," Sara said.

"Still got one foot out the door then?"

"One foot?" Sara paused, realizing she hadn't even entertained the thought of returning to the Lock. "At this stage, I'm entirely out the door, but still curious about what happens inside."

Heather didn't reply for so long that Sara thought the call might have dropped out.

"So, you don't think you'd ever want to live here again?"

"I dunno," Sara said. "When you put it like that, it seems harsher than it feels in my mind. My entire focus was Teddie. Now I can start to think about, oh you know, everything else in my life. I do feel pretty strongly about that building."

"A castle is ultimately just sand blowing away in the wind," Heather said.

"True," Sara said with a sigh. "But it's starting to feel like this princess ain't done with her castle yet."

Heather laughed. "Well get your tiara ready, and I'll text you with a time for tonight."

As their new car crept silently along the top of Central Park, Sara's eyes darted left and right, familiar sights triggering waves of homesickness on top of nervousness. A humid mist was blowing in the air, swirling in eddies below the streetlights, and she was grateful for the pressure of Silas's hand on her thigh. Despite her assurances that she was going to be safe, Silas was insisting on parking near the building and waiting until she was done. He'd been very clear that it wasn't negotiable. Glancing at his hooded, masked face as he drove, she agreed that there was little chance he'd be recognized.

As they swung onto West End from 106th, she saw the building rising in the distance, the silver night sky reflecting on the windows of her old apartment, which were darkened.

"You doing okay?"

Sara nodded and placed a hand atop his, and they turned left in silence, driving halfway along the block before Silas paused.

"I talked to Heather," Silas said, his voice grave. "If anything goes wrong, I'm coming in. She's going to leave this entrance open. Text me."

"I'm sure it won't come to that," she leaned across the console and kissed him on the lips, full and hard, drawing in his breath through her nostrils. "And when I'm done, I think it's finally time for a rematch in the North Woods."

Silas chuckled and shook his head. "Deal, but for now, Sara, please, focus."

"Yeah, yeah, yeah," she said, opening her door and stepping out. After she closed the door, the car slid off along the street, and Sara cautiously circled the compound. Taking her phone from her pocket, she pretended to be on a call as she entered the darkness of the recessed trash well of the building. Her nervousness gave way to excitement when she saw the low door that led to the Surrender room, and she bent, twisting the ancient metal hasp upwards and pulling the door open. Expecting another sooty crawl, she'd dressed entirely in black courtesy of a quick afternoon trip to Uniqlo, but the passage smelled entirely different as she bent and stepped inside. She pulled the door closed behind her, careful not to lock it, and then moved forward to the point where the ceiling was higher and she could stand, then descended the stairs into the original coal storage room. Light was spilling in further along the hallway and Sara paused, listening for voices, hearing only silence.

The last time she'd been here, she had been too disoriented to take anything in. Sara spun, slowly, looking at each brick, each piece of rusty metal, feeling their age, aware that she put them in place.

Who was she kidding? This was her home.

Filling her lungs, she relished the scents of the building, noticing that this passageway smelled similar to the corridors that linked the buildings of the complex, her complex, with an added layer of disinfectant or cleaning products. She couldn't ignore how great it felt just to be within its walls again.

"What are ye bloody doing in there?" came Heather's voice. "I don't have all night."

"Oh, sorry," Sara pushed ahead down the narrow corridor, then crouched down to get through the opening into the Surrender room ante chamber.

"I tried not to touch anything," she said as she emerged into the room where Heather was busily feeding things into the furnace.

"Oh, don't worry about that," Heather didn't turn around. "You'll not believe it, but I found a Groupon for chimney sweeps and I had the whole thing cleaned."

"I love New York," Sara said as she wrapped Heather in a hug from behind. "What ya burning?"

"Loose ends," Heather said enigmatically. "Just leaving enough of a hole in the paper trail to drive the right people crazy."

Breaking the hug, Sara moved around to face Heather, who only glanced up briefly from her task, light from the flames dancing across her smooth, open face as she continued to feed papers and some full notebooks into the furnace, a smile on her full lips.

"Seems a bit drastic," Sara ventured, and Heather shook her head emphatically.

"Not to me it doesn't," she said. "Sara, I've been watching Rosa very closely. She's way too happy right now."

"That's not a state I ever imagined her in."

"A little bit of spring cleaning never hurt anyone," Heather said as she tossed the last of her papers into the fire and swung the heavy iron door closed. "The coast is clear, we'll be in the small conference room."

Sara felt a wash of relief that they wouldn't be in the big room, where things had gotten so ugly the last time. She followed Heather, pausing at the hallway as her old friend made sure nobody was about. Heather made a quick left, then pressed a finger against a lock on the door and it made some smooth metallic noises and popped open. Heather waited for her to step inside, then followed, closing the door behind her. When she heard the locks grind back into place, Sara felt a mild bite of panic nipping at her heart, and she forced herself to breathe evenly. She had no reason to distrust Heather, at all, but this room did not have a bolthole. She'd be exiting via the door she just came in through.

"I never got around to erasing your prints," Heather said with a sly wink. "Actually, I think you have the full set of permissions."

"Good to know," Sara said, her voice even, as she wondered if Heather was hinting at something. That was the thing with Heather, either you got one of her hints, or she would deny it if you asked. At least Sara felt less trapped than she did a few seconds ago. The informal room looked much the same as it always had. Nobody ever bothered with this room, and it was furnished with nice pieces that had gone out of fashion in very different decades, as evidenced by the heavy brown leather sofa next to a gaudily psychedelic velvet couch that had once been Teddie's prize possession.

"I'll call them down now," Heather said. "I hope they're not too noisy."

A few minutes later, a rustling behind the door caused them both to tense up, then the door opened, revealing Teddie standing behind Imani and Yukari, two sets of eyes widening as they caught sight of Sara, who was pushed aside by Heather, hurrying, a finger to her lips.

"Get inside you lot, not a sound," she hissed as she shooed them in with her palm and closed the door behind them. "The door is closed but we still need to use our church mouse voices."

Imani's heart-shaped, dark face was a picture of shocked happiness, her red lips peeling into her trademark smile, tears spilling from her eyes. To her left, Yukari covered the bottom half of her face with a cupped palm while her other hand struggled to contain a wriggling rabbit, and Sara was doing okay until the first teardrop fell and then her chin began to quiver.

"You're bloody alive," Imani said finally, her voice hoarse, and nodding, Sara stepped forward and opened her arms, and the two women fell into them, and she held them while they wept.

"It's okay," Sara said.

"Now I know why Heather said to bring Sir Hopsalot," Yukari said into Sara's hair as she thrust the squirming rabbit into Sara's arms.

"I missed him too, Yuka," Sara said. The hug went on until Imani released them all.

"Somebody should be filming this," Imani said as she wiped her eyes. "Because I'm fuckin' speechless I am."

"I'll cherish the moment forever," Sara said, kissing the top of Sir Hopsalot's head. "You okay, Yuka?"

Yukari nodded, then gestured at Teddie's old sofa. Sara walked her to the edge of it, and she slumped down, almost in a faint.

"Sara I have been so sad," she said, as if that explained everything.

"Wait," Imani remained standing, looking from Heather to Teddie. "How long have-"

"Don't even try it," Teddie said. "I found out this morning. I haven't been acting."

Her back to them, Heather was fussing with something on the floor beside the leather couch. "I was acting," Heather said. "But it wasn't hard, after that scene in the big room."

When she finally stood up and turned, she was holding two bottles of wine.

"Who needs a drink?"

Sara sat beside Yukari, so close that they created a single lap for the rabbit to stretch across, his eyes closed as Sara scratched his cheek. The rabbit closed his eyes and tilted his head to give Sara better access, making her smile. Imani sat on Sara's other side, her curvy hips pressing softly against her, and Sara felt the familiar security that she only felt around these women. Teddie took the wine bottles from Heather, regarded the labels of both, then set one on the floor, opening the other while Heather handed out glasses which Teddie then filled.

"We don't have a ton of time tonight," Heather said as she took a seat beside Teddie on the other couch. "Long story short, I got Sara out just in time. She bumped into April Veronica outside, and they took off together."

"Oh, that's wonderful," Yukari said. "I've been worried sick about that girl."

"She's fine," Sara said. "She's in no rush to come back, but she's safe."

"Totally understand," Yukari said. "Wow. I'm happy and confused at the same time."

"You guys, I was a fucking wreck," Sara said. "I got here as soon as I could. I had to leave the city, for obvious reasons. You guys, I'm still scared, I don't feel safe."

"Who bloody does?" Imani downed her glass of wine in a gulp, holding the empty glass out to Teddie, who had to open the other bottle to top her off. "Have you told her about the weird pings we are picking up between the Madrid compound and here?"

"I didn't get around to telling Sara that just yet," Heather shot daggers at Imani.

Anger flowed into Sara's veins. "Heather!" she fought to keep her voice low. "You do realize that... oh fuck it, you guys, the guy I'm seeing, he's outside waiting, to make sure we are safe."

"I thought he went back to the... hotel," Heather said, grabbing for her phone. "I'll text him to get out of here."

"Hold up," Imani drained her second glass. "Hold the fuck up. Heather, you know this guy?"

Heather raised a palm, waiting until the text was sent. "Yes, I know him. He helped me save Sara."

"I don't understand," Yukari said, "Can someone just explain this all to me, and make it simple. Is this guy one of us?"

"They," Teddie paused, launched accusatory eyes at Sara and Heather, then continued, "won't tell you but yes, I believe he is."

"Is there a bloody man Lock all of a sudden?" Imani waved her empty glass at Teddie who groaned and just handed her the whole bottle. "Can we all get one?"

"No," Sara said. "Sorry. It's just him. He's like us... he's older than me. He's never killed. He tried to approach me at various times over the years, and this time, he got his foot in the door."

"Mind. Blown." Yukari finished her wine.

"It wasn't his foot, and it wasn't your door," Teddie said. "Heather, is there more wine?"

Laughing, Heather leaned over the side of the couch, returning with another two bottles in one hand.

"I want you guys on the same page as me," Sara said, looking at each of them. "Lock life is not for me any longer. We can't just go on living in these groups, hiding in plain sight in major cities. Sooner or later," she glanced at Teddie, "someone will notice. Even if Teddie vanishes for a decade or longer, the digital record is way more enduring than human memory."

"What's the alternative?" Imani leveled her best stare at Sara, who shrugged.

"Those of us who want the old life to continue can see if that is a possibility. Those of us who want to try something new will have that option too."

"Sara," Yukari twisted herself on the couch so she could see Sara's face. "Do you plan to, please pardon me, like run off with this guy?"

"I plan to be around him, I guess," Sara said. "But that doesn't mean that I don't see a future for all of us in this room, together."

"Oh thank fucking fuck," Imani said. "Why you didn't open with that, I'll never know."

"Yeah, Sara," Teddie said in a needling voice. "Your delivery today sucks. Try starting with the good stuff."

Sara smiled.

"You guys, I have to tell you something. My last thought in the Surrender room was that the only thing that matters is love. And I knew that I had loved you all, so completely. I'm sorry that this has been rough on you, but I needed to heal, and I needed to figure out the next steps."

"Sounds like someone's had an epiphany," Heather said, one eyebrow raised.

"Yeah," Sara nodded. "Me. You guys, while I was gone I met up with Fan and Ama –" A round of gasps filled the room. "Wait – and Stefanya. Most of the elders are united against Desdemona."

"This is top shelf magic," Imani grinned.

Heather dusted her hands together. "Silas is safe, he's insisting on circling until you need him to get you."

Sara nodded. "Thank you. Now can you tell me why you think he was in danger?"

Heather went over to a marble-topped 80s style dresser and opened a drawer, retrieving a sheaf of papers.

"This is the intel that Fran has been picking up. Cell phone traces between the Madrid Lock and six burner phones here in the city."

"I talked to Fran today," Yukari said. "She is still doing her job, despite her alliance with Rosa. I was pretty tough on her.

"That I'd like to see," Imani said, pouring herself another wine and staring at Sara as if she didn't believe she was real.

"Stop it," Yukari said. "I don't have to raise my voice to be heard. Trust me."

"True dat," Imani said. "Sorry Yuka."

"Fran was actually very helpful," Yukari continued. "She's been pinging the phones, they're basic phones, no Bluetooth. It's weird, there's always four in the north of Central Park, and two of them always vanish a block from here. We can see them coming closer, and then they must turn the phones off."

Sara and Teddie exchanged worried glances.

"Fran low-key talked to other sisters in the cybersecurity world and she's pretty confident that all of the Madrid sisters are forbidden from leaving and are all accounted for inside the Madrid compound. We don't know who these phones belong to."

"We need to do a bed-check on every sister, right now?" Imani said.

"I've done that," Heather said. "Everyone that can be counted has been counted, and Fan and Ama have located most of the elders."

"It's the 'most' that makes me nervous."

"They just can't find Christine," Heather said. "Christine has wanted to kill Desdemona for longer than you have, Sara."

"How precise are the locations that we're getting?" Sara looked at Yukari.

"The best person to ask is Fran, but she gave me the impression that because of the triangulation between towers and these burner phones, she's only able to specify a general area. But it's always four in the park, two head toward us then vanish, then reappear an hour or two later, rejoin the others and two more head our way."

"And all sisters are forbidden from going out after dark, or into Central Park, or Riverside Park," Yukari added. "I loosened the rules, we were going crazy."

Sara felt a stab of disappointment when she realized that her planned do-over with Silas in the North Woods had just become a recon mission.

"What was that look, lassie?"

Shit. Heather did not miss a trick.

"Fine," Sara said. "I was plotting to take Silas for a walk in the North Woods when I leave here."

Heather shook her head.

"Silas is Vampire Enemy Number One right now. We have no idea who or what these people are. It's too much of a risk. He will be killed on sight. Then they'll capture you, and serve you up to Desdemona."

"Yeah, that's a no, mom," Teddie reached over and placed a hand on Sara's knee. "I don't want to lose you again."

"Sara, are you still a member of this Lock?" Yukari kept her tone light, but her gaze was intense.

"I never left," Sara said.

"Then, of course, you have a home here, why even question it?"

"I'm not the only person that I'm responsible for," Sara said. "He insisted on coming back with me, when I heard that Teddie was talking Surrender."

"Bring him in here, the more the merrier," Imani said.

"Not yet," Yukari said. "I'm sorry Sara. We need to focus on a very real threat. Silas is a distraction, he could be our undoing."

Sara nodded. "I understand completely."

"Heather," Yukari's voice was quietly commanding, "Do we own any property that's not compromised?"

"I offered all the tenants in these buildings a buyout as soon as Desdemona came back, the day after, you know," Heather said. "The last few tenants left last weekend."

"In New York City?" Teddie marveled. "Nothing short of a miracle."

"It was a very handsome relocation package," Heather said mysteriously. "The entire compound is empty."

"It's fine, you guys," Sara said. "We have options too. We can also drive out of town overnight. Get back in touch tomorrow."

"Heather, do we have any spare walkie-talkies?" Sara was impressed at how strategically Yukari was handling herself as Lock mother. Heather nodded. "Please give one to Sara. Sara, if you're in range, only use walkie talkie, no phones at all. Also, please turn off your Wi-Fi and Bluetooth."

Sara nodded. "Yes, boss."

"Hey," Yukari laughed. "That's what I used to say to you."

"Sara," Imani's voice was thick with emotion. "This feels so bloody right, just us all laughing our way through another crisis. Glad to have you back."

Sara looked at the faces in the room, ending on Teddie's, relieved to see happiness and forgiveness there.

"It's good to be home."

Chapter Seventeen

Heather watched the screen of her iPad in silence while Sara texted with Silas.

"There, they're all back in their apartments, and I've placed an override on all the locks, nobody can move about," Heather said at last. "I'm sorry, pet, I thought my little Airbnb would be safe enough, but they're right. I'm not a hundred per cent, so it's not worth the risk."

"Don't worry about it, we can head over to Jersey City."

"Okay love," Heather stood and gave her a long hug. "Fran says that she's getting pings on four phones, and they're all east of us, the closest is headed this way, on Central Park West. Normally only two of them come at the same time, so get out quick."

"Silas will be there when I get out of the passageway," Sara said. "I'll be fine."

In the ante chamber to the Surrender Room, Heather opened a drawer in the desk and handed Sara a walkie talkie.

"Don't change the settings, it is set up to work," Heather said, pointing at one button. "Press to talk, let go to listen."

"I've used a walkie talkie before," Sara said, crossing her eyes at her old friend. That was how they'd communicated in the compound before the advent of cellphones.

"Lassie, I'd completely forgotten how they worked," Heather chuckled. "Now get out of here while you still can."

Obediently, Sara pulled open the old rusty coal door, and crouched down and stepped through, hearing Heather close and lock it before she could turn and wave goodbye. She continued until she the space opened up and she could almost stand upright. She pulled out her phone to text Silas, but she had no reception. Jamming her phone back into her pocket, she continued to the metal doorway that led to the street, fighting off memories of the last time she'd exited this space.

Easing herself cautiously out of the coal cellar door into the fetid, dark trash alcove, Sara looked up at the security cameras that she knew were hiding in the dark and gave the thumbs up.

Standing upright, she kept perfectly still, merging with the shadows. A gut instinct told her to haul a recycling bin in front of the coal door real quick, so she did that, easily pushing the metal dumpster over the barely visible opening. She pulled out her phone to text Silas when a female voice spoke.

"Is a nice night for a walk, no?"

Muscles tensed, Sara slid her phone back into her pants pocket, turning slowly in the darkness. On the opposite side of the small alley stood a woman, barely visible in the shadows, her stance casual, one hand on a hip, the other near her face. Sara pressed her back against the brick wall, weighing her options.

"You no speak?" the woman asked, her Spanish accent thick.

"I don't speak to strangers, love," Sara said, in a perfect impersonation of Heather.

"Ah come on," the woman said, taking one step closer. "You and I we are sisters, no?"

Sara's mind was racing. This woman was clearly a younger sister from Madrid. She should know her name. She decided to gamble.

"I don't believe that anyone from Madrid has informed us that they're visiting."

"You don't own a city," the woman said, her voice angry.

"I have an idea," Sara said, catching scent of something rotten and gagging. "Take your friends. Leave New York."

"That is something I can't do." The woman remained motionless.

"My name is Heather," Sara said coolly, and a smile flashed across the young woman's lips.

"Mi nombre es Edita," the girl said, taking a step closer.

Sara weighed her options. Fan's taser was in her backpack, along with the walkie talkie, and she'd put both her arms through the straps in order to get out the coalway. She wondered if all six Spaniards were circling the block. She didn't have much time.

"I take you prisoner," The woman said. "My Holy Mother wishes to speak with you in person."

"You'll need to catch me first," Sara leapt up onto the lid of the dumpster she'd just moved, then used her momentum to spring across the alcove. Galvanized into motion by Sara's sudden actions, the woman darted deeper into the darkness of the alcove, and Sara, holding onto metal window grates two stories up, saw another figure materialize at the end of the alcove.

As she prepared to leap back across to the next level window across the alcove, the new arrival shook its head at her, and slowly approached the Spaniard from behind.

In a whirl of movement so fast it looked like a tornado of black velvet, the newcomer leapt at the Spaniard, wrapping one arm around her neck, raising the other arm aloft, something glinting before falling and plunging into her neck. The young woman began to thrash her free arm, and Sara was relieved to see she was not armed. Hanging on by one hand, she lowered herself down from the window security grill to the full extension of her arm, then let go, dropping loudly onto the dumpster, where she paused, trying to keep her adrenalin under control in case she needed it.

"I'm not doing this for your entertainment," came Heather's voice, and Sara leapt down, grabbing the woman's still-flailing arm and bringing it close to her body as they waited for her spasms to stop. Within seconds, the woman fell limp, and since neither Heather nor Sara bothered to catch her, she crumpled to the dirty cement, knees first, before pitching forward onto her face.

"What the hell was that" Sara glanced at the hypodermic in Heather's hand.

"Oh, just some Fentanyl,' Heather said as she glanced nervously around.

"She's not alone," Sara said. "We need to be fast."

"Do we take her or leave her?"

"For now, we take her," Sara said, already heaving the dumpster out of the way of the coal door. When it was open, she grabbed one of the girl's hands and dragged her limp form to the cellar. Sara entered first, backward, then hauled her along roughly. As soon as there was room, Heather climbed in, then turned and pulled the dumpster back in front of the opening, far enough out for the door to open, but enough to hide it in the darkness, then she pulled the door closed and threw the bolt into place.

"I bloody felt it in me waters," Heather said, her voice raspy.

"I'm glad you came along," Sara said.

"She saw you."

"No. I pretended to be you."

"Ooooh get a load of you," Heather gave her an approving smile. "Smart. Yukari is waiting inside, she wants to draw some of her blood."

Standing upright, Heather kicked the young girl in her side.

"What the hell are you doing?"

"Making sure she ain't faking it," Heather sniffed. "I'm not about to bend over and get clocked by her."

"Heather, I don't think she's trained, not like we are."

"Well that's something."

"Not really, Heath. She wanted to kidnap me. You. Whatever."

"We should have expected it," Heather said, looking at the young woman laying broken on the floor, her black hair splayed out below her head.

"Fuck," Sara said. "She was wearing a hat."

"Do you wanna just pop her into the Surrender room before she wakes up?"

"What? No, Heather, that's not who we are.":

"Sara, we are being circled by these women. They're radicalized. Do you think your kidnapping would have been particularly pleasant?"

"We're not killing her," Sara bent and grabbed one of Edita's arms, but as she began to pull her into the more open hallway behind her, the young woman began to spasm, contortions wracking her unconscious body. Sara sped up the dragging, hauling her through into the antechamber just in time for Edita to projectile vomit a hot stream of rancid black gore all down the front of herself. The stench of it hit Sara's nostrils immediately, and the recognition made her gag.

"They're feeding on animals," Sara said. "Oh, Heather, hold your breath."

Emerging into the antechamber, Sara glanced from Heather to Yukari, pressed into the corner of the small room, one hand clutching her leather medical satchel, the other clamped over her mouth and nose. Heather's face was crinkled in disgust, the sleeve of her black sweater pressed against her mouth. On the floor, Edita's convulsions were worsening, and with a visceral groan, she vomited again, this time the fluid was as black as oil. She was covered in it.

"I need to get the blood now," Yukari said. "I want a sample while she's alive."

Removing her hand from her mouth, and retching immediately, Yukari opened her satchel and took out a large silver hypodermic.

"Sara, can you raise her sleeve?"

Sara took one look at the sleeve of Edita's sweater, invisible beneath a thick black film of vomit, and her stomach flopped like a toad.

"Please?" Yukari said.

"I wasn't waiting for manners," Sara said tersely before plunging her hand down onto Edita's wrists and sliding her sleeve up along her arm. Yukari knelt immediately and slid the needle into Edita's arm. As she pulled back on the plunger, Edita began to stir, moaning sickly. The sound made the hairs on Sara's arms raise.

"She's too weak," Yukari said. "She's going to overdose." Whipping the needle out of the girl's arm, Yukari stood, returning to her place in the corner. "I'm gonna run back to my lab and get this tested while it's fresh."

Nodding, Sara turned her attention back to the girl on the floor, she watched as Edita's fingers and toes began to quiver, shaking so quickly they became a blur. Both women had seen this before, the telltale signs of overdose inside her body. Sara began to panic, wondering if the woman was minutes away from becoming a whirling dervish of death, muscles and joints tensing and releasing with such force that her bones would shatter if she hit a brick wall, or someone else's bones would shatter if she hit them first.

"We need to give her blood," Sara said. "Now. She'll die if not."

"Yes, boss," Heather said behind her sleeve before darting out into the hallway. Her own stomach flip-flopping inside her, Sara knelt by

Edita's head and pressed her chin down to her chest with all her might. With her other hand, she reached into the fetid puddle in her mouth and scooped out the foul liquid. With a splutter, Edita coughed, and Sara barely jerked herself back in time to avoid a face full. When her windpipe was clear, the girl inhaled, a deep, long, congested breath and as her lungs filled, her toes and hands began to thrash, slapping up and down against the stone floor with increasing force, her back arching violently. Sara knew she didn't have long before she'd have to abandon the room or risk getting badly injured.

Heather reappeared in the doorway, a blood bag in her hand. Blinking at the stench, she whipped her keys from her pocket, stabbing the bag with a key sharpened just for that purpose, she pressed the pierced corner into Edita's mouth, and the virus took over. Her oily, black lips clamped down on the bag and her cheeks hollowed with the force of the suction she applied, and within seconds, the bag was flat, empty.

In silence, Heather and Sara watched as the motion in the girl's extremities lessened.

"D'ye think it worked?" Heather asked, her eyes darting from the girl's feet to her hands before another groan bent the young woman in two. She vomited up the blood in a scarlet roar, and her hands began to snap back against the floor with renewed force.

"Apparently not" Sara said. "Gimme your keys."

Heather tossed her keys to Sara, who without hesitation plunged the sharpened key into her own wrist, making a small circular hole that took a second before it pumped a shot of blood onto the Surrender room door. "Here goes nothing," Sara said as she presented her bleeding wrist to Edita, who even in her unconscious state was unable to resist, her head rising like lightning, her filthy lips suctioning to Sara's wrist with a sickening wetness. After suckling for a few seconds, Sara felt teeth trying to bite deeper into her flesh, and she jerked her arm back.

Repositioning herself, she pressed a knee onto Edita's forehead and held her wrist just above her mouth. The first couple of pulses of blood were off-target and they sprayed her entire face and chest with a red mist before Sara was able to angle herself and get the blood to pulse directly into her open mouth.

"Don't give her too much, love," Heather cautioned. "We don't want her too strong."

As the unconscious woman's hands and feet went still, Sara lifted her arm away, pressing down on the wound at her wrist with her other hand.

"Yukari's gonna need to stitch that up," Heather said.

Sara stood, careful not to slip in the disgusting liquid that covered the floor, gazing at the mess. Edita's tongue was the only part of her that was moving, snaking out of her mouth and searching for the blood on her chin or lips. Her eyes were open, but only the whites were showing. It was horrific.

"Heather, fuck, Silas will be freaking out, I need to text him."

"Already did, pet," Heather said. "He knows you're fine, he's standing by."

"Now what are we gonna do about this mess?"

"I'll get the paper towels and the Febreze."

Without another word, Heather disappeared into the hallway, leaving Sara alone with the unconscious girl, the only sound her rattling, labored breathing. She looked young, by Sister standards, probably only eighteen or nineteen when she was made, which was definitely too young. Pressing her bleeding wrist hard against her breastbone, Sara yanked a strip from the front of her hoodie and bound her wrist with it, using her mouth to tie it off.

With a resigned sigh, Sara opened the door to the furnace, which was not lit. She turned the knobs to start the gas flow and then pressed the igniter button, enjoying the whoomp as the flames appeared. Turning, she figured out the easiest way to reduce the smell in the room was to burn the girl's clothes, so holding her breath she yanked Edita's sweater up over her head, keeping it carefully bundled until she tossed it into the hungry flames. Shoes and pants followed, then Sara lifted the unconscious girl out of the smeared puddle on the floor, setting her against the door to the Surrender room, spattered red with Sara's own blood.

A knocking at the other end of the coal chamber caused her to freeze, and the sound echoed toward her again, and again.

"Dr Lilian Berger?" came Silas's muffled voice. "Open up."

Sara darted along the hallway and threw the bolt open, and the door opened and there was Silas, crouching low.

"Get in," she hissed, and he obeyed, yanking the door closed behind him and filling the entire hallway as he crawled forward.

"Ah gah that smell," he said, then retched.

"Heather's getting the Febreze," Sara said, walking backwards into the antechamber. "Did you see anybody?"

Silas nodded, his eyes watering. "There's at least three of them. They were walking separately but they've ganged up now. I had to wait til they passed."

"Well we have one in here," Sara stepped aside to let him come in through the half door.

"I'm sorry Sara, I think I'm going to.."

"NO!" Sara yelled, startling him. "Not you too, I can't right now."

Chastened, Silas stood there swallowing his revulsion.

"Okay, okay I'm... in the clear."

The door to the hallway rattled then opened, and Heather appeared, her arms full of rolls of paper towels.

"I'm gonna have to brick up that bloody wall," Heather said. "It's like the high street in here all of a sudden."

"It's good to see you too," Silas said as Heather tossed him an unopened roll of paper towel.

"Now get mopping."

Tearing off the plastic wrap, Silas rapidly unrolled the entire roll into a large cloud of paper that he dumped onto the soiled floor, before reaching for two more rolls and doing it again. After walking on the paper to absorb as much as he could, he gingerly bundled it up, pressing it into a ball with his hands and then pressing it through the opening to the furnace.

"Two more of those should do it," he said. Heather handed him two more rolls.

"I dare say you're the first person to help us clean up a mess in many a blue moon," Heather said.

"I know, right?" Sara nudged Heather in the ribs. "Mom, can we keep him?"

Chapter Eighteen

Dawn was breaking by the time Silas and Sara finished hauling her old mattress through the catacombs that ran around the core of the compound. As the heavy door on their new top-floor apartment, in a building on the north side of the compound, swung shut, Silas leaned back against the hallway wall.

"Thank you for the quintessential New Yorker experience," he said, wiping sweat from his brow with the back of a sleeve. "Clandestine apartment swap."

"No, thank you," Sara said at the opposite end of the mattress. "That was a lot."

"Let's just get it done and then we can shower and lay down," Silas pushed himself off the wall, and in silence they push-pulled the mattress around yet another tight corner where they let it fall flat onto the floor, dust bunnies swirling in the light of the bare bulb on the ceiling.

"I wanted to go get your clothing out of the dryer," Sara said, eyeing Silas up and down, squeezed as he was into a pair of her old trackpants and a sweater that was oversized on her and a midriff top on him.

"Why?" he did a slow pirouette. "Is there a problem with my current ensemble?"

Standing on her tiptoes, Sara kissed him lightly on the lips.

"Actually, those pants are tight in all the right places," she said.

"You are out of control," he said, kissing her back. "Actually, let's just sit for a bit. I'll heat up some blood for you. How's your wrist?"

Sara held up the neatly bandaged limb. "Hurts like a bitch, but that's what you get for being a martyr."

"I did not enjoy watching Yukari sew you up."

"She couldn't stop sneaking peeks at you."

"She was friendly, at least."

"She's a scientist," Sara said. "She was probably dying to ask you for a blood sample."

"As long as she doesn't use a sharpened key on me, she's welcome to it."

Stepping into the living room, Sara felt that strange shifting feeling again. They had carried down a lot of her furniture over the course of the night, and there were boxes of her belongings all over the floor. She wondered for a second if this was her dream becoming real, but there was no foreboding, and as far as she knew, there were no dead kittens anywhere.

She began to look into the hastily packed boxes, seeing clothing, books, photographs, reminders of a life that felt like something that happened between two points of time and had now ended. The fact that the best of her belongings were still in boxes somewhere outside Reykjavik added to her uneasiness.

She heard Silas coming from the kitchen and turned and smiled at the sight of him, in pink and gray sweats, two very full glasses of blood in his hands. He gestured at the couches with his head.

"Take a load off," he said as he shepherded her onto the least obstructed couch, then sat beside her before handing her one of the glasses.

"What a fucking night," Sara said, holding her glass aloft. "Cheers!"

"Cheers," Silas said, rubbing her thigh with his free hand. "And skál."

In silence they both drained their glasses in a single gulp, with Silas quickly taking Sara's empty glass and setting it on the floor before she fell back.

The darkness closed in deep around her, and the wound in her wrist tingled with a light electricity, a pulsing white blossom of pain around a strange internal itch.

"Silas," she muttered, her voice thick, "did I do the right thing?"

"You're gonna have to narrow the field a little…"

"With the girl?"

"You probably did the right thing," he said.

"I couldn't let her die, Silas, she's just a kid."

"I wasn't thinking about her, I was hoping that your wrist will heal."

"Course it will," Sara said, turning to face him. "But now we have a prisoner. This has never happened before."

"That you know of," he said with a smile. "Don't go beating your conscience up over this. It's not like she is innocent."

"I'm not sure what I'm supposed to do next."

"Sleep," Silas kissed her nose. "The answers will be there when we wake up."

Sara smiled, gazing along the worn brown leather of her couch at the handsome face of this unusual man, his long lashes and full lips, a light froth of blood in his whiskers.

"Feels weird to have a man in my apartment," she said, wiping the blood away with a fingertip.

"Felt weird to have a woman in mine," he smiled. "Also felt weird having you at my upstate house, my Connecticut house, the Reykjavik compound, the Akureyri guest house and Heather's weird Airbnb."

"Holy shit, Silas," Sara smiled. "We've covered some ground in a short space of time."

"I didn't hate it," he said. "I wonder how long we will be here?"

"This building was tenanted," Sara explained. "Heather's been evicting tenants since the Marguerite drama."

"I was wondering about that," Silas said. "I didn't want to bring it up."

"The tenants were in danger."

"But isn't it hard to evict a tenant in New York City?"

"Not when you offer them a hundred thousand bucks to soften the blow."

"Heather," Silas said, explaining everything. Noises wafted up from the street below them, the sounds of the city starting its day, and they sat in silence, listening.

"Something about that Spanish woman is bothering me," Sara pushed herself upright. "It doesn't add up. She looks sick, but we've all survived on animal blood at times, and it didn't make me look like that. Heather was going to research her background today. She's also going to check her register of the Madrid women, she seems really young, like a recent make."

"Wouldn't that be a thing? If old ZPG Desdemona has been making new sisters."

"Yeah, and sending them out as what? Imani called them her special ops."

"Mom says that Des has been impossible to talk to. She's not giving up a single scrap of information."

"I can't stay dead forever," Sara said. "I need to confront her."

"You could be the perfect straw to break that vampire's back."

"Thank you," Sara said. "I do my best."

"No, thank you," Silas said, taking her hand. "Thank you for letting me stay inside this, this space. I couldn't deal with it if you were stuck in here, under siege and I wasn't able to help."

"Yeah, you're welcome, I suppose," Sara took his hand. "I'm not gonna lie, this is going to be super weird."

"I figure I'll just work on strengthening this building while you guys all work shit out in the main compound."

"We will see, I don't think most of the women will have a problem with it. And you know what, if we get to establish our new rules and keep the castle, then you're going to be a part of it."

Tears brimmed up suddenly in Silas's eyes and Sara felt responsible. "You're with me, from now on," she said, and a teardrop fell.

She watched as Silas went to speak, but his words got stopped by stammering and a quivering chin.

"Shall we go to bed then?" Sara stood and took his hand. "And Silas, I only ask one thing. That means you'll have to reunite with Liz. And honey, I want a front row seat."

A knock at the door shocked Sara out of a dreamless sleep. Sitting bolt upright, she scoured the wreckage on the bedroom floor for clothing. Spying the sweatpants she'd loaned Silas, she snatched them up and dragged them on, followed by the hoodie he had been wearing.

"Hey, them's my only clothes," he protested, pulling a towel from a box and wrapping it around his waist. "Wait, where's the door?"

Sara blinked. He was right. They'd been using the fake rear wall to get in and out of the apartment all night. She didn't even have keys to the door, wherever it was.

The sound of a key sliding into the lock told her that the door was at the end of the short hall by the kitchen, and she sprinted there, slamming herself against the door as it began to open.

"Watch it," Heather called out, and Sara relaxed, moving away from the door as it opened, revealing Heather, a Fairway bag in one hand, and a duffel in the other. Behind her stood Crina, waving happily, suitcases behind her on the landing.

"We brought bagels," she said, and both women pushed past Sara into the apartment.

"Oh, hi Mom, morning Heather," Silas said as Sara walked into the disaster of a living room in time to see Heather handing the duffel to him.

"These are your clothes from last night, love," she said, then Crina handed him the luggage they'd had since Boston.

"You guys went to the house?" Sara said. The smell of fresh bagels hit her nose and she realized she was starving.

"Yeah," Heather said, clearing a space on the kitchen counter. "We snuck out earlier, didn't want to leave any evidence in case you were followed."

"I didn't bring any plates," Sara said. "I'm sorry, last night was a blur."

Heather reached into the Fairway bag and produced a package of paper plates, then a box of plastic cutlery.

"I hate plastic forks," Silas said with a shudder.

"Shut up and put some clothes on," Crina said. "When this is over you can put some fine silver on your wedding registry."

Growling at his mother, Silas went into the bedroom and closed the door.

"It's too early for you to be a nagging mother in law," Sara said to Crina as she yawned and stretched at the same time. "What time is it anyway

"Almost two," Heather said.

"Makes sense," Sara said. "I haven't known what time it is for weeks, and if we were in Iceland it could be midnight."

"We checked on our lodger," Crina said. "She's still sleeping, her pulse is steady."

Sara shrugged. "You know, I actually don't care," she said. "I just couldn't let her die like that."

"It's ironic," Crina said. "You're the one everyone is against, but you're the purest follower of our rules on this Earth."

"Nope," Sara said. "That would be Teddie."

"Teddie woulda let that bitch die," Heather said. "I promise ye."

"She threw up again, in the surrender room," Crina said, screwing up her face. "Worst damn thing I ever smelled. She's been surviving on animals, so now that she's got some pure blood in her system, she'll be quite busy expelling the other stuff."

"Can this wait until after breakfast?" Silas emerged from the bedroom in jeans and a plain gray t-shirt, so casually handsome that Sara nearly swooned.

In silence, Heather busied herself with clearing the top of the coffee table while Crina fussed with the contents of the Fairway bag.

"We don't have coffee," Sara said.

"Is the coffee maker not in your old apartment?" Heather's eyes narrowed as Sara shook her head. "The only person who should have been in there was me. Teddie slept there a few nights."

"She did?" Sara's felt a pang in her heart, happy that Teddie took her coffee maker.

"She's okay now, pet," Heather set paper-wrapped bagels onto paper plates and the room suddenly filled with the homey scent of fresh bread and the paper itself. Heather whipped her phone out and her thumbs flicked across it for a moment.

"Okay, lovebirds, there'll be a Starbucks delivery at the front door in fifteen to twenty minutes. Silas, it's safe for you to go get it, just make sure you look both ways before you open the door."

Crina sat cross-legged on the floor and unwrapped her bagel.

"We've been watching the footage from all of the surveillance cameras," she said, pausing her sandwich in front of her face. "They all take turns circling the block. After we caught that one last night, they regrouped, first a group of three, and then one of those three walked around the building and met another two. They all took turns trying to scale the wall in the dumpster area where you got caught out. They all tried to open the metal door."

"So, tonight," Heather said with an impish grin, "we will set a trap and hopefully catch another one."

"Or two," Crina said, high fiving Heather as she chewed.

On the couch, Silas nudged Sara, who gave him a quizzical look.

"Silas, if you have something to share...?" The motherly tone in Crina's voice almost made Sara laugh out loud.

"It's nothing mom, it's just funny seeing you two so het up to catch more of these poor bitches. They're starving and they're probably living in Central Park."

"Well then, we'll put a roof over their heads," Heather said with a smirk.

"You're impossible." Silas finally began to eat.

"Is this girl still manageable, or did my blood make her too strong?"

"I'd say that this time, we got lucky," Crina said. "She was so weak that you've course corrected her. She's not a danger."

"Who knows she's there?"

"As of now, just us and Yuka," Heather said. "It's getting harder to get anything done. We can't tell Rosa or Liz, they're still talking to Eleanor."

"Who's left in Madrid?"

Heather glanced nervously at Crina, who set the uneaten half of her bagel on its paper plate, then met Sara's gaze.

"It seems that everyone who should be in Madrid is still in Madrid."

"I'm not following," Sara said.

"You said the girl's name was Edita, right" Heather's voice was sharp. Sara nodded. "There's no Edita on file at Madrid, nor any other bloody Lock."

Confused, Sara sank into a reverie, the possibilities of Edita's existence swirling around her mind. The ringing of Heather's phone jolted her back to reality, and she watched as Heather answered, her brows knitting as she listened. Solemnly she handed the phone to Sara.

"Sara, it's Yuka."

Sara set the phone to speaker.

"Hi, Yuka, what's up?"

"Sara, I don't know how to say this, but..."

"What is it?"

"That girl," Yukari spoke slowly, as if what she needed to say was still formulating in her head. "She isn't... she's not Cursed the way we are."

Panic blossomed in Sara's chest.

"What do you mean, Yuka?"

"The virus in her system isn't the same strain as ours, it's much weaker. I've been testing it over and over, it doesn't replicate and it doesn't gain any strength from blood."

"I don't know what all this means, Yuka."

"She's not cursed," Yukari said. "She's carrying a modified version of what we have, kind of like if someone got a mild flu from a flu shot."

The reality of the situation flooded in on Sara. .

"Wait," she said. "Yukari, have I fucked up. What will my blood do to her?"

"I don't know," the woman said tentatively. "She has a virus similar to ours, but not identical. I don't know if that will be enough to stop the..."

"Oh no," Heather. Crina and Silas exchanged worried glances, then they both looked at Sara. If a non-infected person consumed Cursed blood and the blood made contact with their intestines, it was usually fatal. And incredibly painful. The Cursed men would do it to their enemies, feed them their blood, then watch the victim writhe in agony til they died. They called it Eating The Wolf.

"Yep," Sara said, pushing them memory away with a shudder. "Okay, we have one more thing to deal with. I am with Heather and Crina, we will come see you."

"Can I have an hour? I haven't slept and I'm wiped."

"Sorry, of course you can Yuka. And thank you, so much."

"Sorry the news wasn't better," she said, hanging up.

Sara handed the phone back to Heather, her heart racing.

"I basically killed that girl," Sara said, her voice flat.

"You thought you were saving her life," Heather said. "This is all new territory."

"She came here to kidnap you guys," Silas said. "Who knows what that would have actually meant if it happened."

"I'm gonna go light the furnace," Crina said, standing suddenly and brushing crumbs from her pants. "This is a disaster. It's not your fault Sara, but we can't let her live. It's more humane if we peace her out and let her die before your blood consumes her."

Sara winced

In her heart, Sara knew that Crina was right, that her way was the easy way out, but she just couldn't let it happen.

"Maybe," she began. "Maybe. I would like to talk to her before we make any decision, is that okay?"

Heather shrugged. "The decision has been made by fate, Sara. But if you want to talk to her, you'd best do it sooner than later. You should ask Yukari, she is still Mother."

"She's exhausted, we can let her sleep."

"I need to go see her, before she... I mean, she still might survive." Sara wiped the crumbs from her hands on her pants. "Let's strategize."

"Will you at least take a Slicer?" Heather asked.

"I'll take a taser," Sara said. "You bitches are acting like it's sixteen twenty-three. Get with the times."

"I'm acting like I don't want to lose you again," Heather said. "I'll be standing at the door with a Slicer whether you like it or not."

"I'll let you hold one of the new tasers," Sara said. "It's not negotiable. If she's not cursed, we don't need to worry about an adrenaline frenzy."

"You're not going to win this one," Crina said softly, raising a palm to Heather. "Sara's made her mind up."

"What's that mean?" Sara leaned forward.

"Please bitch, have you ever met a stray you didn't have to save?"

Chapter Nineteen

An hour later, Sara had showered, finished her coffee and ordered an espresso machine online. Sitting on the couch, nervously flipping her phone from one hand to the other, she waited for Heather to text her so she could make her way back down to the Surrender room.

It had been decided that it would be better for the girl to shower and use a bathroom ahead of her session with Sara, and Crina had volunteered for that job. Once the women left the apartment, Silas fell silent, and had been texting in the bedroom ever since.

> I'll be at your door in a minute pet. We're all set. And prepare yourself for a shock, the blood has entered her bloodstream.

A wave of angry self-loathing rushed down Sara's spine at the sight of the text from Heather. She had forced the woman to drink her blood, and as a result she was being eaten alive, from the inside out.

"They're ready for me," Sara called out, and Silas appeared in the bedroom doorway. "She's definitely going to die."

"I'm sorry, Sara, really, I am. And please, please be careful," he said, his eyes imploring her. Standing, she kissed the tip of his nose.

"I will," she said, pressing her forehead against his, her feet on tiptoes. "I've looked after myself for a long time, Silas."

"I know, I'm not saying you need me there, not at all. I'm saying that I want to fight alongside you."

She wrapped her arms around his waist and squeezed him hard.

"Thank you, I just need to see what she knows before...."

Silas nodded.

Heather's trademark one-two knock at the rear door echoed in the apartment, and Sara released Silas, kissed him one more time then rushed to open the door.

"Let's go," Heather said. "I've blocked access to these hallways for the next ten minutes."

"See you when I get back," Sara said, laughing at the normal sounding sentiment, as if she was off to a day at the office instead of a potentially dangerous meeting with a newly created vampire.

"We got a nice present today," Heather said as she hurried ahead of Sara. "From Iceland. It was labeled as jewelry and radios. It's-"

"I know what it is," Sara said. "Fan was very proud of her new inventions."

"They're pretty sweet," Heather said. "It'll take some getting used to."

"The cattle bolt taser?"

"Oh no, that scared me," Heather chuckled. "The rings that turn into a slicer. They're pretty."

"Seems unnecessary to me," Sara sniffed as Heather disappeared around a corner. Sara knew she'd be waiting at the elevator when she caught up to her.

"Going down?"

Sara nodded, and Heather summoned the elevator to take them down to the basement level hallway that led to the Surrender Room. The hallway was always quiet, but today, the silence felt foreboding to Sara. Her footsteps did not echo, as if the ancient walls were absorbing sound. As they approached the door to the antechamber, it swung open and Crina leaned out.

"Oh good, you're here. And you left the boyfriend at home."

"You old bitches are exasperating," Sara said. "Eternity is going to feel like forever if you don't give this shit a rest."

"Our new friend is a sullen piece of work," Crina said. "At least she's nice and clean now."

"Was she cooperative?" Sara's eyes bored into Crina's, who shrugged.

"I held a taser up at her the whole time, so yeah."

Shaking her head, Sara pushed past Crina into the small antechamber room and took a deep breath.

"I'm going in unarmed," Sara announced.

"Told you," Crina said to Heather, who didn't answer, her back to the room as she locked the door to the outer hall.

"If things start to get rowdy in there," Heather finally turned around, "I'm going to light the fire. We will get you out before you black out fully."

Sara nodded. "Again?"

Crina moved to the small table beside the furnace door and handed Sara a pink Stanley cup.

"I'm going to talk to an assassin, not go for a jog."

"It's a smoothie and it contains enough Fentanyl to kill an elephant," Crina said. "Yukari would quote love you more than forever unquote if you got her a decent blood sample while you were in there. She wants to see what our virus did to her virus."

"She's going to die," Sara said tersely. "Yukari can do a full autopsy if she likes."

Heather shrugged, as if to say what's done is done, and they each stood in silence, looking at the floor.

"I'm going in!"

Sara saluted Crina and took the cup in one hand, the satchel in the other, then stood back from the door to the Surrender Room.

"Okay, ready?" she said, watching as Heather and Crina drew tasers, standing between her and the hallway door. They both nodded, and Sara deftly unlatched the heavy outer barricade then opened the door a crack, her shoulder against the metal, her left foot planted behind her.

"Edita, hola?"

"Que, *perra*?"

Behind Sara, Crina tittered.

"I'm going to come in and talk to you," Sara said in Spanish, and entered the room. At the sight of her, Sara froze, taking a second to regain her composure. The young woman, now wearing nothing but a sports bra and underwear, was curled back against the same comfortable chair that Sara blacked out in when she ended her old life. Edita's black hair was a still damp, pulled back from her face. Even though it was just over twelve hours since Sara had fed Edita her blood, she could see that the virus was already consuming her. Dark circles under her eyes reached halfway down her cheeks, which were sunken. Her wounded brown eyes met Sara's for an instant, then darted away.

"Is that alright?" Sara asked.

"What difference can it make if I say no?"

"I will leave if you want me to," Sara said, and Edita nervously glanced at her, and then looked away again.

"You have come to kill me?"

"Sweetheart," Sara slipped into the room and let the door fall closed behind her. She watched as Edita's head tilted, listening for the sound of the latch falling back into place. When no sound came, the corners of her mouth curled up slightly. "If the plan was to kill you, you'd be dead already. And don't try to run, there are two women waiting out there and they are armed."

"So just kill me then, *puta*," Edita said, a look of disgust on her face.

"Here in New York, we don't kill."

"You plan to kill our Holy Mother," Edita said. "She has warned of you."

"I do not plan to kill Desdemona," Sara said, leaning back against the wall beside the fireplace. "She is like a sister to me."

"Dirty liar," Edita spat. "I will not tell you anything, you waste your time. But that's what you bitches do here in New York, right? You need to go work on your art degree and do Pilates and then go on a date?"

"That doesn't sound like a bad day to me, Edita. Why does it sound bad to you?"

"This is not permitted, is as simple as that," Edita said. "The rules are the rules. Following the rules is the key to my salvation."

"I don't know which rules you're talking about, but the rules for all women like us are followed very explicitly here in New York."

"Blah blah blah of course you're going to say that, running all over the city as if you own it. And how come you talk different today?"

Sara didn't answer. Instead she looked down at the broken young woman on the couch, her shoulders tense, her eyes baleful, reminding her of a mistreated dog.

"Where are my clothes, bitch?"

"We burned them, Edita. I'm sorry." Sara watched as a blaze of anger passed across the woman's face, her eyes almost glowing with hate.

"Cabrona," she hissed. "I need my clothes. What about my phone?"

Sara decided to change her approach.

"How are you feeling today?" She kept her voice light.

"What do you mean?"

"Well, last night, you were very sick, you could have died."

"Yeah, because you drugged me."

"Well you did try to kill me and got caught."

"I didn't want to kill you, stupid puta. I wanted to capture you, I wasn't going to hurt you."

"Why would you want to capture me? You could have knocked on the front door."

"Why would I believe you?"

"Because I have nothing to gain by lying," Sara said. "Are you hungry?"

Edita's head jerked up and her eyes widened. Sara knew that Edita was ravenous, the hunger of the early stages of this process was legendary. Still, Edita shook her head, her knotty hair whipping around her cheeks.

"I have a smoothie here, if you'd like."

Edita froze, her eyes wide. She looked from Sara's face down to the pink cup in her hand and back up to meet her eyes.

"No, senora, por favor, I can't trust you. Last night you fed me human blood, I remember this. You've doomed me. You gave me the sacrament, I'm not ready yet, is too soon, much too soon."

"What do you mean, Edita? What do you think this is?" Sara held up her left arm, nodding at the bandage on her wrist. "You fed from me last night, that's how we saved you."

Horrified realization washed over the young girl and she crumpled forward, a guttural moan rising from her, so viscerally miserable it made the hairs on Sara's neck bristle.

"Please, no, tell me you did not do that to me."

"I don't understand, Edita, you would have died."

Sitting violently upright, her head thrown back, Edita wailed again.

"Aiy dios mio, I wish you killed me, lady, why didn't you just kill me? Now I can never go back home."

"Calm down, please, Edita. I don't understand what you're saying."

"I am not pure and worthy for the sacrament," she said, her voice breaking. "You did this to me and now I can never go home, I am impure, I have tasted beyond my entitlement, I am now... " She gazed imploringly at Sara. "Cursed."

"I drank the prohibited blood," Edita said, anguish in her eyes and voice. "I am unclean. Holy Mother will cast me out."

"You drank prohibited blood? You're not allowed to drink blood? Edita, I don't understand. You threw up so much blood, you've been feeding on animals."

"I am a penitent," she said quietly. "Until I have paid for my past, I am not worthy for what you gave to me. Only the Holy Mother can transform a novitiate!"

"Well, that's not actually true," Sara said. "Why would you not be worthy of the food that keeps you alive?"

"In Spain, we drink the blood of the goat, is our salvation."

"How long have you lived on goat blood, Edita?" Sara fought to keep the astonishment out of her voice. How was Desdemona convincing newly made sisters to exist solely on goat blood? Of course, there had been periods in Sara's life when that was the only thing available, centuries earlier, and she still remembered the queasy nausea, the lethargy and the general revulsion that she felt the whole time she subsisted on it. Had Desdemona engineered this new strain?

"It's all I have ever known," Edita said. "Until this time, I come here, but we have stayed longer than we plan, and so I had to..." she paused, shuddering.

"It's okay, Edita, you can tell me."

"No, it's disgusting."

"I promise you, in this life, we've all had to do disgusting things to survive. I'm sorry, it's just a fact."

"You think that all this talking of the truth and promises is going to change my mind? I told you I don't want your help or your..." her conviction wavered "...or your food."

"And I said you didn't have to drink it," Sara said. "I was asking how you have been surviving."

Edita shook her head, and tears escaped her eyes, rolling down her cheeks.

"In the big park," she said. "We eat the animals."

"What? Squirrels?" Sara hated the sound of horror in her voice, and Edita picked up on it.

"See? You know is bad what we had to do."

"It's not bad, Edita. You lived on squirrels?"

"And raccoons, and cats," she said dejectedly, wincing at the memory.

"You can't survive on those things," Sara said. "Do you understand that you have a virus? And that only certain types of blood can keep you alive?"

"I'm not an idiot, perra. Of course I know it. But it is not safe for one at my level, a novitiate, to control. Only Holy Mother has the power to consume the blood of a human."

"Someone hasn't been completely honest with you," Sara said. "How did you become able to survive on goat's blood?"

Exhausted, Edita pushed herself upright, holding her head proudly.

"Either kill me or let me go."

"I'm not going to kill you, like I already said a hundred times. And sure, we will release you, probably tonight."

Edita's eyes narrowed and one eyebrow shot up.

"Why would you release me? Why would anyone release their enemy?"

"Listen, kid. I've known Desdemona since she was your age. Whatever she has you doing, nothing will come of it. She does this from time to time, she goes crazy and makes a mess. This isn't the first time I've been through this."

Sara saw that she was confusing the girl, so she stayed quiet for a moment, letting her process.

"Do you mind if I just set this down?" Sara gestured at the pink cup in her hand. Edita glanced at it and shrugged.

"It's your house, do what you want."

"What I want is to understand you, Edita," Sara said, and the honesty in her voice caused the young woman's head to tilt, as if she was listening for the first time. "What happened to you to make you like this?"

"We are forbidden from telling you, the Holy Mother-" A spasm gripped Edita and she bent double, a sickening groan coming from her throat. "What have you done to me?"

"You're just hungry," Sara lied, her voice soft. "Here, take a few sips of this smoothie, you need something in your stomach."

The spasm subsided and Edita slowly pushed herself back to upright.

"This hurts so much," she said quietly. "I... I can't die here, I want to go home. Please."

"I'm sorry you're scared," Sara said. "I promise I'm not going to hurt you. Just drink some of this smoothie, you'll feel better."

Edita considered Sara's offer, her ragged breathing the only sound in the room.

"You first, you take a sip," she said finally.

With a shrug, Sara raised the straw to her lips and applied gentle suction. When she felt the first drop hit her tongue, she pretended to gulp and swallow. Then she set the cup back on the table.

"It's good," she said. "Now you."

Warily Edita reached for the Stanley cup. Gripping the handle, she brought it to her lips and took a tentative sip, her face registering surprise at the pleasant taste. Before she could take a second sip, another violent spasm rocked her body. The cup tumbled to the floor and the girl grabbed at her stomach.

"What the fuck is happening to me?" she screamed.

"You need to drink more," Sara pleaded, aware that time was running out fast. "Hurry, give your stomach something to digest."

Keeping one eye on the writhing woman, she bent and picked up the cup. As she went to hand it to her, Edita stiffened horribly, her back arching as a scream escaped her throat.

"You've poisoned me," she screamed in between spasms, falling from the couch and curling up in the fetal position, her knees pulled tightly to her chest. Sara reached to grab her shoulders, to help her back to sitting, but the flesh that her fingers touched felt like jelly, and a wave of nausea hit her. She had never seen anyone die of this but she had heard the stories, and she knew that the virus was consuming Edita from the inside out. She grabbed the Stanley cup and held the straw at the woman's mouth.

"Edita, trust me this is the only thing that will save you now."

With the last of her strength, Edita hauled her arm back and aimed a punch at Sara, hitting the Stanley cup instead. With a sickening squelch, her knuckles split open on the cup, and she screamed in agony, her smashed hand flapping in pain.

"What the fuck?" Edita said, panicking as she looked at her knuckles, the skin torn raggedly, white bone visible. The wound was not bleeding, not one drop. Sara remembered Ama describing this in her training, that the extremities were the first things to lose their blood. "Why aren't I bleeding?" Edita screamed.

Once again, Sara grabbed the cup and pressed the straw to her lips, and Edita swatted it away. Knowing that she could not watch a child die this way, Sara unscrewed the lid, then threw herself at the woman, overpowering her easily. She pressed her knees into her shoulders, held her forehead back with one hand until her mouth opened, and then poured the smoothie in.

"Drink," she commanded, and after several sputtering attempts at talking, Edita began to swallow. When the cup was empty Sara released her, and set the cup on the mantle.

"Keep it down," she said gently, moving to sit beside her on the floor. "I'm here with you, you're going to be okay."

"I don't feel okay," Edita said, dropping all hostility and instantly becoming a scared teenager. Sara's heart broke and she took the girl's undamaged hand.

"You will, it's just going to take some time, Edita," she said. "I'm gonna stay with you until you feel better, then we will take you to a doctor and then we can send you home."

"I'm scared," the girl said, her voice starting to get fuzzy. "But maybe the pain is less? I'm sorry I tried to kidnap you, I didn't want to come here and do this."

Anger at Desdemona flared up inside Sara and she fought to ignore it, she needed to stay present and help this poor girl at the end of her life.

"It's fine," Sara said. "We've all done dumb things, at least you're going to get better and you can do home."

"Whoa," the girl said, turning to her. "You're nice. Wasn't expecting that. We-" she stopped as another spasm tore through her. "Why can't I feel this?" she asked. "It doesn't hurt any more."

"Good," Sara said. "Let's get you back on the couch and lay you down."

She lifted Edita onto the couch, smoothing her hair over the armrest, forcing herself not to react when she noticed how visible her ribs were already.

"I'm sorry," the girl said, her eyes starting to roll back in her head. "Watch out for the others, they have-"

An explosive spasm rocked Edita, jackknifing her body back and forth, her unconscious head lolling sickeningly, until she was spent and her limp body flopped backwards onto the couch. Inhaling deeply, Sara watched as Edita's skin began to move in waves as the virus consumed her from within. Bruises formed like violet explosions beneath the surface, and then, almost instantly they would fade. Sara reached for her wrist to check for a pulse, gagging when her fingers sank deep into the flesh, feeling the hardened, empty veins beneath the surface now as strong as thin strands of wire.

Turning, Sara pressed her shoulder into the heavy door, and it swung open. Stepping out into the antechamber, she Crina and Heather both checking their phones, tasers sitting beside a glinting Slicer on the little table.

"She's dead," Sara said. "And we need to get her in the furnace fast, unless you want to mop up another puddle."

Without a word, Heather set her phone down and pulled out the lower tray on the furnace, then went into the Surrender room.

"I'm gonna need some help, Crina," she called out. Silently, Crina followed her in.

"Get out of the way, Sara," Heather called, then seconds later, she emerged, carrying Edita by the feet, with Crina following, her arms hooked beneath the dead girl's shoulders.

When they got into the antechamber, Crina turned Edita's body so that they could lay her on the metal grate. Heather lifted her lifeless arms and crossed them on her chest, then slid the drawer closed. Without a word, she punched the ignition button, and they all heard the hefty whomp of the flames catching.

"Could you hear us talking?" Sara said, mainly to break the silence.

Crina shook her head. "No, just the screaming."

"That's gonna haunt me for a long while," Heather said.

"Not as much as watching," Sara said. "You guys, I killed her."

Crina stepped in front of Sara, placing hands on Sara's shoulders.

"I know it hurts, but Desdemona killed that girl. You tried to save her."

"One day I'll believe that," Sara said. "But right now, while she's being cremated three feet away, I'm allowed to have some struggles."

Crina kissed the top of her head. "We will be seeing more bodies before this war is over," she whispered.

This wasn't the reassurance that Sara was looking for, and she stepped away from Crina, readying a reply.

"Piss shit," Heather said. "Rosa has texted me like twenty times. I told her I'm rebooting the security codes. I need to open shit up. Can you get back to your love nest lassie?"

"Yes, of course."

"Okay, sorry that was horrible, I need to get back to me gaff." Blowing them kisses, Heather let herself out the door. When it closed behind her, anger settled over Sara's heart and she turned to Crina.

"Crina, I've been meaning to check in with you on something."

"Uh oh, that sounds like an official email. Do I need to go see HR?"

"That's such a mom joke."

"Live, laugh, love," Crina said, cackling.

"Seriously, if you can please, what are we going to do about Teddie and Silas?"

"You mean the secret son part?"

Sara nodded slowly.

Crina exhaled slowly, loudly, then shrugged.

"I wish I knew the right answer," she said. "That's still my greatest weakness, my best-kept secret."

"Yep. Knew all that."

"And I know how important Teddie is to you..."

"Isn't she just as important to you?"

To Sara's surprise, Crina shook her head. "She and I are not close the way you and she are. To be honest, I welcomed your decision to make her, because it freed me up to spend time with Silas."

"Yeah, all of that fell into place once I found out."

"So what do you want me to do, Sara?"

"I want you to put your money where your mouth is," Sara said firmly. "If we're leaving the Lock system behind, you don't need your big secret anymore."

Sara was shocked when Crina actually flinched.

"It's still my secret, Sara."

"Barely," Sara said, taking Crina's hand. "His cover is blown. The news that you're his mother might actually save his life."

"Or end it." Crina released Sara's hand and turned for the door.

"Crina, my relationship with Teddie is as important as yours with Silas," Sara said quietly, stopping Crina in her tracks. "I'm free to take whatever actions I need to keep that relationship safe."

"I can't believe you're blackmailing me."

"I'm not, at all," Sara said. "It's just time to bring your actions into line with your words. This is a you job."

With that, Sara slipped past Crina and walked down the hall, her heart racing with the satisfaction of beating a parent at their own game.

Chapter Twenty

Inside the elevator that would take her back to Silas, Sara pressed the close doors button and blinked away a wave of tiredness. Edita's death had drained her emotionally, and suddenly, the weight of the past twenty-four hours landed on her like a brick. With a soft hydraulic sound, the elevator arrived at the fifth floor, and she stepped out into the hallway that ran behind her old apartment. Sara made a right, toward the hallway that led to the rear door of the apartment she was in now.

"Get the fuck out of here," came a familiar voice, and Sara spun around to see Fran, in black yoga pants and a loose gray sweater almost the same shade as her hair, leaning against the wall at the other end of the hallway. Sara felt an influx of adrenaline to her system and forced herself to remain calm.

"Sara, is it really you?" Fran's face contorted in shocked happiness as she took four steps closer to Sara, her hands moving absently in front of her, as if she was wringing an answer from the air.

"It is, Fran," Sara said.

"Oh my god, oh my god," Fran sobbed. "Girl, get over here."

"I'm good here," Sara said. "Kind of on the defensive around you guys these days."

"No, no, no, no no," Fran stumbled another few steps closer, and Sara stepped back. "Sara, I'm not going to hurt you, I'm just so, aw hell, I... I..."

And with that, the woman collapsed into a hunched ball on the floor, ugly sobs wracking her body, her thick, straight silver hair falling over her face like a shroud. Everything in Sara wanted to hug Fran, to comfort her, but she was unarmed, and this could be a trap. Eventually, when she realized a hug was not forthcoming, Fran gathered herself, and slowly unfolded, lifting her tear-soaked face up, pleading at Sara with red eyes.

"How... how are you here?"

"Look, Fran, this isn't ideal, I really don't want Rosa to find out I'm still breathing."

"Well she ain't gonna find out from me," Fran slapped the brick wall with an open palm. "Sara, I give you my word, you can trust me."

"It's going to take a lot more than your word," Sara said, surprised at how angry she was getting. "I could have used some support a few weeks ago, you know, when you all put me to death."

Fran's shoulders slumped and she turned away.

"You're right, yes, you are," she said, and Sara had a flash that of all the sisters she'd cared for, Fran was the one she knew the least. She kept to herself, she worked on their cyber security, and she usually had a cat or two. Sara didn't even know if she currently had a cat.

"Look, I get it," Fran said, still unable to face her. "I don't play the game, I don't hang out with you or Imani or whatever. I'm an outsider. I dunno, I always just thought that a time would come where you and I would be tight, but..."

"But what?"

"You never really wanted to hang out or anything," Fran turned back to face Sara, but could only hold her gaze for a second before looking at the floor.

"I got wrapped up in my own shit," Sara said. "And I just figured that you were a lone wolf who loved cats."

"I am, Sara, but I am still a person, and I've been waiting sixty years for anyone in this building to talk to me when they don't need me to reset their fucking VPN."

"Look, Fran, I'm sorry to hear all of this, really I am, but in terms of what I wanted to happen today, this is pretty bad for me. I don't want Desdemona to know I'm alive."

"Well that murdering bitch ain't gonna hear it from me," Fran spat. "Look, it's not safe for you to be walking the back hallways. Everyone's talking about how the security access changes every five minutes. The halls are blocked almost constantly but..."

"Wait, how do you know all this?"

"Sara, I'm a fucking hacker, or did you forget? Now look, I'm not the only one who's noticing Heather playing with the security permissions. Where were you headed? Are you staying in your own apartment?"

"Yes," Sara lied hurriedly. "What's left of it at least."

Fran extended a hand. "Help a bitch up?"

Sara walked to where the woman was sitting and extended a hand, her other hand tensed in case this was a trick. Fran grabbed her hand and sprung to her feet.

"I need a handkerchief," the woman said, wiping her face with the back of a sleeve. "Nobody carries handkerchiefs anymore."

"Would you like to go to your place?" Sara asked. Surprise dawned across Fran's birdlike features as she nodded.

"Follow me but let me go ahead in case anyone else is using the hallways."

Without waiting, Fran sped to the far end of the hallway, then turned and gave her a thumbs up signal, then darted ahead, using her finger to unlock the door, which swung out, obscuring her as Sara approached. Slowing, Sara braced again as she stepped around the heavy brick and iron door, but as she came around, she saw that Fran step inside a doorway.

"C'mon in," she called out as Sara reached her door. Pulling the door closed behind her, Sara inhaled the complicated aromas of incense, coffee and something sharp and metallic. The first bedroom that Sara passed was Fran's work set up, tables on three sides, all topped with monitors, all showing coding tickertape that Sara didn't understand. The ozone smell she'd sensed was emanating from this room. Probably all the CPUs, she figured.

The second bedroom door was closed.

"Fran, I'm super paranoid, can I peek in your bedroom?"

"Totally understandable, go ahead, sorry the bed's not made."

Sara opened the door, and an enormous white Persian cat hissed and vanished beneath the unmade bed.

"Sorry, I startled your cat," Sara said.

"Don't worry, everything scares Olivia," Fran said from down the hall. Sara followed her voice and found her in the kitchen, warming up a gleaming espresso machine.

"Sorry I'm so jumpy," Sara said.

"A near death experience'll do that to ya," Fran said. As the words left her mouth, she paused, a small espresso cup in one hand, and her face softened. "I'm sorry to joke about it, Sara. I'm sure it wasn't a pleasant ride. Do you mind me asking how you got out?"

"Heather," Sara said.

"And how far did she let it go?"

"I lit the fire Fran. I thought my time was up. I blacked out."

Fran blinked slowly, and when her blue eyes opened again, she set the little cup on the counter and hugged Sara, tight.

"There are no words for how sorry I am, Sara."

"Fran, really, it's okay. There's blame all over the place for that one, but most of it rests with me."

Fran let her go and resumed making their coffees.

"Take a seat," she said as the machine hissed and whirred, and the smell of a very robust, dark coffee overpowered everything else. "So who all knows you're alive?"

"Well now, everyone except Rosa, Eleanor and Liz."

"Oh shit, how did Teddie take it?"

"Vaguely resentful."

"She'll get over it," Fran walked into the living room with two cups of coffee on a small tray, bowing to let Sara take one before she settled herself cross-legged on the couch opposite. "I'm sure she's really happy deep down."

"I hope so," Sara said, inhaling her coffee.

"Look, I need to clear the air here, I have done so much meditating and reflecting since that night in the big meeting room, not to mention the way those women have been talking since then, and Sara, I got played."

"We all did, to a degree," Sara said, putting the hot cup on the coffee table between them. "But please, I interrupted."

"Look, I'm still in favor of making no more sisters. Every single one of us poses an incredible risk to the rest of the human race. It's not a bad idea to have us die off. What I didn't know in any way shape or form was that Desdemona was planning to... expedite the process."

"Fran," Sara fought to contain the excitement in her voice. "Fran, do you know what Desdemona's plan is?"

Fran shook her head. "Sorry, no, I wasn't ever privy to the real gossip. Rosa knows more than anyone. Eleanor is with Desdemona, she was at all the Surrenders. She's been quiet on the text circle I'm in with them. And they don't tell Liz a damn thing, they always laugh at her behind her back. I probably know more than Liz but that's not saying much."

"Anything helps," Sara said. "We can't keep her here forever."

"I know Rosa is certain she will ultimately be Lock Mother," Fran said bluntly. "She's said it several times. They want us to become as draconian as Madrid."

Sara wasn't convinced that Fran's change of heart was legitimate. Anyone could have guessed that Rosa was on a Desdemona-fueled power trip. Something was still tripping her suspicions, and she didn't know Fran well enough to figure out what it was.

"There must be something more," Sara said, unsure how much to reveal. "There has been a lot of chatter about a satellite monastery outside Madrid."

Fran jerked her head up in surprise, convincing Sara that at the very least, what she said about not being in Rosa's inner circle was true.

"Yep," Sara said. "We aren't sure what she's doing with the young women. Which is why Heather has to be so crazy with the fingerprint locks and changing the access unpredictably."

"I wondered why she was being so brazen about it all," Fran tucked a strand of her hair behind an ear. "That's why I hacked into our security system, I wanted to make sure it wasn't the cyber girl in Madrid, whatsername? I can't remember her Nominee but her hacker name is El Chapulín. She's good but I see her coming five miles out. She leaves digital fingerprints everywhere."

Sara took a sip of her coffee, enjoying the burn on her tongue.

"What else has this Chapulín been trying to get into?"

"The usual," Fran said. "Our email, servers, storage. That's what's surprising. She's been really predictable, and our firewall is pretty impervious. Which is the kind of thinking that leads to vulnerability, which is why I never sleep." Fran paused, chuckling at her own joke. "Still, she hasn't gone for cellphones, she hasn't done anything complicated. I couldn't believe it, they literally sent me a spam email with spyware embedded. As if I'd panic that my AOL password has been compromised and click that link."

Fran made herself laugh again, this time more loudly. "As if, right?"

"Erm, right?" Sara said, because the last time she'd been in this apartment, she had literally just clicked on such an email. Sara watched Fran's face change in slow-motion as she realized the same thing, and her laughter stopped dead.

"Sorry, yeah, I forgot about that too." Fran sipped her coffee and the silence spun out for two beats before she leapt back in. "Anyway, Chapulín has been leaving digital tracks all over the place, and I'm following the breadcrumbs. I've been talking to Heather, we're trying to find out how many active passports are connected with Madrid, and then we can locate the women, make sure they're all where they're supposed to be."

Sara paused mid-sip, wondering if Fran knew about the Spanish women in the City.

"And are they?" she asked, her voice even.

"Don't know yet, it's pretty slow hacking. Heather told me to hurry up, so I'm working with my girl in Ukraine, we should know in a day or two. On top of that, I'm close to their security system, I can see it, but I can't be sure of their firewall and I don't want to alarm them."

"Do you know if they have surveillance cameras?"

"They've had them for as long as we have, they save them to a hardwired drive, and they don't back up. It's an intranet."

"Makes sense," Sara said. "That's what we have."

"Right, but all their stuff is built on older versions of software and hardware and that means vulnerabilities for me to exploit."

A wave of panic washed over Sara.

"Do you monitor our cameras?" she asked, her voice flat.

"The old system, yes," Fran said. "They're all external, the streets and roof and stuff, the entryways."

"What about the inside stuff?"

Fran's face went dark. "Heather has all that hardwired to the server in her office," the woman said angrily. "Apparently I'm not to be trusted with it. But you know what? Who cares? If I wanted to get in, I could easily do it."

"Well I think it's time for you and me to have a talk with Heather, huh?"

Fran wasn't easily soothed.

"It's like her stupid fingerprint locks. She keeps it all on her iPad, but Sara, I'll tell you something, I hacked that shit without breaking a sweat."

Sara froze, then set a smile on her poker face.

"Does Heather know?"

Fran shook her head, her long silver hair swaying from side to side. "Fuck no, but seriously, walking around with your iPad connected to the Wi-Fi and also with your Bluetooth on? Don't threaten me with a good time."

"You do realize how dangerous that would be if you were working with Rosa?"

"Exactly," Fran said. "And if I was working with Rosa, would I be telling you?"

"So, you've gotten inside the fingerprint locks?"

Fran nodded. "That's how I caught you sneaking about."

"Did you see anything else weird?"

"Yeah, kinda. There are too many sets of fingerprints registered. Now I know that one print belongs to you."

Sara shrugged noncommittally. "I don't really understand how it works," she lied. "Could one be Marguerite?"

"Only if she's not dead too," Fran said with a terse laugh. "It got used last night, only once, on the rear door to your apartment."

"You saw my movements, right?" Fran nodded. "I was in and out last night." Since the other fingerprint was Silas, Sara threw up a smokescreen. "Last night got a bit crazy. I nearly got caught out on the street by one of Desdemona's girls."

Fran gasped. "What the hell are you talking about?"

"Exactly that," she said, the shock on Fran's face again convincing Sara that Fran wasn't lying and didn't know about the infected women in Central Park. "Apparently there are six of Desdemona's women here in New York and they're out there trying to kidnap one of us, or worse."

"And I'm not trustworthy enough to help on this?" Fran's jaw set as she clenched her teeth in frustration.

"Look, Fran, I know it stings but everyone thinks you're in with Rosa and her crew."

"I know, I know, I get it, Jesus Christ I get it, but think for one damn second, Sara. If there are women in this town, don't you think it would be smart to get your resident hacker involved?"

"Not if the hacker might be helping the enemy. Rosa would let them in, and until twenty minutes ago, I would have said the same about you."

"I don't know what I have to do to prove this to you guys, I'm on the side of love and light and freedom and honesty. I always have been. And if we are at war, as you say, then you guys need me working my pussy to the wood to get the intel."

"Your pussy to the wood?"

"I know," Fran cackled. "Great, right? Joan Jett said that to me once at CBGB."

"You went to CBGB? I never saw you there."

"No, remember, because you always went with Teddie and we couldn't go out in groups."

Sara nodded, her eye catching a framed Grateful Dead poster on the wall above Fran. She'd been in this apartment several times, but she mainly went into the computer room, the purpose of her visits. Now she could see the psychedelic poster was signed, and each of the members had said something personal about Fran.

"Fran, I'm just now noticing that your Grateful Dead poster isn't just signed, they are all saying very personal things to you. Wait, Jerry Garcia is calling you the original acid queen? I'm sorry, but I'm impressed."

"Do you not remember when Yukari whipped up that batch of LSD425?"

"Fran, you'd be surprised at the number of things that happened in this house without my knowledge."

"No," she said, her voice less playful. "I wouldn't. Sara, we all got up to murder behind your back. Metaphorically speaking, murder."

"Yes, that's become increasingly clear since my death," she said with a dry chuckle. She glanced at Fran, realizing that she was considerably more interesting than Sara had ever taken the time to discover.

"I'm glad," Sara said. "Once this is all over, if you're into it, I'd really like to spend some time listening to your stories."

A smile spread across Fran's face, and she nodded as she considered Sara's words.

"I would like that very much. Now tell me everything you know about these interlopers and I'll hit the hacker circuit."

Chapter Twenty-One

After hiding out in her old apartment and frantically texting Heather to come open the door to the residential building in order to not alert Fran, Sara finally made it to her apartment.

"I thought you'd left for good," Silas said.

"Complications," Sara said as she locked the door behind her. "Why are there always complications?"

Turning into the apartment, Sara stopped dead. In place of the disarray she'd left, the apartment was organized and spotless, vases of flowers everywhere and something delicious was cooking in the kitchen.

Silas, stirring a pot at the stove, set his spoon down and came to hug her.

"Mom told me what happened," he whispered. "Are you okay?"

"I'm better now," she said, kissing his neck. "You've been busy. I didn't think you were going out."

"It's raining, so I wore a hood and a facemask. No troubles at all. I just figured you'd be having a stressy day and I wanted to spoil you."

Wriggling out of his arms, Sara leaned over the bubbling pot, inhaling the fragrant steam, notes of spices clashing with something she knew but couldn't place.

"I'm making boat noodles," Silas said. "Have you ever had them?"

"Don't think so," Sara said. "Where did you find all the spices?"

"Over on Lex," Silas pulled her back to him. "Can you smell the secret ingredient?"

Sniffing the air again, Sara shook her head.

"It's a blood-based broth," Silas said proudly. "Recipe says cow. I use human."

"I can't with you," Sara said. "You do blood-based cooking?"

"Not all of us have the time to get all dressed up and do a ritual every time we need a fix."

"You should have your own cooking show," Sara said, kissing him on the nose.

"How do you feel after talking to that girl?"

"I feel wretched about killing her," Sara said. "She didn't really drop any truth bombs, but just before she died she was about to warn me about something the other Spanish women have."

"Desdemona sent them here as kamikaze pilots," Silas raised a hand to Sara's face and moved a strand of hair behind her ear. "Desdemona sealed her fate, not you."

Gazing into Silas's concerned eyes, she simply didn't have the stamina for more talk about Edita.

"I had a good talk with your mother."

Silas cocked his head. "Oh really?"

"Yeah, she has to tell Teddie the whole truth. About you."

"Whoah, that's huge," Silas said. "Feels a bit weird."

"Why?" Sara brought her arms inside the hug, crossing them against his chest and pushing herself back so she could see his face.

"The spotlight is already on me, this could be bad for her."

"Teddie is trustworthy."

"Yeah, that's not it. It's just that every time you share a secret, you weaken the floor underneath you. I mean, you've seen the setup in Iceland, you know where we'd go if the shit hit the fan. I just don't think my mother is ready for the amount of attention that information will bring her if it gets out."

"She can handle it," Sara said. "I know she can. Also, I got intercepted by Fran on my way here, and had to spend a half hour with her in her apartment."

"Which brings us to our next point," Silas reached into his pocket and pulled out one of the air tags Heather had given them. "This goes with you wherever you go, from now on."

"Typical man, gets girlfriend, demands to know her whereabouts at all times."

"You haven't carried it since Heather gave it to you," Silas admonished her. "I'll set up yours and mine on our new phones and laptops."

"You went and bought spices, phones and laptops?"

"That's just the half of it," Silas kissed her forehead. "Sara, don't tell me you've never jumped on an e-scooter."

"There are a lot of things I've never jumped on," Sara escaped his arms and wandered into the living room. "I gotta say, our first place together has come together pretty nicely."

Silas came up behind her, wrapping his arms around her waist. "I literally brought a U-Haul on our second date, huh?"

"I prefer to think of it as love during wartime."

Silas chuckled and let her go, returning to the kitchen. Sara turned slowly, taking in her belongings, things she'd acquired over centuries, and her comfy couch she'd bought at a showroom in the pristine new version of the meatpacking district only a few years earlier. Silas had done a good job of fitting it all together, but it looked like someone else's version of her place, not her own. Flopping onto the couch, she thought about a regular night, any regular night, where the two of them would just be sitting there, looking at each other, and she felt stifled by responsibility. Again.

As if Silas read her mind, he turned to her.

"This feels weird, right? I've never really lived with a partner," he said, his expression neutral.

"I was just thinking that," Sara said. "Literally."

"I think that's why I went a bit crazy out there. I guess subconsciously, I used flowers as a smokescreen."

"It almost worked, Silas," Sara smiled at him, then gazed at the riotous floral arrangements that covered every surface around the room. "I love fresh flowers, this whole place feels so... I dunno, welcoming. The flowers, the food, the... the you."

"Don't go getting mushy on me," he walked over and took her hand, holding it gently, his thumb brushing across the back of her palm, and then he just stood while she sat, her arm raised.

"I think we are going to try to trap a few more vampires tonight," Sara said.

"Can I help?"

"Dunno, maybe? Out on the street maybe?"

"Sure, just tell me where and when."

"Just did. On the street, later tonight."

"Thanks."

"So do you feel weird about us living together at this lightning pace?"

Silas sat beside her without letting go of her hand. "I don't really call this set up 'living together,' this is kind of like emergency housing.

Once this is done, we can go back to the space and distance thing. This is temporary."

At his words, Sara felt a lead weight lift from her chest.

"What?" Silas looked mildly panicked. "Did I say the wrong thing?"

"The opposite," Sara said. "How much attention do you have to give to your boiling cauldron of human blood over there?"

Confused Silas looked into the kitchen and back. "I don't have to do much, it's simmering for a while."

"Oh good," Sara leaned against him. "Because I was wondering if you'd like to show me what you've done to the bedroom."

"Oh, nothing, I just... oh wait, okay, uh, do you want me to carry you in?"

"I wasn't asking, but now that you've mentioned it, I will say that nobody has ever carried me into a bedroom."

Before she knew it, Sara felt Silas's arms beneath her and she was airborne. She felt like a little kid, her emotions all tilting the wrong way, alongside her sense of balance.

"I was joking," she laughed as Silas pretended she was heavy for two steps, then sprinted to the side of the bed, twisting as he fell, Sara landing on top of him. As he reached down to slip her pants down, the phone in her pocket dinged.

"Ignore it," she said as she felt her pants slide over her butt and she worked her knees to get them down past her ankles. As her pants fell to the floor, another ding sounded, and then another, and then, a strangely monotone chorus of dings filled the room.

"Oh come on," Sara groaned. "Someone's added me to a fucking group chat."

"Can we ignore group chats?" Silas asked as he nibbled her neck.

"Not during wartime," Sara heaved herself off him and snatched her pants from the floor, pulling her phone angrily from the pocket.

Silas watched her as she read, then began to turn her pants right side out.

"I gather you've got to go somewhere? Something's on fire?"

Sara shook her head. "Your mother has decided that we are having a secret meeting. Now. With you."

"I don't understand."

"She's lost her fucking mind," Sara said, her eyes narrowing. "She doesn't just want to tell Teddie, she wants you to meet them all."

"No way in hell she does," Silas fell back on the bed, a strange grimace on his face.

"What?" Sara asked.

"I didn't make enough blood soup for everyone."

"Good, because we are gonna make them wait while we eat it. After we finish what we started here."

An hour later, Heather met them at the end of the hallway behind their building. Sara could tell immediately that she was in a mood.

"You seem a bit cranky," she ventured as Heather waved them through like cattle then closed the brick door behind them.

"Well you two took your bloody time," she snapped. "On top of everything else, I've got Fran fucking hacking me and I have to come and let you two in and out like your own personal doorman because your mother wants to host her own vampire episode of Jerry Springer"

"Doorperson," Silas corrected her, cracking Sara up until Heather glared at her.

"I'm not in the mood for you, lad," Heather said, striding ahead of them. "What's going to happen is, you'll wait in my spare room. If things don't go well, you can just stay there. Read a book or something, god knows you know how to fill your spare time."

"Did you eat?" Sara said.

"Course I bloody didn't."

"Heather you should have said something, Silas made this crazy noodle thing with blood."

"Oh, you made her your boat noodles did you?"

"Sure did, come for leftovers. If we survive this meeting."

Heather turned and smiled. "I'm going to hold you to that." Then she scurried ahead again, called the elevator and tapped her foot until they got in. It took longer for the door to close than it took to go down the one floor to the level her apartment was on, and she was off again, opening the rear door to her apartment, and tapping her foot again.

"You are stressing me out," Sara said.

"I'm stressing you out?" Heather glared at both of them. "I am, am I? Well I'm dreadfully sorry. Is there anything I can do to calm ye down? Let me just pop that onto my to-do list and I'll-"

Sara threw her arms around Heather and hugged her tight, smiling when Heather fought against her.

"What is this? I don't have time for a hug."

"Heather, we are all stressed, and a lot of your stress is me-based."

"It's not that, love. It's really not. It's just... I never thought I'd have to guard my shit against bloody Fran, and yet, here we are."

"Don't hate her, Heath," Sara said. "She is just good at her job. And she's on our side."

"She's coming tonight?" Silas asked, and Sara felt Heather tense up in her arms so she turned to him.

"No, your mom didn't want to invite her. Now get into the bedroom and be quiet."

"I've been waiting to hear that all day and.."

Sara let go of Heather, placed a hand on Silas's chest and pushed him through the first doorway, then pulled it closed.

"He's so annoying," Heather said loudly.

"Am not," came Silas's voice through the door, and Heather rolled her eyes then hurried down the hall. As soon as Sara entered the room, she smelled the blood that Heather was warming.

"Don't bite my head off," she said, "but might I be able to take a glass through to our surprise guest?"

"Two steps ahead of you love," Heather bent and retrieved a lowball glass from the warmer, full almost to the brim with dark crimson blood. "Here," she handed it to Sara. "Go give him it while I straighten up."

From the hallway, Sara heard Heather plumping cushions and moving things around nervously. She opened the door, startling Silas who was already laying on the bed with his shoes off, channel surfing on the television that took up most of the wall opposite the bed.

"Room service," she said, handing him the glass. He took it and sipped about a quarter of the glass in one gulp.

"In my country, it's customary to tip."

"Get out," Silas said. "We are not getting busy in Heather's spare room."

"Actually, gimme some of that," Sara leapt onto the bed and brought the glass to her lips, taking a quick gulp.

"You can forget about a tip now," Silas said in a fake angry voice. "Get out of here and let me watch my stories."

When she walked back into the living room, Heather was on a stepladder waving a Swiffer at some cobwebs on the ceiling.

"Stop, please, you're making me nervous," Sara placed her hands on Heather's hips, guiding her down from the ladder. She took the Swiffer from Heather's hands and set it in the gap beside the fridge.

"It doesn't go there," Heather said.

"It does now," Sara smiled. Heather went to reply but was distracted by the doorbell.

"Oh god, no turning back now," Heather bustled into the vestibule and opened the door and Sara watched as Imani, Yukari and Crina, all in mismatched yogawear with their hair tied back, bent to kiss Heather then slid past her into the living room. Suddenly uneasy, Sara retreated to the kitchen, unloading the glasses of blood from the warmer. She searched the counter for a tray, didn't find one, and turned and began handing out glasses.

"Sara, what the hell are you doing?" Heather was at her side in an instant. "Teddie's not even here yet." A knock sounded at the back of the apartment.

"She is now," Sara said as Heather grimaced and went to let her in.

"Hi ladies," Sara walked into the living room where everyone was seated.

"Sit by me," Yukari said. "I'm so happy that you're…"

"Alive?" Sara said as she took the seat next to Yukari, who slapped her with the back of her free hand.

"No, I'm so happy you're back."

Sara squeezed her hand. "Me too." She looked up to see Teddie entering the room behind Heather. Seeing Sara, Teddie gave a little wave and blew her a kiss. Maybe the evening wouldn't be too terrible. In short order, Heather gave Teddie her drink and Teddie settled next to Imani and Heather climbed into her ancient love seat, legs tucked beneath her.

Crina, sitting on the arm of the couch beside Yukari, raised her glass.

"Ladies, thank you for all coming here on such short notice."

"Who needs notice?" Imani laughed her raspy laugh. "All these lockdowns serving me 2020 realness."

"Still, thanks," Crina continued. "We have a lot to update you on, and as you can see, I've left some people out. We will have to have a full Lock meeting, probably tomorrow, but if we can push it a day or two, that would be better. Uh... do you guys want to do the whole convening and never have I killed thing?"

Imani raised her glass to her mouth, finishing it in one gulp. "Let's keep it informal then eh?"

A flutter of laughter went around the room, then each woman downed their blood, then sat back as it went to work in their systems. Sara was still coming around when she felt Heather pluck her glass from her hand, followed by the sound of glasses being placed in the sink. Blinking away the darkness, Sara pressed herself upright. Crina caught her eye and gave her a wink.

"Okay, well here goes nothing," Crina said, and Sara heard the nervousness in her voice. "The first thing that I want to tell you is that last night, Sara was almost kidnapped or worse by someone from the Madrid Lock."

"Yeah, we know, guv," Imani laughed. "Yuka told Teddie told me."

"I'd expect nothing else. Yuka, did you tell them what happened next?"

"No, no," Yukari said.

"Right," Crina continued. "To capture her, Heather drugged her and she responded poorly. In our panic, we fed her our own blood. The problem is, she was not Cursed."

"And she is now?" There was panic in Teddie's voice and Sara felt a pang of disappointment that the meeting would likely go off the rails before Crina got around to dropping the Silas bombshell.

"No, Theodora, she is dead." Crina said, a chorus of gasps echoing in the room. "The wolf ate her."

"No," Teddie said, horrified. "You guys let her die?"

Crina glanced at Sara, indicating that she should step in. Sara remained silent.

"She presented like a Cursed woman," Crina explained, clearly annoyed that her big announcement was getting sidetracked. "She had been living on animal blood, and the opioids made her throw it all up, and she was overdosing. Sara tried to save her life."

Bracing herself for an attack from Teddie, Sara kept her gaze on the carpet.

"Is that why there's a bandage on your arm, mom?" Teddie's voice was soft, and Sara raised her head, nodding.

"She was not a member of the Madrid Lock," Crina continued. "There are still five more of these women living in Central Park. They are patrolling the building nightly."

"So," Teddie's voice was low. "These women, they're not Cursed? And they're definitely Desdemona's?"

"I've been testing blood all day," Yukari said. "The virus is in a similar family to ours, but it's a substantially different strain. I think it's a natural virus, not a lab-made one."

"Thanks Yuka," Imani said, waving her hand at Heather and pointing at the warming oven, ordering more blood. Heather shook her head no. Rolling her eyes, Imani continued. "Desdemona has somehow obtained a new version of the virus and she's infecting women with it, and using them as what? Her army?"

"We don't know the full story yet," Crina said, "but that seems to be likely."

Talking broke out between the sisters, and Sara sat quietly, watching and listening as anxiety chewed on her nerves.

"So," Sara interrupted. "While I have your attention, someone else found out I'm alive today. Fran. It went surprisingly well."

"I can't see how, frankly," Imani's face was sour.

"She got duped. You guys, it's the same as it was with Marguerite. Years go by and people get lonely. She was horrified to hear what Desdemona has done."

"Did she spill anything about Rosa?" Yukari looked almost hopeful. "Does she know what they're planning?"

Sara shook her head. "Sorry, no they've been keeping her at arm's length too."

"Then why isn't she here?" Teddie pursed her lips defiantly.

"That's actually by my choosing," Crina stood up. "I actually have the people that I want to have here, because I have something to share with you all."

Silence fell in the room. Nobody even fidgeted.

Crina's chest rose as she inhaled deeply, then held a breath, her palms smoothing the front of her sheer burgundy athleisure hoodie. Sara couldn't recall seeing her so nervous. It was weird.

"Secrets are a strange thing," she began, looking each of them in the eye in turn. "When you first have a secret, there's no way of knowing how potent or powerful that secret can become. At the start, it's just a secret."

A siren wailed, blocks away. Nobody took their eyes from Crina.

"But then, as years pass and the secret doesn't become any less important but life gets weirder, more complicated, times will arise when you need to share your secret with someone. And each time you share it, you feel a lot more vulnerable. And that's where I am tonight. We are in the middle of a time of profound change for our kind, some of you have said war. But that's not why I'm choosing to tell you all my secret. I'm telling you my most precious secret because I love you all, very deeply, probably more than some of you even realize. And that kind of love deserves nothing but transparency and honesty, no matter the cost."

Crina paused, her breathing shallow. "Heather, do you think I could get a wine or a shot of whisky?"

"Anybody else want something while I'm up?"

Everyone raised their hand.

"Whisky it is," Heather got up and went to the kitchen.

"So," Crina continued. "What I am about to tell you is going to shake you up. I just ask that you remember the spirit of the information, the origin of it. Over the years, I took Heather into my confidences. I also told a few elders, most of them are gone now. Anyway, here I am at a point where not sharing my secret will be more damaging than keeping it. I do not want this group of wonderful, warm, intelligent women to be torn apart by resentment, or any toxic feelings, so please –"

Heather interrupted Crina by placing a full shot glass in her hand, which Crina threw back, handing the empty glass back to Heather.

"Okay, and wow this is hard. I... I lied to my maker. When she made me, I had already had a child."

Sara glanced around the room, at the wide eyes on each woman.

"Go on," Teddie said, her voice neutral.

"You can probably guess the rest, but I hid my son from Stefanya, I hid him for many years. And then, I made him one of us."

The room erupted.

Yukari and Imani both started asking questions, over the top of each other, and Crina raised palms at them as she tried to understand what they were saying. Heather darted in and out handing shot glasses of whisky to people, each of them taking the glass, shooting it and handing it back. Sara kept her eyes on Teddie, who sat perfectly still, her face surveying the action like a cat.

When the chatter died down, Teddie turned to Crina.

"Silas is your son, isn't he?"

A chilling silence descended on the room as Crina faced Teddie and very slowly began to nod.

"So there you have it," Crina's voice shook. "You now have the information that is most sacred to me, information that can destroy me." She looked at Sara. "And I think I might throw up."

Sara stood and wrapped her arms around Crina, and together they faced the shocked faces of their friends.

Imani fidgeted on the couch, then raised a hand, swirling an accusing finger at Sara, a half smile playing on her lips.

"Soooooooooo," she said almost comically. "Can I set something straight here. Sara, are you dating a Cursed man?"

"Yep," Sara nodded. "I sure am."

Imani patted the space on the couch beside her. "Then come sit here girl, because, Crina, thanks for your confidence, and don't think we won't come back to you, but Sara, bitch, I got *preguntas*."

Yukari tittered and offered Imani the gentlest high-five that Sara had ever seen, but rather than take the seat that Imani offered, she turned to Teddie.

"I'm just going to say it," she said, her palms open."All of this is happening because we love you and having secrets from you was killing me. Almost literally, as it turned out."

"Not funny," Teddie said. Sara looked her up and down but nothing about her stance or expression was giving anything away.

"So, basically," Crina said, "what this means is, if this is a problem to any one of you, then we totally understand, and as soon as we can, we will leave."

"That's not what I want," Teddie said, her voice steel. "I mean, thanks for the honestly, and Crina, I get it, I do. The thing is, I'm not shocked. Sara, this all falls into place. Didn't you think to yourself, oh this isn't just a bad idea, this is a fucking nuclear bomb and I'm gonna bounce it around the Lock and see what happens?"

"That's not how it happened," Sara said. "You can be as angry as you want, but I swear to you, every word from my mouth will be the truth. I found out that Silas was like us the night before you saw us in Brooklyn. Until then, I had no idea. I treated him for almost two years, unknowing. And I'd like to clear up something else, that thing I wrote in my letter that you found. I did taste fresh blood. My patient slit her wrists while I was trying to help her. I must have forgotten to take my heems, I can't explain it, there was just so much blood, everywhere, and I blacked out and when I came to, I was feeding on a dead woman's arm." Sara blinked at the memory.

Teddie inhaled and exhaled in silence, her eyes never leaving Sara's.

"It's a thing," Yukari said. "It's a part of the virus that I can't figure out. That's why I'm such a narc about always remembering your heems. Sara, I'm sorry, there's every chance I miscalculated, for all of us, the minimum amount of actual blood we need to stay out of danger."

"Bloody rough," Imani said. "Sorry boss. But I don't understand why you didn't tell us?"

"She was ashamed," Crina said. "Yukari, if you stay in the Mother role, you'll learn. It's parenting, and it's a selfless role. Let me ask you this, each of you. How many times have you come to Sara with a problem? And now ask yourself, how many times did you ask if she was okay, if she needed any support? This woman here did a backbreaking job for way too long, and before you judge her, all I can say is you better hope it never happens to you."

"Crina's right," Sara said, her voice thick with resignation. "I felt like I fucked up. My levels were sky high. I had to go running at night, in the park, just to try to burn up the fuel. I felt like a superhero, strengthwise, and an idiot, emotionally. After so many years, all I knew how to be was a Lock Mother, and all of a sudden, I was the worst failure of a Lock mother in history."

"I'd say Desdemona still has that ribbon, boss," Imani winked at Sara.

"I thought you trusted me," Teddie said, her voice still infuriatingly neutral.

"I did. I do. It's nothing to do with trust. Teddie, you're my child. I never let you be someone I could confide my weakness in. Not your fault. I had issues. I tried to deal with them."

"Don't even try to turn it around and bury me with it," Teddie said, a hint of anger in her voice. Sara felt relief, at least she knew which direction it was going in.

"We can talk about this in private if you like," she began, but Teddie waved a finger at her.

"Hell nah, Sara, you wanted to do the big group hug honestly bullshit, let's do it here." Teddie's voice rose louder with each word.

"I'm not going to yell," Sara said. "Look at your anger. Because I finally put myself first?"

"No, it's because you literally risked our entire Lock for a fucking guy."

"Actually," Sara took two steps in Teddie's direction, her eyes boring into her daughter's. "If you hadn't been so gung-ho about killing me when I got back that weekend, I would have announced that I was leaving the Lock. Going Scholar or whatever that means. I found something I wanted to do."

"Or someone," Teddie never backed down. Sara was used to it. "And it's supposed to make me feel better that you met some guy and immediately wanted to just up and leave me?"

As Sara was about to reply, she saw movement in the hallway over Teddie's shoulder, shadows moving, and then Silas appeared. Sara's guts turned to ice.

"I'm not just some guy, Teddie," he said, his expression solemn, his hands hanging defenselessly at his sides, his palms open to them.

"I'm dead," Imani said, falling on Yukari, who wriggled beneath her but didn't take her eyes off Silas.

Teddie leapt to her feet, backing away from him.

"You stay right there, *son*," she hissed. "I fucking mean it. You bitches are fucking crazy, bringing him here."

"Is it okay if I explain myself?" Silas took a step back, and Teddie stepped forward, her eyes blazing.

"Everything in me, every day of my life, I've been taught that right now, I must kill you."

"Yep. I get that." Silas was doing his best to speak peacefully.

"I'm short circuiting right now," Teddie said, her eyes changing subtly from anger to pleading. "Who all in this room knew about this guy, and when, and keep it hunned."

Crina went to speak, and Teddie shut her down.

"Not you, C. You I got."

"You got me too," Sara said. "I've already told you."

Heather, who'd been hanging back in the entry way to the kitchen stepped forward with her hand aloft. "I've known for about a century," she said. "And I know nobody listens to me, but for once, try. Silas has followed the rules of our order better than any one of you, so before you start gunning for him, do a little introspection, and then, if you're still certain, come for him." She paused, looking around the room before locking eyes with Teddie. "But you'll have to go through me."

"I met him last night,' Yukari said. "But I didn't know the son thing."

"Look, I know this is your space," Silas said, facing Teddie. "I'm only here because the city is crawling with fucking vampires, and if it's what you want, once it's safe for me to leave, I can vanish."

"Me too," Sara said.

"So you are leaving," Teddie said. "With him."

Sara shrugged, and Teddie looked at Imani and Yukari.

"Are you guys fine with this? The anger was back in her voice.

"I'm not sure if fine is the right word," Imani said, very seriously. "However, I do *not* feel threatened, and I *am* intrigued. I'd like to hear more."

"I'm fine with it," Yukari said, surprising everyone. "The bamboo that bends is stronger than the oak that breaks. I've been saying this for years. We have been inflexible for five centuries. What we are seeing is the result of that inflexibility. If this is the first step to a new way of life for us all, then I am happy."

"Arigato gozaimas, Yukari-san," Silas clasped his hands and bowed.

"Shi haana tano chi o kenkyuu shitai desu." Yukari smiled and bowed.

"Hai shi ha sore o kyoka shima su," Silas said to her.

"Are you going to charm all of us?" Teddie was getting bristly. Sara, too distracted by Silas's apparent fluent Japanese, ignored her.

"Teddie, would it be okay if we talked privately?"

"Oh yeah right," she stepped back again. "I'm not gullible like these bitches."

"Steady on," Imani fanned the air in Teddie's direction.

"Nomine Silas, and never have I killed."

"Does this asshole know everything about us?" Teddie spun to face Crina.

"I dunno," she replied coolly. "Ask the asshole."

"I was raised on the periphery of Lock life," he said. "My mother taught me well. I would hope that my values are in line with yours. I would like a minute of your time. If it doesn't help you, then I promise, I won't bother you again."

"Grrrrrrr, you all know how much I hate giving in," Teddie said. "Fine. Where do you want to talk?"

"Heather, can we use your bedroom?"

"Fine by me," Heather sniffed. "Just don't get any blood on the quilt. It's Frette."

"You go first," Teddie said, nodding in the direction of the hallway. Obediently, Silas turned and left the room. Teddie held a raised middle finger aloft, directing it at each person in turn before walking into the hallway, then they heard the bedroom door close.

"Well that went well," Imani said. "I gotta say, you two have me shook."

"This is a good thing," Yukari said. "Heather, I would like some more whisky please."

"I'm making cocktails this time," Heather said, turning and opening her liquor cupboard.

"Aren't you worried?" Sara turned to Crina.

"Are you crazy? Those two are the biggest pussies in the whole Lock world. If they can get over themselves, they'll probably end up watching a romcom and gossiping about you."

"I'd rather they fought," Sara said sourly.

"Crina, block your ears," Imani leaned forward. "Sara, he is fucking hot."

Yukari nodded in agreement.

"Well thanks, I guess, but you guys, when he first came in as a patient, I dunno, he looked different, he didn't look like that."

"You were both very unhappy at the same time, for a long time," Crina said. "You both looked so depressed."

"Hang on a minute," Imani said. "If we're sharing secrets, where the hell is April Veronica?"

Sara glanced at Crina.

"You're not going to believe this," she said. "But she's off training."

"Training?" Yukari said. "Who is training her?"

"Amitra and Fan, mainly," Sara said. "And Stefanya."

"Hurry up with the booze, Heather," Yukari crossed her eyes. "This is too much."

"Where the hell is this happening?" Imani said. "Nobody has seen them in years."

"The elders all keep in touch," Crina said, avoiding answering the location question. "After everything she has been through, it seemed to me that the best place for her was with Fan and Ama."

"Where are they then?" Imani was relentless.

"Right now? I have no clue. And I know you have more questions, but I'm going to ask you to hold onto them, just for a while longer."

"If we aren't able to contain these Spanish women," Sara said, "we may need to ask Fan and Amitra to help us out. Which is a vaguely terrifying thought, those women in New York, but they have seen the storm clouds of war on the horizon for a long time, and they're eager to act."

"I can't believe April Veronica is with the elders," Yukari said. "I miss her so much but that is a great place for her to be."

"They're training her to fight then?" Imani whistled. "That's bad fucking ass. Are they accepting new students, because I know I'm rusty?"

The bedroom door clicked in the hallway, and Teddie reentered the room, her cheeks wet from crying. She went over to Sara and slowly encircled her in a hug.

"I'm sorry I was a baby, mom," she said. "I'm gonna need a minute to get my head around all this new shizz, but he's okay."

Silas appeared in the hallway.

"Heather, make mine a double."

Chapter Twenty-Two

As soon as they got back to the apartment, Sara spun around as Silas was locking the door.

"What the hell did you say to Teddie?"

Ducking around her, Silas darted into the living room.

"You'll have to ask her."

"Oh you have got to be kidding me," Sara lunged for Silas but he danced around the coffee table.

"You have two options, Silas," Sara faced him down. "The kitchen or the bedroom. Both of them are dead ends."

"Yes, but..." Without breaking eye contact, Silas leapt for the bedroom, slamming the door behind him. Sara sprung over the coffee table and grabbed at the doorknob, but it was locked, and a temper that she had almost forgotten flew into overdrive. Suddenly, she was angrier than she could remember being.

"Silas don't do this," she said into the doorjamb. "I mean it, just tell me. I'm getting really pissed out here."

"Nope."

Sara's shoulders tightened and her anger boiled up inside her throat like bile. She decided to lean into it.

"We agreed on total honesty, Silas."

"I didn't lie. Ask Teddie. She asked me not to say anything. Sara, this is just the price of peace."

That was it. Sara pressed her palms against the thin wood of the door that separated her from the man she wanted to yell at directly. She knew she could put her fist through it easily. She also knew she'd feel stupid tomorrow. Right now that was secondary.

"I'll give you five seconds to open this door or I'm coming through it."

"No, vampire lady, I didn't invite you in. Stay outside."

The thought that Silas was laughing at her from behind the door caused Sara to clench her jaw so hard she felt something pop inside her left ear. She visualized a spot just above the handle and drew her right elbow back, palm flat and facing the door.

"This is your last warning, Silas."

"Are you gonna huff and puff and"

With a furious growl, Sara threw her hand at the door, which opened just before she could splinter it, momentum spinning her off balance, and before she knew it, the end of the mattress hit her ankles and she half-fell-half-sat hard on the bed.

"Sara, no! Are you okay?" Silas's face was horrified.

"Do not laugh at me," she spat. "This isn't funny, so don't fucking laugh."

Silas laughed.

Digging her fingernails into the bedding, she felt the cotton sheets tear, and her anger intensified.

"So much for transparency," she spat at him. "Fucking first time you have a secret from me and it's something for you to laugh about?"

"Oh brother," Silas said, his voice calm.

"Wait," Sara sat bolt upright on the bed. "That's how you react? *Oh brother*? No yelling? No recriminations?"

Shaking his head, a half-smile playing on his face, Silas reached a hand down.

"I'm not going to yell at you, probably ever," he said. "Would you like some help to get up? Or would you like it more if I sat down beside you?"

"Neither," Sara said, feeling very juvenile all of a sudden. "I just need to be angry at you."

"Is that something that you want me here for, or is it a solo activity?"

"Okay just stop being so fucking accommodating," Sara said, as the anger melted as quickly as it arrived. "Fuck! I just… I mean, you –" she paused, twisting her head from side to side until she got an audible crack. "Do you have any idea how horribly stressed I was about the whole you and Teddie thing? I've been having nightmares about it for weeks and then you think that taking her into a room and sharing secrets is the answer?"

"It wasn't designed as a secret, I just wanted to talk to her confidentially."

"It's clearly freaking me out, Silas. Just tell me."

"Sara, you're not the only one in this discussion who has guilt and baggage around what happened." Silas's voice remained even and calm.

Dropping her gaze to the floorboards, Sara tried to find her footing in the argument, and she had a fleeting thought that she was jealous, which hit her like a gut punch. She sat in silence, ruminating.

"Would you like some space?"

She shook her head.

"I'd like to stop acting like a fucking child," she said eventually. "Silas, I felt left out."

"I'm sorry, Sara. You know that would never be my intention."

"Well I thought that's what I knew until I had some nonsense attack of jealousy. Silas, I haven't been jealous of anything in so long, I didn't even think I could be jealous anymore."

"Can I sit?"

Sara nodded, but didn't look up as she felt the weight of Silas's body on the mattress rock her from side to side.

"Sara be kind to yourself. Tonight was just the first weird night. There will be a lot more in the months ahead. I promise I will try to be more mindful of making you feel included and informed."

"How the hell were you single for so long?"

"For the same reasons you were," Silas said, and she felt the weight of his arm around her shoulders and Sara leaned against him, her thoughts still swirling but now it felt like there was something beneath them, a cloud or a safety net.

"Was that our first fight?"

"You were pretty angry," Silas ruffled her hair.

"Came out of nowhere."

"No, it came out of somewhere, and I swear, I won't put you in that position again."

"Thanks."

"But while we're here, and you've already ruined the sheets, how's about I get some lovin'"

"You are such a dude. I invited Heather for boat noodles, she's just off dealing with Fran."

"Sara, I just brokered the vampire equivalent of peace in the Middle East, and you're holding out."

"I'm not holding out," Sara turned her face to his, kissing his lips lightly.

"I feel like I'm walking into a trap," Silas said, kissing her back.

"Maybe," Sara said, letting herself fall back onto the bed. Turning, Silas placed his hands either side of her and began to crawl up her body to kiss her again when his phone began to ring in his pocket.

"Ignore it," Sara said. "Kisses are exactly what I need right now."

"Can't," Silas said with an eyeroll. "It's Embla's ringtone." Sitting beside her with his back against the wall, Silas straightened his leg and pulled his phone out of his pocket. Sara dragged herself up beside him just in time to see Embla's wide, pale face appear on the screen.

"Hey lovebirds," she said. "Hope I'm not interrupting anything."

Sara and Silas exchanged quick glances.

"Oh no," Embla facepalmed. "I am. I'm sorry for my bad timing. Uh, is it okay for us to talk? I'm just taking a break from working with Fan and Ama and they're going nuts with the whole baby vampire thing. What have you learned?"

"I'll hand you over to the expert," Silas passed the phone to Sara.

"It's not good, Embla. Silas told you about Desdemona is infecting new sisters. They have a mild form of our virus. Except the one in the cellar. She's dead now."

"Probably for the best," Embla said. "So there are still five of them in New York. We here were wondering if you will attempt to capture more tonight?"

Sara nodded. "We need to wait until the streets are empty, so we have a few hours yet," she said. "We are going to try to set a trap in the old coal delivery door."

"Fan and Ama say that you should kill them outright. They know too much already."

"I expected that," Sara said. "But," she paused, looking at Silas. "Please remind the elders that I run a no-kill shelter over here."

Embla nodded.

"Yes, that's why they are planning to come to New York."

"Embla, I hate to sound all vampirey but I didn't invite them."

"That's what I told them. They want to talk to you, but they are busy this evening. They ask you to be free tomorrow."

A jumble of solutions and indignant replies crowded Sara's head, and she sat in silence, looking at Embla's patient face on the small screen.

"I'm sorry Sara, have you frozen?"

"No, Embla, I was searching for a response that didn't make me sound like a whiny bitch."

"Please, feel free to be whiny. I don't like the word bitch."

"Sorry," Sara said. "But Embla, you of all people must understand, these are young women that Desdemona has deceived and weaponized, but that doesn't mean we should murder them."

"I understand what you're saying, Sara, but this almost falls in line with ZPG. This is an unprecedented risk. If any of these new infectees got captured, by a policeman for example, or hit by a car, it would be a global catastrophe."

"Not as bad as if it was a full Sister," Sara said. "The police would think they were in a crazy cult."

"We don't know the full extent of their virus. They are an unacceptable risk. And if it is proven that Desdemona infected them and encouraged this terrible risk, then she must also be stopped, by any means necessary."

"You surprise me, Embla."

"Good," the woman laughed. "Sara, I'm a vegan, not a moron."

"And I apologize if I ever made you feel that way," Sara said very graciously. "Embla, that would never be my intention."

"I know, mama, just fuckin' with ya," Embla rocked back, laughing hard. "Oh," she gasped. "Here's another moron that wants to talk to you"

The screen went blurry, then refocused and suddenly Sara was looking at April Veronica's wide smile and green eyes, and a newly buzzed head.

"Your hair," Sara exclaimed.

"In battle, it is a liability," April Veronica said, very formally. "Do you like my Fan impersonation? Anyway, it kept on getting in my eyes so we just shaved it off."

The woman's irrepressible energy was contagious. Sara felt herself smiling despite her weariness.

"It makes your eyes look so enormous," she said, and April blushed.

"Aw shucks," she batted her long eyelashes. "Is everything going okay in New York?"

Now it was Sara's turn to laugh.

"Well, let's see. Where shall I start? First off, I told Teddie I'm alive. That was fun. Then we found out about the halflings in the Park. I accidentally killed one. Silas and I now live together. And just now, Crina told everyone that he's her son."

"Get. The. Fuck. Outta. Here."

"I wish I was joking. And after I talk to you, we are going to go set a trap and see if we can't lure the other halflings into it."

"What do you mean by halflings? I'm sorry I'm still new to your vampire lingo."

"Infected with a virus like ours, but they can't digest human blood, they survive on animals."

"I didn't know that worked."

"It doesn't," came Embla's voice from offscreen.

"Yeah, it's a shitshow," Sara said. "Anyways, how's training?"

"I'm so sore," April Veronica said. "Even with hours of yoga and stretching, I'm so stiff."

As April Veronica spoke, Sara realized that she still had not stretched since they left Iceland, making a mental note to force herself to yoga as soon as she was off the phone. "But it's great," April Veronica continued. "The physical stuff will come in time, the foundations are already there, but what I love the most is how Fan and Amitra just know strategy, like it's part of their DNA. That's what I'm trying to learn. To stand outside of a situation and see it for what it is, and then retain a calculating mind in the middle of any situation."

"Sounds like I could use a refresher course," Sara said.

"Do you need us to come back?"

"It's too dangerous right now," Sara said. "I'd prefer you to stay out of harm's way."

"I don't want to sit out the hard parts," April Veronica's face was serious.

"I'm not asking you to," Sara said. "But I don't want you to walk into an ambush."

"Do you think you've done that?"

"Right now, everyone still thinks I'm dead.'

"But that won't last forever," April Veronica said. "And once you get outed as a living person, shit is gonna get real."

Sighing loudly, Sara felt a wash of exhaustion and suddenly wanted to end the phone call.

"Hey, listen, I'm gonna go and shower. We have to strategize."

"Wait!"

"What?"

"You are not going anywhere until you tell me how it went with Silas meeting the Lock. That shit is history and I am here for it."

"It's not my story to tell," Sara said with a mysterious smile. "Here, I'll hand you to Silas."

Rolling over on the bed, she passed the phone to Silas, then stood, exiting the room, swinging her ass from side to side. Silas smiled and blew her a kiss.

"Hey peanut," he said happily. "How's your five-finger death punch?"

Sara heard laughter coming from the phone as she left the room, and it made her smile. Heading into the kitchen, she shook eight heems onto her palm, swallowing them one at a time with cupped handfuls of tap water. Taking a seat on the couch while she waited for them to work, she fished her phone from her pocket. Two texts. Heather was ready to talk whenever she was, and Teddie wanted to be involved in setting the trap.

In the past, she would have answered them both immediately but nothing felt as urgent anymore. Something else was nagging at her, appearing in fits and flashes ever since her arrival in New York, and that was Desdemona. Despite visualizing countless approaches and their results, she was no closer to feeling confident about how to confront the woman who'd been a constant source of irritation for centuries. Her latest instinct was to ask Heather or Crina, but that felt lazy. She needed to lay a Desdemona trap and she was the only effective bait.

Bouncing off the couch as inspiration struck, she darted back into the bedroom, where Silas was still telling April Veronica about his summit with the women.

"Sorry to interrupt," she said. "But I like this think tank. It's new. And I'd like you all to ponder my problem, so that I can stop chasing my tail like a cross-eyed cat."

Propping himself on an elbow, Silas gave her a curious smile. On the phone in his hand, she saw Embla press her face against April Veronica's so they could both be in the frame.

"What do you need, boss?" April Veronica asked conspiratorially.

"Input," Sara said, suddenly energized and nixing the shower. "I am going to meet with Heather, but can I leave you guys to strategize how I should deal with Desdemona?"

"Are you going to take our advice, or are you just an ask-hole?" Embla said bluntly.

"A what?"

"Silas?" Embla's voice was playful. "Can you please mansplain for us?"

"Sure," Silas groaned. "An ask-hole asks for advice then ignores it and does whatever they originally planned to do."

"You know what? I have been an ask-hole," Sara said. "But this time, I really want your input on how we should trap her." Leaning over, she kissed Silas on his forehead. "I'm going to take some boat noodles to Heather's, but I'll come back for you before we go a-hunting."

After realizing she didn't have any Tupperware, Sara threw on a coat and lifted the entire pot of noodles from the stove and slipped her feet into comfy old ballet flats. She texted Heather that she was on her way with food and she'd need to meet her at the hallway door, then just stood there, focusing on a feeling, a small glowing coal at the center of her chest.

She was happy.

Chapter Twenty-Three

"**I** can't remember a time when I've come to your flat and you haven't offered me a wine," Sara said as she took a seat on Heather's couch, and Heather unceremoniously plonked herself down on the couch opposite.

"Do you need a drink?" Heather leapt to her feet. Sara had never seen her so flustered.

"No, not at all," she said. "You're jumpy?"

"I haven't eaten," Heather said, rising absently and going to the kitchen. "I'm gonna eat these noodles while you talk if that's okay."

"Are you ready for tonight?"

"As ready as I'll ever be," Heather said. "So we have Crina and Teddie on board. I wanted to ask you, should we include Fran?"

"My heart says yes, but my gut says no."

"She is better at the security systems than I am. Might come in handy."

"Then, yes? If you're not still pissed at her."

Heather fired off a quick text to Fran, who answered immediately.

"She'll be here in a minute," Heather said. "So what happened in the brief time that we were apart?"

"We talked to Embla and April Veronica."

"Oh god, you're already a we," Heather said. "If tonight wasn't so damn dangerous, I'd say I needed a cocktail."

"I was wondering why my hint fell on deaf ears," Sara laughed. "Here's something to take your mind off it. If we don't capture all of Desdemona's halflings tonight, Fan and Ama are coming to New York."

"To kill them?"

Sara nodded. "And even Embla is okay with it."

"It's really the safest answer," Heather said absently. "It's a pity, they've been so misled."

"Desdemona is way more ruthless than we expected," Sara said. "We underestimated her."

"She is in the middle of a power play," Heather said. "We don't even know if she's breaking rules. There's nothing about making halflings. She's not infecting them with what we have."

"I disagree," Sara said firmly. "No matter how *mildly* she's infecting these young women, she is still sending them out in the world. It's so dangerous, I literally can't get my head around it."

"At the very least, these halflings could create a new pandemic, and that research could lead to our strain of the virus. Once a single scientist figures out that eternal life is a side-effect, it's game over."

A knock at the front door startled both of them. A few seconds later, as Heather was standing, a knock sounded at the rear of the apartment.

"Before you open that," Heather said, "The involvement of Fran means Silas can't help out."

Sara felt a wash of relief.

"Have you already texted him?"

Heather nodded. "Just did."

"Thanks."

"Well lassie, go let her in, would ye? I'll get Teddie from the front."

Turning the lock, Sara pushed open the brick wall at the end of the hallway, revealing Fran, who definitely understood the assignment, clad in black army boots, black leggings and sweater, her silver-gray hair hidden beneath a black woolen cap.

"Hi Sara," she said warmly. "I just wanted to say that I've really appreciated you today, and I'm so deeply happy and relieved to have you back."

"Thanks, Fran," Sara leaned forward and wrapped her arms around Fran, surprising her. After a short delay, she returned the hug. "The feeling is mutual."

"So what's going on tonight?"

Sara ushered Fran into the hallway and closed the door behind her.

"Desdemona's halflings are trying to get into the building."

"I am still not entirely sure what a halfling is," Fran said as they reached the living room, where Teddie and Crina were already seated on the couch. Sara shot Crina a quizzical look, she wasn't supposed to come down until later.

"What? You think I could nap?" her creator snapped with faux anger.

"Hey everyone," Fran said, standing in the doorway, a hand waving. Teddie stood and walked slowly in her direction.

"Fran," she said quietly, "I... uh... I'm sorry. I hope you can forgive me."

Her chin trembling, Fran outstretched her arms. "Teddie, thank you, but there's no words for how I feel, and how grateful I am that Sara is here. I'm the one who owes an apology."

Arms around each other, they stayed motionless. Heather glanced from Sara to Crina and shrugged.

"Okay, now that we're all here," she said, taking a seat next to Crina, "let's get planning. Fran, thanks for joining us. Halflings are women infected with a new strain of our virus. We believe Desdemona created them, but we don't know where she got the virus."

"Oh, what fuckery," Fran said as she nestled in beside Sara, a hand on her knee. "That's dark."

"Yes," Heather said with a little smile, "yes, it's dark. Anyway, we caught one, but she died in the process. But there are five more. As far as we know, they're living in Central Park, but they're patrolling the compound."

"If you get close to one," Crina leaned in. "You'll know by the smell. They survive on animal blood, and it doesn't agree with them. They smell like rotting meat."

"Those poor women," Fran said, and Teddie nodded.

"So how do we catch them?" Teddie asked.

Crina glanced at Heather, then at Sara, and raised a hand.

"I will be bait," she said. "Fran, can you stay in the security center? I'll need you on all cameras tonight."

"Easy," Fran said. "I can ping their phones, but triangulation isn't too precise. I can try to intercept calls too."

"Good, thank you. So then, I'm not sure if you know, but there's an old coal delivery chute down on 104th, it's disgusting but we were able to trick that girl last night into thinking it's an entry to the building."

"But how will we get her from there to inside?" Teddie looked suspicious.

"There's an entrance down by the furnace," Heather said. "Well, there is now at least."

"I don't remember that," Teddie said, giving Sara a curious look.

"How'd you think we got the coal in?" Crina said, before Sara could speak.

"Anyway," Heather interrupted, "Crina will be circling the block as bait. Fran will be monitoring and reporting back. Sara will be hiding behind the dumpsters in the alcove, or above them," she paused and gave Sara a wink. "Teddie is going to follow them once they leave the park and I will be waiting in the Surrender antechamber to get Crina through in a hurry and then lock them in. Sara will then block the exit with a dumpster until we can subdue them."

"What if you end up trapping the whole pack?" Fran asked, her eyes narrowed in concentration.

"We can keep them in the coal chute until all of us can get there, I suppose," Heather said. "They are very weak. Yukari has some propofol, we can knock them out."

"So Desdemona, queen of zero population growth, has been engaged in infecting women with a virus and sending them out as assassins?" Fran was aghast. "You guys, I'm so sorry. I got sucked in by a bunch of utopian lies."

"That's how they get ya," Crina said with a gentle smile. "We're glad to have you back, Fran, don't feel stupid. If anyone should feel stupid it's me, she's my responsibility. And she's pure evil. She's risking the human race to get what she wants."

"Does Yukari know what's going on?" Teddie looked around the room. "Because, you guys, she's the Mother. She should."

"I talked to her before I came up," Crina nodded. "She's barely slept since she got the blood samples from Edita."

"I need to say something here and now," Sara stood. "The chance of these women surviving this is basically zero. The elders want them dead, and they aren't going to be welcomed back to Madrid with open arms. I don't agree with that, at all, so I'm open to suggestions."

Fran sat back against the couch and pressed her fingertips to her temple.

"I'm sorry you guys, this is just a lot to process."

"Sorry, Franny," Crina rubbed the woman's leg. "It is. I wish Elle and Liz and Rosa were as open-minded as you. I'm real proud of you."

Fran waved away the compliment.

"Well I am," Crina smiled. "And now I need to go be the bait in this trap. Y'all ready?"

Merged with the shadows at the rear of the alcove, Sara shifted her weight from one foot to the other, a restless energy humming through her. Crina, pretending to be on a phone call, circled the block three times, passing Sara without so much as a sideways glance. So far, she had no followers. A chilly wind was blowing up from the Hudson, eddying in a battle with the warm early summer night. Occasional spotlights traced across the low clouds, and Sara wondered if they were from a premiere in Times Square, a part of New York she'd fallen out of love with a long time ago and never given a second chance. Now she wanted to go there with Silas, eat a hot dog, see a musical, be a tourist in her own town.

That was the magic of New York, she thought. It was a million different cities rolled into one, and even now, after centuries, it could still tug at her heart like a fickle lover and she'd do whatever it wanted.

"Fran," she whispered, snapping back into the moment, "can you see Crina?"

"She's lingering on West End," came Fran's voice into her earphones.

"Yeah, slow it down lassie," Heather said, from her vantage point in Silas's parked car on the other side of the compound. "I haven't seen anything yet."

"I might have something," Teddie said. "Three young girls, pretty sad looking, in dark clothes, just crossed Columbus and headed across on 104th. I think it's them, they walking kinda jerky."

"Don't lose sight of them," Fran said. "But don't get close. Tell me when you have them crossing Broadway and I'll pick them up on camera."

"I'm gonna go wait near the dumpsters," Crina whispered. "Continue my fake phone call there."

In her mind, Sara fought the urge to say "Roger. Over. Copy." Now wasn't the time for people pleasing.

"I'll be waiting," she said finally.

"Okay, Fran," Teddie's voice sounded like she was running. "They're speeding up. They're crossing Broadway."

"Got em," Fran said. "They're splitting up, two are heading north, one is coming along 104th."

"Shit," Crina said. "I'm gonna cross the street and work my way back, I'll try to be seen by all three before I come to you, Sara. Radio silence now."

"Got it," said Fran. "Go north on West End then circle back and you should get them all."

Thirty seconds of silence followed, and Sara watched as a haunted young woman, her hair unkempt, her clothes shabby, walked past with an angular gait. She wasn't more than eighteen. Sara's lungs began to burn and she realized she was holding her breath. Exhaling quietly, she watched her vapor hang in the air.

"They've seen you, Crina," Fran said in her earpiece. "Now slowly make your way into the alley where Sara is."

Even though Crina said she wouldn't be speaking, Sara hated the silence on the line.

"You have all three of them watching you, Crina. Hurry to where Sara is waiting."

Shrinking even deeper into the shadows, Sara watched as Crina came into view, her phone raised to her ear. With a dramatic flourish, she said, "Well if that's what you want, then I guess I have no options!" and hung up the phone, stepping into the alcove just yards from Sara. With deliberate slowness, she moved the dumpster that was blocking the entrance to the coal chute, then lifted the heavy metal latch, swinging the door open with a metallic scrape.

"They're across the street, watching you," Fran said. "Get into the opening, move slowly unless I say otherwise."

On cue, Crina bent and, using her hands on the lip of the opening, crawled inside.

Across the street, three figures emerged into a pool of streetlight, slowly advancing toward the pair of legs that were disappearing into the small doorway. Sara's pulse began to race . She regulated her breathing as she watched the young women whisper to each other, advancing as the door pulled closed. For a moment, they stood around the door in silence, then they began to bicker in Spanish, too quietly for Sara to make out what they were saying. One of them pulled tentatively on the metal door latch, her eyes widening as it opened, gesturing angrily that the others should climb inside. The two women shook their heads, resisting. The first woman slapped the woman nearest her hard across the face, then pushed her head into the dark opening. After a brief pause, she climbed inside. The third woman stepped up to the opening and the standing woman nodded with her head. This time, the woman didn't hesitate, vanishing into the darkness in seconds.

Sara watched as a victorious grin spread over the face of the woman who held the door. With a satisfied nod, she bent over, and followed the other two inside, leaving the metal door slightly ajar.

Sara leapt from her hiding spot in the corner, and in one smooth motion, she pushed the door closed, threw the latch into place, then rolled the dumpster back in front of the opening.

Sara heard a flurry of jumbled Spanish from behind the door, pressing her ear against the cold metal in an attempt to decipher what they were saying.

"Is Crina clear?"

"Yes, I'm in the antechamber. The door is locked."

Sara felt a surge of relief as she listened to the women begin to panic inside the coalway. Suddenly one voice rose above the others, closer to her than she'd expected.

"Es una trampa," the voice yelled. "Sacanos de aqui! Ahora!"

Something thumped hard against the metal door, and Sara moved her face away as more heavy blows pounded against it, uselessly. "No puedo abrirlo," said a different voice, higher. "Esta bloqueado."

The banging on the door continued and the volume of the arguing reached a crescendo until the voice that was closest to Sara yelled "No, no lo hagas, por favor, no, no noooooo."

And then Sara smelled something sharp, acrid, bitter and her mind flashed to almonds she'd eaten eons ago at an Italian christening and something burned at her lungs and she threw herself back.

"Cyanide," she hissed. "They've released cyanide. Get out of the antechamber right now."

In Sara's ears, she could hear voices, Teddie, Heather, Crina, Fran, all yelling at once as she lurched away from the grill door, gasping for fresh air, her pulse racing dangerously. This was what Edita was trying to tell her. They have poison. She prayed Crina was okay.

Another noise caught her attention, and she pulled the earphones out of her ears. Sickening screams of the women inside the coal chamber reached a crescendo, then ended suddenly, replaced by choking sounds, and then brief disgusting moaning that stopped suddenly, leaving an awful silence in its wake.

Bending to pick up her earphones from the ground, Sara shoved them back into her ears.

"Are you alright, Sara, are you there?" Teddie sounded hysterical.

"Yes, yes, I'm fine, I'm fine," she said. "Fran, which door can I come in?"

"I'll unlock the one right by you, maintenance entrance."

Stepping cautiously out onto the street, Sara glanced left and right, relieved that the street was empty. As she walked the short distance to the maintenance entrance, she heard the heavy lock click open, and she pushed it so hard that it bounced back at the end of its arc, nearly hitting her on the rebound. Carefully, she pressed it closed, happy when she heard it lock itself remotely.

Just as she was about to ask Fran to open the brick wall door to the passageways, it opened, revealing Fran, her face a rictus of fear.

"Come on," she said. "Thank fuck you're okay."

In a blind panic, Sara could only think of Teddie as she lurched past Fran, and into the hallway where she saw Heather, Crina and Teddie leaning against the bare brick wall, their chests heaving.

"Did any of you breathe it? Did you?" Sara's voice broke as she yelled.

"No, lassie," Heather said. "The door was already bolted on our side. Did you?"

"Just a whiff," Sara said. "I feel like I'm gonna throw up but it's passing."

"She sent them here to kill us," Teddie said. "They weren't going to bargain for her release, they were going to kill us."

"Yep," Sara said. "They were kamikazes. They could never be taken alive."

"I bet we burned a vial of cyanide in Edita's pants last night," Heather said. "So bloody stupid to not check the pockets."

"How could we know?" Sara said, her breathing still uneven. "We needed to get rid of that stink."

"That stink is going to be nothing compared with the mess we have to clean up now," Heather said angrily.

"Can you get another one of them chimney sweep Groupons?"

Sara literally had to duck to avoid the slap that Heather sent her way.

Chapter Twenty-Four

Sara let herself into her apartment, absently noting that all the lights were on, smiling when she heard the tinkling piano of Bill Evans floating out from the bedroom.

"Honey, I'm home," she yelled.

"In here!"

She followed Silas's voice to the bedroom, where she found him sitting in lotus position, his eyes closed, his long lashes brushing his cheeks. It wasn't until he felt her kneeling on the bed that he opened one eye.

"I'm glad you're home," he said, not moving. "I got a bit wound up, so I did an hour of yoga and now I'm getting started on some meditating."

Sara paused midway into a hug. "I can give you some space," she said. "Finish up and I'll be on my phone in the-"

"Nuh uh," Silas cupped a hand behind Sara's head and pulled her the rest of the way down, kissing her warmly. "I can meditate later. To be honest, I was nervous and every siren or blast of hip hop jolted me out."

"I've been a bundle of why the hell did we come back here?" Sara settled on top of Silas's crossed legs. "Silas, tonight was disgusting. And it's sad, those girls, they're dead because of Des..." She let the sentence trail off, then kissed him again, lingering, inhaling him. "I want to be done with all this shit."

"That's Lock life. As soon as you think you're done, they pull you in."

"I'd like to try some Icelandic chores then," she laughed, kissing the tip of his nose.

"As enticing as that sounds, we can't until this current nonsense is over," he said. "and I don't think we're even close to the finish line yet."

"What if this Lock vanished?" Sara propped herself on one elbow. "What if we went full ghost town on it, packed all our bags and shut up shop?"

"It's an interesting option," Silas winked at her. "Tell me more."

"Well, like we talked in Iceland, you said that I hauled this Lock around on my back like a tortoise, that's just the tip of the iceberg. In my conscience, I am hauling all of the Locks with me, I'm always fighting for what's best for everyone, all the women, even the shitty ones."

"Yep, that's clear," Silas uncrossed his legs and hauled Sara up so she was resting her head on his thighs. "So you've finally arrived at the fuck 'em all place?"

"I'd like to think I have," Sara whispered. "I honestly don't care what happens to Liz or Rosa. They can move on, they're both overdue."

"But what's to stop them just starting their own Desdemona-approved Lock here?"

"Damn you," she laughed. "That's the last detail that I can't quite figure out."

"There's an answer," Silas said, ruffling her hair. "There's always an answer."

"My new favorite distraction is itemizing all the tensions that Rosa and Marguerite caused me, daily, and knowing that it was because Desdemona told them to, that's really starting to twist a knife in my guts."

Sara pressed herself upright then crouched to face Silas.

"And don't go taking the blame for this, but I've been really regretting being so welcoming to Liz when San Fran folded."

"But that is my fault." Silas took her hand. "I'm sorry, my love. But everything that is done, it's done. You can't change the past. Our lives don't mix well with regret."

"True, true. I also have something new for you."

"Oooh I love new things," Silas said, clapping his hands together.

"Yukari asked if she can experiment on the halflings that are still in the park. She wants us to capture them."

"Not what I was expecting, but sure, of course she'd want that." Silas smiled. "How do you feel about it?"

"Not good," Sara said. "I understand totally, Yukari is total science brain, she sees research as her purpose, and we've benefited from it so many times. Teddie says it's human animal testing."

"We are in wartime," Silas began, and Sara cut him off.

"Careful, buster," she said with mock severity. "Wartime is a word that men have used for millennia to justify the very worst examples of human cruelty. Just because there's trouble in the air doesn't mean that we can take away a young girl's autonomy."

"I agree," Silas said. "But what if that sanatorium in Spain is full of women like this? What's gonna happen to them? The girls in the park are the only key that Yukari has to possibly unlock a solution, or a cure."

"The samples that Yukari took before Edita died aren't enough for all the tests she needs to run. And I'm not sure what she'll be able to harvest from the puddles in the coal cellar," she paused, shuddering. "Silas it was dreadful. When we finally got in there, they were still twitching, an hour later."

"Horrible," he said. "So, the weaker virus didn't, you know, fling them about?"

Sara shook her head, trying to will herself to not see the spastic pulsing of the three dead women, their faces black, their tongues distended, their limp bodies dancing with weak electricity. "No, and yet, it was somehow worse."

Leaning across, Silas kissed Sara's cheek.

"I'm really sorry that you have to see such nightmarish crap," he said. "I asked Fan and Ama about it once, whether they were haunted by what they saw when they were out killing all the men."

"And?"

"They said it wasn't as haunting as the things they saw the Cursed men do to other people."

"Fair."

"But that wasn't the answer I was looking for, because it wasn't the question I should have asked," Silas said. "I've talked about it with Embla since. I struggle to understand that whole pillar of our existence, the killing part. We've been dedicated to peace for five centuries, but still, our cornerstones for transgressions are all violent. I should have asked Fan and Ama if they think that violence can coexist with peace."

"You already know the answer," Sara whispered, happy when he nodded.

"I do. Violence and peace are mutually exclusive states. So that brings me back to you. You saw Marguerite's body."

"Don't remind me," Sara said. "I was grateful that my New York nightmares knocked that out of my nightmare top ten for a while."

""That's what I mean. Just because you've lived a long while and your roots were in a more violent time, why should you be able to roll with truly horrifying shit? And these scenes with the halflings, they're unimaginable nightmare fodder, they're literally things you shouldn't be seeing and yet, here you are, seeing them and you're supposed to be okay with it because you're what? A vampire? Because you're really old?"

"I've thought about that a lot over the years," Sara said pensively. "If you take a step back, there's a lot of stuff that is grandfathered into our lives, based on events from the dark ages. It's no different out in the real world, we still use capital punishment and solitary confinement, we still use brutality in war."

"So, to switch tacks, can you see a functional vampire society where violence and punishment are not part of the fabric?"

Sara thought about Silas's words, letting the concept roll around in her mind while she tried to poke holes in the logic of a peaceful, functioning Lock structure. She couldn't think of a reason against it.

"Sure," she said finally. "But that raises a huge question, and let's use Desdemona as an example. In that new framework, what do you do when a person turns rotten, the way she has?"

"Kick her out," Silas said. "She can live by herself, she can see if another Lock will take her. Her journey would cease to be tied to any specific Lock."

"Survey says zero respondents," Sara joked. "Right now, no Lock would take Desdemona. If she lost her resources, and became a loose cannon, how do we solve this problem without violence?"

"We don't," Silas sighed. "Right now, I'm more concerned about this non-stop trauma being piled on top of you."

Sara let out a matching sigh.

"Not gonna lie," she said. "Your concern freaks me out. It's easier for me to sail past these horrifying events and just keep busy, just keep moving."

Silas went to speak and she held up a finger.

"That's not what I'm doing this time," she said, raising her eyes to his. "To use therapy-speak, I feel very supported right now and I trust you enough to believe that you will be there for me if and when this shit gets too much for me."

Silas nodded. "That's probably the nicest thing anyone's ever said to me," he said and they both cracked up, laughing. As Sara was getting her breath back, her phone dinged. It was Teddie.

> Mom you home? I'm okay but I gotta tell you some shit.

> Sure. Meet you at the end of the fifth-floor corridor. Just past my old door.

As soon as the text was sent, Sara realized that she'd just invited Teddie into her apartment, the one she was sharing with Silas. What should have been normal in anyone's life was momentous in hers and her stomach churned.

"What now?" Silas asked.

"Teddie needs to tell me something urgent."

"And she's coming here?"

Sara nodded.

"And am I staying?"

Sara nodded again.

"I love you Sara," Silas said.

"I love that for you," Sara said, bouncing off the bed to avoid Silas grabbing for her. "We don't have time for wrestling now," she quipped, skipping to the bedroom door. Turning she blew him a kiss. "I love you too."

After meeting Teddie at the end of their corridor, Sara ushered her back to the apartment.

"You're okay with this?" she asked as they approached the door. Teddie, in a black BLM hoodie, gray Peloton sweats, a Diop wrap around her hair and a reusable shopping bag with a chihuahua on it in one hand, paused and smiled.

"I am if you are, Little Miss Nervous."

"Whatever," Sara said as she threw her shoulder into the heavy brick door, pushing it open. Stepping into the rear of the living room, she saw Silas cross legged on the couch, an open bottle of Guinness on the coffee table flanked by three glasses.

"Don't get up," Teddie said, waving amiably at him.

"I could never be so gauche," Silas said, unfolding his legs and leaping to his feet. "Are we at hugging yet?"

"Oh, she didn't tell me you were a hugger," Teddie said warily, hanging back.

"No worries," Silas said, his arms still extended, he pivoted, lifting the bottle of stout.

"Get over here," Teddie said, stepping to him and opening her arms. "I was just playing with you."

Laughing, Silas set the Guinness back down and stepped into the hug.

"I was just trying to freak out Miss Thing here," she said as they broke apart.

"Oh she's already freaked," Silas said.

"You guys, I'm right here," Sara said, moving apprehensively to a spot on the couch beside Silas. Teddie took the beer Silas was handing to her and then sat cross legged on the floor, across from them.

"Thanks for coming over," Silas began.

"Are you crazy?" Teddie smiled, sipping her beer. "I have a million questions. A million."

"I'm an open book," Silas said. "Actually, I'm an open book with one chapter missing. It has nothing to do with you, but we are at war and there's one thing I need to guard. I just don't want to lie to you."

"Everybody got their secrets," Teddie snapped her fingers in the air. "I can respect that. Wait. Is it Liz? Because I'm so curious about Liz."

Rolling his eyes, Silas laughed. "No, you can ask about Liz. Or I can just tell you. She was drinking a lot, in the same bar night after night, and I was worried she was getting sloppy. So I just started talking to her, at first it was so that she didn't spill anything to the wrong person. Then, she asked me on a date, so I went. No, nothing ever happened."

"We aren't Eskimo cousins," Sara said and Teddie sat upright.

"Girl, how many times are we Eskimo cousins?" she yelled. "I guess that's alright, you just don't want to share your man with Lizzy. I get it."

"Wait what?" Silas said.

"Oh, I'm sorry, that chapter is sealed," Teddie laughed, finishing her beer. "Feel me?"

"Does that mean when I tell you the missing chapter, you'll tell me yours?"

To Sara's horror, Teddie leaned across the coffee table and shook Silas's hand. "Deal."

The now familiar warmth of happiness blossomed in Sara's chest, and she sat back and soaked in the image of Silas and Teddie getting along. If Silas and Teddie could find peace, she thought, maybe this impossible situation will resolve itself.

Don't get your hopes up, she thought.

"So, Teddie, let's get business out of the way and then we can do the ask me anything thing."

"Shoot," she said, draining her second glass. Sara got up and went to the kitchen to get another bottle.

"Sara asked me about the about the fate of the two halflings in the park," Silas said, "and how you, rightly, think they should be treated with care, not killed. I agree."

"I just met you today," Teddie laughed. "And now you wanna co-parent some vampires with me?"

"No, I just want to donate to your GoFundMe," Silas said, winking at Sara as she poured him a fresh glass.

"Whatcha got?"

"I have a place, upstate. I would like to offer it to you, as a place where you can work on, you know, rehabbing these poor girls. It's secure. As fuck."

"What is it? A secret laboratory?"

"No, Ted," Sara sat back down. "It's breathtaking. Silas, that would be incredible."

"I'm doing this for a couple reasons," Silas continued. "Obviously, I think these women should be given a chance. I've spent a lot of time around Fan and Ama, and for all their radical vegan feminism, they're still the same women who brutally wiped out all the Cursed men."

"Asterisk almost all the Cursed men," Teddie joked. Sara was elated to see her so comfortable.

"They didn't know about me for a long time," Silas said. "They had calmed down a lot by the time we met. They're like my batty aunts."

"That's simultaneously hilarious and terrifying," Teddie said,"and I always enjoy a bat metaphor."

Silas doffed an imaginary hat and nodded in agreement.

"Anyway, I realize there is a big trust gap between us, there's no way there can't be. So, I wanted to offer this to you as like a first step, a vulnerability on my part, and also, it would be a very calm setting for you to do some difficult work, and also, you're still trending on socials so you'd be very well hidden."

"Did you put him up to this?" Teddie glanced at Sara who shook her head.

"Nope, this is my first time hearing it."

"Dang, well thank you, Silas, you strange, mysterious man. You don't got no brothers hiding out at your upstate house?"

"Wait, brothers or brothers?" he laughed. "Actually it doesn't matter, there aren't any hidden siblings, and as far as I know, I'm the only Cursed man."

Sara returned with two bottles of Guinness and three goblets of blood on a wooden cutting board.

"My vintage mirrored serving tray was missing from my apartment," she sniffed as she sat on the other side of Teddie.

"Guilty," Teddie said.

"Are you keeping it?"

"Do you want it back?"

Sara thought for a moment, then shook her head.

"You keep it. But Ted, what was so urgent?"

Grimacing, Teddie looked at the drinks on the coffee table, then back to Sara.

"Can it wait? I'm enjoying this."

"I don't know? Can it?"

"Okay fine, mom. Fuck it. Desdemona sent me a message asking if I'd seen the newspaper today. So, after Imani made two trips to various bodegas below 72nd Street," she paused and Sara laughed, recognizing her rule that even casual shopping had to happen at least a mile from the compound, "I saw this." Teddie grabbed her little shopping bag from the floor and pulled out that day's edition of the NY Post, flicking several pages in before turning it to Sara, who, already annoyed that Desdemona had messaged Teddie, gasped.

A quarter page news story devoted to the Instagram sensation of the ageless woman greeted her. As well as the images of Teddie at CBGB's and the Village Vanguard, there was a photo of an older Latina.

"They interviewed one of my coworkers," Teddie said. "She said that when she saw the photos she thought it was me. Mom, this is bad right?"

Sara scanned the article briefly. There didn't seem to be any additional information that could identify Teddie.

"What did you say when you quit?"

"I said I had to go take care of my aunt in Haiti."

"Good, that will be enough of a smokescreen," Sara said. "So Desdemona texted you about the article? How the hell did she see it?"

Teddie shrugged.

"I'd say Rosa told her," she said, and Sara heard her voice tighten, which meant that Teddie had more to say, and she was nervous.

"What else, Ted?"

"She wrote me that I have put the entire Cursed world at risk and that all of the European Locks want me to go live in Madrid. And she wants me to call her."

"Shouldn't she have called Yukari?" Silas leaned forward and passed goblets of blood to Sara and Teddie.

"Fucking Desdemona," Teddie said. "She says I can't tell Yukari or anyone here, not even Rosa."

"That's weird," Sara said. "Are you thinking of calling her?"

"That's why I'm here," Teddie said. "I didn't tell anyone else. Mom, what should I do?"

"Lemme think for a sec," Sara downed her blood, leaving a thin red mustache on her upper lip. Silas reached across and wiped it away with his thumb, then turned to Teddie.

"If I may say something," he said, waiting for a nod from Teddie before continuing, "I managed five centuries of invisibility. Ted, do not feel any pressure to go anywhere you don't want to go. I'll volunteer a little more. I have properties around the world where you could go. The three of us could go. You probably need to leave New York for fifty years or so, but there's a whole world out there."

"Thanks, Silas, that actually makes me feel a little better," Teddie's voice was still small, and Sara's heart juggled immense love on top of the anger she felt towards Desdemona. "I gotta tell ya, it just feels so strange that there are options outside of the other Locks. No offense mom, but if any of those places looked halfway decent, I might have moved away a long time ago. Nowhere looks as good as here. Nowhere."

Sara smiled and took Teddie's hand. "I've seen a couple of Silas's places now, and they're better than here. Trust me on this."

"And you don't mind me tagging along?" Teddie's tone returned to playful. "Did she tell you she was a single mom?"

"More than once," Silas said with a chuckle. "More than once."

"You guys," Sara interrupted. "Let's just do it. I mean, if you're up to it, Ted, just text her and say you're alone and you can talk for the next ten minutes. Otherwise she'll rant at you for hours."

"Sure," Teddie shrugged. "I'm not as bothered by her as you are. I can handle her."

"Okay, kiddo," Sara reached for her Guinness. "Set it up."

"How should I be?" The look on Teddie's face broke Sara's heart.

"Be you, Theodora," she said quietly. "Don't try anything fancy, she'll get wary. Suspicious is her normal state."

"I thought her normal state was jealous," Silas said.

"Either or," Sara said, weighing her hands in front of her like a set of scales.

"I messaged her," Teddie said, and Silas snatched up his phone and killed the music and they sat in silence, looking anywhere but at each other until a light dinging came from Teddie's phone.

Squaring her shoulders back and taking a deep breath, Teddie answered the call, quickly putting it on speaker.

"What, bitch?" Teddie said with a broad smile as Silas and Sara fought to contain shocked laughter.

"Being famous has ruined you darling." The sound of Desdemona's unctuous voice made Sara's blood boil.

"Like I said, you murdering bitch, what do you want?"

"If you're going to speak like the spoiled brat that you are, I will hang up," Desdemona's edge frayed a little. "You'd think after endangering our entire kind with your lack of responsibility, you'd be more welcoming of an escape hatch that doesn't end with you suffocated on the floor."

"Oh right, Des," Teddie turned her back to Sara and Silas before continuing. "You came in here and stole my mother's fucking skull. And that was after you murdered Marguerite. You really must forgive me, I've completely forgotten my manners. How does a monster like you wish to be addressed?"

"I have some advice for you, if your mother had been better at advice, you wouldn't be in this trouble. My advice to you, right now, is to shut your mouth and listen."

"Mouth shut, ears open."

"Espera, are you alone?"

"Yes, Desdemona, as requested."

"Then why am I on speaker?"

"Because I just painted my nails."

"But of course you did," Desdemona laughed sarcastically. "Teddie, I have talked to all of the European Lock mothers today and they are all very concerned about your new level of fame. All Locks are in agreement that you must immediately transfer to the Madrid Lock."

"Isn't this a conversation you should be having with Yukari?"

"No, because she will side with you, she will insist that it's safe to keep you there."

"Well, there's your answer. Anyway, it's been great but-"

"Mouth shut, ears open," Desdemona said angrily. "I wanted to talk to you about what I'm offering. Your life in Madrid would be better than anything you could hope for. You will of course have to spend the next decade or two out of sight. During that time, I'd like to offer you a position in our clinics, working with the lost girls of Madrid."

"I wasn't applying for a position with you, Des," Teddie said. Sara was hoping that Teddie could keep the conversation going now that Des was revealing stuff, if she was even telling the truth. "Now you want me to work in what? Some clinic? I thought you needed me off the streets."

"The clinics are as secure as any Lock," Desdemona said. "We are taking in the lost girls from the streets, giving them a second chance."

"Desdemona, what kind of second chance can a girl get at a clinic?" Sara gave Teddie a thumbs up and Teddie smiled.

"Unlike your city, my women never gave up on the religious aspect of our order."

"Honey, the nun stuff was just drag so we could be safe."

"You wouldn't know, you weren't there."

"Anyway, what are you offering, Des? You said I was gonna be all locked up and then you offered me a job helping the needy. I'm confused."

Believing she had Teddie's interest, Desdemona softened.

"I know this has been a hard time for you," she said, the manipulation evident in her voice. "But if you join my Lock, you'll learn what it means to have the true purpose of what women like us can do in our long lifetimes."

"Desdemona, you're a cold-blooded killer. You're exactly the opposite of what women like us can do with our lives. If you want to work out your sick messiah complex on a bunch of young women, have at it. They'll see through you soon enough."

"Has nobody ever told you how tiresome you are?"

"No, because I'm a ray of motherfucking sunshine," Teddie said, snapping her fingers twice.

An angry exhale filled the room, and Sara knew that Des had lost her temper.

"You'll be a ray of sunshine with a slicer sticking out the back of your neck if you don't do exactly as I say," Desdemona spat, her accent thickening. "That's not a threat. After we hang up, you will go to Yukari and tell her that you want to transfer to Madrid. Teddie, I promise you will be happy here."

"Doubtful," Teddie said. "On all fronts. I would most definitely not be happy in your weird cult and I won't be passing messages to Yukari for you."

"To be fair," Desdemona was fighting to maintain civility, "I didn't expect you to listen. You've been the golden one for so long. Have you ever killed? Can you even fight? Or is getting your photo taken in public the only thing that you're trained in?"

Teddie let out a long, slow yawn into the phone.

"Sorry, Des, hollow threats bore the shit out of me."

"Entonces, how about a real threat then?"

The steel in Desdemona's voice froze Sara's blood.

"Yes, auntie, I'm waiting."

"If you do not agree to what I say, all Lock mothers will vote for your immediate Surrender."

"Oooh that would be terrifying if I was a member of their Lock, but once again, I'm not. And you're lying. You're powerless."

Unable to resist, Desdemona leaned into it.

"You can't even begin to grasp the extent of my power," she hissed. "I am singlehandedly saving our way of life. And from now until the end of this phone call, I am extending an olive branch, to you. Come here, see how we live. I think you'll like it."

"And I'm sure I won't, and really, Desdemona, you're pathetic. I'm safe here. Unless you're planning to, I don't know, kidnap me or something, then you're just pissing up a rope."

"Good point, Theodora, please watch your back. You'll either be coming to Madrid, or they'll find you with a Slicer between your shoulders. I don't care which. Before I let you go, there's one last thing that I need to share with you."

"Is it a prize? Did I win a prize?"

"Sure, you'll probably see it that way. You wonder where all those photos are coming from? Spoiler, it's me! And you wouldn't believe how many I have. Not just of you. So, if you don't play nice, I'll start releasing more of them. You'll all be trapped inside that building, slowly starving to death. You'll turn on each other. You'll *feed* on each other. And it will be your fault."

"Dang, I was hoping for a puppy," Teddie said with a laugh, and a click sounded. Desdemona had hung up.

As Teddie turned back to face them, Sara reached across and wrapped her arms around her.

"You handled that brilliantly," she said.

"She's nothing but drama," Teddie said.

"No, she's gunning for you," Silas said. "Now that she thinks Sara is dead, she is obsessing over ruining everything that she loved."

"Which is bad for you, too, right?"

Silas nodded.

"Yeah, but she'd have to find me first."

"That would not bother me as much, Silas," Sara wrapped her other arm around him, "if you weren't holed up in the first place she's going to ransack."

"We won't be here that long, right Ted?"

"What does that mean?"

Silas and Teddie exchanged nervous glances.

"What? Is this what you guys talked about in Heather's bedroom?"

Teddie took a deflective slow sip of her beer, not meeting Sara's gaze. Silas gave Teddie an exasperated look.

"Tell her or she'll beat me up when you leave."

"God, fine, whatever," Teddie said. "We need something solid beneath us, or shit is gonna get real crazy."

"That's it?" Sara looked accusingly from one to the other. "That's what your conspiracy is?"

"Basically," Silas said.

"Look mom," Sara loved it when Teddie sounded like an embattled teenager. "Can't you just be grateful that I didn't smuggle a slicer inside my head wrap?"

"I'll always be grateful for that," Sara said primly. "You're getting me back for having secrets by driving me crazy with the secret discussion that transformed you from enemy to ally in a few short minutes."

Teddie let out an agonized sigh.

"All you need to know is that your man here confided some shit to me, and probably for the first time since I met, who now? Probably Heather. For the first time since I met Heather, I met someone who is on the same page as me. It was..." Teddie glanced at Silas. "...refreshing."

"Hey," Silas leaned forward, grinning cheekily, "I thought you had a million questions for me."

"Apparently not while someone's feeling left out," Teddie stood up, walked around the coffee table, sat behind Sara and threw her legs around Sara's waist. "Listen, bitch. I'm so happy that I didn't kill you that you can get away with a lot. But you gotta trust me with your mans."

"You win, you always win," Sara said from her vantage point on the couch where she'd been watching and filing away memories of what was happening in front of her. "I'm beyond happy to see you like this."

Teddie squeezed Sara tight, and Silas took one of her hands inside his and looked into her eyes.

"So," Silas said. "Teddie, how do you like your new Lock?"

Sara sat bolt upright, giving Silas a very definite what the fuck did you just say face.

"What?" he asked innocently. "Teddie, you figured it out already, right?"

Laughing throatily, Teddie nodded. "Yeah, you've been hiding your endgame in plain sight, mom."

"I have been worried sick that you'd reject all this-"

"All this what? Did I pass? Can you tell me everything?"

"Nice try," Sara said. "Silas, when did I find out everything?"

"Hmmm," Silas scratched his chin theatrically. "Without giving too much away, you learned everything after you committed suicide, got rescued, picked up a young hitchhiker, got transported across several state lines and then flew to an undisclosed location, all on trust."

"That does sound about right," Sara said. "And Ted? If it sucked in any way, would I be endorsing it?"

"You would not."

"Correct." Sara leaned her head against Teddie, who wriggled out of the embrace.

"Wait, I do have some questions," she said. "So, there are definitely no more Cursed men hiding out in your secret lair?"

Sara shook her head, her eyes widening as Silas continued the chin scratching. "Well, no," he said. "No men. But we do have a relatively new sister, and she's a trans woman."

"Fuck yeah," Teddie yelled. "Once again, you guys need to start leading with the good stuff. All in. I'm fucking all in."

Chapter Twenty-Five

Waking gently from a nightmare-free slumber, Sara gradually indexed the sensations around her. She felt Silas's arm beneath her pillow, supporting her neck. His other arm was draped across her waist. She felt the hair on his tummy bristling against her back as he inhaled, then soft eddies of his breath across her neck as he exhaled, peace spreading through every part of her body. Keeping her eyes closed, she inhaled, lazily identifying the scents of her new home. Cooking smells, faint incense, unindentifiable New York apartment, and floating like a ghost above it all, she could smell Teddie's perfume like a memory that would vanish if you looked directly at it.

Sara let her mind run off, to a future where Teddie was in Iceland with them, or another where Silas lived harmoniously in the New York compound, spending summer weekends at his lake house, the same life as always but with a lightness she could never have envisioned. Occasionally, glimmers of Lock responsibility tried to encroach, and she simply ignored them. The various crises in that world had no place in this world. She wasn't a Mother anymore. Maybe there wouldn't even be Mothers in the new life.

"What you thinkin' about?" Silas's voice was deep, rough with sleep, and vibrated against her back.

"Mmmmmmmmmm," Sara stretched against him. "Oh you know, just random existential crises."

"Oh yeah?" He kissed her between the shoulder blades and her neck arched involuntarily. "No bad dreams?"

"Not a one," she whispered. "I was just thinking happy thoughts and trying not to wake you."

"I like the sound of that," he said. "Can we stay like this all day?"

"Don't see why not," she smiled. "We will be all rested for hunting the halflings."

"First rule of all-day bed club is no mentioning the halflings," Silas said with mock severity. "Second rule is no mention of the D word."

Sara pressed her butt back against his groin, liking what she felt.

"That's the only d-word I plan to use today."

Giving her a wolfish chuckle, Silas moved back and hauled Sara around to facing him, immediately pressing his full lips against hers, dusting them with short sweet kisses.

"What a grand way to wake up," he said, his lips still against hers, every word brushing against her.

"This will sound corny," she said quietly, "but it still feels like I'm dreaming."

"It's not corny, it's pretty fucking great," he said, resuming the kisses.

An urge to check her phone took shape, and Sara tamped it down.

"What's up?" Silas pulled away slightly, his chocolate eyes boring into hers.

"I haven't looked at my phone since Teddie left."

Silas shrugged. "Check it," he smiled. "Stealth mode. If you don't answer anybody, they won't know you're awake."

"That's never stopped anyone," Sara said, reaching for her phone. She wasn't surprised by the tickertape of texts as she blinked twice to get her eyes to focus. Unable to believe what she read when they did focus, she grabbed for Silas's hand.

"Uh, so.." her voice trailed off as she flicked through texts.

"Is all day bed club canceled?"

"Depends on whether you want to invite Fan, Ama, April Veronica and Embla?"

"What now?" Silas pressed himself upright.

"I have over two hundred texts but what I can gather is that the Icelanders arrived yesterday and caught the halflings in the park."

"No way," Silas smiled. "Where is everybody?"

"Hang on," Sara jumped from one text window to another, reading rapidly. "I have Yukari and Heather going mental as well."

A knock at the front door, startled both of them.

"And this is what happens when I don't answer texts," Sara said, her voice tight.

"I'm sorry baby," Silas said, leaning over and grabbing Sara's shorts and t-shirt from the floor and passing them to her. Another knock sounded.

"That's the front door," Sara said. "Go look through the peep hole."

"Yes, boss," Silas stood up, naked and saluting her. Sara's heart swelled.

"Pants, babe," she laughed. "First, put on pants."

Silas jump danced into a pair of yoga shorts and left the room pulling a tank top over his head.

"It's Peanut and Embla," he called out from the hallway, joy in his voice. Leaping from the bed, Sara made it to the hallway in time to see Silas engulf Embla in a hug. Behind her on the landing, April Veronica raised a hand and waved at Sara, who waved back, then rushed to the door, squeezing past the still-hugging human blockade and wrapping her arms around April Veronica's shoulders.

"I knew there'd be an onslaught of hugs," Embla said. "So I was careful to put the coffees and pastries down a few levels."

"Welcome to New York," Sara said. "I'm so happy to see you."

"Yes, we should have come back when you did," Embla said, "It was weird being at home without you guys. I got used to it way too fast."

"I did too," Sara said. "Let's get inside, I'm still antsy out in the open like this."

"Okay," April Veronica broke the hug and turned to pick up a tray of coffees and two very full Fairway bags. "After last night, you don't have much to worry about but I want you to feel safe."

Turning, Sara threaded herself between the still-hugging Silas and Embla and the door jamb, looking over the wreckage of the living room.

"We apologize in advance for the mess," she said, snatching up clothing and miscellaneous crap she still hadn't found a place for. As she hurled the last armload of crap onto the bed, she heard everyone in the kitchen, and turned, a smile spreading across her face. Embla was setting out all the stuff they'd brought, in an orderly arrangement on the countertop. April Veronica was showing Silas some moves she'd learned from Fan. Sara's heart swelled as the younger woman took her boyfriend by surprise, gripping his wrist and spinning herself so that her momentum spun him around completely, his hand now yanked up between his shoulders.

"So far so good," Silas said. "Now what?"

"Now what what?" April Veronica barely got the words out before Silas slumped down, dragging her with him as he twisted. Before April Veronica knew what happened, Silas was sitting on her chest.

"Good start, Peanut," he said, standing and extending an arm. "But a fight doesn't have a pause button."

"You're just like Fan," April Veronica laughed, yanking herself up to standing. "Also, I trained for like four days."

"You bested a barely-trained woman," Embla said, giving Silas some serious side-eye. "Congratulations."

"I was not acting like a man," Silas said to Embla, who just shrugged and returned to serving their food. "Sara, I was just showing her that positions that work on normal folks aren't as crippling to us."

Silas was so earnest it was killing Sara to continue the ribbing but when she saw Embla give her a wink over his shoulder, she couldn't help herself.

"Sorry, was your alpha ego dented by a little girl?"

"Oh my god, Sara!" Silas was as close to angry as she'd ever seen him. "All three of you know that I was just reacting the way a woman trained me to."

"You're so cute when you're mad," April Veronica said.

"I told you his buttons were easy to push," Embla said, finally turning and throwing her arms around Silas, who groaned.

"Also, you haven't trained in a while," April Veronica whispered. "The next move would break a normal man's neck."

"Thank you for sparing him from that," Sara said, blowing Silas a kiss. "Now can you all get in here and tell me what the hell happened last night?"

Sara felt a strange elation at the look of surprise on Embla's face.

"How do you not know?" Embla came into the living room balancing a tray on each hand. Sara took one, then the other, setting them on the coffee table. Embla sat so close to her that their hips were touching.

"I really missed you, Sara," Embla said, her attention focused on handing Sara a coffee.

"I'm not used to that kind of talking," Sara said, taking the coffee. "But I like it. I missed you too. I was worried about you. I felt bad I just dumped a newborn on you."

"A newborn who's been through more in a few months than you went through in a century," April Veronica quipped as she leapt across the coffee table and landed on the other side of Embla.

"Boasting is gauche," Embla said with a smile, wrapping her arm around April Veronica.

"It's tacky too," the girl said, and they both burst out laughing.

Silas pulled a cushion from the couch and sat cross-legged on it, facing the three women.

"So, are you going to tell us why you're here and what you've been up to?"

"Sure," Embla said. "Fan and Ama decided that they couldn't stay away any longer, and we decided to join them."

As if that was explanation enough, Embla leaned forward and helped herself to a toasted bagel. After chewing on it for a few seconds she paused. "Holy shit," she said. "They really do taste different. And better."

"There's not much to report," April Veronica said. "They literally made us wait in the rental car while they went and caught the halflings. They said it wasn't very difficult. We had a fun little drive from the park, with two unconscious women in the back of a Yukon. Heather wasn't happy when we got here. She had to get all nunned up and let us in the front door. So did Yukari."

"I love them both," Embla said around mouthfuls of bagel.

"The halflings?" Silas asked, deliberately stupid.

"No, you ninny," Embla laughed. "Heather and Yukari. Heather was so grumpy and stern. Yukari was like a kid getting a new puppy."

"Where are they now?" Silas asked.

"I presume they're back in their apartments," Embla said, elbowing Sara gently.

Taking pity on Silas, Sara took over the questions.

"So, the halflings are where?"

"Internal room, lower level, not quite sure," April Veronica said. "Fan and Ama are out being tourists. We are all going to live in this building. They're taking over the third floor. We have to pick our apartment. We can be on your floor or below you. What do you recommend?"

"How's fourth floor," Sara offered. "Not beneath us, the other side?"

"Girl, how much fuckin' you doin'?" Embla cracked herself up.

"Not nearly enough," Sara said with a smile. "People keep knocking at our door unexpectedly."

As if on cue, a knock sounded at the rear wall.

"That'll be your mum," Embla said.

"Use your key," Silas yelled, his voice surprisingly loud, and immediately, Sara heard the rear door open.

"Your stuff is in the kitchen," Embla called out, and Sara glanced up, seeing that there was indeed a full Fairway bag on the counter, as well as four additional coffees still sitting in their carrier.

"Psssst."

Silas caught her attention, and their eyes locked, and he mouthed the words "I'm sorry" and Sara shrugged and nodded before Crina, Heather and Yukari all swarmed into a living room that suddenly felt very small.

Looking up instead of standing up, Sara smiled at the new arrivals and raced to figure out what to say to cut them off before they could start on her.

"So, how many crises did I just sleep through?" she asked, her voice cheerful.

"It wasn't that bad," Yukari said, sitting beside her and squeezing her thigh.

"Easy for you to say," Heather yelled from the kitchen. "It wasn't you who'd had a relaxing whisky or two before she was forced into full nun drag at 1am."

"I had two gummies and I was watching the Barbie movie," Yukari laughed. "I just pulled on the main robe and that was as much as I could manage."

"That's what you should call your autobiography," Silas blew her a kiss. "Sleeping Through Crises."

"I might," Sara smiled at him. "It's how I plan to handle them from now on."

"A solid plan," Silas said. "Hey, should we call Teddie?"

"Already did," April Veronica said. "Imani too. Heather, can you add them to the side passage security."

Pausing a bagel midway to her lips, Heather glared at April Veronica for a second and Embla tittered. "She hates you right now," she laughed.

"Just a little bit," Heather said, setting her bagel down and working on her phone. "Done. Now you owe me, and you can repay me by going to let them in."

"Gladly," April Veronica was bouncing down the hallway to the rear of the apartment before Heather finally got to bite into her bagel.

In the middle of the hubbub, Silas met Sara's gaze, then trailed his finger under his eyes and pointed at her own. With a silent nod, he stood and went into the kitchen. Sara turned her attention to the hallway, where girlish screams told her that Imani was very happy to see April, and vice versa.

"How you feeling right now?" Crina said into her ear, startling her.

"Lots of feels," Sara said. "All of them good. Bit of irresponsibility, but mostly, I can't..." she trailed off, her throat constricting.

"This is the future I've seen in my mind, for so many years," Crina said.

"I know," Sara nodded, gazing about the room, as Imani and Teddie filed in, their smiles faltering when they saw Embla, now sitting beside Heather. For a moment, Sara wondered if she should introduce her. Before she could act on the thought, Embla stood.

"Let me guess," she said, pointing a twirling finger at the newcomers. "Because I have been dying to meet you all. You're Teddie," she paused, glancing at Sara. "This one loves you so much. You're Imani, and I hope you're a hugger, because I need to thank you for your mercy dash to save my girl."

Imani's eyes widened in surprise before she was smothered in a hug. When she was done, Embla released the startled woman and stepped back.

"My name is Embla, I was made by Stefanya at the turn of the century, and I have been," Embla paused, and a very uncharacteristic blush crept up her neck and onto her cheeks, "I don't want to fangirl here, but all of you have been... this is a lot. You've all inspired me, all my cursed life."

Tears rimmed Embla's eyes and April Veronica stood and wrapped her arms around her waist.

"I'm okay, takk," Embla composed herself. "I've lived in a very small world, watching you all from afar, and it is overwhelming to be here. I have one last thing to say. I cannot use my nominee name, because I am a transwoman, and that would be deadnaming. Oh, wait. I can say never have I killed. A person I mean. I've eaten meat. But since my.. conversion, I have been vegan."

Sara watched, her heart filled with love, as Teddie wrapped Embla in a hug, and they stood in a circle, all chattering.

Standing, Sara swung by the kitchen and collected a very full mug of blood from Silas.

"There's something I have to do," she whispered. "Nothing serious."

Slipping into the bedroom, Sara fished her phone from her shorts with one hand while bringing the mug to her lips with the other. Before she finished drinking, she had dialed Fran's number.

"Sara, what a lovely surprise. How you doing?"

"I'm good, Frannie. Listen, I have one question for you. And I just want you to be completely honest with me."

"Honest is all I got, man," Fran replied.

"Are you completely trustworthy, to me, right now?"

"One hundred per cent."

"Only a hundred?" Sara said with a laugh.

"It's per cent Sara. By the hundredth. You can't be more than one hundred per cent of yourself."

"Exactly," Sara laughed. "So Frannie? Meet me in the hallway where you found me the other day. Now. Can you?"

"You bet. See you there."

And she was gone. Wiping her lip on the bottom of her shirt, Sara snuck down the hallway to the rear of the apartment and then out into the corridor. When she opened the secret door to her old building, she could hear Frannie's footsteps rushing toward her.

"No need to run," Sara called out. "Nobody's on fire."

The footsteps did not slow, and Frannie, in yoga pants, a cotton top and a meditation shawl, came around the corner.

"Sorry, I forgot shoes," she called out. "I was meditating."

"Forgive my interruption," Sara said as Fran reached her.

"Not at all," Fran said. "There's always time to meditate later. What's going on?"

"I... uh, I didn't think this part though, so I don't know how to handle it. But Fran, in the spirit of you and me and trust and the future, there are some people I want you to meet."

Fran paused midway to the new apartment door.

"I'm not walking into an ambush am I?"

"The opposite," Sara smiled. "Frannie, when was the last time your mind was well and truly blown?"

"Kendrick Lamar at the Garden on shrooms, a couple years back."

"You're a mystery," Sara laughed. "Well, hang onto your hat."

She opened the door and led Fran along the hall. When they emerged into the living room, the hubbub stopped immediately. Sara stepped in immediately.

"Embla, Silas, this is Fran, and-"

"Oh my goodness," Fran exclaimed. "April Veronica, you're back. And you're bald!"

With that, Fran darted over to where April Veronica was standing and threw her arms around her. Without hesitation, April returned the hug, and as she watched, Sara made her way back to the kitchen and into Silas's arms, where she waited as Fran introduced herself to Embla, and then headed their way.

"Fran, this is my boyfriend, Silas," Sara said. "He's like us."

"Nomine Silas, and never have I killed," Silas said, taking Fran's hand and kissing it. "Francesca, it's my pleasure to finally make your acquaintance."

"A vampire and a gentleman," Fran said. "Now there's something you don't see every day. From now on, I'm Frannie, you're Si and we're good."

Crina, a resigned look on her face, appeared at Fran's side. Sara noticed that Fran backed up a little.

"Hey Fran," Crina began, her voice cracking.

"Hey, Crina."

"Oh, yes, hi, sorry, I wasn't saying hey, I was saying like I was about to..." Crina stopped talking, balled her hands into fists, shook them twice and then splayed her fingers. "Frannie, Silas is my son."

Fran placed a hand on each of Crina's shoulders.

"You must be very proud," she said. "And Crina, your trust means more to me than you'll ever know."

Crina burst into tears.

"Aiy ya... fuck..." she said, as Frannie pulled her close and the sobs intensified.

Silas leaned close to Sara's ear.

"So, we're hosting our first party?"

"Guess so," she shrugged. "Quite a lot of crying for a party."

"I better warm up some beverages," he smiled. "Shoot, do we have anything for Embla?"

"There's Guinness in the cupboard."

As Silas began to set out mismatched glasses on the counter, Fran cleared her throat.

"I really, just oh man, I really just want to thank you all so much, for this. I've been in this room five minutes and already this is, you guys, this is what I signed up for."

"Where's the bloody toast?" Imani was jokingly indignant. "Silas!"

"On it, queen," Silas yelled out, not turning around.

"Well, before we get to toast, I really want to say that being in a room with so much love, so much history, I'm really blown away, like totally gone."

April Veronica looked up from her phone.

"Well, you better sit your gone ass down, Frannie. Fan and Ama just got back from their, wait for it, open air bus tour of Soho, and they'll be up here shortly."

"You're kidding, right?" Fran literally stumbled forward, bracing herself on the couch. When April Veronica shook her head, Crina had to help Fran around the couch, lowering her gently, smiling at the genuine shock on the woman's face.

"Silas, I'm gonna need a double."

Chapter Twenty-Six

Stepping back from the buzzing excitement in her new temporary home, Sara watched as seven women and one man frantically cleaned and organized as if they were at a teenage party that just found out that the parents were returning early. Smiling, she pondered whether she should prepare them for the fact that the fierce elders were more likely to be at the teenage party than hanging out with the parents.

She watched as Heather vanished, only to return minutes later with her arms loaded with blood bags like a teenager on an ice run. Yukari and Fran just walked in circles, muttering nervously to each other. Teddie and Imani tag-teamed the finessing of the apartment, making endless jokes at Sara's expense. April Veronica and Embla pushed the couches as far apart as the room would permit, and Silas, aside from checking in on Sara every thirty seconds, was heating an endless procession of blood, in goblets, coffee mugs and finally, in mason jars.

"Absolutely feels like a hipster party now," he whispered, sneaking a jar of blood to Sara.

"I would have been a wreck too," Sara smiled. "If I hadn't just spent time with them and they were about to arrive at my place... uh our place."

"Nice save," Silas booped her on the nose. "I hope they got us a housewarming gift."

"I hope that our housewarming gift is not the severed head of a halfling from the park."

Nodding sagely, Silas kissed her forehead. "You're right. That wasn't on the registry. I hate it when guests go rogue."

And he was gone, handing out what he was calling "pre-gaming shots" to everyone, a tray of small glass jars of blood balancing expertly on one palm.

"He's adorable," Imani mouthed to Sara. "Can we keep him?"

"Sure," Sara called out loudly above the din. "As long as you clean up after him."

Yukari appeared in front of Sara. "Music," she asked nervously, "should there be music?"

Sara wrapped her in a hug. "Don't worry at all, Yuka. You're not going to believe this."

"But that's exactly what I am worried about," she said, tittering at her own joke. Sara went to reply but was derailed by an ominously loud knock at the door that silenced the entire room. She glanced at Silas, who widened his eyes then looked at the door and pointed. With a resigned groan Sara let go of Yukari and moved to the door, flicking the deadbolt and pulling it open.

"Whassup bitches?" Fan, in bondage pants and a FUCK YOU YOU FUCKIN FUCK t-shirt, bounced into the room, her hands filled with shopping bags. Amrita, in a Liberty jersey and sheer neon yellow tights, slipped in behind her, a carton of Guinness under one arm.

"The party has finally arrived," Ama said, rushing over to Embla and smothering her in kisses. Sara turned to watch it all happen via the reactions on the faces of her friends. Imani, Yukari and Fran were slackjawed. Teddie's lips were pursed and Sara wished she could read her mind. Whirling out of the kitchen with a dancer's deftness, Silas scooped the Guinness out from under Ama's arm, setting it on the now very crowded kitchen counter, then turned to Fan.

"Hey Auntie," he grinned. "Want me to take these off your hands?"

"I told you they'd love you," Fan said, handing him the bags, then turning to the room. "So many nights, he cried, 'I wish they'd let me into their Lock' and I just said, Silas, when they meet you they'll love you."

"None of that is true," Silas said loudly.

"Who are you going to trust?" Fan's arms were wide. "An elder or a *man*?"

"Are we supposed to answer?" Yukari's voice was minuscule, and a look of terror spread across her face as Fan engulfed her in a hug.

"Oh Yuka it is an honor to meet you," Fan said. "We have a lot to discuss, but first, I want to honor you. Girl you're a badass scientist." Sara had never seen such a deep blush on Yukari's cheeks.

Ama raised her hand. "You guys, I am Amrita." Then she stepped to each woman, individually calling them by name and kissing them on the forehead. When she got to Heather, she started to jab and weave like a boxer, and to Sara's surprise, Heather fell into step, lunging and fainting until she landed two jabs and an undercut on the laughing woman.

"You still got it, Heather my queen," Ama said, burying her face in Heather's neck.

"Oh wait," Fan called out. "Silas, can you look in the bags? I brought a bunch of the new synthetic. Embla, you must be starving."

"I'm just getting drunk on all this Guinness," Embla said, raising an empty glass.

Once again, Sara felt like an observer, passive and distant, as she watched introductions and heard jokes and laughter. She remembered similar times, but they were in other Locks, in other centuries. Never in New York. But this strange party, for all its laughter and humor, was not doing it for her. She looked at Ama and Fan, ricocheting from person to person, exchanging banter that reduced the women to giggles, and she felt resentment. Before she knew it, she was speaking and her voice was louder than she intended.

"So, ladies, care to tell us what happened last night with the halflings?"

Another silence fell, this one much more awkward than the last one. Without missing a beat, Ama returned to Fan's side.

"I told you she'd be pissed," she whispered, and Fan nodded.

"Sara," she began, her palms outstretched. "Please forgive us, but seriously, we just wanted to get in and get the job done."

"Did you notify Yukari?" Sara's tone was steel.

"Say yes," Fan hissed at Yukari, who said nothing.

"Exactly," Sara said. "You guys, I know you're itching for a war, but we had this under control."

"Correction," Ama said. "If you'd killed all six, the situation would have been controlled, for now. I'm sorry, my loves, and we didn't mean to step on anyone's toes but as soon as we heard they were carrying cyanide, I mean, nope. No way. Can you imagine what would happen if they gassed one of you, out on the street?"

Familiar feelings of inadequacy, failure and judgement surged inside Sara and she blinked twice to make sure no tears had sprung up in their support.

"Understood, but come on, you should have called."

Slowly, Fan sidled over to Sara and slung an arm around her waist.

"We will tell you all what happened, and then we can decide on our punishment," Fan said, her voice light. "We found them in like ten minutes, just after dark. Ama climbed a tree, not even three meters from them. How long did you sit there, my love?"

"Twenty minutes, I guess."

"And what did you hear?"

"It was pretty sad," Ama said. "Nobody was answering their calls in Madrid. They were starving. They don't have any details of their return ticket. I was hoping they'd reveal more about Desdemona, but no. I watched as they prepared to come circle the building, and when they were ready, I jumped down and knocked them both out."

"Yeah, she really surprised me," Fan said. "I kind of drifted into a reverie and all of a sudden, bam, thwok, two unconscious girls."

"You didn't get here until much later," Sara said.

"Right, we just tied them up and gave them a little nightcap, and kept on dialing the numbers in their phone."

"Did anyone answer?" The annoyance in Sara's voice grew clearer with every sentence. Beside her, Fan nodded.

"We finally tried Eleanor's number," Ama said. "They had it saved. She answered."

Now it was Sara's turn to be shocked.

"I pretended to be one of the halflings." Fan said. "She was very kind, very upset that we had been abandoned. She said that she would try to get us back to Spain or get money to us. I told her that Desdemona would know what to do with us, and it got kind of weird. She said that she wasn't in contact with Desdemona."

"What the..." Heather gave Sara a confused look.

"Did she say anything else?" Sara's eyes bored angrily into Ama's.

"She's in Spain, outside Madrid. We couldn't ask much because we didn't want her to suspect us. Their whole call history was unanswered calls. Those girls were abandoned as soon as they got here. Nobody had answered a single call that they'd made to Spain," Fan paused. "Elle said one more weird thing. She told us to stop trying to kidnap the New Yorkers. She said that plan was abandoned."

Crina and Sara exchanged surprise glances.

"I told you that would shut them up," Ama said.

"Eleanor is going to call back tonight," Fan added.

"Where is the phone?" Sara looked at Yukari. "Give it to Yukari."

"My Spanish has too much accent," Yukari said apologetically.

"You're the Mother of this Lock," Sara's voice was firm. "This is all you."

Lifting her jersey, Ama revealed a neon pink fanny pack. She unzipped it and tossed the phone to Yukari, who caught it like it was a hot rock, passing it immediately to Sara.

"Anyways," Fan said, letting go of Sara and moving to the middle of the room, "that's what happened. Then we called Heather, got her into full nun drag and had her meet us out front. We wheeled them in. They're in a room together, but they're very high and they didn't see a thing. Blindfolded from park to bunker, they were."

"I still don't understand how, after all these centuries, you didn't think it prudent to alert us to your plan?"

"What difference would it have made?" Ama's eyes were defiant. "As we discussed... before you left... we are not members of any Lock and we aren't bound by their rules."

A satisfying round of gasps reached Sara's ears, and she faced Ama directly.

"You could have killed them," she said.

"But we didn't," Ama said.

"But you could have," Sara said.

"But we didn't," Fan said, taking her place beside her wife.

"But you could have," Sara said. "And that's the point here. We don't kill."

"Tell that to the three obliterated women in the furnace," Fan said, her voice even. "Look, Sara, everyone, just because something is happening in your city, you don't own it. These women, these weaponized, irresponsibly created poor young women, they don't deserve this. Not at all. But it has happened, the money has been spent. We felt it best if we came and took care of it. Nobody was hurt, nobody was compromised, and now we have a phone that Madrid will answer."

Inhaling deeply, Sara willed her anger to leave her body, but it proved stubbornly disobedient. She looked at Silas, just a few feet away at the other end of the entry to the kitchen, and he blew her a kiss and shrugged. He mouthed "spilt milk" at her, and Sara understood, and the anger finally began to subside.

"Sorry," she said, shaking her shoulders to help dislodge the tension. "It's not your fault those girls died, that's on me."

"No," Teddie walked over and took Sara's hand. "This is all Desdemona's fault. We're lucky that you weren't caught."

"Absolutely," Ama said. "Sara, you know we love you. But girl you ain't even Lock Mother, we wanted to leave you alone in your love nest with our baby boy."

"Somehow you just made it sound so much worse," Silas said.

"Speaking of which," Imani said, waving her empty at Silas, "What's the deal with this whole no Lock thing. Is that allowed?"

"It's actually not in the writings that we have to live in groups," Sara said. "Like what Des is doing, nobody could ever foresee that a woman would go so crazy, so there are no rules, no contingencies."

"Stefanya could never have predicted the way social media turned humans into idiots," Fran said.

"Oh Franny," Ama laughed. "Do you know how many hours of Tik Tok that woman watches daily?"

Gobsmacked, Fran sat in silence.

"You're right though," Ama continued. "She'd be the first to agree with you. Which doesn't stop her from hours of doom scrolling. And when we scold her, she always says that wasting time doesn't mean shit to an immortal. She's a disaster."

"Does this have to be so thorny?" Fan twirled like a ballerina, perfectly on pointe, blowing smiley kisses to everyone. "Because we thought it was a housewarming party slash holy shit there's a boy vampire party slash.."

"She's trying to say we brought presents," Ama interjected, halting Fan mid-twirl.

"We sure did," Fan tiptoed back to the door, opened it, and darted into the landing, letting the door close behind her.

"Silas, can you get some music on?" Ama bustled into the kitchen. "Who wants to try my new synthetic? I have regular and a CBD/THC hybrid that is very relaxing."

Hoisting a reusable shopping bag onto the counter, Ama dug around inside, lifting out a small cooler covered in stickers reading SCIENTIFIC SAMPLE NON-BLOOD PRODUCT.

"I bet the customs form for that was a bitch," Silas laughed, and Ama slugged him.

"You know it, little prince."

"Yeah," Sara sidled up to him. "Little prince."

"How did you all survive so long without a man to humiliate?" Silas wriggled out of Sara's embrace and took a seat on the floor in front of Embla.

"You'll protect me, right?" he whispered and Embla nodded.

A rustling at the front door turned everybody's head. Fan was carrying two bulging bags. Hauling them to the space between the couch and the coffee table, she spun back to Ama.

"I'm fine with cold synthetic," she said. "Anyone else?"

"Just the regular for me," Embla said, raising a hand. "I want to use the CBD tonight to fight the jetlag which is already kicking my arse."

"I'm in," Fran said, her voice cracking nervously.

"Sure," Yukari said. "I might need the CBD, I'm a bit shaky."

"I hate being pressured into being vegan," Imani said with faux severity. "Count me in, guv."

Nodding, Ama turned to preparing the drinks. To Sara's horror she pulled an ice tray from the freezer and added a couple cubes to everyone's goblet, then started passing them out.

While everyone was busy sampling lab-grown plasma, Sara stepped into Silas's arms and he held her tight. Pressing her ear against his chest, she listened to the heavy thudding of his heart, a sound that had echoed through the chamber of his ribs for centuries. It suddenly sounded ephemeral and light to her, this lone engine keeping a man alive for half a millennia, and she pulled him tighter with her arms. In silence he kissed the top of her head.

"I love you Sara."

Morning became afternoon, and Sara drifted between conversations, delighting in the new combinations of friends old and new. Fran and Embla had been locked into a wide-ranging discussion of everything from advanced hacking to the genius of Björk, and after several attempts to join in, Sara gave up and went and sat beside Fan.

"Everyone loved their gifts," she said, looking at the variety of weapons and Icelandic blankets at everyone's feet. "I never knew a miniature cattle punch could make a woman so happy."

"I know, right," Fan completely missed the sarcasm. "So much tidier than a Slicer, I don't know why we didn't think of this years ago."

"I do," Sara smiled. "We stopped killing each other."

"You're angry," Fan said, her voice small. "I was trying to do you a favor."

"I understand," Sara said, choosing her words very carefully. "But you would have killed them."

"They were armed with poison and pistols," Fan said. "They were desperate. We knew we could defuse them. Also," the elder paused, taking Sara's hand, "if you're serious about deconstructing the Lock, then this is it. We have to trust other people. I know you trust us. Once you step back from the dent to your pride, you'll see that we did nothing wrong."

Silently, Sara pondered Fan's words, giving her hand a squeeze. She knew that arguing was pointless, and nobody had been hurt. On top of that, the immediate threat to the Lock had been neutralized.

Raising her eyes to Fan's, Sara nodded.

"You're entirely correct," she said. "You know, I could have used your help a long while ago."

Fan looked her dead in the eye. "But could you have asked for it?"

Sara shook her head with a wan smile.

Yukari appeared in front of them.

"Am I interrupting something?"

"No, Yuka, what's up?"

Crouching on her haunches so she was at their level, Yukari leaned in close.

"Silas said he has somewhere we can take the halflings, Sara."

Sara rolled her eyes. Silas had segued from outsider to BFF with astonishing speed.

"He probably has several places you can take them," she said, not sure of what Silas had told her.

"The upstate house," Fan said. "Ama and I will take Yukari there, and we will guard her from the Spanish girls."

Sara shot her a concerned glance.

"Gently, Sara, Sheesh, we will guard her from them gently."

"Better," Sara said. "When are you going?"

"That's the thing," Yukari blinked nervously. "We need to get them out of here. Rosa is trying to hack her way out of her two-woman lockdown. But I am Lock Mother."

"Doesn't mean you can't leave," Sara said.

"You never did," Yukari countered immediately. "Sorry, I'm on the CBD. That was rude."

"It was accurate," Sara said. "So just go. We got this."

"No. I want to quit. I don't want to think about Lock Mother when I'm working on vaccines."

"Totally understandable," Sara said. "I also don't want the job."

"Good," Yukari said, surprising her. "Can I motion that we become a leaderless democracy?"

Shaken, Sara needed a minute before she nodded. Huge changes happening in split seconds was new to her, but she didn't hate it.

"Arigato," Yukari said with a quick smile before blowing them both kisses and standing.

"Everybody," Yukari said so quietly that Sara was surprised when everyone stopped talking and turned to her. "I need your attention for one minute. I would like to announce that I'm stepping down from the Mother role, and" she raised a palm, "I would like to introduce a motion that from now on, our Lock does not have a mother. I motion that we function as a simple democracy. We all help. We all make decisions."

"This party is totally gone," Fran laughed. "This is what I signed up for!"

"I also would like to include votes from Embla, Silas, Fan, Ama, whoever's in the room."

Sara glanced at Silas, eyes wide in disbelief that something so historic could happen so casually.

"So, do we just raise our hands to vote yes?" Crina asked, and Yukari nodded, and instantly, everyone raised a hand.

History in a split second.

"That was easy," Yukari smiled.

"Enlightenment should always be easy," Ama said, moving to the kitchen. "Embla, I'm going to leave you with enough synthetic for a couple weeks."

"Where are you going now?" Embla asked.

"Me and Fan and Yuka are going to take the halflings away to Silas's house."

"And we are leaving as soon as Yuka can pack up her lab," Fan said. "It has been a joy to be here, and to be a part of such an historic day for you all."

"Once we get everything secured, we will come visit," Ama said. "I did not get enough of any of you today," she paused. "I'm sorry we stayed away so long."

With one final squeeze of Sara's hand, Fan rose and joined the other two women by the door.

"Sorry we are leaving a mess," Ama said. "And Silas, congrats on finally convincing Sara to shack up with you."

Sara watched as a beet red blush washed over Silas's cheeks, surprised when she heard the click of the rear door that told her that Fan, Ama and Yukari had left via the door at the rear of the apartment.

"Are they definitely gone?" Teddie looked up from her phone, a curious expression on her face.

"You never know for sure with those two," Embla offered.

"Well, okay, fuck…" Teddie glanced around nervously.

"What is it, Ted?" Imani's eyes were wide.

"Cone of silence then, everyone?" Teddie stood up and flipped her phone around, revealing a screen of texts.

"Hold it still, Teddie," Fran said. "We can't read it."

"It's Desdemona," Teddie said breathlessly. "She's been texting me for like the last forty minutes."

"Never a dull moment," Imani laughed. "What does that crazy witch want now?"

"She is saying I'm not taking this seriously, that I'm a threat to the Lock world."

"Well it looks like we picked a great time to leave the Lock world," Sara said. "Don't worry, Ted, we will sort it out eventually."

"Or sooner than that," Teddie said. "She's coming to pick me up. Tomorrow!"

The room erupted into outrage, and Sara sat back, watching where she would have once leapt into action. Eventually, quiet returned, and Sara watched as Embla pulled her phone out of her pants pocket.

"What are you doing, Embla?" she asked.

"I'm going to text Fan and Ama, to tell them before they leave."

"No," Sara said. "Please don't tell them. This one," she glanced at Crina, "I think we should handle this one ourselves."

Chapter Twenty-Seven

"Where are Heather and Fran?" Sara asked, exasperated, looking around the rooftop meeting room for any sign of the women she'd been texting for a half hour.

"Haven't seen them boss," Imani said as she passed, carrying a tray of clean goblets.

"I think Embla is with them," April Veronica said, appearing at Sara's side. "Can I help?"

"Thanks, it's not anything specific," Sara said. "I would just feel better if we were all up here."

"The room is secured," April Veronica said, squeezing Sara's shoulder. "There is enough blood and synthetic for everyone. One o' them cute cattle guns is taped to the underside of every throne. Heather has taken the building security offline, Teddie is trying to meditate, and last I heard, your boyfriend was on a weird mission."

"Oh yeah?" Sara's mind raced. "Did he tell you what he was doing?"

"He did drive out to Jersey to buy some bear traps," April Veronica quipped before darting for the door.

"For real?" Sara called after her.

"Nah, just fucking with ya," April called from outside the windows, "he's probably out buying you some more flowers."

Sara watched her silhouette against the black glass of the windows, arms outstretched, spinning beneath the early afternoon sun. It made her happy, the freedoms that these new sisters had. Sunblock, hot and cold water, veganism. The changes were exciting to her, and she felt the threat of Desdemona and her imminent arrival more acutely, high-voltage hatred on behalf of the young women she'd infected, and the draconian lifestyle she imposed on her Lock. A ding from her phone pulled her out of a very attractive reverie. Heather. On her way up.

"I'm losing my mind," she said out loud.

"Do you want solution or comfort?" Imani popped her head up behind the bar.

"Neither," Sara laughed. "It's been a fact for a while. I'm just making friends with it."

"Good job," Imani said. "Me and my mind, we're old mates when it comes to losing each other. There is always a trail of breadcrumbs to lead you back to each other."

"I'm just massively nervous," Sara said, walking to the bar and resting her arms on its cool marble top. "I hate days that feel significant."

"I get you," Imani stood upright, brushing her palms on her lime sweats. "But worrying won't make it any smoother."

At a late-night meeting of the new anti-Lock, Sara was resoundingly outvoted when she volunteered to be the one to ambush Desdemona. She also lost out on telling Desdemona she was still alive, though more narrowly.

"I suppose I should be happy with hiding in the fucking bathroom while the thorn in my side for oh, you know, five fucking centuries, is finally brought to justice."

"Settle petal, passive aggressive don't look good on you," Imani smiled. "I took the liberty of heating us up a nice pick me up." With a wink, Imani opened the warming oven and took out two chunky coffee cups filled to the brim with scarlet blood. She handed one to Sara.

"We've never killed yada yada arriba la bajo y salud!"

Raising her mug carefully, she cheersed it against Sara's and raised it to her lips, swallowing it all in one gulp.

"So that's what we're doing," Sara chuckled, following suit.

"Whoooo," Imani staggered back against the shelf behind her. "Damn fine vintage."

"You won't get this from synthetic," Sara mumbled.

"You sure won't," Imani whispered. "Sara, do you think this will go away? The whole blood thing?"

"I sure don't know," Sara shrugged. "Why?"

"Don't tell anyone, but I kinda like it," Imani said, still whispering. "We've given up so much to be peaceful, to be normal. This high, it's the last thing we have."

"Except for the whole living forever thing. And the strength."

"And the sex, amirite?"

"Do not wink at me, and bitch no, let's not go there."

"Peoples gonna get jealous."

"Which means you're jealous?"

"I dunno," Imani pushed off the back wall and hunkered next to Sara across the bar top. "You tell me. Should I be?"

To Sara's relief the door opened, and Heather, Fran and Embla tumbled in, deep in conversation.

"I just let Desdemona into the building," Heather called out. "She has gone to Rosa's apartment. Liz is there too."

A shiver started in Sara's tummy and emanated outward in all directions, causing her neck to flex and her teeth to chatter.

"How can we tell if she's armed?" Sara glanced at the newcomers.

"She won't do poison," Heather said. "She's not a martyr."

"I wouldn't be surprised if she turned up with guns," Fran said. "She's insane and whatever mess she makes, it's contained in this building. We need to search her."

Heather locked eyes emphatically with Sara.

"This is why we were delayed," she said. "We will be insisting that all three of them strip to their underwear before entering the room."

A short snort laugh escaped Sara's nose.

"Uh, have you told them?"

"Not yet," Embla said. "Nobody wants that job."

"Well, I can't do it," Sara snipped.

"I'll gladly do it," Imani said. "I've been in the training room for the last couple weeks, I'm not as rusty as I feared."

"Thank you, Imani," Heather blew her a kiss. "Now, you, Sara, plus Embla and April, will be with Silas in the upper floor of your old apartment, Sara. There's a little camera hidden above the bar, you'll see it all. Fran set up a big monitor."

"It'll be like going to the bar during a play," Embla said. "You know, how they have it on the televisions in the lobby."

"I'd rather hide in the bathroom," Sara said.

"Don't make us vote on it, love," Heather said with a smile. "It's just unnecessary risk."

There was no argument to be made, so Sara focused on the tension in her shoulders, breathing deeply.

"Promise me, all of you," she said, her voice low. "Nothing can happen to Teddie."

"That bitch won't get within ten feet of her," Fran said. "I have skipped one day of my martial arts training in sixty years, and that was the day Marguerite... was killed."

"Some hippy you turned out to be," Imani chuckled, hugging Fran as she walked to the door.

"Okay, you lot. Time to head over to your hiding place. Heather, you ready for me to go get Teddie?"

Heather nodded, and Imani disappeared.

"I know it's hard, love. But trust me, once she's in custody, you'll get your face to face."

"Promises, promises," Sara said, extending her hand to Embla. "If you'd be so kind to lead an old woman to her hiding place?"

Bowing deeply, Embla took her hand. "Twould be me honor, m'lady."

Curtsying with each step, the pair of them walked out of the rooftop room into the glare of the afternoon sun.

"Ouch, fuck," Sara exclaimed as the sun tore at her exposed skin. "Quick, run!"

Dropping Embla's hand, Sara sprinted across the rooftop to her old flat, the door pulling open as she approached. Sara launched herself into the dark safety, bumping into Silas and sending both of them sprawling onto her old reading couch. She felt his arms around her as they fell, pressing her face into his neck so they didn't crack their teeth together.

"That was dramatic," Embla said as she stepped into the room. "Is April in here?"

"I'm downstairs fixing drinks."

Sara disentangled herself from Silas, pressing up and examining her arms.

"Before you all start," she said. "No, I wasn't wearing sunscreen, it was cloudy when I went up there, and it slipped my mind."

Silas went to speak and she raised a finger.

"I've had a lot on my mind," Sara said. "April Veronica, would you please bring up some aftersun from the bathroom cabinet?"

When April Veronica appeared at the top of the stairs with the bottle of lotion, Silas took it from her and sat beside Sara on the couch.

"You got yourself pretty good," he said quietly, looking from her arms to her face, then squeezing the transparent green gel into his palms and slathering it along one arm, then the other. Then he made a dollop of it in one palm and applied it delicately to Sara's chin, cheeks and forehead with two fingers.

"Hopefully it won't get much worse," he said, kissing her on the top of her head.

April Veronica appeared with two flasks of blood, one red, real, the other oily black, synthetic.

"No cups?" Embla said, her head tilted comically.

"Didn't think we'd need them. Blood for the adults, non-alcoholic for the kids."

Embla smiled, and Sara watched as she gazed at April Veronica in naked admiration, then she turned her attention to the monitor on the coffee table. On the screen, Heather was puttering around the room, arranging thrones, moving them left or right by just an inch or two, and Sara could tell she was nervous.

Glancing at the door briefly, Heather stood upright and looked directly at the camera in the back wall.

"Text me if you can hear me well enough," she said.

"I'll do it," April Veronica pulled her phone from her pocket, and seconds later, they heard Heather's phone ding loudly through the Bluetooth speaker beside the monitor.

"A thumbs up," Heather muttered. "For the record, I bloody hate a thumbs up text."

All four of them pulled out their phones and sent Heather a thumbs up text, laughing at the look on her face when she saw them.

A burst of light flooded the left corner of the screen as the door to the outside opened, and Imani and Teddie, in a black and yellow dashiki and matching head scarf, walked in. She was smiling at something Imani had said, and did not look as drawn or stressed as she had on prior livestreams. Embla fussed with the volume until they could clearly hear inside the rooftop room, which now was just the sounds of furniture moving as Imani, Heather, Fran and Teddie took their seats, their backs to the camera.

"I'm quite nervous," Embla said, and April Veronica threw an arm around her.

"Is it mansplaining if I say we all are?" Silas looked at each of them.

"No," Embla said. "You're not explaining anything. You're admitting a weakness, which is not traditionally a male behavior."

"I was joking," Silas said. "You know, trying to make things less stressful."

"*That's* mansplaining," April Veronica laughed.

"He's still joking," Sara said, kissing Silas behind his ear.

"It's that or shit my pants," Silas said lightly. "I'd feel better if I was in the room."

"To protect us because you're a big strong man?" April Veronica needled.

"For fuck's sake," Silas was finally exasperated. "No. Because I promised Sara I'd do anything to protect Teddie and here I am hiding out with a hot new vampire comedy duo."

"I'm using *humor*, Si," April Veronica slugged him in the upper arm. "We're all twitchy."

A text to all of them from Heather told them that Rosa was bringing Des to the roof now.

"Just breathe, everyone," Sara whispered.

"If anything goes wrong, we're going in right?" Silas squeezed Sara's hand.

"You fucking bet," Embla said loudly. "Except you, April V. You understand."

April Veronica nodded. A flash of light at the bottom of the screen faded, revealing Rosa in a simple shift dress, barefoot, and behind her, barefoot in a black tank top and bike shorts, her hair upswept and her eyes rimmed with kohl, stood Desdemona. The sour set of her mouth as she surveyed the room had the opposite effect on Sara, her mouth turning into a smile.

"Where the fuck is everybody?" she asked. "Is it impossible for this Lock to be punctual?"

"Well hello to you too, Desdemona," Heather said, rising from her throne and walking directly to the newcomers. "If you don't mind, ladies, I'm going to pat you down, and fair warning, if you try anything, you won't be getting out of here alive."

"Do piss off, Heather," Rosa raised an arm. "Do I need to remind you that I'm a member of this Lock?"

"For now," Heather said bluntly. "Now, both of you, turn around and raise your arms."

Slowly, both women obeyed, whispering in Spanish.

"Everyone in this room speaks Spanish," Heather reminded them as she fluttered her palms up and down Desdemona's back and sides, repeating the process on Rosa.

The door opened and Liz stepped in, startling Heather, who spun quickly, landed in battle pose and pulled the cattle prod from the holster on her hip,

"Dramatic," Liz said coldly. "Unnecessary and dramatic. As usual."

"You were told to wear workout gear," Heather said, surveying Liz's ensemble of carpenter pants and bulky jacket.

"And I didn't," Liz said snottily. "What are you going to do about it?"

"Seriously, either strip or leave," Heather said angrily.

"Go and change, you stupid bitch," Rosa barked. Liz gave her a you're kidding face and Rosa shook her head angrily and pointed to the door. "Go, we won't be long."

With the theatricality of a slighted fourteen year old, Liz huffed and spun and left the room, a raised hand flipping them all off.

"Are you finished?" Desdemona began to turn around and Heather gave her a slap to the side of the head.

"Did I say I was finished?"

In silence, Imani stood and handed Heather a metal detector, which she used to wand each woman from top to bottom. Once she was done, she returned to her seat.

"You two can sit up there and tell us what you think is going on," she said, jerking her thumb at the dais.

Warily, the two women stepped up onto the low stage. Desdemona took the first throne, plonking herself down and glaring almost directly into the camera at the back of the room.

"Oooh, she pissed," Sara said.

Rosa took the seat beside her.

"Alrighty then," Heather said. "Desdemona, please tell us the purpose of your visit."

"Why am I talking to you? Isn't Yukari your Lock mother?"

"She's too busy for your bullshit, guv," Imani said, her voice like steel. "So either get started or get going, don't care which, really."

On the dais, Rosa and Desdemona whispered with increasing intensity for almost a minute.

"We don't have all day, ladies," Teddie said, her voice bright and clear.

At the sound of her voice, Desdemona's head snapped up and she glared at Teddie with pure hate.

"Never speak to me like that again, you stupid little slut," Desdemona spat. "You know why I'm here. Your cover is blown. You need to hide out somewhere secure. Madrid is the only answer."

"Nah, not for me," Teddie's voice remained light. "Have you seen your Yelp reviews? Apparently your Lock is past its prime, ugly and dull."

"Much too dull," Imani agreed, crossing her legs and nodding. "Definitely too dull."

"It has been voted on by all Lock Mothers unanimously," Desdemona pushed on. "It is not optional."

"Not sure who you're quoting, Des," Imani was deliberately making her voice sweetly grating. "I made some calls, nobody says they actually voted. At best, you got a few people to agree with you just so they could get you off their phone."

"There is nothing in the writings about what should be done in such an instance," Heather said.

"In discussion, Heather, it has been agreed that being photographed is covered by the rule that forbids any permanent writings."

"Seems a stretch," Imani said. "Writing is an active verb, being photographed unknowingly is a passive action."

"I didn't come here for a linguistics lesson," Desdemona said. "Theodora, you texted that you would be willing to accompany me back to Rome and accept your punishment."

"Oh, right," Teddie smacked herself on the forehead. "Oh wait. I lied."

"Get her," Desdemona said to Rosa. "Bring her to me."

As Rosa stood, so did the four women seated in the room. Rosa began to laugh.

"Oh Frannie, you stupid old bitch, what are you now? A peacenik? An assassin? You guys know she set up all our Signal channels. Frannie, we couldn't have done all this without you."

"Who among us trains every day?" Fran's voice was guttural and angry in a way Sara could never have predicted. "In peace, I have prepared for war. And Rosa?"

"What?"

"Oh nothing," Fran said. "What's the point?"

"Rosa," Desdemona barked. "Grab Teddie, we are leaving."

In the viewing room, Sara realized she'd been holding her breath. Taking a deep inhale, she watched as four women she'd known for eons all fell into battle positions. Deftly, each of them grabbed a cattle prod from under their throne.

"Four against two," Desdemona hissed. "Such cowardice."

"Nah bitch," Imani said. "We just the backup."

Confusion flickered across Desdemona's face and the door beside them opened in a light flare that faded as it closed, leaving only Crina, clad in head to toe racing leathers, a Slicer in each palm.

Not taking her eyes of Desdemona, Sara watched as her mask cracked irreparably, eyes wide in fear.

"Crina..." she began.

"Wait!" Crina commanded. "Rosa, for the last time. Are you a member of this Lock, yes or no?"

Rosa glanced at Desdemona, who nodded at her.

"Yes, I am a sister of the New York Lock."

"Don't just say what she tells you to say," Crina took a step forward. "If you stay, you agree to live by all of our rules."

"Yes, you bitch, yes, I said yes."

"Then sit your ass down," Crina said, nodding at the dais. "And Heather, if she tries anything, kill her."

"Got it boss," Heather smiled, brandishing her cattle prod in Rosa's direction.

Waving the Slicers in the air like scythes, Crina advanced on Desdemona.

"My daughter," she began. "How I've come to regret making you."

"Really, mama?" Desdemona said obsequiously. "Even now that I'm your only child?"

A laugh escaped Crina.

"Yep, and you know what? Sara was everything that you're not, and everything you'll never be. I'm so proud that I made her, and I'm proud of everything she ever did."

"Waaaaaaah," Desdemona actually rubbed her fists in her eyes like a crying child. "There's no point in being proud of the dead. You know what I'm proud of? I got the bitch killed."

"Please remember which one of us is holding a weapon," Crina advanced another step, and Desdemona pushed back into her throne. "I would think nothing of severing your spine right here, watching your face turn black with anger while your body drains itself on the floor."

"Oh you mean like Marguerite's did?" Desdemona smiled.

In the viewing room, April Veronica flipped off the screen with both hands.

"Don't let her get to you," Embla said. "Words are her only weapon. Let them mean nothing."

"I'll ignore that," Crina said. "Unless you'd like me to consider it, in which case, I will be killing you right now, for murdering one of our own on our premises."

"It was a Madrid matter, and now it is a closed case," Desdemona looked at her fingernails as she spoke.

"Is it also a Madrid matter that you have been infecting young women with our virus?"

Desdemona's head snapped up, her eyes wide again.

"Like being photographed in public, it is not outlawed in our writings," she began, a rough edge to her deep voice. "These women were junkies, whores, thieves. Now, they are clean and sober, and we teach them how to live the way we live."

"Asking for a friend," Teddie quipped. "How does this fit in with your whole zero population growth philosophy?"

"You'll find out when I get you to Madrid," Desdemona fired back. "Because, trust me, if you don't come with me today, things will get a lot worse for you."

"No, Desdemona," Crina stepped in front of the dais facing the two women. "The only person who is about to experience a worsening of things is you. Under the newly adopted rules of the New York Lock, I am placing you under arrest, for the creation of sisters without credits."

Rosa began to stand in outrage, and in a blink, Crina had one slicer, horizontally, an inch from her throat.

"I'd sit back down, Rosa," she said coolly. Rosa sat.

"This is how cowards attack," Desdemona said.

"I'm giving you more warning than you gave Marguerite," Crina said. "But if you want a duel, dear child, say the word."

Locking eyes with Crina, Desdemona burned with anger, her chest heaving silently.

"Like I said earlier," Imani called out, "we aren't here for a good time or a long time. Either put up or shut up."

"You're making a mistake," Desdemona said.

Crina looked her up and down with a raised eyebrow.

"I'm looking at the worst mistake I ever made," she said, and Desdemona flew to her feet, then fainted, leaned left and spun a roundhouse kick intended to connect with Crina's arm. In a blur that was impossible to see on the screen, Crina dodged it easily, reappearing behind Des the Slicer now vertically in line with the vertebrae in her neck.

"Extend your hands in front of you," Crina said. "Now."

Wordlessly, Heather reached below her throne and hauled out a set of cast iron cuffs. She carried them to Desdemona, who slowly held out her arms, looking at the floor as Heather closed each cuff around a wrist, the ancient metal clicking deeply as they closed. Imani brought another pair forward, kneeling and locking one around each of Desdemona's ankles. Then she connected the chains between each with two heavy padlocks.

Once Heather and Imani stepped back, Crina slowly lowered the Slicer and turned to Rosa.

"Nobody is to find out what happened today," she said. "You are a member of this Lock. Does this mean we can trust you?"

"You always could," Rosa lied.

"Good," Crina said. "Now return to your apartment. There will be a meeting tomorrow where the fate of this bitch will be decided."

Without a word, Rosa left.

"Heather, Imani, would you be so kind as to help me escort our prisoner to her cell?"

Desdemona inhaled, about to speak.

"Not a word," Crina said. "Do you understand how badly I want to run this slicer from your skull to your asshole? Don't give me the slightest excuse."

On the screen, Heather and Imani each took an arm, and Crina walked behind Desdemona, Slicers drawn.

After they left the room and the door closed, Teddie turned to the camera on the wall.

"You guys, get in here right fucking now. I'll heat up the blood."

Chapter Twenty-Eight

Sara stood at the door to the tiny, windowless room where Desdemona was being held, Heather and Crina by her side. She let a wave of anxiety come and go, her breathing focused and steady.

"You okay, pet?" Heather asked.

"You don't have to do this," Crina said.

"I absolutely need to do this," Sara replied, squaring her shoulders.

They'd spent the last hour strategizing, trying to figure out the best way to get the truth out of Desdemona. Sara insisted on going in alone, and hoping that the shock of seeing her would shake Desdemona deeply enough that she'd make a mistake.

"Ready, Freddy?" Heather smiled impishly.

Standing beside her, Crina unsheathed a Slicer from its thick, dull leather sheath, sliding her fingers through the ringed holes.

"I've always loved the feel of this on my hand," she said, waving it back and forth.

"You'll put someone's eye out with that thing," Heather said.

"I'm almost hoping she gives me a reason to," Crina said. "I so wish I'd never made her."

"Regret is a toxic addiction," Sara said with a wink.

"We start talking like that, we'll be here all day," Heather said brusquely, nodding at Sara to open the door. With a wink, Sara pressed the pad of her index finger onto the wall panel, and the door unlocked with an efficient metallic rasp. Breathing deeply, Sara thought back to the last time she saw Desdemona at the Central Park Boathouse, just months ago. It felt like years.

Anger throbbed in her temple as she relived the meeting, and she tried to distance herself, to see if she could find anything helpful in the way Desdemona had behaved, the way she had lied and covered up what she had done. She saw the same woman she'd known for five centuries, the same insecurities and triggers she'd always had, but it was mixed with something newer that she hadn't picked up on, a glazed, beatific assuredness, so minor she'd overlooked it. Desdemona wasn't normally one for subdued cockiness. She had always been openly competitive and antagonistic. At the lunch meeting, she kept herself above the fray, sailing along in a curious way that, in hindsight, was clearly suspicious. Sara cursed herself for missing it.

"You ready, pet?" Heather's voice jolted her back into the moment.

Sara shook her head. "Keep the door open a crack and listen. If things get wild, come on in."

"If she tries anything, I'm slicing her," Crina whispered, locking eyes with Sara. "I'm not fucking playing."

"And with that," Sara glanced at Heather, who shrugged in agreement, 'I'm going in."

Sara set her face to neutral and slipped inside the first room, a dingy eight by eight room lit by a single bulb inside a metal cage. Against the far wall a doorway led into the room where Desdemona was being held. Glancing around, Sara took in the ancient dust bunnies crowding the spaces where the walls and floor met, and inhaled a dry, dusty and vaguely rotten smell that reminded her of catacombs.

"Who's there?" Desdemona barked. "Crina? You gonna kill me from behind like a coward? Unchain me then, you pinche puta."

Sara paused, shocked at the way Desdemona spoke to Crina, the venom in her voice. She and Crina had never had a heated argument.

"Whatever you do to me, mi madre, you will always live with the knowledge that I killed your favorite."

Sara's eyes rolled so violently that they hurt in their sockets. Desdemona was a five-hundred-year-old toddler. Sara took three quiet steps. She gazed at Desdemona, her bare arms cuffed behind the back of the chair she sat in, a chain running from her wrists to her ankles, her thick black hair a tangled nest. Sara let the moment play out. Slowly, Desdemona turned her head as far as she could, and Sara stepped just outside of her vision.

"I know you're there, Crina. I can recognize your stink anywhere."

Raising the corners of her mouth into a fake smile, Sara silently walked around the chair. Slowly, Desdemona turned to face her.

"Sister, dear," Sara said, relishing the actual jaw dropping shock that settled on Desdemona's face before she could catch herself. "Surprise!"

Desdemona's mouth opened and closed silently, her eyes wide. With a convulsive, angry twitch, she blinked twice and closed her mouth, her upper arms straining against the back of the solid oak chair.

"I'm not a ghost, dear sister," Sara stepped closer. "Happy to see me?"

"Alive, dead, you're nothing to me," Desdemona spat, her eyes burning into Sara's. "Of course you didn't even have the courage to Surrender, not even after all the rules you broke."

Sara gulped down the responses that flooded to her. She was determined to not let Desdemona get to her.

"Mind if I sit?" she asked, her voice pleasant. Without waiting for a reply, Sara turned, taking in the room, bare except for a thin slab of memory foam on the floor. She kicked it with one foot. "I guess this will have to do."

In silence, she circled Desdemona, pausing when she was behind her. She gripped the back of the heavy throne and tilted it back until it was balancing on one leg, then turned it slowly so that it was facing the mattress. Letting go of the back of the chair suddenly, it fell forward and Sara smiled as Desdemona's head snapped back and forth. With deliberate steps she circled the chained woman, then crossed her ankles and sank slowly to sit on the edge of the bare mattress.

"That's better," she said with a smile, adjusting herself until she was comfortable. "So, yes, I'm alive, you're not thrilled about it. That's not why I'm here."

"You're here to kill me," Desdemona deadpanned. "And like a coward, you have me bound like a hog. Just do it then."

"Unlike you, dear sister, I'm not a killer. I'm here to have a chat, you know, catch up with you. Hang out a while. It's been what? Four hundred years since we just shot the shit? I feel like we've become disconnected. Are you sad we grew apart?"

Anger flashed in Desdemona's eyes and her self-control broke. She leaned forward, her hands and feet straining against the shackles that tied her to the chair, her face reddening.

"You treat our lives as a joke," she hissed. "Your joke is about to be very unfunny."

"Such a temper," Sara said, her voice light. "Des, literally, let it go. I came here to talk. I came here to understand."

"Aiy, pinche puta you came here to gloat. At least be honest."

"Okay, I came here to understand *and* to gloat a little. Desdemona, what happened to you? We are blessed. We have seen so much, lived through such incredible times, witnessed things that our mothers would not have been able to imagine."

Desdemona relaxed slightly, pushing herself against the back of the chair, her head cocked slightly as the angry flush drained from her face.

"Do you remember your mother?" Sara continued. "Not Crina, your real mother, your birth mother?"

Desdemona's eyes glanced up and left as she thought.

"As if you care. This is not important."

"Just answer me," Sara kept her voice even. "Please."

"I remember her," she said eventually.

"Think about the life she had," Sara said earnestly. "Her life was short. It was dirty. It only held fleeting spells of magic, and that's if she was very lucky. And then she died. The extent of her learning, of her experience, was survival."

To Sara's surprise, Desdemona nodded slowly.

"The gift of our virus is being able to experience endlessly, to always learn and grow, and waste as much time as we want. It's something that is impossible to value, it's everything to me, to be able to live like a river, just always moving, watching the changes on the banks."

"Rivers change the land that they flow through," Desdemona said softly. "Our creed forbids us from leaving a trace."

"No, dear sister," Sara raised a palm. "That's disingenuous. Every human life leaves traces, changes, echoes. Everyone alters their landscape. And in a century, everything of that life is forgotten, and new lives shape the riverbanks."

"Spare me the cheap philosophy," Desdemona said. "I'm not stupid, I know the value of our gift. To other people, I mean. I've been trying to get you to take this seriously since, I don't know, like when they put the surveillance cameras across London, since everything started being recorded. If a sister makes one slip, one mistake, we will be uncovered. And then, the entire world will want to be infected. We cause the end of civilization."

"So this is why you've been secretly photographing us...?" Sara began.

"I didn't do it secretly, I had Rosa and Marguerite take the photos, two women you know and did not notice as they took photos of you."

"Oh, I saw them," Sara lied. "There's nothing in the writings about photography. I assumed they had hobbies."

Anger literally caused Desdemona's back to arch and a frustrated groan escaped her lips.

"Sara do you understand just how dangerous it would be if any one person in the world discovered our secret?"

"I understand."

"You literally couldn't, Sara. You permit your girls to have relationships, you let them go out to nightclubs and bars. You let them do whatever they want."

"I let them live," Sara said.

"And now your darling Teddie has gone viral. With my help. If you kill me today, the New York media will be flooded with similar photos of all of you. You'll be stuck inside this building and you'll starve."

"You're wrong, because everything is fixable," Sara said, locking eyes with Desdemona. "But our lifestyle didn't go to shit because of some photos in a newspaper. It is going to shit because we have not adapted with the times."

"Oh, here we go..."

"The answer isn't more rules, Des," Sara spoke plainly. "The answer, and you're not going to be able to understand this, is less rules."

"Sure," Desdemona shook her head. "Sara, you're sunburnt." Sara winced, instantly regretting not wearing foundation. "You can't even follow the simplest rules. And now you want to what? Feed on humans? Talk to the press? Make as many sisters as you want? Oh... I get it. You want to start making men."

"You just literally infected who knows how many young women." Sara said. "I actually don't want to start making anyone, I'm very much in favor of pausing that side of our lives."

"I'd prefer you to kill me than continue this bullshit chain of lies."

"What are you talking about?"

"I know your secret, don't try to hide it from me."

"Huh?" Sara said, a confused expression on her face. Realizing Desdemona was alluding to Silas, she set her poker face in granite. "What are you talking about?"

"The man, the man you've been running around with, he is known," Desdemona said dramatically. "Many years ago, we assumed he was hunting for our secret, but now we know that he is infected, and somehow, you're what? His girlfriend?"

Clearing her throat mainly to buy some time, Sara looked at the desperate anger in Desdemona's eyes, then at the cuffs around her wrists and ankles, and something flipped inside her. She held the power here. She could easily either kill Desdemona or let Crina do it. She needed to gamble with the truth, or at least some of it.

"I am his girlfriend," she admitted. Desdemona nodded triumphantly. Fuck it, Sara thought. I'm going for it. "He's a vampire. And Desdemona, he's older than you."

Desdemona's eyes widened as her mouth curled in disgust.

"This is an abomination," she said finally, true horror in her deep voice. "This is everything we are against."

"Actually it's not," Sara said calmly. "He's never killed, he lives by our rules. His only crime is his gender, and I'd like to think at this stage in human evolution, we can acknowledge that gender is a construct."

Desdemona shook her head slowly.

"Don't try to sway me with modern ideology," she said slowly. "Don't get too attached. Every Lock on Earth is aware of his existence, and once his truth is known, he will be killed."

"They'll have to come through me," Sara said coldly.

"You're no match for the elders," Desdemona said. "Do you think you could stand up to Amitra?"

"No, I know she would defeat me," Sara said. "But I don't have to worry about that. Who do you think saved me?"

Desdemona froze, her mouth opening and closing slowly, thoughts withering before they became speech.

"I'll fill in some blanks, Des. I was rescued at the last second by Amitra and Fan."

"You're lying," Desdemona seethed.

"They're here in New York," Sara continued. "And they really want to kill you, which is why I did not tell them that you were coming to town."

Desdemona slumped in her chair. The gravity of her situation hit her all at once, and Sara watched as the fire drained from her eyes.

"Then just kill me yourself," she whispered. "Don't go calling the elders to do the jobs you're not capable of."

"I could easily kill you," Sara said. "Killing you would actually be too easy. But Des, trust me, I don't think you're beyond salvation."

"Only the Lord can save me," Desdemona said.

"You know the nun suits are just drag right?" Sara rose to her feet. "We've watched religion grow and change. We understand what it is and how it works."

Desdemona went to speak and Sara raised a hand.

"I'm not here to discuss theology," she continued. "I'm here because I honestly want to talk to you."

"I'd rather take my chances with Fan."

"I get it," Sara said. "But let's try. I think that you and I have something in common."

"I doubt it," Desdemona spat. "It is impossible."

"What else are you gonna do? You're chained to a chair, your prospects aren't good, let's have a chat." Sara said. "While we've been so focused on running our Locks, a lot of things have been happening that we don't know about."

"Speak for yourself," Desdemona said. "You lost control of your women. I have not."

"If we aren't here for freedom, what are we here for?"

"That's what you don't understand," Desdemona's voice softened, surprising Sara. "We can never have freedom. You've risked the entire world so a handful of women can go out dancing."

"That's an oversimplification and you know it."

"It's not though, Sara. The women who've been part of your Lock do not function after they leave, they are broken by the experience."

"Let's not get sidetracked by the bad Yelp reviews women have left me," Sara said with a grin. "As we know, humans are tricky. What I wanted to talk to you about today is, why the hell are you infecting women and bringing them to my city?"

Desdemona recoiled like a rattlesnake about to strike, her eyes slits.

"Cat got your tongue?"

Desdemona didn't move.

"Well I have some updates for you," Sara continued. "Four of them are dead, three from the cyanide you gave them to kill us with. One of them, well, do you want the good news or the bad news?" Even though she knew Desdemona wouldn't speak, Sara waited a beat before continuing. "Things got complicated with Edita."

Desdemona's head jerked upright at the use of the girl's name.

"We captured her, but she reacted badly to sedation and uh, to save her life, I let her feed on me."

The information hit Desdemona like lightning.

"You stupid, *stupid* bitch," she whispered.

"How was I supposed to know?" Sara said in a cutesie voice. "She presented herself as a full member of your Lock. Anyway, congratulations, she met the wolf and it ate her. She died horribly."

Seething in her chair, Desdemona remained silent.

"Three more tried to suicide bomb us. They only managed to gas themselves. We'll send the bill for the cleanup to your office. And Des, the other two are with Fan and Ama right now."

To Sara's horror, Desdemona shrugged.

"These women, they were junkies, they were whores, begging on the streets, they had no future."

"So you turned them into suicide machines?"

"Call them what you like. They'd all be dead from drugs by now anyway. I don't care what happens to them."

"And I do care," Sara lied. "But here's what's next. Madrid is going to agree to stop making these infected women. Stefanya is in Madrid now."

Desdemona gasped, and Sara smiled and nodded.

"If you don't agree," she continued. "She will be joined by Fan and Ama and they will do a little mini-Purge. Your Lock will cease to exist, like the Cursed men of our time."

Desdemona's eyes widened briefly, and then her face went blank and Sara knew she was hiding her reactions.

"I should also mention, New York has left the Lock community. There's nothing in writing that says we have to remain in any sort of union with the European Locks. We are now autonomous, Desdemona. We will be peaceful, and we will phase out blood use entirely.

But New York is our town, and no Cursed woman may enter the town without our knowledge and our welcome."

"This is nonsense," Desdemona said. "You have the greed and singlemindedness of a man. You are ignoring all the signs." Pausing, Desdemona shook her thick black hair back over her shoulders, her expression softening. "Listen, Sara. You can't see it, but I am doing this for the good of our kind, and the good of the world."

"Doing what? Killing people? Exploiting them?"

"If you'll let me finish, you may agree with me. Yes, we need to die off. There are too many Cursed women, made by women who should not have had that power. Who even knows where Marguerite's newborn is?"

"Me," Sara said brightly. "She's upstairs. And she's going to be an asset to our kind, as you call us."

"Whatever," Desdemona countered. "Unimportant. She's the last woman that will ever get made. Imagine a future where our number is small, manageable, and we get to enjoy life exactly as you say." Desdemona's face lit up persuasively. "This is what I'm working for. We just need our number to be more... manageable."

"There are many ways to shrink our numbers," Sara whispered. "We don't have to push whole Locks into Surrender. Clearly, you've been doing work in virology that you haven't shared, otherwise how did you find this different virus that you gave to the girls?"

"I won't tell you that," Desdemona said. "But you're way off."

"It doesn't matter," Sara waved a dismissive hand as she circled Desdemona. "Yukari is working on a vaccine. If any sister wants to end her life, she will be able to get the shot, and hopefully, go on to age and die like a normal person. That's a beautiful option, one that we've never had before."

"So, you aren't afraid of death?"

Sara sat bolt upright.

"Desdemona, I already died once. It doesn't scare me anymore."

"You make no sense."

"Let me make it clear to you. That night, I accepted Surrender. I went through with the whole thing. I wrote my letter. I took the pills. I lit the fire. Everything went black. That's as close as you can get to death and still live to tell the tale. No matter how we play this, sister, no matter what we do or what we change or who we align with, we're all going to die eventually. Our time isn't endless. And next time I face death, I want to be happy with how I spent my time. Are you happy? Has your censored, restricted, blinkered life made you happy?"

"Not in ways you'd understand."

"You're right, it's subjective," Sara smiled. "I came here today to see if I could connect with you, to really understand you, and honestly, I wanted to see if I'd been wrong in the way I treated you for the last hundred years. I dismissed you, I ignored you, and I didn't have any space for you."

"A hundred years? Try always. You've always treated me like that."

"I'd counter that it's been mutual."

"Not true," Desdemona stared at the ground. "When we met, I was excited, I had heard so much about you. I thought it would be the two of us, the two young sisters shaping our world."

"I never wanted to shape the world. I wanted to protect it."

"I'm gonna throw up from your nonsense," Desdemona raised her face. "Do you remember when you left, after we set up Madrid? You said that you'd come back for me. You went to Paris, then you went to London, and the whole time, I thought that I would join you. Instead, as soon as you could, Crina brought you here, to New Amsterdam."

"That's what all this is about?"

"Think about it, Sara. Did you ever, ever in your life look back-wards?"

Pursing her lips, Sara considered her answer.

"No, not then," she admitted. "But you weren't just sitting around. You were setting up Helsinki, Warsaw, Rome."

"Yeah, the hard ones."

"You didn't do it alone," Sara hissed. "You had legendary women at your side, you should be honored and thrilled to have those adventures in your memories."

"How would you have felt if Crina abandoned you?"

Sara's breath caught in her throat.

"It felt... horrible."

Confusion clouded Desdemona's face.

"I don't think you heard me," she said.

"No, I did," Sara said quietly. "When Crina stepped down as Lock mother in New York, she literally vanished. I absolutely felt aban-doned. The whole time I wondered what I had done that made her leave."

Desdemona raised her head, and they stared at each other in silence.

"So, we are alike then," she said eventually.

"No," Sara said firmly. "I've kept up with the times. You've become radicalized."

Desdemona's face darkened.

"Oh act your age, you sound like a Gen Z."

"Desdemona, we are supposed to sound like the generation that we are in. You're a murderer, you've created an army, and you're trying to subvert the Locks around the world. Please explain to me how that is not radicalized?"

"You don't know me," Desdemona said, her voice weary. "Just tell me what are you going to do with me?"

Sara exhaled slowly through her nose and shrugged.

"You know what? I don't know. That's the truth."

"Well you can't just keep me forever in this... what even is this room?"

"It's a panic room, I guess you'd say. Used to be called a bolthole." Sara glanced around the room. "I like what you've done with the place."

"It's easy to be a smug bitch when I'm chained to this chair," Desdemona said angrily, flexing her arms against the restraints. The ancient chair groaned but held firm.

"Guilty as charged," Sara said, standing in one feline motion. "Which is probably what they'll find you if this goes to tribunal. Dear sister, the evidence is stacked against you, unless you have something up your sleeve that you'd like to share with me."

"Oh, I have something to share with you," Desdemona said with a dry chuckle. "On *my* timetable."

"Well if you want your timetable to extend beyond today, I'd be expediting the timing your announcement."

"Sara, please listen to me." A plain honesty crept into Desdemona's voice, triggering something in Sara.

"I'm listening."

"There is room for you in the future, in my future. I want you to know that."

"What is that future exactly?"

Desdemona's eyes flared and an ugly smile twisted her mouth.

"Untie me and we can talk," she said, the familiar wheedling tone returning to her voice. "I'm not in the habit of confiding in someone while I'm shackled to a chair."

"Oh, okay. So the offer is, join a murderer in her unspecified vision of the future. Got it." Sara stood in one feline motion and stepped around the throne, paused at the doorway to the entry chamber and looked back over her shoulder.

"I'll talk to my boyfriend tonight and see what he thinks. Is there room for him in your future too?"

Chapter Twenty-Nine

"She's just so crazy," Heather, cross-legged on the loveseat in her apartment, said. "All of a sudden she wants you to be a general in her new world order?"

Across the coffee table, Sara and Silas were curled up together at one end of Heather's sofa, with Teddie at the other.

"She just wanted you to untie her," Crina said bitterly from the kitchen, where she was opening the evening's first four bottles of Pinot Noir. "That was some last-ditch rubbish and you know it."

"What was she like when you went back in?" Teddie asked.

"You take it," Crina said to Heather as she circulated, handing very full glasses to each of them.

"She was subdued," Heather said. "She didn't say much."

Crina set a fresh pair of bottles of wine on the coffee table and then sat on the floor beside Heather.

"Desdemona is always scripted," she said. "Nothing comes out of her mouth that she hasn't already rehearsed in her head. You freaked her out, Sara. She was short circuiting."

"That's great," Teddie said, and Sara cut her off.

"No, love, it's not. We can't underestimate her again. All of this that's happening now, it's because we all dismissed her. We took our eyes off her, and she got away with-"

"Murder." Silas said quietly.

"I walked into that one," Sara smiled.

"I'm afraid it's going to turn out to be much worse than murder," Heather said. "I can feel it in me bones."

Everyone took a sip of their wine, and in the silence Heather lifted her iPad from where she had it stuffed down the side of the arm of her seat. Her elfin face illuminated pale blue by the screen she was tapping at, Sara watched intently, wondering what Heather was up to.

"Everyone is in their own apartment," she said finally. "Liz was in Rosa's all afternoon but she just got back to hers."

Heather gave the screen one last, dramatic tap with a finger, and then slid the tablet back between the cushion and the arm of her seat.

"Everyone's locked in for the night."

"Has Fran seen anything on the cameras?" Crina asked.

Heather shook her head. "No, but I think she's going to lose her mind if we don't start helping her out. Every young woman who looks even slightly Spanish that walks by the cameras sets her off."

"I can take a shift tomorrow," Teddie said. "I feel pretty useless right now. It'll be nice to have something to do."

"You do plenty," Sara said. "I was going to ask if you wanted to help me on the roof garden."

Teddie gave Sara a loving look. "I'd love that, mom. Let's do it in the morning and then I'll go help Fran after."

Sara reached across and took her hand.

"It's a date."

Silas's phone dinged and he glanced at it.

"Fan didn't like the sound system at the lake house, you guys," he said with a laugh. "She's bought a whole new set up that's so loud she needs to know how far away the nearest neighbor is."

"Those poor Spanish girls," Sara said, watching Silas tap out his reply.

"Yeah," Teddie said. "Those poor girls that were trying to kill us just a few days ago."

"You wait til you see the lake house," Sara smiled. "There are worse places to be deafened by feminist post-punk."

"I had an interesting text from Yukari," Crina said. "She's been mixing blood from the halflings with her own blood. She said the re-actions that she is observing are interesting. She said our blood doesn't react for a period of time, and then it attacks the other blood cells."

"What does that bloody mean?" Heather waved her glass in the air for emphasis.

"Give her some time," Crina said. "She had to order a bunch of equipment. One thing she did say that was interesting was that the two halflings had slightly different variants of whatever virus they have."

"That's more than interesting," Silas said. "All of us OG's have the same virus, no?"

Teddie nodded. "Yeah, it's basic genealogy. Sara made me, so I have her virus."

"And I have yours," Sara said to Crina.

"Me too," Silas said.

"Yeah, we haven't had any new strands since the initial infections," Heather said. "April Veronica's virus would be the same as Mar-guerite's."

"And Embla's is the same as Stefanya's." Teddie said. "Actually, it's probably worth getting a blood sample from both of them."

"Good thinking," Sara said. "Let's also get one from Des, and while we're at it, we should probably all give a pint. Maybe Silas could take you out to the lake house to deliver them, Ted?"

"Too dangerous," Crina said. "Teddie is the conspiracy crowd's latest pin-up girl."

"Yeah, I can't mom."

The ever-present feeling of parental failure surged up inside Sara, once again she'd been so wrapped up in her own drama she hadn't checked in with Teddie about her photo scandal.

"How bad is it?" she asked meekly.

Teddie shrugged and scratched absently at her scalp.

"It's not good," she said finally. "I made Fox News last night."

"Teddie, why didn't you tell me?"

"Because it doesn't matter," Teddie said, staring into her eyes. "If I stay in these walls, I'm good. But even on the roof deck, I'm going to start wearing a burka. If that works, I'll be able to go out into the streets eventually, but I'm on lockdown for the next, oh I don't know, three to five years?"

"I'm sorry, Ted, really, I am."

"It ain't no thing, mom," Teddie laughed. "I've always wanted to learn Navajo, and while Fan and Ama are around, it's time I brushed up on my battle skills."

"Do you remember the decades we spent learning everything?" Crina said, rising to top off everyone's wine. "We'd pay those scholars to teach us to write, to read?"

"It was so scandalous," Heather said with a laugh.

"Why was it scandalous?" Teddie's eyes widened.

"Hands up if you dated a scholar?" Heather said, raising her hand, with Sara and Crina raising theirs slowly.

"It was either that or a journeyman craftsman," Sara said, glancing at Silas.

"Or both," Crina said, laughing as she sat back down.

"And then, when they fell in love with you, it was ten years of lockdown," Sara said. "After that they'd either have moved on or died."

"Sounds romantic," Teddie said. "At least you guys got to date."

"You dated," Crina said. "If anything, it's because of you that we figured out the alternate identities and off-site love nests."

"And for that we are eternally grateful," Heather said, raising her glass. They all followed suit.

"And I had my own lockdown," Teddie said.

"In *Paris*!" the other three women said, laughing.

"So," Teddie looked around the room. "Can I have my next lockdown wherever you were when you vanished, mom?"

Shrugging noncommittally, Sara looked at Silas.

"Do not throw me under that bus," he said to Sara, before turning to Teddie. "But yes, of course you can."

"But you won't tell me where it is," she needled, and Silas shook his head.

"Ted," Sara said. "Do you know when I found out where this place was?"

Teddie shook her head.

"When I got to the gate at the airport," Sara said.

"But you didn't use your Lillian Berger passport," Teddie said. "And yes, der, of course I checked."

"Maybe I didn't need a passport," Sara quipped, and everyone laughed.

As the laughter died off, a burbling electronic sound began to emanate from the kitchen, and everyone cocked their head as they tried to figure out its origin.

"O' hell," Heather exclaimed, leaping up and rushing to the kitchen counter. She turned to face them, holding up an ancient iPhone.

"It's the phone we got from the halflings," she whispered.

"Then put on your best bloody Spanish accent and answer it," Crina said, snapping her fingers.

Sliding the screen with her finger, Heather put the phone to her ear.

"Hola," she said timidly as everyone leaned forward on their seats. "No, no, Edita no esta aqui ahora mismo."

The person at the other end of the line spoke rapidly, and Heather's mouth fell open.

"Yes, Eleanor, this is Heather."

As the shock ricocheted around the room, Heather took the phone from her ear and put it on speaker, setting it on the table.

"Eleanor, you're on with me and Crina," Heather said, unnecessarily, putting her finger over her lips and glaring at Sara, Teddie and Silas.

"Oh, no, Crina, you're there too?" Eleanor's voice was hoarse, panicked, and her Israeli accent, normally so faint, was so pronounced that Sara immediately knew she was in trouble.

"I am here, Elle," Crina said gently. "Are you okay?"

"No, I'm pretty messed up," Eleanor said. "They had me locked up, but I just... I... I escaped. I'm in the woods, but it'll be dawn soon, I have to find a hiding place, I don't have sunscreen and it's hot."

"Calm down, pet," Heather said. "Where are these woods?"

"I'm in Spain, somewhere outside Madrid."

"Turn on Find My Friends," Crina said. "Do it now."

"Okay," Eleanor went silent, the sound of her fingertaps echoing in the apartment as five people stared at each other. "It's done."

"Gimme a sec," Heather picked up the phone, saved the location, took a screenshot, then set the phone back down. "Gotcha. Now turn it off again."

"Done," Eleanor said. "I will be near this place all day, there are mountains, I will find a cave, but tonight I have to move."

"Don't worry about that, pet," Heather said. "Do you mind telling us what's going on?"

Eleanor began to weep into the phone.

"Crina, you will never forgive me," she said eventually, her breath rasping between words.

"Try me, Eleanor."

"I've been so stupid," Eleanor said. "But after Edinburgh, when I saw.. I saw.. what she did, it was the worst thing I've ever seen, and when I spoke up, Desdemona beat me. They tied me up, in the back of a van, and drove me here. They didn't feed me. They told me that I was going to be executed. I don't know what date it is, but I have been listening. Do you have Desdemona?"

Heather glanced at Crina.

"Nice try, Elle. At least we know why you called."

"Nooooooo," Eleanor wailed. "No, no, no, no. I'm not lying."

"That's what all liars say," Crina said bitterly. "Anyway, it's been great to hear from you, we're going to get back to our wine now."

"Desdemona leaked the photos of Teddie," Eleanor spat. "Marguerite and Rosa took those photos!"

"Yes," Crina said. "We figured that out."

"She has photos of all of you," Eleanor continued. "I'm calling to tell you that if you don't release her, the Madrid sisters have been instructed to release all of them."

"We know," Heather said. "Tell us something we don't know."

"Why are you helping us?" Crina's voice was sharp.

"I can't..." Eleanor said, her voice cracking. "This wasn't what I thought I agreed to."

"Eleanor, pet," Heather's voice was soothing. "Just tell us what happened."

They heard Eleanor exhale, a long, rattling sound.

"Edinburgh changed their mind," she said at last. "Heather, I'm so sorry, she... well, she tricked them. She killed them."

Heather's hands began to shake in her lap and she blinked away tears, not meeting anyone's gaze.

"How, Eleanor" Crina's voice was strained. "How did she kill them."

"She told them it was a new synthetic, that's why it tasted weird. It was lethal fentanyl."

Heather put her face in her hands, and began to sob.

"I tried to stop her," Eleanor said.

"Not hard enough," Heather snapped. "You stupid, stupid bitch."

"She didn't tell me she put poison in the synthetic," Eleanor said angrily. "I tried to fight her. I wish you could see me. She ripped half my hair out of my scalp, then hit me in the head with a metal iron. Before my adrenaline could kick in, she had me cuffed hand and foot, and then she just kicked and kicked. I ripped both arms out of their sockets before I passed out. My last thought was that she would poison me while I was out, but when I woke up, I was in the van, they woke me on the ferry to France. I didn't see Des after we got to this place."

"And precisely how did you escape?" Heather's voice was steel.

"After Des stopped answering texts, the sistren all went back to Madrid to prepare to release the photos, and these young women that were guarding me, they're innocent, young. It was easy to get them to relax around me. And when I heard them talking to a squad of them in New York, I knew what I had to do."

"Which was what?"

"I killed them," Eleanor said simply. "Five of them. They had no fight training, they were very weak, but I did it and I grabbed the phone and I ran."

Crina picked the phone up off the table.

"Eleanor, if you're fucking with us, I will kill you."

"I am not, I swear on everything I've ever loved. And you don't have to help me, I do not deserve it."

"Save your battery," Crina said, her voice emotionless. "I will call Stefanya, she will be with you by nightfall."

"Stefanya of Wallachia?"

There was terror in Eleanor's voice. "No, she will kill me."

"She's the only hope you have," Crina said. "But, if this is an ambush, she will be prepared."

"It isn't," Eleanor said before beginning to cry again. "Thank you, Heather, Crina."

"Don't thank me," Heather said tersely. "If it were up to me, I'd slit your throat meself."

"Go, find shelter, save your battery for later," Crina said. "Check your phone hourly."

"Okay," Eleanor paused. "Before I go, write this down, it's the password for a Signal channel that I had, you know, for backup."

"Go," Crina said, and Eleanor recited strings of numbers, an IP address, an email account and a password.

"Got it," Crina replied.

"Log in," Eleanor said. "And Heather? I'm sorry in advance for what you're going to see. Watch it and you'll see I'm telling the truth."

"Anything else?" Crina asked.

"No," Eleanor said. "I'm sorry, that's all."

And she was gone.

"I am going downstairs, right fucking now," Heather stood, her hands balled into fists, face wet with tears. "This stops tonight. I am killing Desdemona."

Crina stood and threw her arms around Heather, holding her in place.

"If anyone's killing her, it has to be me," she said. "But let's talk first."

"We can't worry about the photos," Sara said. "They've been digitized. They'll float around the internet forever, but the public will forget."

"But none of us can be seen in public for decades," Teddie said. "We'd be vulnerable, and inoperable."

"She murdered my friends," Heather said, bursting into tears again.

"They were my friends too, Crina said, rubbing a palm up and down Heather's back.

"Heather?" Silas's voice was gentle. "Where's your laptop?"

"On the nightstand by me bed," she mumbled, and he left to retrieve it.

"We need to log into this Signal account to see if she's telling the truth," Sara said. "In case she is, Heather, do you want to sit this out?"

Heather shook her head angrily.

"No. I need to know."

Silas returned with Heather's laptop. He held it out for her to unlock, then took his seat beside Sara, entering the information from the notes on his own phone.

"I'm in," he said after a few minutes.

On the couch, Teddie and Sara moved closer to him, and Crina guided Heather around to the back of the couch, where they looked over his shoulder.

"There's a message called Edinburgh," he said.

"Open it," Sara said.

"Yes, boss."

"It's a movie file," Silas said. "Are we all sure we want to see it?"

"I need to, kid," Heather sniffed. "Thank you though."

Without a word, Silas clicked on the file and it opened into a full screen view of the Edinburgh meeting room, with the phone recording from the back wall. Unlike the other Surrender videos, when the women began to file in, they were dressed in regular day wear, not white robes. Upbeat chatter filled the room as eleven women took their seats. Sara glanced up at Heather in time to see a fat teardrop fall from her cheek onto the back of the sofa.

Shirley, the Lock mother for over forty years, entered and went up onto the dais.

"Nominee Shirley, and never have I killed," she said, her Irish accent dancing with joy. "It's my distinct pleasure to convene this meeting of the Edinburgh Lock, on the day when we have chosen to live, in peace and harmony with the planet, and begin our transition away from any human-based sustenance."

A smattering of applause sounded in the room, and Shirley nodded, smiling.

"Additionally, I want to thank our friend and mentor, Desdemona, for her understanding of our decision. Des, get up here."

In a flurry of white robes, Desdemona ascended to the small dais. After kissing Shirley on both cheeks, she turned and faced the women – and the camera.

"Women of Edinburgh," she said, "I am so proud of you. Your decisions today will shape the lives of Cursed women for centuries to come. The first Lock to move onto a synthetic food, on top of adopting a creed that forbids the making of any more Cursed women. So brave, so inspiring."

Another round of applause sounded, and Desdemona stood upright, letting it wash over her.

"Those poor women," Heather said.

"Desdemona's white robes should have been a giveaway," Crina said. "They got lazy."

"Not now," Heather snapped.

"It is my distinct pleasure," Desdemona spread her arms wide, "to toast you with the latest synthetic plasma, from our lab in Madrid. This batch, I believe, is the closest we've come to the full effects of human blood. Indeed, you will even get to enjoy the bliss of a good swoon."

More applause, and a few cries of "cheers" and "here here" rang out.

At the side of the screen, Eleanor appeared with a tray of goblets. She held the tray while Shirley took hers, and then she moved along the three rows of thrones, each sister taking a goblet until the tray was bare. Eleanor then moved out of camera again, returning with two more goblets. She handed one to Desdemona and kept the last one for herself.

"My beloved sisters of the Edinburgh Lock, I, Desdemona, mother of the Madrid Lock and friend to you all, toast your bravery, your resilience, and," she paused, "our sisterhood."

Desdemona raised her goblet into the air, and all the women in the room did the same. With dramatic flourish, Desdemona brought her goblet to her lips, and tipped it, her throat bobbing as she swallowed it all in one gulp.

Beside her on the dais, Shirley followed suit then settled into her throne for the effects to take hold, her hands gripping the ends of the wooden armrests.

Suddenly, Shirley's head jerked back and her eyes flew open, a moan escaping from her lips.

"This doesn't feel right," she groaned.

At the bottom of the screen, the seated women began to writhe in their seats.

"This hurts," cried one woman. "What the hell is happening?" wailed another. Painful groans began to grow in volume as the writhing worsened. On the dais, Shirley's face was a rictus of pain, her body bending backwards, and she fought to put her fingers down her throat, trying to rid herself of the synthetic.

"Desdemona," cried a voice. "Something's wrong. Please, help us, please."

Desdemona surveyed the room calmly, her eyes bright. Eleanor appeared at her side.

"Mother, something isn't right, what is going on?"

"They're taking Surrender," Desdemona said. "Like they promised they would."

At the sound of her words, a ghastly look of realization flooded Shirley's face and she threw her clawed hands at Desdemona, who dodged them effortlessly. With spastic movements, Shirley hauled herself to her feet, only to topple off the dais, landing with a sickening thud on top of the women in the front row.

"What the fuck is happening Desdemona?" Eleanor screamed, rushing into the frame. "They voted against Surrender, we need to help them."

"No, we don't," Desdemona said, anger crossing her face when Eleanor bent to tend to Shirley, trying to lift her off the row of dying women.

"STOP IT!" Desdemona yelled. "Eleanor, I mean it, get over there, get away from them. You can't save them."

Ignoring her, Eleanor put her arms around Shirley and began to drag her toward the door. In a rage, Desdemona grabbed Eleanor by the hair, yanking her upwards so rapidly that she dropped Shirley, who slumped to the floor, white foam pouring from her mouth, very clearly dead. The sickening, tearing sound of Eleanor's hair ripping from her scalp was followed by her agonized wail. Tossing the handful of curly brown hair to the side, Desdemona jumped from the dais, returning seconds later with metal cuffs. She knelt on Eleanor's back and roughly cuffed her wrists together as the shrieking woman began to tremble with the tell-tale signs of an adrenaline dump. With only seconds to spare before she became an explosive dervish of death, Desdemona rapidly cuffed Eleanor's ankles with a second set of cuffs. The adrenaline hit her system and Eleanor tensed, an animal scream emanating from her throat. Attempting to stand, she fell backwards onto the bodies in the second row, fighting the restraints in violent thrashes that shattered at least one throne beneath her, the cuffs grinding at the corpses below her, a puddle of blood spreading on the floor. With one sickening pop, an arm dislocated, and Eleanor's screaming became somehow even more raw. Desdemona went back to the dais, watching the horror with appalling satisfaction. When the sound of Eleanor's other shoulder popping out of joint filled the room, Heather leaned forward and slammed the laptop closed.

"Nope," she said. "No more of that. No more of that."

Silence fell in the room, then they all began to cry. Turning, Sara watched as tears poured down Crina's face. She had never seen her cry, never.

"I need to call Stefanya," Heather said, wiping her eyes with the sleeve of her sweater. "We need Eleanor. Alive."

Nodding, Sara pushed herself from the couch.

"We can grieve later," she said, her voice shaking. "We are at war. Heath, yes, call Stef right now. The rest of us, we need to talk to anyone we can trust, anyone in Europe. It's early but we need to wake them.

Silas, sorry, you can't be on that zoom. Teddie, you go get everyone except Rosa and Liz. Tell them what we saw."

"I'll call Fan and Ama," Silas said.

"No," Sara said firmly. "They'll come and kill Des."

Teddie gave Sara a strange look.

"Isn't that what we're going to do?"

Sara shook her head.

"No. We're no kill. I have a much better idea."

Chapter Thirty

After a tense, mostly silent argument consisting mainly of eye contact, Silas settled behind the computer monitor in Heather's office, his face downcast. Battling to center herself, Sara struggled to focus on the purity of Silas's desire to help her, but her mind kept on returning to his defiance, his goddamn stupid maleness, when she tried to get him to leave.

Don't blame his gender.

It was true. Sara wasn't mad at that. She realized with shame that he was the first person who'd stood up to her in a very long time, and she had reacted poorly, from a place of ego. She felt like a bitch, then decided to own it and move forward. Heather had roused three of the four women she was certain they could trust: Lindsey in the London Lock, Yfke from Bucharest and Skye in Paris. They still couldn't get ahold of Christine in Budapest.

"She sleeps like the dead," muttered Crina. "And you two, quit your sulking."

"I'm not sulking," quipped Silas, sounding very sulky indeed. "You know-"

"Shut it," Crina waved a hand at him. "Not now. I want you to focus, not plead your case."

Sara watched with growing rancor as Silas pulled his phone out and started looking at TikTok. Blinking away the angry fog she turned to Crina.

"We need to get this meeting started," she said.

"Teddie is on her way back up," Crina said, barely pausing her work at the keyboard. "I'm about to go live. Si?"

"Yes, mom?"

"Not a fucking sound."

"Wasn't gonna."

Anger flared in Sara until Silas glanced at her and winked and mouthed "good luck" and she suddenly remembered why she had abandoned relationships so long ago. She was too literal and men were too quick to move on from a conflict if you gave them something bright and shiny.

"Heather," Crina yelled. "Get your arse in here."

"I can't stand you when you're cranky," Heather mumbled, appearing at Sara's side with a tray carrying four very full mason jars of blood. "Get 'em while they're hot. There's one for you lad."

She set the tray beside the monitor and passed the jar to Silas.

"Can I have a straw auntie?" he said obsequiously. "You know, so I don't make a noise."

"Ignore him," Crina said, snatching her jar and drinking half of it. "How much blood do we have in store, Heather? It is time for us all to get stronger."

"The way we are going," Heather said seriously, "we'll be out in five days."

Silas raised his hand.

"For fuck's sake," Crina hissed. "What?"

"Today I established a New York department of our offshore research division, and our first delivery will be arriving on Monday," he said with a smile. "It's Thursday night, so we are covered."

"This is why I can't stay mad at you, lad," Heather said, blowing him a kiss.

"We can safely increase our levels, and our strength, without leaving the property."

A ding signaled a text on Sara's phone.

"Teddie is with Fran," Sara said. "She says to start without her."

"Okay, dialing in," Crina said, and several clicks of her trackpad later, the screen divided into four, and they saw the faces of their old friends.

"Before we start," Yfke said, not waiting for any formalities, "I just talked to Stef. I know what's up and-"

"Well that makes one of us," Skye said, rubbing sleep from her eyes.

"Yeah," Lindsey chimed in. "Yfke, have you even been to bed yet?"

"Of course not," Yfke said. "It's summer, the days are for sleeping."

"You guys," Crina snapped. "This doesn't have to be a long meeting. We have a lot to tell you."

Sara, standing out camera range, motioned to come into the frame and Crina gave her a terse head shake.

"Who's on?" asked Lindsey.

Heather leaned in front of the monitor.

"Just me, loves."

"So here's what we know," Crina said, her voice neutral. "And what I'm about to tell you is going to shock you but please, let me finish before you start the questions."

Nobody replied, so Crina pushed forward.

"We have learned that Edinburgh did not take Surrender voluntarily. They changed their minds and Desdemona poisoned them."

Raising a palm, Crina continued.

"Eleanor from our Lock was with her, and when she protested, she was beaten and imprisoned. She has escaped and that's who told us. She sent us video of what happened. I am about to send the video to all of you, and I ask that you wait until the end of this call to watch it. And girls, I'm warning you, it's a hard watch."

"So the reason we're calling," Heather chimed in, "is that we are wondering about Desdemona's end game. She is the one who leaked the photos of our Teddie to the internet, and that she has been collecting photos of all of us, she plans to use them as leverage over us. We don't know if she's focused on New York, or on all Locks."

"Fuck me," Lindsey whistled. "What a cunt."

"Yep," Heather continued. "So our question is, you three all have former members of Madrid in your ranks. What jobs do they have?"

"I'll go first," Skye said. "We have three. One is a scholar, one is a nurse, and one is in charge of our legals."

"Uh that's fucked up," Yfke said. "We have two, and they're in the same roles, nurse and legals."

"Us too," Lindsey said. "Exact same roles. Fuck us, what have we done?"

"That's what I'm worried about," Heather said. "These transplants from Madrid have all gravitated to positions of controlling our real estate and our financials."

"We've walked into a fucking trap," Skye said, tears of frustration rimming her hazel eyes.

"Maybe not," Heather said. "So far it's just a coincidence."

"Desdemona doesn't do coincidences," Crina said. "Ladies, we are starting to see a picture of a very long-range attempt to undermine our Locks."

"No kidding," Yfke said. "I've always hated that fucking beast."

"There's a second issue," Heather said. "Before we get sidetracked. We should have told you before now, but we just don't know who to trust."

"I trust everyone on this call," Lindsey said. "Implicitly."

"Well here goes," Heather said. "Desdemona has been infecting young women with a virus that is similar to ours. She sent a group of them here to kidnap one of us."

Chatter flared up on the call and Crina waved her arms back and forth.

"Mute yourselves," she barked. "If you can't keep it quiet."

"You should have bloody told us," Lindsey said. "Are you sure they're just in New York?"

"We aren't sure of anything, pet," Heather said.

"Lindsey's right," Skye said. "We could all be in danger."

"We are coming to you now," Heather said. "We are telling you everything we know. And we have one more thing to tell you."

Skye sighed loudly.

"Now what?" she asked, slumping to her desk.

Heather gestured at Sara, and she leaned into the camera.

"I'm not dead," she said, waving gaily at three dropping jaws.

Skye and Lindsey fully burst into tears. Yfke waved back.

"I already knew, Stef told me."

Crina and Heather exchanged knowing glances and shook their heads.

"So anyway, here I am and you guys, I met with Des today and she is absolutely ready to destroy us all."

"Oh fuck," Yfke clapped her hands together and tossed her strawberry blond hair away from her face, gazing at the camera intently. "How the hell did that go?"

"It was before I knew about Edinburgh," Sara said. "So it was just a nasty little chat."

"Disappointing," Skye said. "Sara, I'm so overwhelmed that you're alive. Like in a good way."

"Me too," said Lindsey, wiping her eyes. "And I'm glad you called when I wasn't wearing mascara, This could have been a disaster."

"It *is* a disaster," Crina butted in. "We don't have time for joking around. Sorry. We have to put the screws on Des, and we have to do it fast. We are planning to give her a trial tomorrow, and we will threaten her with surrender and hopefully that will break her."

"Doubt it," Lindsey said. "She always has a contingency."

"She's still an egomaniac," Crina said. "And she's changed, she's more manic, more erratic than I've ever seen her."

"We're hoping to exploit these weaknesses," Sara said. "And if we fail, we'll try starving her."

On screen, all three women shuddered in unison.

"Why don't you just kill her?" Skye asked with a shrug.

"Because," Sara knelt on the floor beside Heather and looked directly into the cameras. "Because after this, you guys, we are leaving the Lock world, and one of our unbreakable tenets is that we don't kill. Anybody. Anything."

"So start that the day after you kill Des," Lindsey said with a grin.

"We can't," Sara continued. "The old ways, they're so brutal. They need to evolve, and they need to be peaceful."

"What if Madrid tried to invade New York?"

"Skye, I dunno," Sara said. "We'd try to sort it out peacefully. Also, remember, this is a war involving less than a hundred human beings."

"And how many of these infected women does Desdemona have?" Skye's voice went up an octave. "How will you defend yourself against that?"

"We don't know how many there are," Crina said.

"Stefanya says there is at least two hundred," Yfke said, not looking up from her phone. "Sara, what if she killed Teddie? Would you kill her then?"

"Let me make this clear," Sara's voice was steel. "No killing. No how."

In the silence that followed, Sara looked at the women on the screen, women she had known, from a distance, for so long, and they looked like strangers. They'd shared a virus, an experience, and little more. She felt the sense of sisterhood dissolving around her, a strange chill around her heart.

"I'm not sure why that's being met with such resistance," she said finally.

"I think it's a great idea," Skye said. "I wish I was in a Lock that would support a move such as this."

"I'm not doubting your ideology," Lindsey said. "I just don't think I have the bandwidth to be discussing this kind of thing when all I want to do is get off this call and watch this video."

"We don't have anything else to share with you," Heather said. "You can hop off, love."

"Before you go," Sara raised a hand. "There is one more thing, full disclosure and all that. We captured two of the six infected women. Four died. But the two surviving ones are in a secure location with Yukari from our Lock and she is testing their blood. I'll be sharing the information with you all as soon as it comes to hand."

"Now this, I did not know," Yfke said, her eyes wide.

"Right, because we didn't tell Stef yet," Crina said with a chuckle. "And for now, please keep it that way."

"My head is splitting," Skye said. "I haven't had this much new information in... oh, in forever, literally, like I've never had this much information in one phone call."

"Life is speeding up," Heather said.

"I don't like it," Skye said with a wan smile. "No ma'am."

A knock at Heather's rear door made them all jump, and Heather leapt to her feet and vanished down the hallway.

"What's going on?" Lindsey asked.

"It's probably Teddie," Sara replied.

A burble of voices got closer, and then Heather, Teddie and Fran appeared in the doorway. Fran looked like she was having a heart attack.

"What is it, Frannie," Crina stood and rushed to her.

"I'm gonna throw up," Fran said, and Crina ushered her to the chair she'd been seated in.

"Francesca," Yfke called out. "Hey. Oh shit, honey, what the fuck happened to you?"

"I started checking our donations," Fran said, her voice hoarse. "You know, the usual, the Black Lives Matter and the scholarship funds and the various legal defense funds. All the donations were canceled a few years back and the amounts have been going to something called the Calle Sagrada, a church in Spain."

"Fucking hell," Skye spat. "What about your holdings?"

Fran inhaled deeply.

"You guys, you need to run, do whatever you can, They're trying to... they...she, I mean, Rosa, at least just Rosa..."

Crina wrapped Fran in a hug.

"Just breathe," she whispered. "And tell us what you found."

"I think I stopped it, I'll have to go down to City Hall later, but you guys, she's in the process of transferring all our holdings over to this Sagrada whatever."

Dead silence fell.

"She's drained a lot of our accounts, and the titles of all of our properties are in the midst of transfers to this Spanish church LLC."

"Is that all you know, Frannie?" Lindsey's voice was sharp.

"All I could find out was New York based, but just in case, get the fuck off this call and just call your local property records office, just enquire about your title. It might just be here, I don't know for sure."

"And you were able to stop it?" Sara's voice was tight with panic.

"I think so," Fran said. "But we are almost out of cash."

A cold sweat broke out on Sara's forehead and one foot began to tap rapidly on the floor as she catalogued what she knew of their financial portfolio, and rapidly realized she had largely left its management to Rosa for much longer than she should have.

"How bad is it?"

"Hard to tell," Fran said, very slowly. "But conservatively, it's very bad."

Behind the monitor in front of Fran, Silas moved suddenly, waving his arms and startling Fran, who jolted upright, sending an almost empty mason jar skittering across the table, a spray of blood spattering the monitor.

"Oh god, you scared the shit out of me Silas-"

Moving at lightning speed, Crina's arm shot out, grabbed the trackpad and clicked on the red disconnect button, ending the call.

"Silas!" Crina thundered at her son. "What part of sit there and be silent did you not understand?"

Before Silas could reply, Heather snatched the trackpad and began to reconnect the call.

"This time, laddie," she said, her voice weary, "Frannie, please just say that I'm sitting Yukari's rabbit and it scared you."

"Sorry guys," Fran said, still catching her breath. "And you," she pointed at Silas, "Sir Hopsalot, you really need to work on letting us know you're here. Since rabbits like you are new in this building."

Nodding silently, Silas wrapped his arms around himself and gazed at the floor penitently and Sara suddenly felt terrible. Clearly overexcited by something, Silas had lost sight of the gravity of the situation. She wondered if he thought he had ruined his chances of joining the Lock. She tried to get his attention, just to smile or something, but at that moment the zoom reconnected.

"Sorry, you guys," Fran said. "Yukari's rabbit scared the shit out of me."

"That's an excuse you don't hear everyday," Skye said with a laugh.

"Speak for yourself," Yfke said, cracking herself up, a snort laugh escaping her nose and making her laugh harder. Sara wondered if she was drunk.

"Ladies," Heather said firmly, "I just got us all back on to reiterate that you need to get onto this five minutes ago. Shit is going down. Figure out who you can trust, and get into those accounts. Lock them, freeze them, whatever. And be at your offices of property titles as soon as they open, and see what's going on with your holdings. Do it online if you can."

"Property in the U.K. online?" Lindsey scoffed. "We're not America."

"Well then, lassies, it's time to get off this call and make sure you're all okay," Crina said, her finger hovering over the trackpad. "I'm nominating myself as your point person, I'll be awake all night, please keep me posted via secure channel."

After a round of quick goodbyes, Crina terminated the call.

"I'm so sorry, you guys," Silas said, his voice heavy.

"Well no," Fran said. "Don't worry, nothing came of it. What was so damn important anyway?"

"Oh, nothing. I just wanted to say that I have more than enough investments and whatnot to keep New York afloat."

"Oh honey," Fran laughed. "I've always wanted a sugar daddy."

Chapter Thirty-One

After walking in silence back to their apartment, Sara unlocked the door, holding it open for Silas as he sheepishly sidled past her. Following him along the hallway, Sara took in his hangdog gait and the way his arms flopped miserably at his sides. It was almost comical, except for the fact that she knew he was deeply upset over what happened during the zoom, and her heart ached for him. She didn't know whether to punish him further, because what he did could have really messed things up, or to just let it slide without any further drama. He'd just gotten too excited to be able to help.

"Would you like some blood?"

Glancing up, she saw he was standing in the kitchen, two empty mugs in his hand. After thinking for a moment, Sara shook her head.

"Hit me with a Guinness if we got it," she said with a smile.

Without a word, Silas turned and set the mugs on the counter, then retrieved the cans of Guinness from the cupboard. Unable to hold back, she stepped behind him and wrapped her arms around his stomach, resting her cheek against his back.

"I love you," she said quietly, and she felt him relax against her.

"Good to know," he whispered, pouring the stout into the mugs. "Thought I mighta blown it in there."

"Oh you almost did," Sara said, releasing him and spinning him around to face her. "But it didn't happen and even if it did, we'd just have to figure out a new Plan B."

Smiling, he handed a full can of Guinness to her, then cheersed her, his eyes gazing into hers.

"I'm not big on excuses," he said. "We were both there. I feel dumb, is all that I can say. After so long of my autopilot defaulting to high caution, I lost my shit because an old hippy felt bad."

"And that's a wonderful reason to lose your shit," Sara said, taking him by the hand and leading him to the couch. She set her drink on the coffee table and then took his from him, setting it by hers. Then she guided him onto to the couch, his back against the arm rest, and she curled up between his legs, her arms on his chest.

"I only panicked because deep down, you're my secret," she said. "Your mom has got me all crazy with the cloak and dagger secret son thing."

"It's literally the backbone of her life," Silas said, and Sara nodded.

"It had to be, but after that happened, when I calmed down, I thought about it, and basically, if you get discovered, we just disappear. It's a huge planet and we can vanish pretty effectively."

"Sure, but that's not what you want to do, right?"

Sara couldn't tell if Silas's question was hopeful or not, whether he was fishing.

"I don't know," she said honestly. "You want us to go back to Iceland, I know that much."

"Well that's not entirely true," Silas said, kissing her forehead. "These past few days, being an ad hoc member of a Lock, you know what it's meant to me."

Sara nodded and cupped his cheek with her palm.

"I do, and watching it unfold has been the greatest thing I've ever seen outside of my time with Teddie."

"So you're not .. you know.. angry with me?"

"Never said I was," Sara smiled. "Pass me my beer?"

Groaning loudly, Silas stretched his long arm out and snatched up a can, handing it to her with another kiss on the forehead.

"Good, because I'd like to stay here for a while," Silas continued, resting his arm across Sara's stomach. "Bounce around the East Coast, explore New York together, share our favorite places. You know, do couples stuff."

"That does sound pretty divine," Sara said. "It's the most attractive rabbit hole I've wanted to disappear into in a while."

"I smell a but," Silas said, cracking himself up.

"What the hell are you going on about?" Sara pressed herself up, an elbow digging into Silas's chest. He was laughing so hard he didn't notice.

"You're about to give me the but," he said between laughs.

"Silas, you're not five. What's going on?"

Blinking and gasping away the laughter, Silas wiped the tears from his eyes.

"You're about to tell me why we can't be five-hundred-year-old young lovers doing all the couple things in New York."

"You know why we can't, " Sara said, taking a long draught of her beer. "She's shackled downstairs."

"I have to say, I'm really getting tired of your sister interfering in our relationship."

Sara cuffed him with her spare hand.

"Technically, Des is much more your sister than mine."

"Yeah, let's not go down this path, because then you're my sister and this is all wrong so let's stop."

"Drink your beer..." Sara paused, because in the comedic beat she was going for, she would call Silas by his last name. She didn't know it. She tried to remember Crina's nominee name and couldn't.

"You trailed off," he said quietly. "When you trail off like that, I tend to think something bad is about to happen."

"Not this time," Sara said. "I just realized that I don't know your last name. Like your actual one."

"Join the club," Silas said. "The genesis is foggy at best, mom and I had to have one the first time she put me in a school, in Bucharest. We came up with Funar, but she says that was actually a family name on her side, or it was the name of the family she left me with."

"That's fascinating," Sara said, running a finger through his thick curly hair. "You know what I'd love to do? Spend some time just talking about that stuff, we must have a lot of weird overlap."

"Not to creep you out, but you've figured out that I would see you from time to time?"

"Yeah, but I got over that weirdness at the lake house, if anything it makes me feel really unobservant, when I was supposed to be this vigilant secret vampire."

"If it makes you feel any better, it was very rarely up close. It was more like me stumbling along a path and then seeing you and mom and maybe Stef in the distance so I'd hide until you passed."

They both sat silently, digesting information and each feeling the other's heart beating.

"So what are you going to do about Desdemona?"

Sara took so long to answer that Silas began to fidget beneath her.

"Silas, I told her about you," she said eventually. "I got fucking boastful and if I had said nothing, then it would be different."

"Nope," he said. "That photo is out there in the world, it's shared. Every Lock has seen me now. They know I'm something, they just don't know exactly what."

"Desdemona knows the exactly what," Sara said bitterly. "Because of me. She just doesn't know who your mom is."

"It doesn't matter," Silas said calmly. "It's the same as what happened with me and Fran tonight. What's done is done and we roll with it. If we have to delay our New York In Springtime moment for fifty years, a hundred years, then so be it."

"Do you not watch the news, Silas Funar?" Sara gave him an exaggerated stare.

"What now?"

"New York is sinking," Sara said. "Who knows what will be left in fifty years?"

"Then we will take part in the great northern migration," Silas said, kissing her again. "I've always wanted to live in Norway. We could buy out an entire island, take whoever wants to come with us."

Sara felt a glow in her heart.

"So," Silas said. "back to Desdemona..."

The glow went out.

"I can barely say it," she began.

"Yes?"

"The easiest thing is to kill her," Sara said, and silence hung in the air.

"Sara, I love it that you call New York a no-kill shelter."

"And I loved the women of Edinburgh. And Helsinki. And Warsaw."

"Killing her won't bring them back."

"I know that," Sara half-snapped. "But it will prevent the same thing from happening in Rome. There might even be hope for Madrid, in time."

"Do you remember telling me, in therapy, that I can't save everyone?"

Sara nodded.

"Well it's not your job either," Silas said.

"Fine, what if I just fucking hate Desdemona and the best thing for everyone is if she's dead."

"Then why haven't you already called Fan and Ama?"

"Because I'm a no kill shelter kind of girl. I just can't."

Chuckling, Sara finished her beer and handed her mug to Silas who set it back on the coffee table.

"Sara, can I speak freely?"

Sara giggled. "Of course you can! What is this? 1875?"

"Whatever," Silas wrapped his arms around her, speaking into her ear. "Sara, one of the bonds that I was able to make with Teddie is that we are both committed to never killing. She and I are literally talking about living on synthetic and seeing if it works. It's the one promise I made to her, the thing that made her accept me. Being present while Desdemona is killed is the opposite of that promise. She and I want to find a peaceful resolution, or at least a scenario in which that awful murderous witch is transported back to Madrid. It's worth everything to us."

"Even if it costs us New York?"

She felt him nodding against her cheek.

"Even if it costs me my life."

Sara closed her eyes, her mind racing as her heart wanted a death, and the two people she trusted most in the world wanted to save that life at any cost.

"Fine," she said eventually. "We will send that bitch home. But Silas?"

"Yes, my love?"

"I need some alone time. I'm working on a little gift to send her home with."

Chapter Thirty-Two

Sara paced the perimeter of the basement meeting room, trailing a hand behind her, fingers dragging along the uneven plaster wall, cold and ancient. No noise ever escaped the room, a fact that usually calmed her. Today, the room felt like a tomb where sound died, bouncing around forever in a chamber of brick until it ceased to exist. With a blink, she saw herself in the moment, Shakespearean and gloomy, Lady Macbeth on the parapet, drowning in metaphor. A small laugh escaped her.

She loved lapsing into being theatrical, and she knew Crina would have been laughing hysterically at her, if Crina wasn't preparing to subdue Desdemona, just a few rooms down the hallway. Countless strands of thought from the day pulled at Sara, and she struggled to focus and put them into order ahead of the meeting, which was due to start in – she checked her smart watch – fourteen minutes.

Busying herself, she pushed away from the wall and checked the stockpile around her throne on the dais. On a small coffee table sat a television, plugged in via a long extension cord, its screen a deep flat blue. An Apple TV was plugged into it. A pair of remotes nestled beside it on the table. One the carpeted floor beside the rear leg of her throne lay a large, ancient book. Two Slicers, unholstered, were hidden inside the pages, their bulkier knuckle rings protruding from the pages. She went and stood in the center of the room, studying the spine of the book to make sure that nobody would suspect the book's contents. No matter how directly she wanted to intimidate Desdemona, Fan had always taught her that a hidden threat was infinitely more dangerous than an obvious one.

On a small carved teak table on the other side of her throne was a metal insulated mug containing blood laced with enough Fentanyl to knock Desdemona out. A smaller second cup sat beside it, destined for the lips of Rosa and Liz, if they chose to follow Desdemona back to Spain. The plan was to sentence them all to death, and force them to drink what they would think would be a lethal dose. They would wake up in a Boston airport motel room with nothing but a passport and a one-way ticket to Madrid. The thought of them going through the same ordeal that she did gave Sara much more pleasure than she wanted to admit.

Indulging in one last bit of rewarding drama, Sara took the stage and collapsed in a dead faint onto her throne, head thrown back, limbs limp.

Silas's voice, booming inside the room, made her jump.

"And the Oscar goes to…"

"I wasn't entirely acting," Sara sniffed, arranging herself on the chair. "A dramatic fainting does wonders for your tension."

"So does a kiss."

Smiling, he crossed the room, took her hand, kissed it, then sat cross-legged on the floor in front of her, setting a solidly packed duffel bag on the floor beside him.

"Yep. That worked." Sara said. "What's in the bag?"

"Oh you know," he said jovially. "The usual. Weapons. Chain mail. A helmet."

"For a modern man, you sure pack like it's sixteen ninety-two."

"Would you rather I kept bees and competed in beard competitions in Brooklyn?"

"I'd rather things were peaceful enough that we could even consider such hipster activities," Sara laughed. "Now get into that there storage cupboard and get your battle gear on. Heather will be unlocking the hallway doors soon and people will start to arrive."

Nodding, Silas stood, stretching his long legs in a pair of Carhartt work pants that were very flattering from all angles.

"Oh wait," he said, pausing. "I just talked to Stef. She found Elle, she's pretty beat up but she's stable. They're in a hotel, and they'll all come here, when she's well enough to travel. Stef says she'll need a wig, half her hair is missing."

"That will serve as a good reminder to her," Sara said. "You know, for what she did. But I don't think she should be coming back."

"Me either," Silas said. "We can vote on it later."

Sara nodded.

"Okay, it's time for me to hide and get ready." Silas blew her a kiss and turned away. Sara watched his ass until Silas pulled the heavy wooden door of the storage closet closed behind him. Motion at the hallway door caught her eye and she leapt up in mild panic.

"Settle down pet," Heather, in an ancient chain mail tunic, laughed. "It's just me popping me head in before I go assist poor Crina."

"I'm officially jumpy," Sara smiled. "Good news I hope?"

Heather nodded. "We lost a lot of money, but I was able to kill most of the property transfers."

"The most part is scaring me," Sara fought to keep her voice light.

"She started with some of the out of state properties and it was too late to save them. Looks like Liz finally gets to move back to the West Coast. But I was able to shut down all of our New York property transactions at the last minute." Heather stepped into the room, a vision in heavy medieval leather armor, and spun around daintily. "This old pile of stones is safe. We still have a home."

"No thanks to Rosa," Sara said with a groan. "So the plan is to not tell her, right?"

"I think we should wait until we have Desdemona in the room with her, don't you?"

"I never disagree with you, Heather," Sara stood and crossed the room quickly, wrapping her arms around her old friend. "Please be careful with Des."

"Look at what I'm wearing, love. I'd survive a nuclear blast."

"Like I said," Sara released the hug and stared into Heather's eyes. "Keep your wits about you. It's not nukes I'm worried about. She's gotten this far."

"And it's far as she's going to get," Heather turned to the hallway. "When it's time, have Teddie come let us know and we'll bring her in."

Saluting dramatically, Sara turned and walked back to her throne, running her fingers along the arms of Teddie's throne, and then Imani's as she passed, spurring memories of countless meetings in this room, with so many sisters who had either moved on, or taken Surrender. They'd had Fran's welcome ceremony down here, because the roof had been deeply snowed in, and suddenly, Sara was reliving that night. She saw smiling faces, happy women dancing and drinking, all wearing Courreges and Gucci, bright 60s colors, and Fran, the happiest she'd ever seen her, looking so young as to belie her gray hair. Sixty years vanishing in a whirl of memory, she let her feet skip slightly as she remembered the music playing that night, even though she couldn't name it.

"That looks like one helluva memory, guv."

Pausing mid step, Sara turned and blew a kiss to Imani, striking in all-black racing leathers, one arm tucked through a glossy black motorcycle helmet.

"I see you took the assignment seriously," Sara said, continuing to her throne.

"I didn't live this long just to get clocked by your crazy-arse sister."

"Why does everyone call her that?" Sara groaned.

"I was hoping the three of you would make a sitcom," Imani settled into her throne, setting the helmet beside her on the floor. "Now that you also have a brother that you're dating."

"Lols," Sara said drily. "I was hoping today might actually be a snuff movie."

"Remember when they were a thing?" Imani let out a chuckle and they both sat there in silence until the sound of footsteps in the hallway caused them both to look up.

Teddie and Fran waltzed in, wearing matching, billowing long-sleeved chiffon dresses over what looked like dark gray wetsuits.

"We're giving tactical haute couture Hamptons," Teddie purred, raising Fran's arm up while Fran did a tidy pirouette.

"No helmets?" Sara's voice was stern.

"No need," Fran said. "We won't be getting close to her."

"Isn't she in chains?" Teddie walked Fran to her throne.

"I'd be worried if she was neck deep in cement," Sara quipped, looking at her phone. "Hurry and sit down, Liz and Rosa are on their way."

"These are Kevlar body suits, Sara," Fran said.

"Great," Sara said, her voice mildly sarcastic. "If this turns into a gun battle, you'll be fine."

"I told you she wouldn't like them," Teddy whispered as they took their seats. Sara ignored them, and a hush settled, broken only by the occasional creak from an ancient chair caused by a nervous fidget.

Hushed chatter from the hallway told them that Rosa and Liz were on their way, and at once, every sister in the room straightened in her throne. Nobody turned their head when the pair entered the room, but Sara raised her eyes, meeting Rosa's for a second before she looked away.

"Welcome," Sara said neutrally. "If you can take your seats, we will begin."

"Everybody is not here yet," Liz said.

"Everybody who can be here is here, Liz," Sara said, standing and facing them all.

"My name is Sara," she said, her voice strong. "I have killed. I regret it, and it was not intentional, but I have killed. And it is time to put the pretense behind us. All of us are afflicted by a virus that controls us, and that virus can force us to kill."

"Yeah, if you let it get out of control," Rosa said loudly. "Like everything else in your life."

"I'd bench that attitude," Sara cautioned. "We've been through this before. You decided to stay. So play the fuck along."

"Whatever," Rosa snarled.

"As a Lock, we will learn by my mistakes, and we will be better guarded against them in the future."

"Why are you even bothering with this bullshit," Liz said irritably. "You have the votes to do whatever you want with her."

"By the end of this meeting, Elizabeth, you'll be voting alongside me."

"Fat chance," Liz said, her arms crossed angrily.

"Firstly, I do want to reconfirm that you, Rosa and you, Elizabeth, intend to remain as members of this Lock."

They both nodded sullenly.

Sara pursed her lips briefly, then continued.

"That brings us to our second matter. Our sister April Veronica has returned, and she has brought with her a fellow neophyte. April, Embla, would you like to come in?"

Liz and Rosa spun around in unison. Sara watched as they stared as the two young women entered the room and walked down the aisle.

"Join me up here, would you," Sara said, and they obeyed, Embla leaping up onto the dais, then turning and extending a hand to April Veronica. When they turned to face the room, Sara watched as Rosa slowly looked Embla up and down, her body trembling with anger. She made the sign of the evil eye at Embla, and spat between her fingers, the spit landing on the floor at Embla's feet.

"Abomination," Rosa hissed dramatically.

"Whatever, transphobe," Embla said dismissively, causing April Veronica to giggle and flip off Rosa, who glared theatrically, her face blood red.

"There's plenty of room for old-fashioned bigots like you in Madrid, Rosa," Sara said. "Liz, do you have a problem with Embla?"

Liz shrugged and shook her head, and Rosa elbowed her sharply.

"What?" Liz elbowed her back. "Gender is a construct, I'm surprised it took this long."

Rosa attempted a hissed whisper in Liz's ear, and Liz shoved her away with her palm.

"I was a founding member of the San Francisco Lock, Rosa," she said tersely. "You're getting pretty close to bigotry here."

Rosa inhaled, but before she could speak, Liz pressed a finger to Rosa's lips.

"Shhhhhh," she said. "Now is a listening time."

Batting Liz's hand away from her face, Rosa glared from Liz to Embla to Sara, then back to Liz.

"I will remember this," Rosa said, her voice steel.

"Hey Liz," Fran called out. "Wanna come sit over by me?"

After a nervous glance at Rosa, Liz shook her head.

"Thanks, though, Frannie."

Sara smiled as confused glances were shared around the room.

"Anyway, everyone, April Veronica and Embla are full members of the New York Lock and they will be voting at today's hearing."

"This is such bullshit," Rosa said. Sara raised a palm. "This is fixed voting."

Grateful that Rosa didn't say "rigged", Sara ignored her.

"Before we bring in Desdemona, there is something I'd like to share with you."

Sara nodded at Teddie and Fran, who stood and walked to opposite corners of the room. Teddie killed the lights and Fran switched on the small television with a remote from her pocket, then cast a video to the screen. As the video of the Edinburgh Surrender began to play, Sara did not take her eyes from Rosa and Liz. She saw the anger in Rosa's face increase, in the set of her jaw and the flare of her nostrils. Liz seemed confused, her head tilted as her horror dawned across her face. It told Sara everything she needed to know.

As the video played on, Embla and April Veronica rose and left the room, fingers in their ears. Imani, Fran and Teddie all bowed their heads, refusing to watch the slaughter a second time.

Like a hawk Sara watched the horrifying realization wash over Liz, first a lone tear spilled down her face, then her chin began to tremble and her face contorted in pain.

"But..." she stammered. "This is... this is...."

"Desdemona murdered them," Sara said, her voice low. "She murdered our sisters, our friends, our lovers."

Liz collapsed in a sobbing heap in her throne, her blonde locks tumbling forward, hiding her face.

Beside her, Rosa leapt to her feet. Before she could do anything, Imani grabbed her from behind, pinning her arms at her sides. A wolf's howl tore from Rosa's throat, and she flicked her head back, trying to dislodge Imani, who quickly moved her own head out of the way, then used the momentum to let go of Rosa then thread her arms behind her elbows, yanking them together behind her back. The howl turned into a scream of pain.

"One more fuckin' headbutt and I'll break both your arms," Imani said, and Rosa fell still, her head hanging down, her breathing ragged. Silently, Teddie moved in and locked metal cuffs above each of Rosa's elbows, forcing her chest forward and her head up until finally, her eyes met Sara's.

"Rosa, today we will be charging you with murder alongside Desdemona," she said.

"For fucks sake," Rosa said with an angry laugh. "Will you ever get over yourself?"

"Doesn't look like you're going to be around to find out, guv," Imani said, releasing her grip on Rosa and pushing her forward so that she fell between two thrones and landed painfully on her side in front of Sara.

"I didn't know," Liz said, her face still hidden, her voice breaking. "I didn't know."

Switching the television off, Fran went to her side.

"We got played, honey," she said quietly, wrapping an arm around Liz's heaving shoulders. "You didn't know."

Sara kept her focus on Rosa, now kneeling, her head whipping left and right. Sara wondered if she was trying to trigger an adrenaline dump, turn herself into a human suicide bomb. She didn't know whether to abandon the plan or continue and risk it.

Movement at the doorway distracted Sara, and she glanced up to see April Veronica and Embla walking slowly back in, both of them in tears. They went and stood by Liz, each placing a hand on her shoulders, and Sara knew that she had to press ahead.

"Teddie, would you please go and tell them it's time for Desdemona to come to her trial?"

Chapter Thirty-Three

Sara kept her eye on Rosa when the sound of Desdemona's footsteps echoed from the end of the hallway. Rosa's shallow breathing grew more rapid, and a fervent gleam shone in her eyes. At every step, Desdemona's chains clanked and Rosa's eyes widened, then narrowed. With disgust, Sara recognized the hollow worship in the zealot's gaze on Rosa's face.

The woman was vibrating with excitement at the thought of being reunited with Desdemona, and in a brief flash of panic, Sara realized that this was what Desdemona had done. Somehow, she'd risen to the role of a god in the eyes of her sisters. Dealing with Madrid was going to be much more complicated than she imagined.

Sara knew that Desdemona had appeared in the doorway because Rosa's panting stopped and a beatific smile spread across her face. Raising her gaze, Sara saw Desdemona, her face defiant, walking toward her in a long black t-shirt, her raven hair matted and wild, hands cuffed in front of her. Behind her walked Heather and Crina, each wielding a Slicer..

"Put her over there," Sara said, pointing at the corner of the room opposite Rosa, and Crina gave Des a nudge, forcing her in that direction. When she reached the corner of the dais, Desdemona went to step up onto it.

"No you fucking don't," Sara snapped. "You're not worthy of a place on this stage."

"I knew you'd be dramatic," Desdemona rolled her eyes. "That's your problem. You're predictable. That's why I've always been five years ahead of you. I've been the architect of all of your misfortune, for the past century. No matter what you do to me today, you can't undo that."

"And yet, I'm not the one facing Surrender," Sara said coldly.

"I thought you didn't kill?"

"ELEANOR SOLD YOU OUT," Rosa screamed from across the room, and Sara saw shock flicker over Desdemona's face. "SHE TOLD THEM EVERYTHING."

"Calm down, lapdog," Sara said unctuously. "But yes, Des, the cat's out of the bag. This tribunal isn't to judge you on, you know, the technicalities of murdering Marguerite and making an army of halflings. Today, you're also facing justice for murdering the women of Edinburgh."

Desdemona's face remained disappointingly passive, and she looked at Rosa and shrugged, making Rosa giggle.

"Is that it?" Desdemona looked from Sara to Crina.

"I'm going to enjoy pushing that button," Crina said.

"Before you do," Desdemona purred, "mother, dearest..."

Crina bristled, her shoulders widening, a vein standing out in her neck.

"Do not use that word on me," she whispered, murder in her voice.

Desdemona laughed.

"Lord, Sara, I see where you get it from," she said jovially. "Anyhoo, before anyone presses any buttons, Rosa, I guess we should tell them about the... the consequences."

Rising to her feet, her eyes fixed on Desdemona, Rosa, grinning madly, began to speak.

"As of today, this whole building and every holding of the New York Lock has been transferred out of your hands." Rosa's head turned slowly and her eyes burned into Sara's. "Everything is now property of La Iglesia Del Camino Sagrado."

"Of which," Desdemona said, indulging in a little theatricality of her own, "I am Madre Superiora."

Gasps from April Veronica and Embla drew Desdemona's attention to them.

"And as the new owner of this building and mother of this church, you filthy little abominations will be the first things I kill. Now, Rosa, tell them what will happen if they don't let us go right now."

"The property will be sold to developers. There is a preliminary contract in place. If I don't withdraw it by midnight, you'll all be homeless," she started to laugh. "And broke. And starving."

"So," Desdemona raised her arms. "Who wants to unlock these pinche cuffs?"

Heather stood slowly, setting her Slicer on the floor beside her throne. She dug in her pocket and withdrew the key to the handcuffs and took a few steps in Desdemona's direction, a smug grin lighting up Desdemona's face.

When she was still several feet from Desdemona she paused and turned to Sara.

"Do you want to tell her or shall I, pet?"

Smiling, Sara shrugged. "I don't care, Heather. Actually, why don't you do it?"

"Sure," Heather said. "So, Rosa, did you get any confirmations that your transfers went through?"

"Yes, yes I did."

"I doubt that's entirely accurate," Heather said, her voice sweet. "Since I was able to kill most of them overnight. I will congratulate you on your success with a small section of our stock portfolio, and I let you have the building in Red Hook. You will be able to enjoy the easy life in your San Diego compound. If you'd opened the confirmation emails, you would have seen the details of just what the... what was it? The Camino Sagrado owns in New York."

The look on Desdemona's face was finally the one that Sara wanted to see.

"You're lying," Rosa said nervously.

"No, pet, I'm not," Heather slipped the key back into her pocket and walked over to Rosa. "No funny business now," she said, reaching into Rosa's jeans pocket and pulling out her phone. She held it to Rosa's face to unlock it, and then flicked at the screen until she found what she wanted. Holding the phone in front of Rosa's face, she glanced at Desdemona.

"What does it say, Rosa?" Desdemona's voice was taut.

Angry sobs shook Rosa from her core, and she turned her face to the floor.

"I'd say that she's confirming that I'm not a liar," Heather said. "So, unless you have a plan B, Des, I guess we can move along with your... Sara is it a trial or a tribunal?"

"You know, Heather, I'm not sure it's either," Sara smiled. "Des, you killed Marguerite and directly or indirectly you've killed countless sisters. You're going to die now. And Rosa, I watched you during the video. You knew what she was planning to do. You'll be in the Surrender room with her."

Desdemona bowed her head, hiding her face behind a veil of black hair, and the only sound in the room was Rosa's guttural crying.

"This is weird," Teddie said, with a wink at Sara. "So, do we just load em into the Surrender room?"

"Dunno, mate," Imani said. "It's not like this mob give two shits about protocol."

"And my button pushin' finger is itchy," Crina said, standing and stretching.

"Well, I guess that settles that," Sara said. "If nobody else has anything to say-"

"I do," Liz stumbled to her feet, shaking off Fran's arm on her way up. Breathing loudly, she took slow, measured steps to Desdemona, who slowly raised her head.

"This'll be good," she croaked. "Great, the last person I get to speak to is you, Liz. The stupidest, most easily led sister of all,"

Liz's arm swung so fast even Desdemona didn't see it coming until the palm smacked her face sideways, the slap echoing throughout the conference room. The force of the blow nearly knocked Desdemona over and she fought to keep her balance, blinking at the pain.

"How fucking DARE YOU," Rosa screamed.

"Oh, I'm not even done yet," Liz said, and she braced her back foot, pulled her right arm back and delivered a brutal uppercut to Desdemona's jaw, sending her backwards off her feet. As the woman landed, Liz rushed to her fallen form, readying a kick aimed at her ribs.

A brutal scream tore through the room but it wasn't Desdemona. Sara spun around in time to see Rosa's eyes roll back in her head and her shoulders flex, forcing against the metal restraints that bound her upper arms. Aghast, Sara watched as the metal cut into Rosa's arms, and blood began to pour freely, splatting wetly on the carpet, until, with a sharp POP! the chain binding the cuffs snapped and Rosa launched herself at Liz, snatching her heel mid-kick and spinning her around so that she landed on top of Desdemona, who groaned loudly, then grabbed Liz tightly by one wrist.

Rosa, still wailing, grabbed a handful of Liz's hair and yanked her off of Desdemona, whose nails dug into Liz's wrist, slashing it open and causing Liz to screech in pain, thrashing as Rosa dragged her across the room, right past the dais.

Sara, her mind racing to figure out how to save Liz, glanced at her Lock for support. To her horror, she saw April Veronica and Embla's eyes glaze over as the aroma of Liz's blood reached them, and blood lust began to set in. She needed to move fast or they'd both black out and feast on Liz. Nodding at Crina, she leapt for Rosa, who backed herself against the far wall, hauling Liz up to standing and wrapping one arm around her neck. Rosa dug into her back pocket with her spare hand and pulled out a small case.

"Stop right there," she screamed, glancing maniacally from Sara to Crina. "Another step and she's dead."

Liz's terrified blue eyes pleaded at Sara, and she paused, raising a palm in peace.

"Don't hurt her Rosa," she said.

"Don't move," Rosa said, bringing the case to her mouth and opening it with her lips. As it opened, Rosa snatched the contents out, silver flashing in her hand as the case tumbled to the floor. Sara's panic ratcheted up a notch when she realized it was a pair of the silver teeth, razor sharp and glinting malevolently. Rosa deftly slipped them over her teeth and smiled, the light bouncing off the razor-sharp blade across her front teeth.

"You don't bring a knife to a gun fight," she said, her voice furry as she kept her tongue away from the blade in her mouth.

"What the fuck is happening? Liz cried.

"I'm gonna turn you into the biggest fucking mess this Lock has ever seen," Rosa croaked, violently pulling Liz's head to the side, exposing her throat.

Sara put her weight into one leg, preparing to launch herself at Rosa, but in a split second, the door beside Rosa burst open, and Silas lurched out, snatching Rosa's hair and kicking her legs out from under her. In shock, Rosa released Liz, who spun to the floor then bounced immediately to her feet, landing in a combat pose. Recognition and then horror flickered across her face as she took in Silas.

Sara's heart was in her throat as she watched Silas, his only protection a motorcycle helmet and chainmail vest, lock his legs around Rosa and thread his arms in hers, until he was flat on the floor beneath her, and she whipped her head from side to side, snapping at the air like an animal. Blood spurted from her lacerated tongue, and Rosa had to cough it out of her mouth in order to breathe, the blood landing on Silas's face, the stench of it filling the air. In seconds, Crina was beside them, a Slicer at Rosa's throat.

"Let her go, Silas" she said. "Rosa, get up. Don't try anything."

Releasing his legs from her waist, Silas pushed himself up to his knees, then rocked himself up to standing, lifting Rosa painfully with him.

"I said, let her go," Crina's voice was steel. Without another word, Silas released Rosa's arms. Crina stepped back, expecting Rosa to attack her. Instead, the blood-soaked woman spun to face Silas, raw hate contorting her face as she coiled to strike him. Rosa flexed her knees and leapt at Silas, her feet leaving the floor as she threw herself at him. Without thinking, Sara launched herself across the room, things moving in slow motion, women getting out of her way, thrones being thrown aside by her arms. She saw the blood streaked silver razor grille in Rosa's mouth, Silas dropping as dead weight to avoid her, Rosa's arms closing around nothing in the space where Silas had been a split second before.

As Sara landed on the carpet beside Rosa and prepared to take her down, she saw the glint of a Slicer raised high, before it descended like a guillotine, lengthwise, hitting Rosa just below the skull, slicing her spine down the length of her neck continuing between her shoulder blades.

With a horrifying gurgling sound, Rosa collapsed down and backwards, her mouth still snapping, confusion in her eyes. April Veronica screamed, but to Sara it sounded like she was beneath the ocean. Crina stood motionless, the Slicer in her hand, its blade wet and crimson, her chest heaving. All Sara cared about was Silas and she tried to pivot, to get to him but something heavy smashed into her, knocking her sideways, momentum working against her until she thudded painfully against Rosa's throne. In horror she saw that it was Desdemona, wild-eyed victory on her face.

In an instant, Desdemona, arms still cuffed, grabbed Silas by the chest. She lifted him effortlessly, his legs flailing uselessly, too disoriented to defend himself. Before he knew it, Desdemona had let go of his chest, and flipped him around and dropped her arms over his shoulders, imprisoning him against her. Sara's adrenaline begin to spike. Her vision darkened and she fought to blink the virus away.

She couldn't afford to lose control now.

"Do not hurt him," she yelled.

Desdemona winked at her, then bent her head and bit violently into Silas's neck, and he screamed in agony. Instead of releasing him, Desdemona started to chew on the flesh of his neck as he whipped his head in agony. The sound of Crina's screams joined the din. A thick spill of blood poured from the wound, coursing over Silas's chain mail. Stopping suddenly, Desdemona looked up, her chin red.

"I avoided the jugular," she said, her chest heaving. "Unlock me right fucking now or he dies. And Crina? Mom? Take ten steps back or I'll do it anyway."

"Heather," Crina yelled as she stepped backwards, her eyes burning into Desdemona's. "The key, get the fucking key."

Dropping her Slicer, Heather whipped the key out of her pocket and moved closer to Desdemona.

"Sara," Heather said. "You hold her head back. Imani, grab his shirt. Pull him as soon as I unlock."

A guttural noise caught everyone's attention, and Sara glanced right, seeing April Veronica's eyes rolling back in her head, and a white foam at Embla's lips as they lost themselves to the blood lust. Deeply triggered, Sara watched as they fell to all fours and began to drag themselves to Rosa's body to feed.

"Teddie, Fran," she barked, "Get them the fuck out of here."

"Lock one in the Surrender room, put the other in the room we had Des in," Heather yelled. Sara turned her attention back to Silas, standing motionless in Desdemona's arms, blood pouring from a jagged tear in his neck. "I love you," he mouthed to her and something deep inside her broke.

Stepping forward, she pulled Desdemona's hair back with one hand, so roughly that her vertebrae cracked, then placed the other palm on her forehead, pressing it against the wall.

"Ready," she said.

"You ready, Imani?" Heather glanced at Imani, who nodded, grabbing a handful of Silas's bloody chainmail. Forgotten on the floor, Rosa made a ghastly gurgling sound then was quiet.

"Okay," Heather stepped in close and unlocked one of Desdemona's wrists. As soon as it was free, Imani hauled Silas away from Desdemona, and he landed in Rosa's old throne, next to Liz.

"We can talk later," he said to Liz, placing a hand over his bleeding neck.

"I don't even care," Liz said, not looking at him.

Motion in the doorway caught Sara's eye and she turned to see Teddie coming back.

"The kids are alright mom," she called out.

"Get out of here, Ted."

"No," Teddie walked over. "I want to be here for this. I want to see the bitch die. I want to press the button. I want to lose my no-kill card on this fucking worthless maniac."

"Fair," Sara said, spitting at the floor at Desdemona's feet.

"No," Crina said, stepping forward, Desdemona's face registering shock as she met her maker's gaze. "We are a no-kill Lock. That means no death penalty. No matter how hateful the crime."

"You know what?" Desdemona rolled her eyes. "I'd rather be dead than have to listen to this new-age hippy bullshit."

"I know you would, dear daughter," Crina came ever closer to her, and Sara put even more pressure into holding Desdemona's head back. "Which is why we came up with something worse for you."

Finally, fear registered in Desdemona's eyes.

"And then we will send you home," Crina said, her voice steel. "Won't we Heather?"

Sara nodded at Crina, who gave a thumbs up to Heather. Without another word, Heather left the room for a moment, returning with a small rolling travel bag and a shopping bag which she upended onto the seat of her throne. A nun's habit tumbled out.

"Only fitting that the Madre Superiora of The Camino Sagrado returns to Madrid in her ceremonial robes," Heather said with a sniff. "We'll get you washed up and you can put this on. Your passport is in the suitcase."

Sara felt Desdemona relax, her weight slumping slightly as the tension ebbed from her.

"Hold her tight now," Crina said to Sara, and Sara obeyed, putting so much weight onto Desdemona's head that she groaned in pain.

"I have one last gift for you," Crina said. "A little something to send you on your way."

Beside her, Heather held a folded leather satchel, the same one that they'd used at April Veronica's conversion. Crina flipped it open, and Sara was surprised to see a small modern hypodermic instead of the traditional metal one that usually resided in that case.

Crina plucked the syringe from the satchel and flicked it with a fingernail, then jabbed it unceremoniously into Desdemona's shoulder, depressing the plunger fully.

"What the fuck have you done to me?" Desdemona said, pressing against Sara.

"A little gift from Yukari," Crina said. "And a lot of payback for what you did to those girls. Congratulations on being the first person on earth to ever be vaccinated against our Curse."

Horror dawned on Desdemona's face, slowly, and her breathing became irregular. Sara wondered suddenly if she would turn to a pile of dust..

"What is going to happen to me?" Desdemona said finally, her voice constricted.

"Like I said," Heather quipped. "We'll get you washed up and onto a flight to Madrid later tonight."

"I meant with this fucking vaccine," Desdemona spat.

"Oh, that," Crina said lightly, gripping Desdemona's free hand and pushing it down while Heather replaced the handcuff. "Nobody knows. Yukari would really appreciate it if you could keep her posted.

If she's right, the vaccine will strip the protein shield on the virus, and it will either die or lose its potency."

Desdemona's face paled.

"The fun part," Crina continued, "is that after that, it's all new ground. I guess you could die on the flight home. Or you'll just get to age normally. Like I said, if you could keep Yukari informed, your her most precious guinea pig right now."

"I've always hated you," Desdemona whispered.

"That's not true," Crina said, turning away from Desdemona. "But you know what I love about this, Des? You have finally gotten the one thing you always wanted and never were."

"What's that, you bitch?"

"You're finally one of a kind," Crina said, turning and blowing her a kiss. "You're finally *special*."

Chapter Thirty-Four

Three months later

Fighting a crush of late afternoon commuters, Sara emerged from the 96th St Subway station into the swirling gray of a New York twilight. Crisp yellow leaves swirled in little tornados between buildings and the air had a hint of frost. Pulling her jacket tight around her throat with one hand, patting the small box in her pocket with the other, she decided to cut across and walk up the less crowded West End Avenue.

A nagging thought that she'd forgotten something, whether it was an ingredient or a task she wasn't sure, followed her down the hill. It wasn't important, she decided. And if it was, it would be a nice evening for a walk with Silas, and they could take care of the thing together. Whatever it was.

Together.

She paused, hung up on the weirdness of the word in her life. They'd remained in their wartime apartment, as Silas was fond of calling it. Silas painted it and they'd decorated it together, like a new couple, doing weekends in Connecticut and Vermont, scoping out antique barns and artisans. Together. After a life of enforced solitude, the word was proving to be a bigger hurdle than the act. She loved living with him, she loved waking up with him and she loved being honest with him. It helped that he had an almost preternatural sense of the perfect time to give her space, vanishing frequently to help or hang out with the women of his Lock.

Realizing she was standing like a statue at the corner of 96th and West End, Sara shook away the cobwebs and began the uphill trek to the compound, making a list of the things she needed to do for the evening. Firstly, she needed to call Teddie, who'd been with Yukari at Silas's upstate place for the past three months. She had unanswered messages from Crina and Heather in Iceland, and Fan and Ama in Madrid, as well as evening invites from the kids, as Silas had taken to calling April Veronica and Embla, who were exploring New York at a level she'd never been able to. Something in Gowanus was "essential" for them to all attend, around midnight.

She just wanted to sit on the couch with Silas and watch a movie. The breeze intensified to wind, bringing billowing golden leaves. The temperature plummeted along with the failing of the light, and she was suddenly transported back to the night she fed on Laura. Her footsteps faltered, but she did not lose her pace. The anniversary of that night was approaching. Flushing the shadows of that memory away with light, she thought of the adventures she'd had since that night, the good, the bad, the ghastly, finally able to focus on the good. Her heart was full on a daily basis in ways she'd never thought possible. Mistakes, she joked to herself, weren't as bad as she'd always feared. She could make mistakes now. Mistakes, she smiled, can always be fixed.

Arriving at the building door, she held her phone to the security lock and it ground open, the door springing ajar with a satisfying click, and she let herself inside, pressing the door closed behind her.

Sniffing at the air, she smelled chicken roasting and smiled. Silas had started dinner. They were the only carnivores in the building. Her tummy grumbled and she started up the stairs. By the second floor, she heard music, a pounding beat and a guitar solo, that she couldn't quite place but was certain she knew.

At the top floor, she held her phone to the sensor on the door and it opened, bathing her in music and scents, and the view of Silas and Fran, her hair recently dyed a pale lilac by April Veronica, at opposite ends of the couch, lost in the music in the air.

"Honey, I'm home," she called out, startling Fran. Silas opened his eyes slowly and a smile spread across his face. He held up a "please wait' finger and lifted the stereo remote from the coffee table, turning the sound down. Then he leapt up and wrapped her in a hug, kissing her hard on the lips.

"Frannie's been teaching me all about the Grateful Dead," he said, kissing the tip of her nose then bouncing into the kitchen. Sara turned to Fran and blew her a kiss.

"Don't you go turning my boyfriend into a Deadhead," she said with a laugh.

"Oh too late, sister," Frannie said, returning the kiss. "He's gone. Man, he's gone."

"Wait," Sara looked from one to the other. "Are you guys high?"

"Not yet," Silas appeared in front of her with a very full glass of red wine. "We were waiting for you to get home to see what the night was looking like."

In her old life, Sara would have immediately accommodated Fran, but she wasn't about that life anymore.

"Actually, sorry to be a party pooper, but I kind of want to snuggle and be quiet and be weird with my man, Frannie. Is that okay? Can we raincheck, because I also never was able to crack The Dead."

"Not a problem at all," Frannie tipped the remainder of her drink down her throat and stood. "You do realize this means you're forcing me to go to some happening in Gowanus with the kids?"

"Forcing you, huh?" Sara gave her a hug.

"Forcing me," Fran said with a laugh and a tightening of the hug. "Which means I can actually go take a nap. The thing they're taking me to doesn't start until midnight."

"Don't forget your homework, Frannie," Silas called from the couch.

"Australian punk, nineteen seventy-six to the present," Fran said, saluting him.

"I ordered you a bunch of vinyl, it'll start turning up tomorrow," Silas said.

"Thanks," Frannie quipped, letting herself out the rear door into the passageway. "Enjoy your flix'n'fux."

And she was gone.

"Are we flixin' and fuxin'?" Silas rose from the couch and wrapped his arms around Sara's waist.

"Something like that," she said, twisting herself from his embrace and sitting on the couch, facing sideways. "Sit."

She nodded at the couch and Silas sat down, trepidation on his face.

"I feel like I'm about to get in trouble."

"The opposite," Sara said. "Quite the opposite."

On the turntable, the silenced LP reached the end of its side and the needle began an irritating clicking.

"Is it okay if I get that?" Silas asked and Sara nodded. Bouncing from the couch, Silas lifted the needle, cradled the tone arm and was back in his seat in the blink of an eye. "Where were we?"

"We were here," Sara took his hand. "In our home. Together. Alone. And there's something I want to say to you."

Silas bit his lips together, a smile playing at the corners of his mouth, nodding her to continue. His childlike innocence, and the fact that he still possessed it, made her heart swell.

"I want to thank you," Sara said, her eyes looking deep into his. "I know this wasn't easy, and I know also that I made it harder than it needed to be."

"You don't have to apologize."

"I'm not apologizing," Sara said, "I'm acknowledging, and I'm telling you that I appreciate everything you have done for me. I'm talking every step of your long game, everything that you did, with my safety in mind. When I think about it all, I am humbled beyond measure."

Tears began to well in his eyes.

"Which brings me to now," Sara continued. "It's almost year since I.. since I lost control of my... levels. And I forced your hand. And you risked it all for me. And against the odds, here we are. The story is vast, the strands are many, but simply, all I have to say is, Atenase Funar-"

Silas chuckled at the use of his birth name.

"Better known as Silas, if that's better, all I have to say is, thank you, and I love you."

A tear fell from Silas's bottom lashes and landed with a soft splot on the couch. He reached for Sara's other hand, and she pulled both hands away.

"No, I need them for another minute," Sara smiled, reaching into her pocket.

"This might be me making a huge assumption," she continued, looking into his eyes. "Because seriously, Crina, Stefanya, Ama, Fan, nobody will talk. But the consensus is that you've never dated seriously, and that's my fault."

"I dated seriously," Silas said. "But somewhat infrequently."

"Either way, I'm hoping this is a first."

Reaching into her pocket, Sara pulled out a handmade wooden box, and presented it to Silas, whose mouth was now opening and closing in confusion.

"I.." he stammered. "I...uh, I think you're supposed to say something before I take it."

"Right," Sara said, her voice breaking. "I don't think anyone's every given you a ring before."

"That much is correct," Silas said, his lip trembling.

"This ring is a symbol, Silas. There's never been a marriage in our kind, and I don't know if we need to haul that cliché into our world, at least not yet. But this," she paused, opening the box, Inside, on a bed of black velvet, lay a simple gold ring crowned by a round, pocked black stone. "This is my decision ring, Silas. Together, we have decided to do this life, this adventure, together. And, I don't know, it just felt really significant and like something I needed to..."

"Lock down?" Silas laughed and sobbed at the same time, crumpling forward and throwing his arms around her.

"Sure," she said into his neck. "I'm locking you down. Here."

Sara lifted the ring from the velvet and pressed herself back from him, holding the ring between them. With a sniff, he pushed his ring finger through the center of the ring, until it slipped over his knuckle.

"It fits perfectly," he whispered. "Sara, it feels fucking wonderful."

She rested her forehead against his, then lifted her chin until their lips met, and they kissed, tenderly, endlessly. His hands found hers, and she let her fingers feel the ring on his finger.

"I've never been so happy," he said quietly.

"Me either," she replied, and he pressed her backward, laying on top of her as the kissing continued. "The stone is a piece of lava I picked up in Iceland."

Silas took Sara's head in both hands and pulled her to him, beginning a kiss that didn't end for several hours.

The sound of a phone buzzing nearby woke Sara, and she fought to disentangle her legs and arms from Silas's, and groggily, he tried to assist her.

"What is it?" he mumbled.

"Hold please," Sara lifted her jeans from the pile of clothing and fished her phone out of the pocket. It was Imani.

"Hey Imani," she said.

"I need you here immediately," Imani said, and something in her voice filled Sara with instant fear.

"Where are you?"

"Front vestibule, church entrance."

"Are you okay?"

"Yes, Sara. Wait. Do you still speak Romanian?"

"Haven't for years, really. I'm a bit rusty."

"Then bring Silas. Now."

The line went dead. Dragging on her jeans, Sara picked up the pile of clothes and tossed it onto the couch, snatching her shirt from mid-air and putting it on.

"Get dressed," she said, worry in her voice. "Imani has a problem at the front door and she needs both of us."

Without a word, Silas saluted her with a goofy smile. Half asleep, with dried blood turning the edges of his mustache to rust, he blew her a kiss then slipped into floor jeans and shirt. Barefoot, he made for the rear door. Grabbing the keys, Sara fell in behind him.

"Any hints?" he asked as they made their way around to the front of the building.

"Imani sounded shook," Sara said, holding open the door to the fifth-floor landing, just outside the door to her old apartment. As soon as they stepped out, they could hear the deep voice of a man echoing up the stairwell. They were unable to make out what he was saying due to Imani saying, "I'm really sorry I can't understand you," every time he tried to speak.

"A Romanian man?" Silas asked.

"Sounds like," Sara said, pushing past him and leaping down the stairs two and three at a time until they rounded the final flight of stairs and saw Imani, in a hastily thrown together nun habit, and an average sized man, Mediterranean skin and tousled black hair, an expression somewhere between panicked and pleading on his face. Seeing Sara and Silas, he turned, and said, in Romanian.

"Greetings, friends, do you understand me?"

Nodding, Sara stepped closer to him.

"Yes," she replied in Romanian. "The man and I speak the mother tongue. Are you in need of help?"

Nodding, the man looked at Silas.

"She says you speak Romanian."

"She speaks the truth," Silas replied. "It is ill manners to speak of a woman as if she is a liar, in her own home."

"Good, good," the man said, switching to barely-accented English. "Is there somewhere we can speak in private?"

"After all that you speak English?" Imani was pissed. "You better not be fucking racist."

"Not at all," the man raised a placating hand. "I was told to only speak to the couple who speak Romanian. I didn't mean to offend you."

"Well you did," Imani said. "Absolutely got off on the wrong foot you did."

"Again, I apologize," the man said. "Is there somewhere we can speak candidly?"

"She's coming with us," Sara said, nodding at Imani. The man shrugged and picked up the worn black duffel bag at his feet.

"I'll take that," Silas said, in Romanian, and the man surrendered it in silence.

"Can you open 1A?" Sara asked, and Imani nodded, holding her phone to the door by the mailboxes. It clicked and Imani twisted the handle, pushing the door open and letting out a very dusty, stale smell. This room, where they did most of their nun business in the old life, clearly hadn't been aired out in a while. It was still decorated with furniture that had been purchased just after the second world war, a burgundy wool couch and a two stiff high-backed chairs with leather upholstery.

"Sit there," Imani pointed at one of the chairs, and the man sat. Silas and Sara took the couch, and Imani remained standing.

"I have a strange story to tell you," the man began, making eye contact with each of them. "And if I wasn't so desperate, I would not be telling it."

Something about his cadence, his posture, was starting to worry Sara. He seemed scared but resigned.

"Open the duffel," she said to Silas.

"I already did a squeeze test," he said. "Feels like clothing."

"You're not in danger," the man said. "At least not from the bag."

"Then what do you want?" Imani was still irritable.

"I need your help," the man said simply. "Please, let me begin."

Sara nodded, and the man stood.

"My name is Toma," he said. "I was born in Bucharest, thirty-eight years ago. I studied abroad, that's where I learned English. But for the last ten years I have been an adventure guide. Several months ago, I was contacted by a wealthy woman. She wanted me to lead an expedition along the Arges River."

Silas and Sara's heads jerked up.

"She offered me a fortune," the man continued, his eyes darting from Sara's to Silas's. "She had scientists with her, and they were looking for something, but she didn't say what. The money, it was too good to refuse, so I said yes."

The hairs on Sara's neck were prickling uncomfortably. She had swum in the Arges as a child.

"We searched by night, going deep into caves, crevasses, and ruins. She began to trap bats, conducting tests on them."

"How long ago was this?" Sara interrupted.

"We set out two months ago," the man said. "Two weeks ago, they overpowered me while I was asleep in my tent." The man hung his head in shame.

"Come on then," Imani snapped impatiently.

"They gashed my arm, here" the man pushed up a sleeve, showing a bare forearm. "There is no scar. Not now, anyway."

"Oh no," Silas whispered.

"They poured blood into the cut, and then, I remember no more, at least not that night,"

Imani's eyes widened in realization, and she glanced at Sara and Silas, who nodded.

"And what brings you here, friend?" Silas asked in Romanian.

"I am sick," the man said. "I have to take pills or I am consumed by incredible pain."

"Do you have the pills?"

The man nodded at the bag beside Silas, on the floor. He opened it and jammed his hand inside until he felt the bottle. None of them showed any surprise when he held it aloft. Heems.

"Is that all you have taken for this illness?" Silas grabbed the man by the shoulder.

Shamefully he shook his head.

"No."

A shiver ran through the man and he began to cry.

"They let the pain get so bad, they said only one thing would save me."

"They give you blood, mate?" Imani kept her tone even.

Sobbing, the man nodded, and all three of them exchanged worried glances. He was fully cursed. Desdemona had found a natural source of the virus.

Imani went into the small bathroom, returning with a wad of toilet paper that she handed to the man. While he was wiping his eyes, Imani looked at Sara and Silas and mouthed "Surrender?" Sara shook her head and mouthed "not yet."

"I didn't want to come here," the man whispered. "She said you are murderers."

"I'm a fucking nun, mate," Imani said, and the man's head jerked up and he crossed himself.

"I apologize, sister," his voice was earnest. "I am telling what the lady said to me, that's all."

"Did she say we would murder you?" Sara tried to keep her voice light. Unsurprisingly, the man nodded.

"Then why did you come here?"

Inhaling deeply, the man clasped his hands together and looked at the floor.

"I am a twin," Toma said gravely, as if sharing the information was physically painful. "If I do not do as this woman says, then she will also infect my brother."

Anger flared inside Sara and she fought to keep her face passive.

"And what does she want you to do?"

"I am to deliver a message."

"Okay, then," Imani stepped threateningly close to the strange man. "Out with it."

"It's on my phone," Toma said. "In my pocket."

"Slowly remove your phone from your pocket," Sara said gravely. "And don't try anything else."

Without taking his eyes from Sara's, Toma took his phone from his pocket and unlocked it, tapped the screen a few times, then turned the screen to face Sara, who gasped at the sight of Desdemona's face as she inhaled before speaking. The face that she had known for centuries had changed, very slightly. There were lines at the corners of her eyes and mouth. Sara glanced quickly at Imani and Silas, who both nodded, eyes wide. They saw it too. In only three months, Desdemona had begun to age.

"Dear sister," Desdemona said, her voice dripping venom. "How do you like Toma? I was thinking, why should you be the only one in New York with a boyfriend? That's why I sent him to you, knowing he will be safely cared for in your no-kill shelter."

Sara stole a quick look at Toma, clearly confused.

"So anyway, congratulations on your new member, but here's the thing. If you don't have Yukari reverse the poison you put in me, I'm going to send you a new infected man, every Friday, until Yukari finds a way to restore my..." Desdemona paused, thinking, "...my power, if you know what I mean. And there's another thing I wanted to tell you. Toma is the last one that will have your address. You'll have to find the others, you know, before they get hungry and do something... regrettable."

Desdemona smiled a sickening grin, and Sara looked away for a second until Des continued.

"I'll make it easier for you," she cooed. "I'll have their drivers drop them in..." she cackled, "...or near The North Woods."

Sara's heart sank and a chill settled in her bones.

"Anyways," Desdemona said, then actually winked at the camera, "you can always get me via the number in this phone. Adios, mi hermana, vaya con dios. And don't fuck this up."

On the screen, Sara watched as Desdemona's control over her expression faltered slightly as she directed her fingertip to stop the recording, and wrinkles became visible on her neck and forehead. The video stopped and silence descended on the room.

"She's going to do this to my brother?" Toma wailed, letting the phone fall to the floor. "She promised that I was buying his safety. This is why I came even though she told me that you would kill me."

"She's just being dramatic, my friend," Silas said in Romanian, stepping close to the panicking man and putting himself between Toma and Sara. "Just come with me, I'll get you set up in a room, you can sleep and we can start work on helping your brother in the morning."

Exhaustion rippled through Toma and he nodded slowly. Silas took him by the upper arm and began to lead him to the door before stopping suddenly and twisting the man's arm behind him painfully. Toma screamed briefly, before Silas threw his other arm around Toma's neck and began to squeeze. Thrashingly wildly, Toma smacked his heels back against Silas's shins but Silas held tight until unconsciousness clouded Toma's vision and he went limp.

After gently laying the unconscious man onto the floor, Silas turned to Sara.

"She's going to send an army of full vampires into New York City?"

Sara nodded slowly.

"This is my fault," Silas said, his deep voice shaking, and in the midst of her panic, Sara melted when she saw the look on his face.

"It's not, guv," Imani said, her voice small.

Looking from Silas to Imani to the unconscious man on the floor, Sara felt the familiar pull of responsibility, this time tangled with deep love for the people standing in front of her, their eyes boring into hers, waiting for an answer, a solution. Breathing deeply to slow her racing thoughts, Sara leaned into responsibility.

"Silas, literally none of this is your fault," she said. "But I'd love it if you could carry our sleeping friend to the little room we had Des in. Imani and I need to make some calls. I'll see you back at home in, oh, half an hour?"

Without a word, Silas bent and hoisted Toma's limp body up and onto his shoulders.

"I'll get the door," Imani said, moving to the rear of the room and pulling open a brick door, instantly filling the air with the catacomb scent of the hallway beyond it. Pausing at the doorway, Silas turned.

"I'm sorry," he said. "No matter what caused this, she's not just threatening us, she's threatening all of New York City."

Nodding slowly, Sara pondered his words, then decided to lie.

"It's Desdemona," she said, not breaking eye contact with him. "How many crazy threats has that bitch made over the years?"

"She's just desperate," Imani said, looking up from her phone. "Sara, I have Lindsey, Skye, Yfke and Christine ready to jump on a call, which means you-" she glanced at Silas, "-need to vanish before I connect it."

Nodding, Silas stepped into the darkness of the hallway, Toma's dirty boots whacking against the wall on their way out. Holding her phone in one hand, Imani used her other hand to push the door closed. As soon as it clicked closed, she hit call and handed her phone to Sara, who waited until all the little squares on the screen were filled by worried faces of women she had known for centuries.

"You guys," she said, her voice strong. "We have a little problem on our hands."

By the time Sara finished the video conference, weak dawn sun was cutting through the venetians. Exhausted, she handed the phone back to Imani, slumped on the couch beside her.

"We're gonna have a houseful," Imani said. "If they all come here..."

When Imani didn't finish, Sara turned to face her.

"Yes?"

"It feels like a trap," Imani said finally. "It feels like she's pulled a stunt knowing that it will get all of her enemies in one place."

"Yeah, I thought of that too," Sara said. "But right now, the most important thing is that we have enough people scouring the park for these men, if she sends them. Crina and Heather will be back tomorrow. Can we tell Fan and Ama when we wake up? I don't have the energy for that right now?"

"Great idea," Imani said, pushing herself to her feet and turning and extending a hand to Sara, who grabbed it and pulled herself up. "Because I don't know if I can sleep right now, but I bloody well want to give it a shot."

Sara nodded, and was surprised when Imani threw her arms around her and hugged her tight.

"We got this, guv," Imani said. "And I don't say it often enough, but how do I love thee, Sara whatever your last name is."

"We do got this," Sara said, kissing Imani on the neck. "I better get upstairs, Silas is going to be losing his mind."

"Go, I'll lock up down here."

Disentangling herself from Imani's arms, Sara let herself out into the foyer, then walked up the eight stairs to her old apartment, pausing in the wreckage of her old kitchen, saddened by the disrepair. She'd really loved living here, but now it was just an empty space dusty with too many ghosts.

Sighing, she exited into the hallway behind it and made her way to her new home. The door was unlocked, one of Silas's most infuriating habits, and she let herself inside.

"Sorry that took so long," she called out. When no reply was forthcoming, she assumed Silas was asleep, which made her feel slightly angry jealous until she got to the living room and saw the note on the coffee table. As she read it, she heard Silas's voice saying the words inside her head.

"Sara, I'm sorry. I talked to Stef and we are gonna set this right. I'll call as soon as I land. Don't worry about me. I got this. And I got you. I love you so much. Silas."

Her world began to tilt crazily, and Sara steadied herself on the couch before falling onto it, her eyes never leaving the note on the table, her mind refusing to process the information it contained.

Silas was gone.

Acknowledgements

Hi!

This book was written under a cloud of grief. Just weeks after I published From Him To Eternity, friends started dying. People whose presence in my life was huge, loving, formative and vital. I'd like to start these acknowledgements by naming them, in the order in which they passed. They are with me always, in my heart and in my memory.

Beverly Rayburn

Nicholas Harding

Jake Taylor

Megan Pigram

Lynne Watkins

Nolan Pate

David Morley

Ken Taylor

I kept a very small circle around me while I grieved and worked on this book. I rarely left the house and I didn't see a lot of people. Some weeks it was just me, my husband and my dogs. And that was okay. Dogs make everything okay, and mine, Miss Tuna, Graciela and Olivia, cheered me up when that didn't seem possible.

This book is dedicated to Skye Pyman. She's been my rock, my cousin, my sister and so much more, since the day she was born. She worked on this book with me, editing each and every draft with her excellent eye. I literally couldn't have done this book without her. Thanks, Skye, I love you more.

I also relied really heavily on my home team cheer squad, because they are awesome and they have my back. So, thank you to my husband George Castro, a certified gold medalist in keeping me afloat, and my spectacular friend Lindsey Kelk, a unicorn among humans who somehow keeps me sane.

Endless love, as always, to Heather Taylor, my rock. Everyone deserves a friend this magical, and I am lucky to have had Heather in my life since I was a teenager.

Mad love to the magical force of nature that is Christine Beidel. She does the audiobooks for this series, and on top of that, she brings so much joy to my life.

Oaky Tyree over at Tell Me About Your Book podcast gets a shoutout. Her enthusiasm and deep soul buoyed me at a time when I really needed it.

Huge thanks to Steve Gidlow, who always helps my projects in new ways, from directing music videos to styling to photography, he's an amazing friend and creative force.

Thanks to Sitaram, Bhava and Goenka for getting me on the right path. It took me a long time to get here, and I recognize that it was like getting an octopus to walk a tightrope. Saadhu.

And lastly, to the small crew of friends who cheered me on and cheered me up while I worked, in alphabetical order: Paul Amirault, Hugues Barbier, Adriane & Tom Boat, Rosa Castro, Tammy Germani, Larry Hardy, Christine Linardon, Joan Oexman, Felix Schliebitz & Emily Thompson, Patricia Stone, Liz Tooley, Yfke Van Berckelaer and Priscilla Wardlow. You're all rock stars.

And you. Thank you for reading this book. I appreciate it more than you'll ever know.

with love,

KJD

About the author

Kevin Dickson is an Australian-American author who lives in Los Angeles with his husband George, three spectacular dogs, Miss Tuna, Graciela and Olivia, and an irascible parrot named Chapulin. After working as an entertainment journalist in Australia, Dickson relocated to Los Angeles in the late 90s, and found himself in the epicenter of the reality TV explosion. Bouncing between LA and New York for the next twenty years, he had a ringside seat for some of the most scandalous media events in recent history. Dickson exorcised his demons from that time in the thinly veiled tell-all bestseller Blind Item and its sequel, Guilty Pleasure. After a brief stint in a punk rock band that toured and recorded a well-received album, Dickson once again turned his attention to the written word, and the Vampire State series was born. These days, Dickson divides his time between writing, hiking, traveling and devouring films, books and music, and running a screen printing business with his husband.

The author does not endorse or enjoy social media.

Any official accounts will be poorly and sporadically managed at best.

To contact the author please email vampirestatebooks@gmail.com

Also by Kevin Dickson

From Him To Eternity: Vampire State book one

Seasons Of Blood: Vampire State book two

The North Woods: Vampire State book three (Summer 2025)

Blind Item (co-author)

Guilty Pleasure (co-author)